Doghouse Blues 3

Clive Radford

Published by Rogue Phoenix Press, LLP

ISBN: 978-1-62420-632-0

Editor: Amanda Armstrong

Dedication

To all satire lovers.

Contents

Chapter 1: The Road goes on Forever

Absurdity and modern life seemed to be inextricably linked as far as Roger Fraser could make out.

Ever amazed or disheartened by the deluge of ill-considered edicts and pronouncements, flying out of the mouths of ill-equipped power-players and mediocrities alike, long ago he took it for granted the capable and the gifted had been removed from the field of play by subjective laws and positive discrimination in favour of self-interested cliques, out to irretrievably change England into shapes of their choosing. Leveraging such a resolute grip on society at large, avoiding the impact of the new breed's agenda proved impossible.

It had got to the point whereby he intended to employ meditation as an antidote to combat his 'not in control of his own destiny' complex. Accordingly, come 2012, he set great store in evading doghouse blues servitude by becoming a contemplation practitioner.

After the Firm's Christmas party shenanigans involving false revelations regarding Roger's assignation with Maria Sharapova, and him going toe to toe with local vicar, the Right Reverend Reddick, 'Big Dick' as Roger kept mispronouncing his name, on the thorny theme of the church versus the financial sector, at the Fraser's Hazelwood house on Christmas Day evening, he anticipated the New Year's Eve watershed with relish as the advent for a lifelong fix to his dilemma.

In Roger's mindset, come 1st January 2012, he'd log-on to Amazon.co.uk and invest in a plethora of meditation self-help books to empower him with a look-over-the-horizon capability to dodge contentious social mantraps, and failing that, provide the means to fight the agony when he became caught in some unfortunate social web resulting in a merciless haranguing from his wife Charlotte's acid tongue.

With the extra demands created by his trouble-shooter role at The Firm, Roger concluded he needed to be at his best to effectively and efficiently address them, meaning a clear mind free from concerns, as well as an unfluctuating robust body to manage the incurred workload and attendant strain.

Over his years in investment banking, he had seen honest and dedicated good men suffer premature burnout through overload excess. Having no counterpoint to balance out the crippling aftermath of sleepless nights, meals consumed on the hoof, and cramming twenty-six hours work into a twenty-four-hour day, the jitters arose, cold sweats and delirium drowning the victim in a pungent bath of touchiness and agitation. Butterflies in the stomach stoked up fluster and impatience. Fidgetiness became a daily distraction to control. Fear of others seeing decline into the abyss, the final calamity culminated in the shakes and neurasthenia.

Roger had always promised himself it would not happen to him, foresight ringing the alarm bell way before irreparable damage set in, his innate sense of survival making him throttle-back, take stock and reappraise his call to duty.

However, supplementary to taking notice of his sensations, without doubt he had to quell pent up frustrations and anger by artificial means. His rudimentary knowledge of meditation suggested regular sessions of cleansing his mind of amplified anxieties and worries could be the difference between retaining his sanity and going completely Tonto.

Undeniably, his alpha-male social activities went a long way to relieving tension, especially those associated with Kappa Corinthians Rugby Club and the Hazelwood & District Gentlemen's Club. Alcohol played a pivotal part in the assuaging mechanism as well, but its residual downside could be just as decimating in terms of hangover pain and long-term body degeneracy as stress.

Back in the autumn, he had visioned out some long-term ambitions to be fulfilled when the Fraser children left home and before he approached mandatory retirement age at The Firm. For these to become reality, more than ever, he recognised John Barleycorn and Harry Hop only offered partial relief from built-up anxiety to brace his volition and his being. For the road to go on forever, he hoped meditation filled the rejuvenation gap, and sustained him in his hours of need when work and domestic pressures overwhelmed him.

Chapter 2: New Year's Eve

Early on New Year's Eve morning, the Fraser offspring comprising eldest daughter Wendy, son James and youngest daughter Heather set out with Roger and Charlotte in the family MPV for Buckingham, immemorial home of Charlotte's parents Valentine, and Davina, otherwise known as Lady Macbeth.

Whilst keeping a watch out for 1.3 Escort and Astra vans driven by West London wide boys, flashing him to move over and mouthing 'Get out of the fackin' way, you cant,' as the MPV sped along the Essex section of the M25, Roger hummed a few choruses of *I've got the Chicken Shack, Fleetwood Mac, John Mayall can't fail blues* to himself.

"Can we have some real music?" James beseeched on hearing his father's refrain for the umpteenth time.

"I have a wide selection of quality jazz and rock on a memory stick plugged into the MPV audio system. Anything in particular you'd like to hear?"

"Oh, Roger," Charlotte petitioned, "nothing too loud and startling please."

"Well, we could always listen to classical music on Radio 4 or Classic FM, if it's more to your liking."

"I not sure I want anything intellectual so early in the morning."

"I thought I made the request," James insisted.

"Patience, son," Roger counselled. "This is an iterative process with your mother. You have to allow her a while to become accustomed to the idea."

"Have you got any preferences, Wendy?" Charlotte enquired.

"Do you have anything by Adele or Lady Gaga, Dad?"

"*No*," he single-mindedly replied.

"How about Katy Perry or Ed Sheeran."

"Certainly not. That last name sounds more like a footballer than a pop star. He's not one of those virtual artists who makes recordings, singing with paper and comb for accompaniment, is he?"

"No," Wendy vindicated. "I showed you a photograph of him in the *Telegraph*'s arts section."

"When?"

"Mid-November."

"What, the one-man Chaz & Dave tribute act, the Worzel Gummidge Doppelganger in the making?"

"He only looks like Worzel Gummidge from some angles."

"Well from the angle I saw him, he mirrored as a dead ringer. He's a ginger tosser as well, like that obnoxious mediocrity, Chris Evans. He who clogs up the airwaves with his self-centred diatribes about ginger people with frail voices being lampooned by society."

"*Roger*!" Charlotte admonished, "Mind your language in front of the children."

"It's alright, Mum," Wendy rejoindered, "we all know what a tosser is." She paused before endorsing, "Elton John likes Ed Sheeran."

"And *that's* a recommendation?" Roger grilled, his note ringing with ridicule.

"Your father doesn't like Elton John," Charlotte advised. "He thinks he has an ambiguous sexual orientation."

"He's a puff, isn't he?" James wisecracked.

"We don't use offensive terms such as 'puff' anymore, James," scolded his mother. "He's a homosexual."

"What's a—" Heather began.

"*Don't* even go there," Charlotte implored, cutting off her youngest daughter. "It's also too early in the morning for you to be tabling your penetrating w-questions."

"I was only going to ask, what is a virtual artist?" Heather certified. "I already know what a homosexual is."

Frowning, Roger turned to Charlotte. "Does she?"

"They covered sexual orientation in their sex education classes in the autumn term at junior school."

Astounded, he challenged, "what on Earth for?"

"So children don't see homosexuals as sexual deviants," Charlotte whispered.

"But they are," Roger maintained.

"I thought we were talking about making a music selection," James reminded his family.

"Indeed we were, son," Roger brightly responded. "Now what's it going to be? The mellow syncopating tones of Miles Davis and John Coltrane, or alternatively, the awesome potency of the Rolling Stones, the Who and Led Zeppelin?"

"You still haven't told me what a virtual artist is," Heather complained.

"*Oohh*, not now," Charlotte returned. "Maybe later when I'm feeling more perky."

"Allow me to finalise the earlier precis," Roger intervened. "A virtual artist is a modern, saddo, freak-geek phenomenon. Someone failing to secure a record deal through hard gigging, who then resorts to barricading himself in his bedroom, singing silly ditties accompanied by a washboard when he's not blowing a paper and comb, and subjecting an unsuspecting public to the dross on-line."

Several annoying hours later, the MPV rolled into the driveway at Vespers in Buckingham, Charlotte's parents' ancestral home. Annoying, because the Minister for Transport had taken advantage of the relatively low traffic density on New Year's Eve to repair a dislodged apex piece on a concrete wall, adjacent to the Potters Bar junction, bringing traffic to a near standstill. Incredulously, the simple one-man repair necessitated Health & Safety bureaucrats to reduce the west-bound motorway down to one lane, the restriction causing a tailback to Waltham Abbey, significantly adding to journey time.

After the usual all-round hugs and kisses, the family retired to the lounge for late morning refreshments, specifically, alcohol for the adults and Wendy, and soft drinks for James and Heather.

"Since it's New Year's Eve, can I have a snorter?" James appealed.

"You can have some wine with your lunch," Charlotte told him.

"Ugh, I'm not a kid anymore, you know."

Cogitating for a moment, his mother bartered, "I'll do a trade with you, James. You delete the incriminating video of my Greenwich Park contretemps from your iPhone, and I will permit you a glass of beer."

"Is it a good bargain I ask myself. How do I know you won't subordinate me to the same doghouse blues punishments you inflict on Dad when he's been caught with his pants down?"

"What's that about me being caught with my pants down?" Roger piped up, catching the rump of the conversation.

"Nevermind," Charlotte fended. She rotated her attention to her son. "Well, James, do we have a deal?"

"Oh, alright then," he conceded, producing a resigned phiz. Activating his iPhone, he trawled through its contents' menu.

Having heard the odd word of their chat concurrent with talking to Wendy and Heather, Davina investigated, "what's James doing?"

"It doesn't matter, Mother," Charlotte steadfastly instructed.

"I'm searching for an incriminating video of your daughter, Grandmother," James chipped in.

"What did you say?" Valentine explored, breaking off talking to Roger.

"Our grandson has a prosecutable video, starring our daughter," Davina clarified.

"Oh, *really*." Valentine's lineaments lit up. "Might we see this impeaching feature before it is confined to the recycle bin?"

"Absolutely *not*," Charlotte blasted. "And it won't be the recycle bin. It has to be deleted."

"Oh, don't be coy, Charlotte," Roger importuned. "I'm sure your parents will discern it with academic interest, and not become judgmental." Flaunting a winning smile at her, he entreated, "come on, what harm can be done? and after all, it is New Year's Eve."

"New Year's Eve or not, the incident engendered a lot of embarrassment I do not need repeating in the presence of my parents."

"Charlotte," Davina pressed in her most persuasive voice, "please."

Breathing out heavily she relented. "Oh, very well then."

"We can't all crowd around my iPhone to monitor it," James contested. "Dad, have you got your laptop with you?"

"Indeed I have."

"Right. I'll connect my iPhone to a USB port on your laptop and run the video. The screen is big enough for all of us to see it together."

"And you will delete the video from your iPhone afterwards," Charlotte reiterated.

"I will."

After James had consummated the steps, the family gathered around the laptop.

"Ready?" James tested.

"As ready as I'll ever be," his mother retorted.

Initiating the video, the Greenwich Park incident came to life replete with grunts and groans, Charlotte seen in *Full Metal Jacket* mode doing battle with a humongous-sized, beetroot-red faced woman, whilst bystanders stared at the best-of-ten bouts action.

"*Good grief*, Charlotte," Valentine trilled, "I didn't realise you had acquired kick-boxer skills."

"Nor had I at the time," Roger lamented, the comment deriving a decimating glare from his wife aimed at his inner being, her Superman-like X-ray vision frying his loins.

As the exposé took hold, including Roger becoming floored by a stray punch after travailing to break up the fight, and the police arriving, Charlotte's parents' consternation grew.

"You didn't get arrested, did you?" Davina yelped.

"No…Roger intervened."

"Oh yes," Valentine chimed. "I see we're at the point where Roger is pleading with you to stop attacking three burly policemen with your brolly. Ohh…I say!"

At the end of the spectacle Davina canvassed, "what incited this fracas, Charlotte?"

"I had a squabble with a bunch of protestors not wanting to see Greenwich Park taken apart to accommodate the 2012 London Olympic Games equestrian event."

"Doesn't sound too serious," Valentine credited. "Why did it end up in fisticuffs?"

"Because the lard…" She bit her lip trying not to come out with a swear word. "…large, rear-ended woman called me stupid."

"But you were," Roger began, before realising the implications of his criticism and breaking off.

"Were what, Roger?" Charlotte barked, glaring at her husband.

"Nothing, darling."

~ * ~

After Davina's palatial lunch, the children retired to the study to text friends or watch TV, leaving the lounge free for the adults.

"Tell me, Roger," Valentine began, "what did you make of the Government selling Northern Rock to Virgin Money?"

"It was undervalued at £747million, but inevitable."

"Why?"

"After the collapse of Northern Rock in 2008, Gordon Brown's nationalisation ensured members didn't lose their savings, however, Northern Rock has been slow to recover and regain independence. When the Coalition took jurisdiction in May 2010 and Cameron and George Osbourne found the Treasury cupboard bare, they recognised little scope existed to featherbed failing financial institutions. With Northern Rock exhibiting no signs of recovery, it became clear a buyer needed to be found, probably exacting a knockdown price to take on the risk."

"Hhmm, will Branson make a goer of it?"

"Indisputably he has a plan to restore the Northern Rock part of Virgin Money into profitability, but his liability is not complete yet. There's still plenty of toxic debt on Northern Rock's books needing to be dealt with over financial year 2012-13. But er—" Suddenly twigging, he frowned. "You haven't got money tied up in Northern Rock, have you?"

"Yes, some shares from 2002."

"Yikes, I wish you'd told me, Valentine. As your broker, I'd have advocated you sold your shares in 2006."

"Well, Branson had inaugurated interest in Northern Rock, so I figured when he procured the bank provoking a rising share price and thereby my dividends, I'd be okay."

"But then the nasty stuff hit the fan in 2008."

"Quite, and my stake has been in limbo ever since."

"Might I quiz what degree of exposure we're talking about?"

"A little over £120,000."

"Oh, based on what I know about your other investments, the hit is not too bad then."

"No, it represents less than five per cent of my portfolio, but it still hurts to see my money go down the drain."

"What's your stock holding currently worth?"

"About £40,000."

"And you're hoping with the Virgin Money purchase of Northern Rock, eventually the share price will recover?"

"Indeed I am, Roger."

"Reckless *blaggards*," Davina wailed. "If I had my way, those responsible for the dire financial situation at Northern Rock would be hung, drawn and quartered, and their severed heads put on spikes outside the London Stock Exchange as a warning to other board executives, thinking of indulging in playing the stock market with other peoples' money."

"As I've said before, Davina, don't sugarcoat it," Roger quipped. "Tell us what you really think."

"Well, if you're questing for a less drastic method, but nonetheless similarly finite in its effect, I'd employ my brother Les' solution to all anti-social degenerates."

"What does Les prescribe, Mother?" Charlotte probed.

"A helicopter job."

"Meaning?"

"Gather all the offending miscreants together."

"Yes."

"Shove them into an EH 101 Merlin chopper."

"And?"

"Fly it out over the North Sea."

"Go on."

"Then release its trap door, and the miscreants drop out…end of problem."

"Brilliant," Roger applauded.

"*Roger*!" Charlotte exclaimed. "It's barbaric."

"Maybe," he accorded, "but it's efficacious." Thoughtfully he appended, "come to think of it, there are other candidates I'd like to propose for a one-way EH-101 trip over the North Sea."

"No doubt they are all members of the Labour Party."

"*Au contraire*, ruffled wife of mine. I am distinctly unimpressed by the wishy-washy, imprudent policies of the Coalition Government, chiefly created by 'Cleggover' and his bunch of sanctimonious Lib-Dem elitists."

"*Damn it*!" Davina blurted. "Don't get me launched on that heap of pious, insincere, self-satisfied, shifty, smug, hypocritical company of traitors. The Clegg person spends more cycles with Muslims and every so-called minority group under the sun, licking their rear-ends and making excuses for their dreadful behaviour, than doing what he was elected for, and paid to do."

"And what's that?" Roger flippantly tabled, trying to rile her further.

"Rescuing England from the clutches of the EU. Preventing this sacred island from being invaded by a never-ending stream of so-called asylum seekers and economic migrants. Standing up for England, not denigrating her at every opportunity he has to make a public address. The man is a scoundrel, and should be hounded out of Parliament, and preferably out of England."

Turning to Valentine, Roger jested, "she's definitely not sugar-coating it, and she hasn't lost any of the vitriol I witnessed in the summer, when the Speaker incurred her wrath."

Amused by the witticism, Valentine couldn't help but grin at his son-in-law's precise assessment. "Yes, I learnt long ago, it's fatal to err into the area of scurrilous politicians with Davina in the discourse."

"Oh, Mother," Charlotte rebuked, "the Lib-Dems are there to reign in the heinous excesses of the Tories."

"*What* excesses?" Davina objected, her Lady Macbeth mantle

visibly growing. "I don't see any difference between the trendy, let's feed the undivided world at English taxpayers' expense rhetoric of Gordon Brown, and that Goody Two-Shoes excuse for a Prime Minister, David Cameron. Quite rightly, he prescribes a tightening of the public purse strings to guarantee the national debt does not increase, but disingenuously, he then deepens the Overseas Development Agency budget, and does nothing to reduce the UK's trillion pounds per day contribution to the EU, or recoup our gargantuan payments made to date."

"He has promised an in-out EU referendum during the course of this Parliament," Valentine reminded her.

"Balderdash," she jeered. "Pie in the sky, and if it does happen, Cameron will rig the outcome to clinch England is harnessed to the EU for evermore.

"Mark my words," she demanded. "It's plain to see Cameron is a liberal and a Europhile. Any prominent Conservative front bencher opposing closer EU union and an end to subsidising that corrupt, undemocratic machine has been marginalised and banished to the back benches. If David Davis had been elected as Conservative Party guardian, we'd have exited the fiendish EU by now. He's one of the very few politicians who are trustworthy and loyal to England."

"As a matter of academic interest, Davina," Roger began, "who'd be acceptable to you as prime minister?"

"I'd have thought it was obvious."

"Genghis Khan perhaps," Roger facetiously introduced.

"Don't be ridiculous," she fired off.

"How about Caligula?"

"Patently even more impertinent, Roger. Hereinafter, you'll be proposing Maximilien Robespierre or Ivan the Terrible."

"I'm just labouring to bring a little bit of levity to proceedings, mother-in-law dear. It's New Year's Eve. We shouldn't be getting heated about articles beyond our control."

"Well, you started it, Roger, when you broached the 'Cleggover' contention, as you call him."

"I know, and I regret it. How about if we delve into a lighter and less controversial topic?"

"Such as?"

"An abstract treatise, such as the declining calibre of proper English in newspapers?"

"Alright." She leaned frontwards in her easy chair. "By the way, my acceptable choice for prime minister is Michael Gove."

Refraining from arguing about her mother's choice, albeit Charlotte glowered in a dismissive retort.

Also not wanting a repeat of Lady Macbeth's virulent opinions on the Coalition Government, Roger stayed focused on his prescribed substance. "In my humble judgement, internet blogs, publications and such-like use a very elemental style of English language, often festooned with the invalid use of words, bad grammar, wrong punctuation and a low-grade concentration requirement appealing to the lowest common denominator, rather than toiling to raise the collective average."

"Yes, for once, Roger, I couldn't agree more with you," Davina saluted. "The infernal use of texting has not helped the appropriate continuance of the Queen's English, because it's eventuated in people using silly abbreviations in email communications and even conventional hard copy letters."

"What do you think, Valentine?" Roger solicited.

"I'm inclined to concur with both of you. Recently, I've noticed instead of using graphic detail in newspaper sports reports like, 'Michael Owen sliced through the defence and unleashed an unerring shot, the ball flying past the keeper for the opening goal', we get, 'the man put the ball in the net'. And *that's* in the broadsheets, let alone the red tops!"

"Typical," Charlotte carped. "As usual, I'm going to be in the minority on this discussion."

"Yes, it's because you've lost your common sense, as I told you in the summer," Davina asserted. "All this adoption of swank leftie morality has inhibited your natural ability to see the wood from the trees. I sometimes think it was an utter waste of money sending you to Cambridge to study architecture."

"I was a different creature then, Mother, still under your influence and yet to find alternate viewpoints on a vast profusion of polemics."

"Codswallop," Davina scoffed. "Roger, I don't know why you

allow your wife to attend those arts & crafts courses at your local tech. All her bolshiness has come about since then."

"I didn't have any choice, Mother-in-law. Charlotte has become very independently-minded. Incontestably, in part she's escaped the shackles of domesticity, and until this 'everything left of centre is good' exploration has come full circle, I've surrendered myself to yielding to her rejection of the mainstay, conservative establishment mindset."

"Well, bless my soul. You're not condoning her standpoints, are you?"

"I'm neither condoning nor condemning. My darling wife is an adult, with a free spirit and mind to adopt any discipline and doctrine of her choosing. It never interferes with the smooth running of our house, or the bringing up of our children, so I haven't really got an excuse to bludgeon her to death, have I?"

Scowling, Davina then trained on her daughter. "What were you going to say, Charlotte?"

"Only this so-called lowering of English language standards has not had the detrimental impact on the nation's fortunes that you three imply. I could support the case, computing and mobile amenities have freed up millions of people to communicate, who prior to their advent, found it difficult to express themselves."

"Maybe, but fundamentally, it's because they're well below par," Roger submitted, "when it comes to the required hallmark of paradigm written and verbal language to be competent."

"Maybe so but the stem inducement is the education system has failed them."

"Oh, what fatuous nonsense," Davina slated. "Education is on tap for all. If those on the receiving end can't be bothered to take advantage of the freebie, then they must take the consequence in their adult lives. If you ask me, Charlotte, what you are saying is a convenient get-out clause used by the PC crowd to justify the comprehensive scheme, and correspondingly bring down attainment levels."

"Mother, that's simply not true."

"*Oh yes it is*. PC people can't take the truth. They hate the truth, and will do anything they can to mask off brass tacks, embracing wholesale historical revisionism. They denigrate those seeking veracity, and deny them free speech." Pausing, she peered at her son-in-law. "Correct, isn't it, Roger?"

Almost daring him to come down against her, and face the knock-on doghouse consequences, Charlotte fulminated at her husband.

"Well, er…golly—" Not wishing to have two fiery women on his tail, he issued Davina an accommodating simper. "Truth is an interesting concept. Often, instead of being binary, the shades of controversy give credence to truth. Like being in a hall of mirrors takes a leap of faith to believe where you actually are before you move. Remaining still, enters into a perfect ambiguity with no answers, and only more themes arising. The trapped voyager has to retreat to the entrance, or rise above their presupposed limitations."

"You're blathering, Roger," Davina bitingly impeached.

"Am I?"

"Yes. Why are you blathering?"

"Well, er, I could argue you're mistaking candid philosophy for blathering."

"Allow me to help you," she vigorously proposed. "Far too many people are in the habit of using abstract concepts to engage in debate, rather than the pure essence of black and white proof. I didn't take you for one of these catch-all, internationalist Muppets, spouting one-liner slogans and psycho-babble configured to evade the cold light of truth."

"Got any prima facie evidence to bolster the supposition?"

"The prima facie evidence is all around you, in every walk of daily life."

"If I might interject?" Valentine requested.

"Please," Roger encouraged with a welcoming gesture. "This altercation could do with some wise words from the president of the clan."

"*Hah*. Thank you, Roger. It's not often I'm elevated to the zenith of the household." Charged with vim, he twinkled warmly. "Whether the proposition is couched in either deductive or inductive terms, if any reasoned conclusion is to result, it beholds both parties to carefully examine each side of the argument."

"Dad's right," Charlotte piped up. "Arguments are meant to be convincing, so philosophers must be sensitive to what makes an argument convincing or not."

"Quite, clever daughter of mine. Now—" Gathering momentum, he lifted his hands in an astute manner, his expression certain, emulating that of an erudite professor. "A statement is an unambiguous declarative sentence of fact or non-fact about the world, whereas an argument is a series of pronouncements constructed to establish a claim. And, in inductive terms, tenable arguments must be strong and cogent, whereas bad arguments are weak and muddled."

"Okay Socrates," Davina japed, "so where does it leave Roger, blatherer or philosopher?"

Ruminating, he smirked at Roger. "I think a bit of both. I know you are sometimes tough-minded, Davina, reducing your sensitivity to spot sincere human traits, but I also know you do not lack for intellect or a high I.Q. If your antennae had been on receive, you might have detected Roger straining to fortify Charlotte, whilst simultaneously, not belittling your rather rumbustious attack on her current set of beliefs."

"Was I?" Roger rebutted. "I didn't think I was that clever."

"Aah, ever the modest broker hey?" Valentine complimented.

"Anyway, Mother," Charlotte interrupted, "yours is an asymmetrical argument."

"What do you mean?"

"I mean, it's biased towards one pole, as opposed to imparting balanced symmetry."

"On the contrary, Charlotte. I've already considered both sides of the English yardsticks contention, and concluded one side is preachy, un-thought out, unstructured dribble, whilst the other is uncoloured and free from political correctness. Adopting this paragon of leftist-liberal virtue cuts no cake with me."

"Oh, Mother, you're impossible."

"Not so," Davina contended. "My darling girl, I learnt decades ago, appearances can be very deceptive. For example, Dirk Bogarde was a gorgeous man, much admired by women, but secretly he led the life of a whoopsie!"

"Oh surely," Roger endorsed, "but his sexuality did not detract from his outstanding film career. *The Spanish Gardener*, *Campbell's Kingdom*, *Death in Venice* and *The Night Porter* readily come to mind, and Bogarde was a fine actor, capable of both dramatic and comedic roles."

"Yes, you're right, Roger, but it's not the point I'm making."

"Just what is the point you're making, my dear?" Valentine intervened.

"Things are not always what they seem. Gourmet coffee promises the sensational, but the only spectacular thing about it is, the in-vogue, chic name. The rest is just what your imagination cares to conjure up in response to its highly inflated price tag. President Blair positioned himself as a British patriot, but authorised England to be swamped by immigrants. Cameron also professes to be a patriot, but he has sanctioned the invasion to carry on unabated. Applied to Blair and Cameron, their left hands are waving in the plundering hordes, while their right hands signal to the British not to be apprehensive our country is being ethnically changed to the extent whereby we don't recognise it anymore." She threw an abrasive glint at her listeners. "You follow?"

"I concede you have an unarguable point there," Roger congratulated. "In this age of inconsequential, flimflam bunkum, bogus messiahs and soundbite politics, there's little genuine authenticity of incontestable sureness. Long gone are the days when if Churchill spoke, the whole world listened and took note, because they knew his message had the ring of credence."

"For sure," Valentine affirmed. "Churchill was the tectonic plate. If he moved, everyone moved." Swivelling to prospect Charlotte, he begged, "forgive your father for saying so, my dear, but today, world bigwigs explicitly comprising Cameron, are perpetually caught up in wrangles no one understands, have no relevance to the wellbeing of England, and are evidently designed to prolong politicians' careers and their places in the history books. For most people, to use your mother's phrase, the edicts and decrees they spout are just abstract concepts, unconditionally adjacent to verity."

"Exactly," Roger backed. "And often, and I admit this is my own hobby horse, the rhetoric is fashioned by absurdity bordering on dementia."

"You mean, there's a component of psychosis?"

"Yes I do, Valentine."

"*Incredible*," Charlotte thundered. "So what you three are saying is, anyone in the prevailing public domain, proposing change without rationale to validate it, is a charlatan out for their own ends?"

"*Yes*," Davina, Valentine and Roger emphatically cooed in unison.

~ * ~

When the children returned to the lounge, the residue of the day transposed into an 'all our yesterdays' type review, Heather recalling she had a notably testing 2011 with underperforming stuffed animal contestants on her versions of *The Weakest Link* and *Britain's Got Talent*, James moaning he is never allowed to participate in grownup activities, and inevitably Charlotte complaining the uncut world is reactionary to her adopted anything-left-of-centre doctrine. On a much more positive note, Wendy adjudged it had been a watershed year for her in terms of social interaction and went on to outline her future educational and career plans. Also striking an implicit note, Roger disclosed despite being confined to the doghouse by his lovely wife for the most marginal misdemeanours, his social calendar had provided some stimulating episodes, and his newly acquired trouble-shooter mandate at The Firm extra to his stock analyst functions had delivered many memorable experiences.

"How about you two," Roger ticketed the hosts. "What were your decisive takes on 2011?"

"Well, after the falling out we had early in the year, and my subsequent homecoming to the marital nest," Valentine substantiated glancing at his wife, "I think I can safely say on behalf of Davina and myself, a business as usual atmosphere has resumed."

Rising from her comfy chair, Charlotte affectionately embraced her mother. "I'm so pleased. Both of you had me very worried for a while."

"Oh, darling," Davina tenderly entreated, "your father and I have been together for far too long to let a silly disagreement end our marriage."

"Quite right," Valentine approved. "I behaved like a total arse and your mother forgave me."

"*Valentine*!" Davina chided. She nodded in the direction of the children.

"It's only the same word Charlotte narrowly avoided using to describe her opponent in the Greenwich Park kickboxer fight."

"Nonetheless." Grimacing at him, her body language ordained an apology.

"I'm very sorry, children."

"It's alright, Grandfather," Wendy granted.

"I've heard far worse from adults," James reminisced.

"*That's right*," Heather rang out. "You should hear some of the language Mummy comes out with when someone has upset her, mainly Daddy."

"Heather!" Charlotte murmured.

"Well it's true, Mummy. I've heard you say something rhyming with clucking on lots of occasions. 'Clucking idiot,' or 'What the cluck do you think you're doing?' or 'Cluck that.'"

Charlotte's mouth dropped open.

"And you're just as bad, Daddy," she decried, giving him a disapproving blaze. "You use the word rhyming with anchor a lot. 'Stupid anchor,' or 'They're a complete bunch of anchors,' when referring to Mummy's art class teachers. I even heard you refer to the Right Reverend Reddick as 'A self-righteous anchor,' when you told Uncle Steve about the church choir's visit to our house on Christmas Day evening."

Roger's mouth also dropped open.

~ * ~

Come the evening, the entire family dressed to celebrate the New Year, everybody emerging as either high-class, or breathtaking, or both in their best togs, the standout attraction being Roger. Clad in a tartan kilt with accompanying regalia incorporating white dress shirt, black bowtie, black, three-quarter length, single-breasted jacket, white upper-calf length socks and shiny black shoes, he stole the upmarket show.

"Where on Earth did you get that apparel from?" Charlotte curtly enquired as he made his grand entry into the lounge, everyone amazed at his Celtic epiphany.

"I hired it from Gates & Humphrey in Fenchurch Street yesterday."

"Why?" she acerbically tested.

"A, because I wear a business suit nearly every day of my life, and b, in the past, I've always worn a business suit or a penguin suit on New Year's Eve. This year, I thought I'd ring in the changes."

"I see. Well, it's a good job you've got good legs."

"Oh, Roger," Davina pealed, struck by her son-in-law's outfit, "you do look august." She walked all the way around him. "My, it really suits you."

"Thank you, darling monster er, mother-in-law. I distinguished you'd appreciate the sentiment."

"Well, Roger," Valentine declared, "you must have a touch of Scottish blood in you."

"Interesting thought, but I can assure you my heart only beats out pure English blood of the Royal Cheshire strain."

Pointing to his blue and green with red and white vertical and horizontal pinstripes kilt, Valentine interrogated, "what's the clan?"

"I'm reliably informed it's the Clan Ross, hailing from Ross & Cromarty."

"Not the McFraser then?"

"Heavens no!" He chuckled. "It's also the Clan Ross coat of arms on my sporran."

"Has it got any money in it?"

"Don't be silly, Valentine, I'm in unmitigated Scotsman mode."

"Ha, ha. Yes, they're renowned for their tightness."

Latching on to the archetypal slight, Roger hatched, "what's the difference between a tightrope and a Scotsman?"

"Go on."

"A tightrope sometimes gives."

"Ho, ho, ho, jesum crow, ha, ha, ha…"

"Someone at The Firm told me about a Scotsman who was so mean," Roger brought to mind, "when his suit needed cleaning, he donated it to a charity shop…then repurchased it at a knockdown price when they had cleaned and pressed it."

"Dear me," Valentine cackled, holding a handkerchief to his watering blinkers. "Stop it."

"Just one more. A business associate from New York told me this one. They say a 'True Scot' in North America, is one whose ancestors came from Scotland, but were born in North America to save the fare."

"Do stop it, Roger," Valentine pleaded, tears dripping down his cheek. "I'm getting stomach cramps through uncontrollable mirth."

"What's making you two laugh so much?" James posed blending into the gathering.

"Your father has been telling me the most hilarious tight Scotsman jokes," Valentine disseminated.

"Oh, I've got a good one, Grandfather."

"No, please, James," Valentine supplicated, assuming a defensive posture. "Anymore laughing and I will end up with a hernia."

After dinner, the entire family gathered in the lounge, everyone feeling a buzz sequent from wolfing down Valentine's special Caribbean Rum Punch. Heather of course abstained when Charlotte offered her a sip, citing rum was made from sugarcane, and sugarcane farms had eroded the habitats of wild animals. No matter what the grownups said to guarantee it wasn't the case, she abided adamant, stating all farming was anti-wild animal. Not wanting the squabble to go on all evening, the grownups acquiesced to her claim.

"So," Davina began, "it's time for everyone to outline their New Year's resolutions. Heather darling, you go first?"

"Yes, Grandmother." Cogitating, she brought topics to mind and disseminated she discriminated her parents wanted her to confront. "Above all, I'm going to promise not to put Fozzie Bear, Miss Piggy or any other of my stuffed animals in Mummy's washing machine when they don't give the right answers on *The Weakest Link*. I also promise not to bash Adelaide Perrett when she is wrong and I am right."

"There's one other item, isn't there?" Charlotte prompted.

"Oh yes, and I promise not to watch naughty films like *Pulp Fiction* without Mummy's permission."

"Yes, I have to sign up for the last one as well," Roger confessed, simpering.

"Very commendable, Heather," her grandfather felicitated. "Now, how about you, James?"

"I'm pretty much absolved of sin, Grandfather, so I don't have to make any resolutions."

"Oh yes you do," Charlotte pressured, fixing her son with a trenchant gaze.

"Well, erm, *hah*—" He glistened. "I surmise I have to promise not to video Mother when she gets into fights with women disagreeing with her perspectives."

"Fights," Davina parroted, fixing Charlotte with a condemning lour. "Does he mean, there have been more fights than just the one at Greenwich Park?"

"Nevermind, Mother. Go on, James, you have a further commitment to promise."

"Do I have to?"

"*Yes*," she vehemently ordered.

"But it's embarrassing."

"James, I'm not going to tell you again."

"Very well." Biting his bottom lip in vexation, he frowned. "I promise not to stare at girl's chests while I'm talking to them."

"And," Charlotte annexed.

"Take photos of them at any future garden parties we have."

Titillated by the pledge, Valentine and Roger exchanged a crafty smirk before solemnity devoured their faces.

"What else?" Charlotte persisted.

Glaring, James responded, "I will try very hard not to let *The Inbetweeners* influence my attitude towards—" His features filled with submissive lines. "Everything."

"Over to you, Wendy," Davina induced.

"I'm not sure I have any bad habits to stop like Heather and James do, so I'll commit to helping Mother more around the house."

"And," Roger coerced.

"Oh, Dad, you're not going to command me to stay away from boys, are you?"

"Only the ones answering to the name Sly, and any others from higher educational institutions knocking on our door, wanting to take you out."

"So, I am permitted to have boyfriends from Chelsfield Grammar School for Boys?"

"Who do you have in mind?" Roger snapped out, already thinking his Purdey might have to be brought into action again to deter suitors.

"I haven't decided yet."

"Right, the junior members of the family have been covered," Davina appraised. "Now for the adults. Charlotte."

"Oh, Mother, I thought we had settled I'd be exempt from making resolutions this year."

"You're referring to the telephone powwow we had yesterday?"

"Yes."

"Boo-hoo, a ruse," she boasted. "I'm surprised you fell for it. Come on, out with it."

Aggrieved she'd been bamboozled, Charlotte huffed and puffed. "Very well. I promise to be tolerant of people not holding the same views as me, and not to get infuriated with traffic wardens and inanimate objects not obeying me." She beamed profusely at her mother. "There."

"Oh, Charlotte," Roger began, "you've only just scratched the surface. There's a myriad of foibles and quirks needing to be exorcised from your inner being."

"*What*!" she blasted, scowling, her Superman X-ray vision once again primed and ready to take enormous swathes of flesh from her husband's sensitive body.

"How about promising to ditch the New Age witches brew you still occasionally present to us for dinner, and afford yours truly a freer reign over my social calendar?"

"There are limits, Roger, and I don't intend to let you use this forum as a means to gain liberties ultimately getting you into a lot of trouble."

"Trouble at Kappa Corinthians Rugby Club?" Valentine intoned, "or trouble with you?"

"Both," she uncompromisingly verified.

"Okay, Charlotte, you've suffered enough," Davina acknowledged. "You're off the hook, and Roger's on it."

"I discerned I'd not evade this little charade," he voiced, glowering at Valentine.

"Come on, Roger," Davina enlivened, "tell us what vices you're going to give up for 2012."

"Vices," he repeated. "Hhmm, I'm not sure I have any vices."

"Oh yes you have," Charlotte upheld.

"Such as?"

"Weaseling out of domestic chores, pretending you have an urgent business appointment when we're due to go to the supermarket, treating some of my friends with downright disdain."

"Some of them deserve it," he whispered to Valentine.

"Engaging in lewd and boisterous pastimes with the Hazelwood & District Gentlemen's Club—

"Sounds good, Roger," Valentine praised, "I'd like to join one of those sessions."

"Coming home from celebrations at the rugby club, ragged and tatty. Making fun of some of the less than ideal articles coming out of my arts & crafts course." She paused. "Shall I go on?"

"No," Davina directed. "We've got the picture."

"Well, Roger," Charlotte badgered, "what are you going to do about it."

"How about I become a Trappist monk, and give up life altogether?"

Chapter 3: Out of Bounds

On his return to The Firm, Analysts Department PA April Harrington reminded Roger Fraser he was due to go on a short but intensive outward-bound course centred on team bonding the second week in January.

"But it's the middle of winter, April," Fraser moaned. "Surely the dates are invalid."

She re-read the joining instructions. "No, you're to report to the British Army Blandford Camp at 18:00 hours, Sunday, 8th January. Your contact is Captain W.J. Lethbridge."

"Can we send someone else, one of those delinquent Essex boy brokers for example?"

"Because of your trouble-shooter standing, Mister Chalcroft has insisted you go, and Mister Jacques has approved your absence for three days. Oh—" She read more of the instructions.

"What?"

"And don't forget, you have a medical with the company doctor tomorrow at nine, to make sure you are fit to join the course."

"*Wonderful,*" Fraser griped.

Subdued, he strolled down to his office mumbling about his discontent.

Moments later, Lawrence Springs, one of Fraser's least favourite Essex boy traders bounded in. "Hey, Rog, baby—" He clocked Fraser's depressed shape. "You're a bit glum this morning."

"Ten out of ten for observation, Lawrence."

"What's happened? Has your copy of the latest US Federal Reserve stock market forecast caught fire through spontaneous combustion, leaving you stranded without a stock analysts' bible to cling to?"

"Huh, very droll, as my friend Gordon Anderson would say." Irritated, he peeped up from his sedentary position. "Toby Chalcroft has put me on a team bonding outward bound course."

"*What*!" Recoiling, he proclaimed, "I'm dazed Top Cat even lets you stray from Canary Wharf for a few minutes, what with your trouble-shooter responsibility and promotion to director of market analysis."

"Well, TC thinks such a course will aid my trouble-shooter credentials. Anyway—" Fraser frowned. "No doubt you are hunting for top-quality hot leads to furnish the readies to pamper your invidious lifestyle."

Thoughtfully staring at the ceiling, like the archangel Gabriel had descended from heaven above and imbued him with the ability to hold an inquest, Springs canvassed, "what does invidious mean?"

"Forget it. Its nuance meaning will be beyond your obsolete intellectual equipment."

Thunderstruck, the dealer developed an even more disconcerted phiz. "What does nuance mean?"

"Good grief, Lawrence, with commission and bonuses, you must earn at least £750,000 a year, yet your understanding of the English language is equivalent to the repartee of a fully-retarded moron."

"Actually, I didn't think it was that good."

"You're not a Chelsea devotee, are you?" Fraser probed, delivering him a damning sulk. "They tend to imbecilic speech patterns."

"No, West Ham. All the Essex boys support the Hammers."

"And by the way, contrary to what you imagine, let me correct you on a few misconceptions. Physiology is not the study of fizzy drinks. The Tea Party is not a collegiate of chimps from the Typhoo Tea advert, and the axiomatic message behind altruism is not search, trap and destroy." Slow-witted, Springs descended into a confounded rank. "Check them out on Google, or better still, the Encyclopaedia Britannica."

"Oh, right," he sheepishly mumbled. "Anyway, what gems have you got to feed my ravenous appetite for the commodities markets?"

Fraser made a few keystrokes on his laptop. "There's some high-yield opportunities arising on the London Metal Exchange for molybdenum and aluminium. If you want to venture further afield, take a gander at Brent crude on the Intercontinental Exchange, and rapeseed on the EURONEXT." Glimpsing up, he warned, "if you do venture into Brent crude, be careful. Currently, there's a potential red flag on long term earnings against the stock. It's thought in some quarters, mine inclusive, the Chinese market might very well go into decline over the forthcoming few years, and their rapacious thirst for oil will markedly decrease, causing a worldwide plunge in the price of oil."

"How do you know these things, Roger?" Springs quizzed developing a puzzled mug.

"You mean, how can I make judgements or concur with others regarding the health of the markets?"

"Yes."

"It takes a world-class analytical brain, years of study, sustained dedication to task, paying tribute to the Zen masters of the universe who determine all our fortunes, and most of all—" He narrowed his blinkers. "A clear, in-depth comprehension of the English language for verbal and written communication purposes." With a profound frontage adorning his face, Fraser rammed home, "evidently a facility you and your Essex-boy trader brethren had surgically removed at birth."

~ * ~

Still inclined not to participate in the Blandford event, late morning Fraser went to see Equities Director Toby Chalcroft up in the dizzying heights of his forty-fifth floor executive suite.

"I've got a very heavy schedule over the upcoming few weeks, Toby. Rather than going on this outward-bound course, time spent parsing the markets will be more productive."

"*Nonsense*," he inflexibly contended. "You're a gifted analyst, never fazed by any workload, including extra trouble-shooter demands."

"But—"

Unyieldingly, Top Cat elevated a dismissive hand, a sign Fraser had seen on numerous occasions. It meant, no, as in no debate, no compromise and indubitably, no get-out clause.

"Roger, why do you think The Firm is sending you on this course?"

"To hone my trouble-shooter capabilities."

"Precisely." Rising from the seated station behind his mammoth executive desk, Chalcroft clasped his hands behind his back and walked to the vast window expanse giving an aerial panorama of the Isle of Dogs financial district and west into the heart of the City of London. "I ought not to be telling you this, because it is yet to be officially announced, and it might not come off anyway." Ogling Fraser, still sitting on the other side of his desk, he relayed, "The Firm is going to make a bid to take over one of our major rivals."

"Can you say who?"

With caution in mind, TC grimaced. "I've revealed too much already, and please keep it to yourself. Don't even tell Henry Jacques. If it does come off, I foresee your trouble-shooting activities enlarging." He took a deep breath before slowly exhaling, the token indicating he remained in two minds as to whether to take the trouble-shooter deeper into his confidence. "Let's call this possible acquisition, Company X, and please don't guess it's identity. If you can work out who's in the frame, don't voice it to me. Clear?"

"Clear, Toby."

"I happen to know Company X has similar convoluted and out-of-the-ordinary challenges facing The Firm. Assuredly, they fall into trouble-shooter territory. Should the purchase succeed, you'll quickly find yourself taxed to perform missions on behalf of The Firm and Company X." Pertinently, he gestured a symbol of latitude. "Under such a circumstance, we must forensically focus on cutting to the essence of business limiting inhibitors and nip them in the bud, or the venture could fail."

"Quite," Fraser validated, then inwardly thought he'd been far too quick to agree, Chalcroft's silky sales skills drawing him into his landing net, the buttering up process coming thereafter.

"I know you're an excellent problem solver and communicator, as well as a first-rate diplomat, Roger…" *Yes, here it comes*, Fraser recognised. "…but dealing with the executive layer in Company X will even test your skills, particularly your patience. The Firm will be the senior partner in the takeover. As such, Company X executives might not like you being designated to wash their dirty linen."

"Does Company X have dirty linen?"

"All enterprise scale investment houses have dirty linen to cleanse, some more than others. I'm not saying Company X falls into the delinquent category, merely pointing out The Firm will inherit their abnormal business conundrums to resolve, as and when, but—" Frowning TC developed his well-known menacing persona. "Having an outsider come in to clean the stables, meaning you, could produce some resistance in their executive sphere." Moving towards his desk, he came to rest behind his executive chair, his deportment blown into full assertiveness. "Principally, it's why you are going on this team bonding course with the military. Bembridge and I think it will endow you with the skills and knowhow to handle Company X trouble-shooter type obstacles."

"And if The Firm does not appropriate Company X?"

"Those skills will still be useful to you for trouble-shooting assignments with The Firm."

"Right," Fraser accepted. "Looks like I'll be Blandford bound this Sunday."

"Good luck, Roger. Oh, and by the way—" Top Cat's hard physiognomy relaxed into a smile. "You'll be having company on the course from another Firm employee."

"Oh, who?"

"Walter Hoskyns. We liked the way you worked with him on the Guatemala affair. Based on the homework we've done, we think some Company X business enigmas will need a commercial man to help you tackle them."

~ * ~

Faithful to his convictions, Fraser acquired half a dozen meditation books, some grounded on the teachings of Buddhism and the Dalai Lama, others of a practical bent, giving instruction on meditation technique. Noting the wisdom did not fall into the twenty-minute, quick physical workout bracket, he quickly realised for the student to achieve the desired state of tranquility, a lifetime's perseverance was required. Often, practitioners spent months curled up in the lotus position, trying to attain oneness with the deity, Fraser not bargaining for such rigid devotion. In his mindset, meditation took place at convenient spells when vital obligations allowed, the measure taking no more than a few tens of minutes. Resigning himself to compromise, he intended to practice the discipline before breakfast, at lunchtime and after dinner, family and work commitments permitting.

His introductory attempts to cleanse his mind of the clutter consequent from stress were not successful. Lighting a perfumed candle at the onset, he then sat in the *I Ching* posture and practiced the required breathing exercises whilst imagining his muscles relaxing, *ab initio* in his feet and legs, then his body and arms and finally his neck and face. Shadowing the physical initiation, he then immersed his mind in a good memory, typically a place he had known, his vision closed off and his breathing steady during the enactment. Having a low threshold of boredom, after less than ten minutes his concentration diminished, the place he mentally revisited losing its definition as other thoughts permeated his consciousness, his peepers involuntary opening, breaking the trance-like interlude.

Never one to give up without a fight, Fraser persisted with his chosen path on the basis like with most things, practice made perfect.

~ * ~

On a bright and unusually warm for the time of the year afternoon, Fraser piloted his beloved BMW M3 down to Blandford Camp, two miles north-east of Blandford Forum, Dorset. Still having reservations about his ability to survive the ordeal, he had reiterated to Charlotte his last will and testament was to be found in the bottom drawer of his study desk at their Hazelwood house. She had found his somewhat grave notice quaint, told him not to be such a drama queen, and favoured nothing untoward befalling him.

Since their trip to sort out The Firm's investments in Guatemala, Fraser had infrequently seen Commercial Manager Walter Hoskyns. Though in terms of confidence Hoskyns had lurched into the pueblo as a church mouse and marched out as a mountain lion, Fraser ascertained from their brief liaisons the commercial manager's self-belief had waned. During the drive to Dorset, he pondered how Hoskyns had reacted to the news he was Blandford bound. Had it sent him scrambling for the Valium bottle, or did he take it in his stride?

Latterly, Blandford Camp housed the British Army's Royal Corps of Signals Regiment and had also become home to their advanced officer team training unit. Ancillary to officer recruit full-induction training at Sandhurst, periodically and as new methodologies evolved, many long-term serving officers joined the unit's outward-bound courses, their content centring on developing team bonding skills under simulated theatre battlefield conditions. In line with Government-MoD strategies to make such specialised units pay for themselves, their exclusive brand of skills was made available to the private sector, mercantile companies recognising the army could put their executive and middle managers through a regime not available in civvy street. Triumphant on an enviable array of offerings, Blandford had gained a much-vaunted reputation for empowering course participants with the necessary acumen and ingenuity enabling them to settle any business puzzler involving team bonding and had received multiple plaudits from highly satisfied company corporate executives.

When The Firm's London-based VP Investment Banking Luther Bembridge and Toby Chalcroft had discussed the need to beef up Fraser's trouble-shooter skills in response to the possible capture of Company X, Bembridge cited a Morgan Stanley board member friend of his attached colossal importance to Blandford's reputation. Making discreet enquiries with the Blandford advanced officer team training unit adjutant, *vis-à-vis* client references, Chalcroft found in addition to Morgan Stanley, other financial institutions and a host of industrial companies awarded Blandford superlative reviews and recommendations.

Halting the M3 outside the Blandford Camp main gate sentry point, Fraser showed his letter of introduction and passport to a guard, freeing him to drive into the core of the military base. Following signposts for the civilian accommodation block, within minutes he parked the coupé outside his temporary lodgings. Adjacent to the block, he saw the advanced officer team training unit building, the slogan-sign over its entrance proclaiming, 'We aim to make you a better officer'.

Entering the block, an NCO verified his registration details, allocated him a room on the third floor, and told him dinner served in the officers' mess commenced at 20:00 hours.

"Has Mister Hoskyns, also of The Firm, checked in yet?"

"Just let me see, sir." Scanning through a list of attendees for the three-day course, the NCO affirmed, "he has arrived, sir. He's in room 214. If you wish to talk to him, there's an internal phone network connecting all the accommodation rooms, and reception. Just dial his room number."

"Many thanks."

After acclimatising himself to his room, Fraser called Hoskyns.

"Walter, it's Roger Fraser."

"Hello, Roger."

"All set for some team bonding?"

"To answer the motion competently, I'd need to know what it means."

"Surely Chalcroft gave you the same information pack he gave me explaining the nature and objectives of the course?"

"Indeed he did, but I can't see how this fits in with my commercial manager job description."

Unlike for him, Fraser deduced Top Cat had not let on about Company X being the stimulant behind both of them being sent on the course.

"I think you were nominated because of the excellent job you did in Guatemala."

"Yes, Chalcroft did allude to it as being the reason."

"If I were you, Walter, I'd take your inclusion as a huge compliment."

"He articulated a phrase like that, as well."

"Right, a quick shower and shave, and I'll see you for dinner."

Captain Lethbridge, DSO and bar, and an Afghanistan conflict veteran, warmly greeted The Firm's pair in the officers' mess, Fraser immediately taking to his genial personality. During the course of the dinner, they met their fellow civilian course members, Fraser judging like him, all the participants were aged thirty to fifty, were middle to senior line managers working for blue-chip organisations, and had never been anywhere near an army base in their entire lives. Few possessed the sheen of sportsmen, most exhibiting the effects of too much food and alcohol intake. Albeit Fraser could be accused of the same indulgence, at least he still played rugby, and on occasion did a few torturous press-ups.

Catching Hoskyns note he gibed, "if a man's success can be gauged by the size of his waistline, then I'd suggest most of our new comrades in arms have been extremely successful."

"An astute observation, Roger. For my part, notwithstanding I've always been on the slim side, I could never boast an overabundance of physical energy. The most exertion I get is from moving chess pieces, and pulling newspaper broadsheet pages apart."

During dinner, the grape flowed freely, breaking down inhibition barriers and establishing camaraderie. Eventually sauntering to their rooms, everyone felt the grand buzz of expectation pervading their beings. Chilled to the point of floppiness, Fraser fell asleep very quickly.

He got a rude awakening when the alarm clock went off like a demented Claxton at 05:30. As his spiers struggled to open, initially he couldn't figure out his surroundings. Then his mind kicked in and he remembered the previous evening Captain Lethbridge apprised course members, trailing breakfast served at 06:00 hours, the course formally began at 06:30. Drawing the room curtains uncovered pitch blackness outside, and no sign of the sun.

"Ye gods," he muttered to himself.

Quickly dressing in the thermal underwear, army camouflage clothing, boots and beret he'd found in his room on arrival, he then pinned his identification tag to his breast pocket and made for the canteen. After breakfast, hands in pockets and bleating about the chilly dawn, the civilians assembled on the floodlit barrack square opposite to the advanced officer team training unit building.

Self-consumed, they were still complaining about getting up in the middle of the night and the Arctic environment, colder than a well-driller's arse, when a voice boomed out, "*get in line*."

Craning their necks to the blast fount, everyone clocked a well-built, tall man, with a weather-beaten, rugged face, dressed as they were, and stood to attention with a swagger stick under his arm.

"I said, *get inline*. Move yourselves, move yourselves. You should be there by now!"

Spurred into action, the thirty early morning risers formed a line abreast.

"My name is Colour Sergeant Kilroy. That's spelt, b-a-s-t-a-r-d."

Classically comical, his duel announcement brought a few snickers and grimaces, the name Kilroy associated with facetious dido's and fictitious literary characters, whereas the translated articulation of his surname made no bones about his intolerance to indiscipline.

"I didn't petition for comments," Kilroy barked. "Form three ranks. Tallest on the right, shortest on the left."

In an effort to establish height credentials, the entrants stumbled about before coalescing into three, ten-man ranks.

"Atten-*tion*."

They came to a faltering attention.

Unimpressed, Kilroy examined them with muted regard. "Stand at ease."

They did so, beginning to realise they were mistaken, if they expected a holiday camp.

"Platoon, platoon atten-tion."

They did so again.

"Better." Squinting at them he instructed, "you will address me as Colour Sergeant Kilroy, not sir, not that bolshie bastard, or any other derogatory names associated with my rank and reputation. Clear?"

"Clear, Colour Sergeant Kilroy," the partakers echoed.

Studying his charges with cynicism, Kilroy went along the ranks, inspecting them as if classifying a piece of high-grade bone China for impurities, and occasionally making acid comments about someone's longer than army regulation hair, or their out of shape semblance.

Regressing to his frontal position, he stood the platoon at ease then issued more criticisms about their presentation and their obvious calorie over-consumption. Seeing Captain Lethbridge departing the building, he stood the platoon to attention. When Lethbridge came to a halt, Kilroy saluted him, Lethbridge emulating the honour before addressing the platoon.

"Good morning, gentlemen. I trust you all had a good night's sleep, and are ready to commence your team bonding training. Course Chief Instructor Colour Sergeant Kilroy will be your overarching mentor and coach. Over the contiguous three days, you'll be subordinated to some testing sorties calling for teamwork and cooperation if you're going to pass this schooling with flying colours. We're all for individual achievement, but you'll find conjoint responsibility and collaboration will pull you through. You'll be split into three ten-man sections, competing in a series of tests. There will be rewards for the winning section. However, whether first, second or third, to accomplish a pass, every team member has to finish the duty. This is a team game, gentlemen. To win an event, all team members must pass the winning post. Accomplishing the goal will call for drive, determination and most of all, team spirit. Team spirit will result from bonding and a shared purpose. Substantively, it is these attributes we're seeking to expose, nurture and measure in the newcomer. If you have any difficulties, I'm available through the company adjutant. Good luck, and I hope all of you receive certificates of completion for the team bonding training course." Finished, he turned to Kilroy. "Carry on, Colour Sergeant."

"Sir."

Exchanging salutes, Lethbridge then strode off to his office.

"Right," Kilroy began, "let's get you sorted into three sections. A-Section will comprise…" He read out ten names, their owners forming A-Section forward of the platoon, B-Section and C-Section similarly formed, Hoskyns attached to A-Section, Fraser to C-Section.

Unaccustomed to the regimentation and finding it amusing, one or two chortles arose from the ranks, Kilroy homing in on the gravest culprit.

"Name?"

"Magnus Farquhar, Colour Sergeant," the offender answered, his effeminate moniker bringing smirks from those nearest to him, Kilroy tarrying stoic.

"As well as being able to snigger, Mister Farquhar, are you tough?"

Such a juxtaposed ask, the barbed query made simpers broaden, the dichotomy between Farquhar's name and notions of toughness, unimaginable.

Sobering up, Farquhar tabled, "why do you ask, Colour Sergeant?"

"Just prodding to get a mental map of where you fit on the aggression scale, if in fact, you fit at all."

"Gentlemen, let me be crystal," Kilroy elucidated, resuming his berth at the head of the platoon. "I am famous for my lack of humour, both on the parade ground and during manoeuvres. You will have a toilsome enough job matriculating from this course with a pass, let alone higher honours. The last thing you want to do is test me and get on my bad side." Theatrically holding out his swagger stick, he warned, "there's a notch on this stick for every disrespectful, smart-arsed, know-it-all braggart, thinking they can breeze through our testing courses, and have dramatically fluffed making the required standard." Replacing the stick under his right arm, he advocated, "if any of you feel you cannot commit to a military regime, step forward now, and we'll happily dispatch you to Civvy Street."

Peering along the ranks, he noted no one stepped frontward, their expressions resting neutral.

"I'll take that as a full commitment."

Marching them off to a wooded zone in Blandford Camp, the light extended by the parade ground floodlights vanished behind them. Bringing the platoon to a halt by a hut, he stood them at ease, went inside and came out with three torches.

"Right." Shining a torch at an area with a few very long logs and some shorter pollarded tree branches, then into two alike spaces containing the same tree parts, before illuminating a wet ditch about ten feet deep and six feet wide, he tutored, "using the wood available, each section will come up with a way to cross the dyke, taking all the wood with them to the other side." Randomly selecting one man in each section to be given a torch, he then stood bolt upright. "You have ten minutes to make it to the other side. Fall out."

Forming three huddles, most section members mooted solutions as to how the undertaking could be fulfilled, but gained little abetment from their colleagues.

"The clock is ticking, gentlemen," Kilroy advised. "You have less than seven minutes to execute the task."

Under pressure, each section agreed on an approach, then ran around like scolded chickens straining to assemble the wood parts to form a crude bridge. During their assays to fabricate the make-shift, and get all section members across the ditch with all the wood ending up in the far side, most fell off their compositions into the ravine and got a soaking.

"Times up, gentleman, and I see all three sections have failed the test."

Distinctly unmoved, he gaped around the panting platoon with a vexed mien, the disorderly foot soldiers exasperated or bemused staring at their pitiful deeds to build a solid bridge construction.

"Now, why do you think you all flunked?" Kilroy hit them with a hard stare. "Anyone."

"Because we were disorganised," someone let slip.

"Yes. What else?"

"Because we didn't analyse the situation properly before engaging a plan," another incensed platoon member asserted.

"Yes. What else?"

"Because we didn't elect a team leader, and buy into a rock-solid plan quickly enough," Fraser contended.

"Yes." Obviously pleased, he pointed his swagger stick at Fraser. "All the inducers tabled are valid, but the cardinal foundation is you didn't elect a bossman and most essentially bond with him and your section members. Without hegemony and binding, no team mission and certainly no battle can be won." Lighting up, he professed, "you've just learnt your first valuable lesson, gentlemen."

For seasoned civvy streetwise managers, the remark came as a damning indictment of their insular and somewhat cosy worlds. Used to sitting in air-conditioned chambers, with wall-to-wall secretaries and a surfeit of willing supernumeraries to do their bidding, they all realised when it came to leftfield spectres in their experience, they were like babes in the wood, only marginally more qualified than army raw recruits.

"*Fall in*," Kilroy sharply bayed.

Reverting to platoon formation, the three sections were then stood to attention.

"Your real training will now begin."

"Colour Sergeant Kilroy," someone from B-Section began, "can we withdraw to the accommodation block to put some dry clothes on?"

"What makes you think you have any clothes other than the ones you're standing in?" Without waiting for a reply, he roared, "platoon, platoon right turn." They did so. "Quick march…left, left, left, right, left…"

During the remnant of the morning, Kilroy deputised a corporal trainer from his team to each section to act as their section mentor, the three sections then subjected to competitive burdens, all practical and centred on solving typical, in-the-field military quandaries with minimal equipment and within a timed period. Observing the units going through their enterprises, their mentors occasionally gave limited advice. Having learnt from their disastrous ditch debacle, each section appointed a team guv'nor for every toil to delegate assignments and manage the workout. With each succeeding test, collective proving led to cooperative teamwork fertilising team bonding, strangers fused into a collegial unit with a common purpose. After four hours of solid graft, the sections had developed better execution, drawing a few encouraging remarks from mentors at the culmination of the calling. Impervious to their improvement, Kilroy's countenance persevered deadpan and impassive.

With most of the participants gone to seed, by lunchtime, enthusiasm had given way to fatigue, Colour Sergeant Kilroy's relentless goading to go the extra mile to consummate targets adding to the draining of energies.

Sitting alongside Fraser during lunch, Johnson Matthey Sales Director, Rex Downey, grumbled, "who the hell is that guy? Darth Vader mixed in with Freddie Kruger?"

"To quote from the film *An Officer and a Gentleman*," Fraser replied, "he's 'your mama and your papa' for the adjoining two and a half days."

"Jeepers, you're right. Maybe he has a Gunnery Sergeant Folly fixation. Slackers will be submitted to, 'I want your DOR, boy.'"

"Yes, drop on request." Browsing his associate course members, Fraser imparted, "somehow, I don't think anyone is going to take such an option. Everyone now knows who everyone else works for, and being dropped on request is tantamount to a black mark against their company."

"*Hah*!"

"What?"

"If Foley—" He tutted at the mistake. "Er, Kilroy, puts us on a route march this afternoon, I'd not be astounded if he inaugurated the, 'I don't know but its bin said, Air Force wings are made of lead. I don't know but I've bin told, Navy wings are made of gold' routine."

"Yeah, changing Navy for Army."

"And those notches on his swagger stick are pure Sergeant Foley."

"Ahh, it's where cinema and actuality diverge. Foley's adoption of the intimidation is pre-owned. British Army trainers have been chipping away at their swagger sticks since the Anglo-Zulu Wars."

After further in-the-field, military problem-solving drills, the launching day session terminated at 18:30 hours, the twelve-hour working day with only a half-hour lunch break coming as a severe step change in terms of workload intensity for many participants. Even the high stamina and forever very busy Fraser felt the burn.

During dinner, Fraser talked to Hoskyns.

"So, Walter, how did you find today's session?"

"Are you kidding, Roger?" Putting down his knife and fork, Hoskyns gave him a disconcerted glare. "It was the most onerous day I've ever experienced in my working life. I had to take a Valium tablet when I retired to my room. Guatemala was a piece of cake in comparison."

"Yes, I must say, the amount and sheer ferocity of the pursuits took its pound of flesh out of me."

"So exhausted, one guy in A-Section threw up midway through

the final discharge. I pride myself on keeping my body weight under control through a careful diet, but it damn near wasted me. It's why I had to have a fix. I haven't taken Valium since the day we flew to Guatemala. I always keep a bottle of them with me as a kind of safety blanket, but this is the only juncture I've taken one since. All the confidence you imbued me with conducting business with the Guatemalans seeped away. If there had been another toil sequent to the ultimate one, I'd have dissolved."

"Steady, Walter, we all felt it today. An intense outward-bound course comes as a shock to the system. It takes acclimatisation to get used to it. Tomorrow will be easier. Your mind and body will know what to expect."

"You really think so?"

"*I do*," he inveterated, inwardly knowing he had pulled the wool, and there'd be no let up to the intensity, or getting used to both mental and physical demands over the course period.

In his youth, Fraser had engaged in a myriad of testing outward bound courses through Chelsfield Grammar School for Boys, the school presently attended by his son James. As a junior player, Kappa Corinthians Rugby Club had also put him through the outward-bound course mill. On each occasion, he had gone into an intensive training regime beforehand, so as to make the transition from everyday life to the high-adrenaline pumping requisitions of the process less of a jolt to his body. Though fit, his pre-course preparation never seemed to fully accomplish the aim, the severity of whatever he'd signed up to, testing him to his limits.

Before daybreak the next morning, the platoon stood at ease listening to Colour Sergeant Kilroy's instructions for the starting exercise.

"Shortly, each section will climb aboard a six-tonne transport vehicle and be dropped off ten miles from Blandford Camp in open country. Each section will be given a different compass heading drop off point, so you're kept well apart. Your objective is to pass through the camp gates by 12:00 hours. As usual, all section members must cross the camp threshold by the watershed for the entire section to pass the test. Your mobiles and money will be temporarily confiscated. Timepieces will be endorsed so long as they do not house a GPS function. Any questions?"

"Will we be given a map, Colour-Sergeant?" a B-Section member enquired.

"You won't need a map. The sun will rise at 08:02. Using a combination of the sun's position and a compass, you'll be able to roughly work out which way is Blandford Camp."

"Doesn't it rather depend on whether we're dropped off north or south of the camp, Colour-Sergeant Kilroy?" Fraser queried.

"Indeed it does. So you will need a third factor to compute where you have been dropped off. It will be down to teamwork and initiative to derive the third component. You may use any scheme you wish, so long as it's lawful." Pausing, he then silkily communicated, "a word of advice. You'll have more tasks in front of you this afternoon, so don't expend all your energy on this stint."

Cognizant of the warning, three transport vehicles departed the camp containing the sections in fully-enclosed rears with their mentor.

As soon as the vehicle transporting C-Section pulled away, Fraser pleaded to mentor Corporal Lancing, "can we have the compass now?"

"Nice try, Mister Fraser." Lancing grinned. "However, it'd give you the ability to see our direction and backtrack to the camp from your inception point."

"I thought you might say that," Fraser verbalised, duplicating the grin.

"Since you've taken the quintessential move, Roger," Rex Downey began, "how about you steer this activity?"

"My pleasure." Lingering, he matured a thoughtful aspect. "Surmising we get to the outset point by 07:30, it gives us four and a half hours to retrace our outbound journey to Blandford. Allowing say fifteen minutes to get our bearings, leaves twenty-six and a half minutes per mile, if we have to walk it."

"What do you mean by, if we have to walk it?" John Laing Engineering Director, Harry Burdett tendered.

"Kilroy didn't say we couldn't use motorised transport," Fraser submitted, staring at Corporal Lancing.

Lancing smirked. "You're learning."

"So what do you propose?" Downey combed.

"I think it's safe to assume we'll not be dropped on a road, because we could quickly survey for road signs giving a clue apropos Blandford's whereabouts." Shuffling about on the surround bench seat they all sat on, he postulated, "no, our genesis destination will be a lane or a field, so here's what I propose. As soon as we're dropped off, let's reconnoitre for farm house lights. I intend to barter a deal with a farmer to take us to Blandford in exchange for some form of negotiated remuneration, payable when the course is over. On the basis we might not get a positive reaction from the first farmer approached, I'll send out six men in search of a lift. As an alternate, the residual four of us will scout the sector searching for road signs, just in case if we can't get any takers. I'll ascribe thirty minutes to those sent out to rejoin us with their offers. If there are no takers, it will mean fast walking to the camp at a rate of a mile every twenty-four minutes." Pinpointing Corporal Lancing, he broached, "a point of clarification, if I may?"

"Go on."

"Ten miles is not as the crow flies. It's ten miles by road, isn't it?"

"That I can't confirm, Mister Fraser."

"Mmmm, your response might indicate there is scope to cover the home journey cross country, hence the issuing of a compass."

"Which means if we walk along roads," Burdett calculated, "the actual distance travelled might be more than ten miles to the base."

"Quite," Fraser acceded. "It means we'd have to run until we found a signpost with a precise distance to Blandford on it, and with the time outstanding, maintain a proportionate minutes per mile rate."

"Sounds tough," Burdett allotted. "Fingers crossed we can find a responsive farmer."

When the six-tonne transport vehicle abandoned C-Section at the drop point, they found themselves on a narrow gravel lane, surrounded by fields with hedgerows and trees and in pitch blackness, the feeling of sheer isolation stunning them into silence.

"I can't see a damned thing," Arcadia Group Sales Director, Austin Haskett whispered, as if sensing the need to dwell quiet. "It's bloody cold as well."

"I can't even make the hands out on my Breitling," Downey piped up. "This has become more of an out of bounds endeavour, than an outward-bound course."

"I checked my watch just before the truck stopped," Fraser reviewed. "It read 07:25. So it's about thirty-seven minutes to sun up."

"I can't see any farmyard lights," Mott MacDonald Business Development Director, Nick Logan enlightened.

"Right," Fraser acknowledged, "we'll have to take a chance, and move on a course as a group, either up or down this lane keeping tabs for farm lights as we go."

"Let's use the truck's course," Haskett suggested. "Eventually it must buttress on to a road."

Tramping along the lane, they did not appreciate a deep trench run by its side. Inadvertently, Logan stepped to near its edge, tumbling into it and emitting a loud, "*aarrgghhh*!"

Hearing his shout, the residuum of C-Section went to his aid. Pulling him out, Logan thanked them before attempting to stand up straight and feeling a sharp pain in his right ankle.

"Damn it," he screeched. "I think I twisted my foot when I fell in."

Fraser and Downey supported his weight.

"Try a few steps," Fraser encouraged.

He did so, but collapsed under the effort. "Holy cow, I don't think I can walk."

"Well, we could always put you out of your misery by clubbing you to death," Haskett mocked, his black humour making Fraser scintillate. "But we'd fail the test."

"We'll have to carry him," Fraser nominated, "until we can find a makeshift stretcher."

Pentland Group Business Futures Director, Loyd Uttley stepped forward. "I'll give him a piggy-back."

"Many thanks, Loyd," Fraser praised. "Great teamwork."

Continuing down the lane, eventually the hedge row to their right gave way to a clear spectacle across a matrix of fields.

"Bugger me," Haskett blurted, pointing over the undulating land.

"There's a light. It *must* be a farm house."

"Yep," Fraser responded. "Can you go and investigate, Austin?"

"Sure." Accelerating away, he legged it across the fields in the direction of the light.

"It's the only light on the horizon," Downy observed. "Let's hope the farmer is receptive to making a few quid."

A while later, Haskett reappeared. Out of breath, he panted out his words. "I spoke to the farmer's wife…told her who we are and our undertaking. The farmer…her husband George, has a tractor capable of hitching up to a cart. She reckons he will take us to Blandford for £300."

"Splendid. Well done, Austin. Metered out, it's thirty-pounds per person."

"The only thing is, the farmer has already gone off in the tractor, and won't be returning until about nine-thirty."

"No problem. Still gives us plenty of time." Fraser beheld the sky. "It's starting to lighten. Come on, let's get to this farmhouse."

"Did you find out where we are, from the farmer's wife?" Fraser solicited Haskett as they made their way across the fields.

"Yes. Their farm is two miles south of the A35 at Bloxworth. We're south of Blandford. She said Bloxworth might be ten miles as the crow flies from Blandford, but by road it's nearer to fifteen."

"Yikes, so walking back to cross the finish by noon is very difficult, if not impossible."

"Yes. To succeed, we'd need to acquire some transport."

"Kilroy insisted success would be down to teamwork and initiative. I'm thinking providing each section with a compass and alluding to a third factor to compute where we were dropped off were red herrings."

By mid-morning, C-Section were aboard the cart, Fraser standing on a footplate behind the farmer sat in the tractor driving seat.

"George, I'll write you out a cheque for £300, and drop it by the farm house Wednesday evening. Okay?"

"No need, Mister Fraser." Reaching into a glovebox-like gap in the tractor dashboard array, he pulled out a business card, handing it to Fraser. "Just send the cheque to the farm."

"Very trustworthy of you, George."

"Ah well, us country folk can tell a good egg from a villain. Besides, if you reneged, I could always get your details from the army."

"Be assured, a cheque will be winging its way to you by Thursday."

"That's good enough for me."

"It was very considerate of you to go out of your way to accommodate us."

"No worries. Me and the wife are old hands at this."

"How do you mean, *old hands*?" Fraser muttered, puzzled by the remark.

"You're the third lot from Blandford Camp coming knocking on the farmhouse door over the past year."

"Oh, I see." Fraser twigged. "And er, how much have you levied other beached course participants?"

"You're a businessman, Mister Fraser. I'm sure you keep your cards close to your chest in your business dealings." Glancing behind, he simpered. "Suffice to say, the price goes up with every new Blandford intake."

Fraser laughed. "I thought there were some sharks in my world of investment banking, but we're novices compared to country folk when it comes to maximising profit."

Converging on Black Lane connecting to Blandford Camp, Fraser tapped the tractor driver on the arm. "George, you can drop us off here. We'll walk the rest of the way for effect."

Waving the farmer goodbye, C-Section then made their way to the camp, less than half a mile away, three of the section propping the injured Logan. Ahead at the entrance, they saw Colour-Sergeant Kilroy holding a clipboard.

As the last C-Section man crossed the threshold, Kilroy noted the section's time of arrival, then called for medics to take Logan to the medical centre for treatment.

"Good," he commended Fraser, "you got all of the section over the finishing line before noon, so I can award you maximum points."

"Have Sections A and B returned yet, Colour-Sergeant Kilroy?"

"Not yet, laddie, but they still have time." Noting the dishevelled deportment of C-Section, he advised, "if I were you, I'd get yourselves cleaned up before lunch, and much more importantly, for the afternoon workouts."

When Fraser talked to Hoskyns during lunch, it transpired A-Section had been dropped off near King's Stag to the west of Blandford. They too had figured a farm conveyance afforded the best home bound option, their benevolent farmer also taking a £300 fee. Moseying into the canteen midway through lunch, B-Section had made it to the finish line with seconds to go. Dropped off at Rockbourne, north-east of Blandford, they elected to walk before happening on a road sign displaying Blandford Forum fourteen miles. Eventually, they too found a friendly farmer. When someone from A-Section pumped how much the other sections were burdened, and the reply identified £300, Fraser adjudged a neat cartel of self-interested farmers like George existed all around Blandford Camp, ready, willing and able to come to the rescue of stranded out-of-bounds course participants.

Similarly testing in terms of sovereignty and team bonding, Kilroy's afternoon sessions took place in the camp. Appertaining to solving typical army in-theatre brainteasers with minimal assets, other than those of the human variety, everyone evaluated unlike their office environments distinguished by an overabundance of every resource, soldiers on the battlefield had to invent on the spot to fulfil the demand, predominantly staying alive.

~ * ~

After a sumptuous dinner in the officer's mess, Fraser talked to Captain Lethbridge.

"Colour-Sergeant Killjoy, er, sorry, Kilroy, really drove us to the hilt today. Some of the course participants are looking down-at-the-heel."

"True, but doubtless, they will be fitter."

"Funny you saying that. When I put my suit on tonight, it felt looser on me. I must have lost some weight."

"Over the three-day course, on average, participants lose about twelve pounds."

"*Get away*!"

"It's true. A combination of the intense physical regime coupled with being driven to pass the team bonding course, results in more weight being shed than in usual exercise. Plus, we ensure everyone eats healthily."

"Maybe I'll get my rugby club to take a dose of your training." Producing a bashful face, he reproached, "unlike me, some of them are very overweight," Lethbridge sparkling at the amusing proposition.

"Tell me, Captain Lethbridge, what's the story on Colour-Sergeant Kilroy. He's a very hard taskmaster, but he has the respect of every platoon member."

"Ahh, interesting." Sending the inquisitive civilian a riveting shine, he catechized, "guess his age?"

"Ohh…er…he's weather-beaten, but I'd say mid-thirties."

"He's forty-eight and has nourished the same body weight since joining the army, aged sixteen. Kilroy is the fittest man on this entire camp. In the gym every day, he also adheres to a strict calorie intake regime, and only drinks alcohol on official occasions."

"Wow, pretty much the archetypal role model for army entrants."

"Precisely. He's also seen action from the Falklands War onwards." Breaking off, Lethbridge adopted a very sincere visage. "I don't know how familiar you are with ribbons worn on uniforms signifying medal awards, but if you browse Colour-Sergeant Kilroy's ribbons, you'll see amongst a superabundance of campaign medals, he has also been awarded the Victoria Cross and the George Cross."

"The two highest awards for valour in the face of the enemy."

"Quite. They were won during Operation Desert Storm and Operation Enduring Freedom."

Noisily blowing out through his mouth, Fraser pursed his lips in admiration. "A powerful piece of manpower then?"

"They don't come any better." Lethbridge radiated. "*Hah*…I know a lot of young officers sent on these courses think he's the perennial winner of the UK bar-steward of the year award, and he's got an uncanny knack to make a stressful calling even more taxing, but like all colour-sergeants, Kilroy is also eminently capable of making the most hilarious remarks."

"Really."

"Put it this way, lilies have never been so gilded."

"But he told us on day one, he is famous for his lack of humour."

"Oh, that's just a seasoned colour-sergeants' trick used to instil discipline in the ranks," Lethbridge declared, grinning.

The closing day of the course saw attendees undertake more testing exploits designed to maximise team bonding in order to accomplish expectations. Like in the other sections, Fraser and his fellow C-Section compatriots got better and better at executing the practices as inter-bonding took paramount hold. Knowing each other's capabilities and talents, objectives were achieved on-time under the command of saddled skippers. Fraser likened it to the intimacy of rugby players optimising team performance under the jurisdiction of the team captain and thus winning matches.

At the course finish, Captain Lethbridge called the platoon for a final wash-up in the admin centre at 17:30, the civilians disclosing they had discovered hidden depths in their makeup over the three-day training period, and felt better equipped to handle business missions needing team bonding to guard success.

"The good news is, gentlemen," Lethbridge elucidated with pride, "all of you have passed, some with distinction. The attainment has been down to your own perseverance to succeed and Colour-Sergeant Kilroy's motivational skills." Studying Kilroy admiringly, sat at the rear of the room, he congratulated, "well done, Colour-Sergeant."

Kilroy stood up. "Sir," he boomed in recognition of the praise.

Sitting at the front, Harland Gourlay, Director of Global Business for Bibby Line, the most senior participant on the course, caught Lethbridge's eye. "May I say something, Captain Lethbridge?"

"The floor is yours. Mister Gourlay."

Getting to his feet, Gourlay recounted, "when we landed at Blandford Camp, all of us underestimated the challenge before us. Without Colour-Sergeant Kilroy's guidance and occasional metaphorical boot up the behind, none of us would have capped the course. I'd like to call on all delegates to express their gratitude with a round of applause for the Colour-Sergeant."

Everyone in the room stood, rotated to regard Kilroy and clapped, the Colour-Sergeant rapt suitably in a choked comportment.

As the adulation died away, Lethbridge joked, "you'll be making our renowned chief course instructor blush in a minute, but many thanks gentlemen."

After collecting their certificates and making farewells to course members, Fraser and Hoskyns ambled off to the accommodation block for a shower before setting off for home.

"It has really renewed the vigour I had after Guatemala," Hoskyns edified.

"Yes, I must say, it has enlivened me. I feel quite sparky."

"What are your crowning thoughts about the team bonding course, Roger?"

"I think I'd categorise it as about as much fun as you will get these days with your trousers on and fully zipped."

Chapter 4: The Night Watch

Roger came home from Blandford to some startling news, Charlotte quick to tell him about a transgender teacher at Gravesend Grammar.

"I think someone is having you on, darling," he entreated, chuckling at the notion.

"It's authentic, Roger. When I collected Heather from school yesterday, Marian Pender told me about it. Her eldest daughter is at Gravesend Grammar."

"Marian's got a vivid imagination," Roger contradicted, sneering dismissively. "She'll have misunderstood whatever gossip she picked up."

"Well, Trisha Hollingswood confirmed it. Her daughter Kaitlyn is also at Gravesend Grammar, and she came home with the same story."

"It's a wind up," he conjectured, guffawing. "You know what adolescent schoolgirls and schoolboys are like. Remember when James came home claiming Mister Copley, the PE Master at Chelsfield Grammar was a member of MI5 and he worked undercover to root out subversives in the student fraternity!" Dismissively furrowing his brow he guaranteed, "whatever it is at Gravesend Grammar, will be hearsay."

"Oh yes." She handed him the current edition of the Orpington & District Gazette. "I bought this on the way home today. Check out page five."

When Roger did so, the strapline glaring at him read, 'Teacher vamooses for Christmas as Lionel then begins spring term as Laura'. "*Good god*," Roger wailed. "'Principal teacher at Gravesend Grammar School for Girls, Missus Gloria Jackman,'" he read aloud, "'says the school board of governors and the Department for Education cannot terminate Lionel Lavery's, aka Laura Lavery's contract of employment on grounds of false declaration of gender, because it contravenes EU Human Rights Laws. Horrified parents formed a hanging party at the school gates, ready to nab the transgender teacher and stretch his-her neck, only to be ushered away by the police.'" As his alarm grew, his disbelief mushroomed. "I owe you an apology," he meekly articulated. "Incredible. Beggars belief."

"You want to be careful when you resume your business studies evening sessions at Wendy's school," Charlotte tipped. "There are one or two limp-wristed masters skulking about who could be transgender candidates."

"Why, Charlotte," Roger mockingly began, "you do surprise me. I'd have thought with your adopted liberal-lefty agenda, you'd uphold transgenderism. Hardly PC, is it, darling?"

"I do have my limits, Roger, and the thought of a mister becoming a miss, or graver, a miss becoming a mister, is too much for even me to stomach. I'd hate to think Wendy could be exposed to that kind of thing, and worse still, Heather in a few years when she goes to Chelsfield Grammar. Think of the never-ending mass of w-questions emanating from her after she found out!"

"Quite."

"Found out what, Mummy?"

Roger and Charlotte whirled about to see Heather standing in the lounge doorway clutching Kermit the Frog.

"Oh, nothing, darling," Charlotte bonded. "Couldn't you sleep?"

"I had a bad dream about me being marooned on an island where nobody speaks English. It woke me up." Running to her mother, she climbed into her lap.

"Ouch, very poignant," Roger acknowledged. "Not speaking English is fast becoming the *de facto* state of affairs in England, especially London."

"Mummy," Heather pressed, "what is it I shouldn't find out about?"

"Oh, nothing, darling. Daddy and I were just having a general conversation."

"About what?"

"Nothing important."

"I heard you say something about a mister becoming a miss."

"Well…er—" Searching Roger imploringly, she nodded for him to intervene.

Reacting, he made a perplexed face, noncommittal his intention.

"Has it got to do with Mister Lavery at Gravesend Grammar School?"

Gulping, Charlotte murmured, "er, yes. Apparently, Mister Lavery has become Miss Lavery."

"How's it possible?"

"Well, you see, darling, Mister Lavery has undergone transgender surgery."

"Is a transgender the same as Grayson Perry, the man we were talking about at Daddy's Aunt Jemina's house, after last year's Summer Exhibition at the Royal Academy of Arts?"

"No, darling," Roger jubilantly refuted. "He's a transvestite."

Frowning at her husband's forthrightness, Charlotte counselled, "now, Heather, we don't want you to become alarmed at—"

She cut her mother off abruptly. "It's alright, I know all about Mister Lavery turning into Miss Lavery."

"*What*?" Charlotte snapped, thrown by her youngest daughter's enunciation.

"Zoey Harvey told me after she heard her mother talking about it."

Exchanging bewildered kissers, both her parents dissolved into ambiguity. If the newspaper strapline had jolted them, Heather's knowledge of the bone of contention blew apart any notions they had apposite young schoolchildren being kept away from such gory disclosures!

~ * ~

After Roger's autumn supplementary A-level business studies night school sessions success, both Missus Greenwood, Wendy's school headmistress, and Charlotte, had incessantly pressured him into delivering a further set of classes.

Under extreme pressure during the opening few weeks of the New Year, in the end, he relented, agreeing to engage the little darlings again in what he dubbed, 'the night watch.' Thrusting an imaginary sword upward in heartfelt Henry V fashion and quipping, 'Once more into the breach, dear friends, once more', only for Charlotte to deflate his balloon with a caustic comment about keeping out of the clutches of his charges, he mentally prepared for combat.

Like for the previous term sessions, after scrutinising the A-level business studies curriculum, Roger prepared complementary course addendums, e-mailing the content to Business Studies Master Mister Bryant for printing and distributing to the evening class students, the girls requested to digest the stuff before the two-hour sessions scheduled for Tuesday and Thursday evenings over two weeks began. With the intended aid of an overhead projector linked to his laptop, and a white board, Roger planned the session subject matter dovetailing into a Q&A session for the spring term themes, including enterprise scale management techniques, investment planning options and some *avant garde*, go-to-market disciplines, such as boulder removing marketing and critical path analysis.

Using his 'ancient school year terminology', he soon unearthed additional to some GCSE candidates intending to do A-level business studies the following academic year, the usual suspects from the 'upper' and 'lower sixth' inhabited his class. Whereas the previous term he virtually had to spoon-feed the girls with superintendence, this term they were much more switched on, Roger finding he only had to apply a slight stimulus to get a massive step response, leaving him agape at their quick take-up of his new material. Recognising the young and still terminally wet behind the ears Mister Bryant had been doing a good job during the daytime sessions, Roger concluded some of his acumen had washed off on him. Despite his novice-like appraisal of real business practice when they first met, Bryant now counted as worldlier, enabling him to append some associated expediency to the baseline curriculum, clearly benefiting the girls understanding of the business studies genre.

Quickly, it became clear the class had not only honed their knowledge base, they'd also become capable of making intuitive comments and conveying original interpretations, boding well for avoiding examination textbook answers, and conversely displaying aptitude, Roger envisioning the adjudicators frothing with joy when they cast their dissecting mincers on perceptive responses to age-old mind-twisters. As per the autumn term, Mister Bryant sat at the rear of the class, also taking in the subsidiary text. Promptly, Roger noticed he seemed much more relaxed, like he had grown into daytime teaching and found enjoyment in his profession.

To his everlasting amazement, the revelations were most evident when making ready to begin the maiden session. He coughed to draw their gaze, and thirty pairs of peepers, incorporating Wendy's, swivelled frontwards. Blown away by the unexpected and swift response, he nearly jumped up Basil Fawlty style.

Seizing on the moment he adopted a forthright, no nonsense, I'm in command and you're not going to flummox me this term timbre. "Right…I know you all have a good comprehension of classic marketing precepts." Stopping, he peeped into the heart of the class. "That is right, isn't it?"

A chorus of, "yes, Mister Fraser," came back at him embodying the deep tenor intonation of Mister Bryant. *Maybe his balls have finally dropped,* Roger concluded.

"Good. We're going to explore an innovative scheme used to liberate sales obstacles and substantially ramp up business revenues," he introduced. "Boulder removing marketing is about finding ways to unlock barriers preventing sales channel access and thereby company growth. It's a concept centred around gaining thought leadership, and if used in conjunction with critical path analysis; a project management method requiring the mapping out of every key task necessary to complete the project, can generate explosive dividends. What we're going to investigate, is how if boulders are removed, company growth zooms very quickly."

Ostensibly, the girls had largely got over their sexual innuendo phase, even the vivacious Zoey Dunbar, aka Lolita, had stopped baiting

Roger. More focused on the examinations, less than six months away, they consequently hung on his every word.

"A pivotal element within this method is vision lock selling. You'll see in your handout sheets, VLS is about being first to create a market segment category, name it, define its attributes and promote differentiated benefits. What we're talking about here is winning in the market first with thought leadership." Again halting, he studied their luminous youthful faces, outwardly transfixed by the motif. "Now, can anyone give me an example of a company acknowledged to be the market pacesetter in their business vertical?"

"How about Proctor & Gamble for FMCG?" Patricia Ellison nominated.

"Yes, an excellent example, Patricia. Can we have some others?"

One of the upper-sixth girls, Gina Zaccardelli extended her hand. Of Italian parentage but born in Blighty and English through and through, she resembled a young Sophia Loren in the making, graceful and jaw-dropping but very respectful of Roger's position. One of the few girls from the earlier evening sessions, who didn't use her overt sensuality to bait him, she had seeped into his good books and stayed there, Roger using her as a shining example of the devoted business studies student to Missus Greenwood, when she quizzed him about the girls ability to knuckle down to the chore.

"Yes, Gina," Roger buoyantly licensed, forever encouraging the girls to express themselves.

"Mister Fraser, I'd suggest Coca-Cola is the trailblazer in the soft drinks and beverages market."

"Yes, in general you're right. Pepsi occasionally sneaks into the lead, but other cola and soft drink brands lag far behind. Anymore?"

"Nationwide for mortgages," Abigail Mortimer tabled.

"Yes, one from my world. Very good Abigail. Anymore?"

His darling daughter Wendy hoisted a fluttering hand.

"Yes, Wendy?"

"Estee Lauder in cosmetics, Dad, er, I mean Mister Fraser."

Titillated by the indiscretion, the rest of the class twinkled, Wendy still finding it hard to make the transition from parent label to classroom title.

Beaming a *I love you so much, and it must be difficult for a student to have her father as the teacher* physiognomy at her, he replied, "quite correct. Now, we could go on, because I know you're a clever lot, but let's just determine what all these brands have in common. Any ideas?"

"Customer perception they're dealing with the market front-runner," Roxanne Harrison funneled.

Despite her burgeoning sexuality and use of it to wind the male of the species around her little finger, Roxanne had a top-notch business brain. Of all the students Roger thought might do well in the real world of commerce, she'd be the best. Brains and beauty cutting across traditional male demarcation barriers and petty PC jealousies from coyote-ugly women. If she learnt to handle herself, he could see her ending up as a chief executive officer. Stimulated by the deliberation, he pondered, it'd be interesting to re-visit her in twenty years, to see if his assessment had worked out.

"Excellent, Roxanne."

"The player who sets trends, influences others, and drives the market forward," submitted Catherine Walmsley, another upper-sixth member.

"Absolutely right, Catherine."

Stirred by the responses, the class reigned down auxiliary examples, Roger bowled over by their accurate answers delivered with tangible enthusiasm.

"My, you girls have unequivocally been doing your homework. Very good to everybody. Very good."

Taking a peek over at Mister Bryant, he saw an air of satisfaction emblazoned across his still developing face, hallmarked by embryonic bumfluff replacing the finishing vestiges of pimples and spots, a definitive portent he'd found his feet and handled the girls with enhanced confidence.

"I'll propound one more example for your consideration," Roger ventured. "In the mid-1950s, vacuum cleaners became a colossal business with the rise of the domestic appliance market. Through its cutting-edge technology and catchy, 'it beats as it sweeps as it cleans' slogan, the

Hoover Company attained clear market big cheese status. Customers went into electrical appliance stores and didn't buy a vacuum cleaner, they bought a 'hoover'. The term 'hoover' largely replaced both vacuum cleaner and sweeper in the psyche and vocabulary of the buying public. It became one of the most lauded examples of thought leadership and brand awareness ever to emerge in the world of commerce."

"But consumers don't buy hoovers today, Mister Fraser," Felicity Mendham alleged, another student from Wendy's lower-sixth form.

I love to see the girls right on the rim, in step with me in terms of their topic appreciation, Roger fleetingly machinated. *It makes my job easy, and gives me enormous pride the class gained benefits from the foregoing evening sessions.* Extrapolating the contemplation, he knew he must never confess the judgment to Missus Greenwood, or she'd have him at Chelsfield Grammar School for Girls every evening during the term. Pleasant it might be, he had other responsibilities, foremost enlarged workload at The Firm since his trouble-shooter appointment, family demands, and training for the Kappa Corinthians veteran matches, trusting he was picked to represent what in rugby circles was Kent's premier amateur rugby club, exhausting his energies.

"Quite right, Felicity. Undoubtedly a fabulous *tour de force*, the Hoover Company fell away. Why do you think it happened?"

"Because Hoover rested on their laurels. Because they overlooked sustaining their reputation through longer-term technological advancement and clever advertising."

Quiet as a reserved nun during Roger's preceding sessions, through deep study and dedication to task, Felicity had been transformed into a Sir John Harvey Jones in the making. His cup of delight runneth over with joy.

"I couldn't have put it better myself," Roger congratulated, discharging the exceptionally smart student his very best smile. "Well done, Felicity." Gawking around the class, he catechized, "now, to complete this singular picture, who did become the rising star of the vacuum cleaner market, the housewife's sweeper of choice?"

"Dyson," Wendy and Abigail requited in unison.

"Definitely. James Dyson took the market by storm with a series of very unique technical innovations, bestowing a wealth of benefits and advantages to the user. Though more expensive, the ROI on a Dyson far outstrips other brands, proving the point, lowest price does not necessarily equate with best buy." Tickled, an example of price-performance came to his mind. "In my own life, a relatively expensive purchase has proved to be a long-term winner. I've always had a penchant for quality shoes. Before Wendy and her brother and sister were born, my wife and I were in my home county of Cheshire. I bought a pair of Swiss-made Bally shoes from Hobson & Gormley in Chester, costing seventy pounds, over twice the price of most other men's shoes. However, despite frequent use, they bide in fine fettle, and nineteen years later, I'll get many more years of service from them."

"Have you had them soled and heeled, Mister Fraser?" Felicity investigated.

"Just once, about five years ago, but even building the repair price into the total cost of ownership…I think the repair cost fifteen pounds…the total life cycle cost to date is less than investing in cheaper footwear, needing recurrent refurbishment before being binned after a few years. Shucks—" He glistened.

"*Oh no,*" Wendy muttered to herself. "He's going to recite one of his not-so-funny tales."

"If you'll indulge me," Roger pleaded. "Talking about shoe repairs has reminded me of an aphorism." Resting he got his ducks in a row. "Snoopy Anton finds an old trunk in the family house attic. Rifling through it, he discovers his father's World War II uniform. Just for fun, he tries it on. Before taking it off, he puts his hands in the trouser pockets and pulls out a ticket. Inspecting it, he finds it's a shoe repair ticket for Henriks on Church Road, Bromley, dated 14th January 1942. He can barely believe it. An unclaimed ticket, fifty-five years old. Weeks later, Anton happens to be in Church Road and finds the shoe repair shop is still there. Wandering inside, he tells the story of finding the ticket to an old man behind the counter, who says his name is Henrik, and he has owned the shop for sixty years. 'Give me the ticket,' Henrik implores and meanders into the core of the shop. Astonished, Anton thinks, what good fortune, what a coincidence." Hunching his shoulders Roger enacted

Anton's awe. "Henrik saunters to the counter. 'I've got your shoes,' he declares. 'They'll be done tomorrow!'"

Glimmering at his ironic gag, the whole gathering, encompassing Wendy, who had not heard the yarn before, burst into laughter, Mister Bryant still guffawing after the girls stopped and trained their alertness on him. Becoming cognizant of their staggered features, he cleared his throat and instantly regained decorum, his embarrassment producing a reddish glow in his cheeks.

Resurrecting the subject matter, the workshop continued with parleys on market shape and size pronouncement brokers, price-point optimization, and the importance of boulder-removing marketing contrivances to unlock markets.

During the session's second hour, when Roger covered corporate and middle management hegemony aspects and traits, without rhyme or reason, Abigail suddenly brought a television reality show into play.

"Mister Fraser."

"Yes, Abigail."

"Don't you think belligerence, aggressiveness and self-belief are the indispensable weapons of choice for middle managers and corporate execs these days?"

"Why do you say that?" he petitioned, withdrawing resultant from the acidity of the sentiment.

"On *The Apprentice*, Lord Sugar always comes across as a hard man, badgering and browbeating his workforce into doing what he wants, and that's why he's been successful."

"Yes, I concur with Abigail, Mister Fraser," Catherine backed. "Business studies qualifications are fine, but to succeed, don't you also need a prodigious amount of dynamism allied to belligerence?"

Being careful not to deflate their bubbling zeal, Roger made a calculated riposte. "I'd suggest you could be misinterpreting reality show business behaviour as being representative of the real business world."

"How do you mean?" Abigail enquired.

"Alan Sugar is a self-taught and self-made businessman. Part of his success has been acquired from being single-minded, but—" He waggled a reprimanding finger. "*The Apprentice* is a television reality programme, not a fly-on-the-wall mode documentary. It has to be show-biz impelled to capture the non-business audience. To accomplish the objective, it is artificially hyped up to furnish drama, conflict, and in Sugar's paradigm, a fire-breathing, intolerant dictator, his broad message being, 'it's either my way or the highway.'" Strolling up and down perpendicular to the class, he let the dissection sink in. "Sugar is playing a role and he does it very well, engendering tension and most importantly spectator participation, the epigrammatic fundamentals nurturing viewer loyalty; customer loyalty in the more general business sense, so they tune in for the hereinafter week's episode. The same proficiency to heighten onlookers' curiosity has been used in soap operas since the early 1950s in the United States." Squinting at the class, he recorded chimerical exclamation marks popping up over their craniums, their facial mannerisms indicating a revelatory flash. "Call to mind from our earlier discussions on brand management, the sole destination of an advertisement or advertorial is to create the desire and the aspirational need to own the product, and by inference association with a perceived peer group."

"So, are you saying," Gina set forth, "to succeed in business, you don't necessarily need to be overly domineering and dictatorial?"

"I am, Gina. Business practice is not a precise science. You can't apply the same proficiencies to a given set of circumstances and reproduce the same outcome every time. Yes, sometimes an autocratic *modus operandi* does work, but I'd suggest—" He paused. "No, better still, I'd endorse the opinion that in general, good employee performance comes about through leading by example. It wins over people willingly, rather than by intimidation or threat. The institutions and organisations experiencing uninterrupted longevity were built on principles of leadership by example. You have to adopt the Douglas Bader approach."

"How do you mean?" Felicity supplicated.

"Group Captain Sir Douglas Bader was a Battle of Britain pilot who had lost his legs in an earlier flying accident. He got about on what he called his 'tin legs'. When he took charge of a sceptical RAF squadron who assumed he couldn't fly because of his impediment, he demonstrated just how good his flying skills were in a Spitfire. Straightaway, he gained the esteem of the entire squadron, walking the talk by example, not by using his rank and being truculent. Of course, having a very effervescent nature helped Bader develop team work as well."

"You mean, by a manager doing what expects of their team, they're airing ascendancy and thereby the team will replicate their example, notably, if they're well-liked by the team?" Felicity voiced.

"Exactly. Don't be fooled into thinking the way to boost your career is to be unnecessarily combative, like those asinine 'Apprentice' candidates. As with Sugar, to some extent, they're caught up in reality show business, but it's not how business people behave in the real world. Think assertive in place of aggressive. Think conciliatory in place of muscle. After all, the primary function of a resource manager is to get his team onside with a willing attitude." Holding up a supportive hand, more like Tonto about to say 'how', rather than the intended approbation of his recommendation, he prescribed, "think about applying the Douglas Bader strategy."

I'm gilding the lily a little bit here, Roger thought, *but no need to de-focus the girl's impression of the right technique with lurid examples of the belligerent management criterion from my world, utilised by the Firm's Ayatollah Luther Bembridge or Dwight Armstrong at Zicon General.*

"One final piece of advice *vis-à-vis The Apprentice*. When compiling your curriculum vitaes, do not cosset the outrageous and ridiculous claims made by those silly wannabe candidates. Phrases like, 'I'm the best salesman since sliced bread', 'I always give 110 per cent'...physically impossible and 'I'm responsible for a company turnover of a trillion pounds', only serve to bring amusement to seasoned interviewers. Granted, such idiotic depositions are part of the required show-biz rhetoric, albeit the BBC ought to warn televiewers beforehand, so as not to give the falsehood, such contentions are real."

"Mister Fraser."

He faced Abigail. "Yes?"

"What should we put in our CVs, and what should we dodge?"

"As a guiding rule, think if you were the interviewer reading your CV, what dazzled you. Begin with a profile outlining your mission statement, ambition, skills and summary qualifications, then accompany with details of your education and work experience numbering employment history, references and interests, and finally your personal data and contact details. Keep it to no more than two pages and factual throughout."

"Anything else?"

"Yes, and admittedly this is a pet hate, do not use the words 'cool' and 'awesome' to embellish your accomplishments, and above all, don't drift into trendy clichés and abbreviations, like using the term 'uni' for university. They just make you come across as a 'me-too' adherent, a sheep shadowing the crowd. Think of your CV as a document identifying your singularity, *ipso facto*, a narrative making you stand out as having the uncommon. Interviewers and assessors constantly seek the X-factor, that special, unique integrant setting the candidate apart."

"But how can we be unique, if we are all using the same prescription?" Wendy tendered.

"Good probe, astute daughter of mine." Delighted, he radiated at her approvingly. "One of the great things about being English, is the opportunity to build on a long history and heritage of individual attainment. Though our renowned English military heroes, philosophers, scientists, engineers, artists and writers, and dare I say it, business entrepreneurs, appear to be products of conformity and stalwarts of the Establishment, dig beneath the surface gloss, and you'll find many exhibited highly idiosyncratic and even non-conformist peculiarities." Raising his arms, he emphasised the revelation. "We are all special and excel in our own way. Never think you are run-of-the-mill and have nothing extraordinary to offer the world. Everyone is capable of esoteric achievement. The trick, if there is one, is developing the interpersonal and communications skills to highlight your uniqueness."

Scanning around the class, he proffered, "what I see before me is a group of lively scholars, coming together for a common purpose, not a herd of gormless nonentities, strained into attendance through coercion and threat. You're here, because you chose to be here, illustrating you made a visceral decision. It symbolises the fount from which profound development grows, and whilst you will all matriculate from the

Grammar with pinnacle marks in A-level business studies, nonetheless, each one of you will be different in your character and outlook. But bear in mind—" Pinpointing the essence of his avowal, his body language became prescriptive. "Gaining A-star grades at GCSE A-Level, or any other subsequent qualification, is not the end game."

"In what way?" Catherine canvassed.

"There's a huge difference between the ability to memorise and recount information for valuation purposes, and the ability to make learned decisions based on the material available."

"You mean, the eggheads on the television programme of the same name might be able to answer questions, but not necessarily grasp the significance of their content?"

"Indeed. Intellect is much more about the ability to interpret and comprehend, rather than possessing an astronomic repository for storing gospel truth." Shifting through their ranks, he interpolated, "by way of example, let me ask you another brainteaser. What is the value of history?"

"To learn from the past," Abigail unerringly burst out.

"Affirmative," he certified pointing a praising finger at her. "O-Level history might centre around the regurgitation of dates and events for examination purposes, but at A-level and beyond, the history student is challenged to deduce why events occurred, could they have been avoided, and most importantly, lessons learnt so as to evade making the same mistakes. Of course, in practice, those in the saddle take little note of the historians' counsels, and the same mistakes are perennially made, but that's the keynote of another discipline we won't go into now."

"So, what you're saying," Roxanne began, "is to help display individuality to an interviewer, we need to be able to rationalise and deduce from verities?"

"Exactly. It will significantly set you apart. But as a maxim, customarily ask yourself, am I going to be an applauder or a performer? There's a capacious difference, and I'm sure all of you can work out to succeed in any walk of life, you need to be a performer. To use a sporting term, it's the difference between being good and being a game changer. Don't let life slither by without you appending weighty triumph addendums to your CV."

"Will you help us write our CVs, Mister Fraser?" Zoey beseeched.

Chortling, he cogitated *fell into that one, didn't I*? "Why not?"

"Can we have your private email address then, Mister Fraser?" Roxanne pushed.

"What?"

"We'll need to submit our CVs to you."

Suddenly his mind went into overdrive, generating images of the girls sending him expressive, even wanton photos of themselves, or telling him their innermost thoughts pertaining to how they'd like to explore his mind, and more dangerously, his body! Extrapolating the nightmare, he conjured up a perception of Charlotte happening on the salacious messages, and in response him suffering all kinds of doghouse blues penance. Even more acute, James might hack into his email account, lay open the girls' emails and blackmail his father into coughing up vast sums of pocket money, or face the emails being sent onto his tawdry friends. Like 'Billy the Mountain' Swan, and the incriminating evidence going viral at Chelsfield Grammar School for Boys, culminating in his Hazelwood home being blitzed by rampaging, rapacious reporters, intent on dissecting the gory details for newspaper front page headlines and the lead television story on *News at Ten*. More seriously, the inevitable knock-on fallout meant instant dismissal from The Firm, excommunication from his hallowed Kappa Corinthians Rugby Club, being thrown out of his domicile and a long, protracted divorce in the law courts. Yoked as a social outcast, he'd never see his wife and children again, and end up in the gutter with all the other down-and-outs and Chelsea supporters; the clear-cut dregs of society.

"*Aaaahhh*!" Roger involuntary let out. Shaking his noodle, he dislodged the fancy. "Sorry—" Baring his teeth, he invited empathy. "Just a bit of cramp coming on in my left thigh."

Mystified by his outburst, Mister Bryant and the girls looked clueless.

"So what about your email address, Mister Fraser?" Roxanne reprised.

"I think it'd be wise to submit any CVs for review via Wendy."

Mopping his brow, he pivoted away from the class and mumbled, "so I will avert a fate worse than death."

~ * ~

During the ensuing session, Roger went through how national and global economics work, a concern close to his heart because it formed the footing of either a black or red balance sheet.

"Can anyone tell me, what any social community's future has been predicated on since time immemorial?"

"Trade, Mister Fraser," Wendy articulated, successfully abstaining from the 'Dad' moniker.

"Undeniably spot-on, darling, er, I mean, Wendy."

His formality slip brought smirks from the other girls, even Mister Bryant letting out a chuckle. Sensing the mirth, Roger felt predisposed to join in, emitting a minor laugh.

"Homo sapiens have been trading through barter, exchange of goods and ultimately through monetary regimes since man crawled out of the slime," Roger proclaimed. "It's been geared up to form the customary way in which the exhaustive world has evolved in terms of interconnected economics, the ebb and flow of currency dependent on ever-changing market coefficients, political drivers and buyer trends. However, this paints a somewhat romantic picture of a steady-state system, untouched by external and often unexplained constituents propagating catastrophic effects. Predictability is ambiguous, future goals based more on extrapolating statistics rather than formulaic theories." Designedly, his slant became disarming, his words delivered with saccharine-like authenticity. "But one thing is certain, for a given community, whether it be a household, a business, or a country, balancing the books is axiomatic to nurse well-being. Drifting into the red, preeminently through over-borrowing, has been the cancer marking the demise and death-knell of every community since Julius Caesar ruled the world. The key to evading such a draconian event is preserving capital reserves to cover debt, a necessary instrument, *blatantly* and repeatedly sidelined by those in charge of governance." Moving into the nucleus of the class, he hypothesised, "it's a little like posing the conundrum, strikingly in light of current market turmoil and the country's structural debt, what's the easiest way to make a small fortune? Answer: start off with a large one!" Appraising his well-intentioned directive might have segued into being highly prescriptive, he begged, "sorry for being verbose girls, but economic book balancing needs to be everybody's bible, worldwide." Disseminating an exacting gander, he propositioned, "let me pose a further enigma. What do you think has been the systemic cause of the economic depression sweeping across the world since 2008?"

At least twenty hands shot up. Spoilt for choice Roger selected Amanda Ludlow, Mandy to her friends, a new GCSE year entrant to the evening sessions, electing to do A-level business studies next year.

Mandy, Roger ruminated, *the name stimulates memories*. During the mid-1990s, Mandy Wilkins, her from *Game On* played by the luscious Samantha Janus was Kappa Corinthians pin-up girl. If it had not been for Charlotte, he'd have gone for the delightfully, sexy Mandy, 'like a rat up a drainpipe' to use an Anglo-Saxon phrase from the TV series.

"Yes, Amanda."

"Toxic debt."

"Completely right. Go to the top of the class." Slowly pacing up and down adjacent to the white board, a mechanism he used when wanting to emphasise crucial points, usually lessons learnt to wayward Gordon-Gekko-wannabe traders like The Firm's Lawrence Springs and Brendan Kirkman, he progressed the lesson. "The simple truth is, in any economic archetype borrowings cannot outstrip income in terms of the ability to shelter the debt, and preferably, in principle, debt is to be eternally sidestepped. Once debt begins to spiral without the means to reverse the trend, then disaster quickly befalls, although in-government politicians invariably persist in denial and try to keep fiscal debt a rigorously guarded secret."

"Are you saying enduring in the black has become neglected," Roxanne grilled, her siren-like mooning from the autumn term replaced with a business-like expression, "and there is a worldwide debt epidemic, driving balance sheets into the red?"

"Indeed I am, Roxanne. The cardinal culprits are administrations, borrowing more and more money to quote, 'spend their way out of recession.'" Lifting a reproachful finger, like in prior sessions the class and Mister Bryant followed its movement. "Now, if you had a credit card, and went into the red through purchase excesses, consider how your parents might respond if you announced you intended to clear the debt by spending even more. Anyone."

"My parents would hit the roof," Abigail advised.

"Mine too," Patricia favoured.

"And mine," Wendy also appended with a slender sniggle.

"Quite," Roger upheld, sending a pleasant mien to his daughter. "So, what's the antidote to get out of credit card debt?"

"Economise," Amanda figured.

"And how is such a measure accomplished?"

"By reducing or even stopping spending on non-essential acquisitions, until the debt is cleared through the income stream."

"Very good, in fact excellent. Let's build on the theme. Backtracking, how's it possible to settle that you never incur monthly credit card interest charges?"

"By paying off the bill in total every month," Wendy stipulated.

"And the how?"

"By safeguarding outgoings never exceed income."

Roger couldn't help but break into a jubilant mug. He felt like saying, 'girls, you can see why I love my daughter so much,' but resisted the temptation.

Residing business-like and strictly impartial he corroborated, "quite correct, Wendy," then winked.

With a combination of an outstretched paw and a pleading facial nuance, Desdemona Rhodes, another new student to the evening sessions, attracted his cognizance.

"Yes, Desdemona?"

"Can you give an opinion on how consortiums can circumvent getting into the red, when they're drawn into the maelstrom of a global recession?"

"What a brilliant poser," Roger enthused. "It's been a perennial ask, testing all businesses." Resting, his articulation took on the mantle of an Oxbridge don, rather than a street-wise, book-smart stock market analyst. "I want to get this right, so please indulge me for a jiffy." As if compiling his best response, he gazed into the metaphorical distance. "Monetary gearing or stress testing is the crux to obviating debt, meaning ensuring liquidity is always managed so as to lock-in a net positive cash flow into the commonwealth, after tallying outgoings. The granularity of the discipline substantively needs to equal the temperament of the business. FMCG is at the high volume, low unit price end, whereas high-tech, long term projects represent the high worth end of the wide-ranging spectrum. The economic health of a FMCG company might need to be measured in terms of daily outgoings versus revenue income, and adjustments proportionately made to the business exemplar to nail down positive cash flow. Large scale engineering and scientific project providers have longer periods between outgoings and incomings, but still need to monitor the direction of money flow." Halting his response, he developed an incongruous face. "Of course, despite the good governance observed by a responsible financial director, human frailty in the form of ego drive in the executive plane can be the culprit behind toxic debt. CEOs, managing directors and even unabridged boards of over-ambitious directors, induced to reap or sustain kudos, and thereby gain applause from their correspondents and competitors, often bankrupt their company through high borrowings without the liquidity to even belt and brace the interest payments." Observing the class like a wise old owl, he solicited, "does that begin to decipher the stumper?"

"Yes, Mister Fraser," Desdemona affirmed.

~ * ~

As the evening sessions went on, Roger's conviction the girls had traversed through their sexual baiting of him phase cemented, and they'd become motivated to concentrate purely on his business studies supplementary classes content.

Howbeit, the certitude evaporated when he walked down a school corridor with Mister Bryant for the concluding session. Enthusiastic as ever, the girls had already gathered outside the classroom, awaiting their arrival. Instead of the relatively modest attire they had been wearing to the preceding sessions, the little minxes had adorned their developing bodies in St. Trinians vogue revealing schoolgirl uniforms, subsuming Wendy, who as usual, had gone on ahead of her father with her friends. To complement the shortened and tightened in all the right or wrong places uniforms, dependent upon whether the evaluator was a schoolgirl or an adult, they wore stockings and high heels.

"*Oh my god*," Roger muttered. "I thought they'd got over their man-baiting period."

"The school allows the girls to wear pretty much what they like for extra-curricular activities, Mister Fraser. Are you objecting to the length of their skirts?"

"More like the lack of length."

Deciding on an unfazed comeback to the spectacle, Roger boomed out, "good evening girls. Ready for our final session?" the frisky contingent bursting into giggles and yelps, as if he implied a diversion beyond the business studies curriculum.

"Good evening, Mister Fraser," Zoey near-to breathed at him as he passed her. Catching his nostrils, he weighed her perfume to be a lethal combination of all the ingredients required to disarm the male of the species. "Yes, we're all prepared for you."

Keeping his cool, when Mister Bryant unlocked the classroom door and the girls piled inside, Zoey's seductive redress yielding more hilarity, he maintained an oblivious disposition to their mischievous demeanour.

Inaugurating the first hour of the session founded on the complexities of investments and investor mentality, Roger heedfully specified as his opening remark, "demystifying the financial services sector into logical terms is a near-to impossible undertaking." Hesitating, he envisioned the vamps to his forefront interrupting him with lewd and lascivious suggestions. Notwithstanding, his pause produced nothing but attentive faces. "Business is about risk versus confidence. Any change to circumstances must be communicated to all stakeholders or confidence is lost, arousing waves resulting in amplified costs and putting profits at risk. Old school thought always centred on using someone else's money to underwrite business ventures, meaning, using the banking and investment network." Again, he stopped, anticipating the baiting to begin, but the class appeared thunderstruck by his review. Distrustful, thinking it to be a feint, he peered at Bryant, but the master too acted as if entranced by the treatise. "Such a scheme is fine under stable economic conditions," he moved, "but we've been subjected to the peaks and troughs of double-dip recession for numerous years, with borrowers consequently incurring widely differing interest rates, impacting their own business model. Resourcing a new business venture via organic growth is a less risky bet because lenders can foreclose on any investment of their choosing at a moment's notice. This particularly applies to small businesses. Why, you might ask?" Knowingly, his rhetorical question drew no responses. "Other than min-max ROIs and market analysis used to minimise risk, there's little science applied to the investment market. It's more driven by emotions and undefined feelings. And let's not kid ourselves this doctrine is exclusively the domain of the capitalist West. The Russian Federation and Red China use the same min-max ROI projections and illogical, even impulsive emotions to pull the plug on investments. Whether in the West or the East, it generates subsequent borrower attrition for inexact and *prima facie*, invalid reasons. Global volatility in government, along with the erratic market price of natural commodities, especially oil, are the foremost variables behind lenders' unpredictable mentality, not their minds but their guts determining their actions."

"Mister Fraser," Amanda interrupted, "what has changed to ignite this fickle lender behaviour?"

"Well, with the advent of e-business and e-commerce software technologies in the late 1990s, we used to talk about business transformation realisation through build, deploy and run systems coupled with open-systems I.T standards, enabling investment banks to build new applications and integrate existing applications and data into a single, cohesive perspective, via business process management platforms.

"It intrinsically gave us a know-your-customer capability, empowering us to slice and dice the investment market into identifiable segments, as well as a refined analytical angle on vertical market behavioural patterns. Accordingly, investment banks geared up their businesses, going out on a limb more with their investments because of the improved helicopter view of the world at large afforded by the new technology, and in the belief investments could be reined in quickly, meaning foreclosing if markets turned sour." Wrinkling his hooter, he acknowledged, "it never quite worked out as per the theory."

"Why?" Amanda delved.

"*Hah*, a vexing qualm," he snapped. "Doubtless, some CEOs became possessed by the same spiel they advocated to financial services clients, their ego drives dizzy with autonomy, their inflated ambitions ungovernable. To observers, their manoeuvres were so transparent, it approached narcissism… 'see me, I'm king of the economic forum castle'. In reality, most couldn't make the Standard and Poor one hundred, but their autonomous power granted by high-earnings-hungry stockholders drove them on unabated. As to other possible reasons, they are legion, springing from motivators such as avarice, over-optimism, craziness, the list is endless."

"Did your CEO get bitten by the narcissism bug?" Abigail cross-examined.

"Aaahh!" Roger chuckled at the thought. "Good enquiry. Benton Pascoe III, The Firm's current CEO has a reputation for aggressive investment strategies, tempered by good corporate governance. In post since 1999, he is a solid thinker, taking council from both The Firm's executive board of directors and external consultants before embarking on any transformative initiatives. He is what the English Establishment call, *sound*. Pascoe has always made sure The Firm is anchored in positive liquidity, without having to be pressed into doing so by the US Federal Reserve. When the 2008 meltdown took off, along with Goldman Sachs and a few other enterprise scale investment houses, The Firm abided sturdy and strong. For sure we have coddled the derivatives market for sold-on debt, but it was a trifling amount of exposure sheltered by stable and secure investments elsewhere."

"In general," Patricia initiated, "how did the financial services sector get to grips with toxic debt?"

"Some debt was so toxic, its risk had to be shared by selling some or all of the debt to other investment houses through derivative investments. Topically, the American sub-prime mortgage crisis was a benchmark in point, because the scale of the US derivatives tactic accelerated at an astronomical rate across investment banking worldwide, until principal casualty Lehman Brothers made banner lines with their demise, and subsequently other cardinal institutions declared bankruptcy by applying appropriate chapters of the bankruptcy code."

"And consecutively," Wendy propounded, "it energised the worldwide recession."

"Yes. Government debt fuelled the stage setting turmoil, but the cataclysmic Lehman's event sent markets into a spiralling downturn. Since the low point, there's been a seismic shift in the nature of investment banking operational procedures and protocols."

"In what respects?" Patricia tested.

"After governments bailed out the chief culprits, and guilty corporate executives like Fred Goodwin, ex-CEO of RBS, were ceremoniously dishonoured, widespread change came about worldwide. Gone were the days when a high street bank could use capital from its retail arm to finance its wholesale banking division's profligacy in casino mirrored investments on the stock market. The US Federal Reserve and their European equivalents, like the Bank of England, have applied stringent regulation and governance to investment banking. Now, every trade above an agreed maximum threshold has to be sanctioned in a multi-layer management approval structure, constantly monitored by Stock Watch and other regulatory bodies. The opportunity for dealers to become latter-day Nick Leeson's has practically been curtailed. But the unknown still is how quickly can prolonged equilibrium be recovered?"

Too young to qualify for credit, undeterred Roxanne delicately debated, "in terms of domestic debt, don't you think advertising is a major anathema in persuading buyers to revel in higher and higher levels of credit card debt?"

"Ah yes, the iconic Madison Avenue adman, part businessman, part scientist, part priest, disseminating the quintessential, new American business lingo and language, transmigrating across the Atlantic to seduce young, impressionable schoolgirls." His sardonic portrayal made Roxanne blush and drew narrow laughter from the class.

Mindful of how fledgling women could be tempted to buy a plenary host of unnecessary trinkets and accessories, he wondered if some of them, not Wendy of course, had fallen for the silky seductiveness of consumerism, reflected in the ever-soaring totals to be paid on their parents' credit card statements!

"Like an infestation of woodlice," he blazed, getting into his stride, "the originative types emerge from Westport Connecticut, then descend on the Big Apple with ambitions to be the supreme purveyor of the one-line, billion-dollar making advertising slogan, or the ringmaster behind the latest aspirational invoking TV adverts. Let's 'imagineer' they say. Let's go with the pathfinder artifice. Let's find the line of consumer least resistance."

Gazing at the enthralled class, he fathomed his graphic rhetoric had become infectious to their green, persuadable minds.

"If Macy's catalogue and Harper's magazine were their bibles in the late 1940s," he appraised, "then television became their alter in the 1950s, platforming daily miracles witnessed by tens of millions, and additional to the introduction of the world wide web, TV still is the adman's holy grail. And in terms of weapons; seduction and aspiration remain the cornerstones of advertising, the hooks pulling at desires and ambitions and the tentacles embracing the drive to acquire material wealth. Without advertising, without selling, nothing from Rolls Royce cars to Persil washing powder could be sold. Advertising is a consumerism fundamental touchstone, its' mightiness to persuade and influence, prized above all other go-to-market tools."

Beholding the quester, he summarised, "so yes, Roxanne, advertising has played a colossal role in fuelling the credit card debt epidemic. It's a little like alcohol is available to all over the age of eighteen, but the wise user drinks moderately." Terminating, he scanned around attentive faces. "You follow the comparison?"

"Yes, Mister Fraser," thumped the airwaves, comprising a tenor response from Mister Bryant, blending in with the girl's soprano voices.

I hope our young business studies master has not been pampering too much credit card self-abuse, Roger mused.

Going on to delve deeper into the investments world

idiosyncrasies, Roger then called a short break. Still emphatically conscious of the girls scantily clad posture, it disturbed him. Based on his experience to date, he foresaw a group of them surrounding him during the break, and teasing him with their foxy charms, whilst Wendy clocked the affray and scribbled copious notes. Quite the converse, they chatted amongst themselves, never throwing an alluring sparkle at their mentor.

"I don't like it," he judiciously mumbled to Bryant.

"Excuse me," the young teacher emitted, puzzled by the comment.

"I feel like Ward Bond in the TV series *Wagon Train* scrutinising the Apaches circling before an imminent attack."

"Sorry." He squinted. "I don't recognise the programme."

"Yes, it was a little before your time, come to that, mine as well."

"Erm, are you implying you expect the girls to attack you?"

"More like compromise me with their glamour."

"Ohh…really, Mister Fraser, you do have an overdeveloped flight of fancy."

"You're not married, are you?" he submitted, throwing a pugnacious gawp at Bryant.

"Er, no."

"Well, when you are, let me assure you, you too will develop hyperactive ingenuity aimed at self-preservation."

Perplexed by the adage, Bryant's consternation grew, Roger gaging his naivety to be quaint, or more pertinently, tragic.

"Nevermind, Mister Bryant. I don't want to spoil your somewhat utopian vista of the world." Sympathetically tapping him on his upper arm, he attached, "you've got all these joys to come."

~ * ~

Roger's terminal evening session hour focused on how government spending burdened the private sector, including the financial services vertical.

"As I said last term," he echoed, "any fool can spend money. Making money takes ingenious skills, grit and dauntlessness. Before the State can spend, taxes have to be levied out of the creative pool.

Unfortunately, like those helter-skelter investment houses who over-geared their businesses we touched on earlier this evening, governments also wallow in borrowings to bankroll their vanity projects. Instead of gearing public spending in line with taxation bearing receipts, since the end of World War II most Western governments have embarked on an irresponsible shopping list of unaffordable luxuries, their price well beyond taxation takings. Inescapably, the knock-on punch has been to augment taxation higher and higher to cover the national debt."

"Is that what halts investment in the commercial sector?" Roxanne canvassed.

"Absolutely," he confirmed. "An ever-expanding phenomenon, periodically, it has immobilised investment in the private sector by investment houses because net profits have been so eroded by the taxation burden, it has limited the borrowers' ability to reimburse the lender." Ticked off at the injustice, he categorised, "and the spiral has deepened since the millennium, HMG bailing out failing retail banks, principally RBS and Lloyds since the 2008 meltdown, because of the inability of borrowers to meet their payment commitments. Nevertheless, it pales before the extravagances of public spending made by the Labour governments of Blair and Brown, and now Cameron's Conservative-led coalition administration. Governments spending their way out of recession is the worst kind of political dogma optimism. Irrefutably, it's psycho-nonsense, just like the silly, Europhile-babble, liberal-elitist do-gooder Ming Campbell spouts. Politicians are pathological about protocol but incredibly, not about veracity. Belief and fact rarely coincide in their vocabulary."

"My father says a country can't be taxed into prosperity," Abigail recalled.

"Unequivocally, your father is right," Roger concurred. "Democratic capitalism has been lassoed by the liberal elitist faction. Free enterprise democracy is being used to subsidise their oppressive brand of one-world socialism. Western taxpayers have been chained into tax slaves, their lives, an unremitting treadmill of coughing up more and more direct and indirect taxes to stake vanity projects such as the EU, the ODA and a plethora of grandiose public works like the proposed HS2 rail link."

Clapping his hands to emphasise his upcoming assertion, he tendered, "in reality, British democracy is soft power regulated and tempered by general elections every five years. To achieve anything over a Parliament, seductive vision has to be sold to the electorate. In the case of the EU, it involves the selling of birthright heritage and at least £50million going from the Exchequer to Brussels on a daily basis, for a nebulous set of chicken feed yields having little to no value for most voters. Return on investment from the lavishness of the ODA sees even less, and little approval from ordinary people. Most believe the politicians and their sycophantic hangers-on are on a massive ego trip to extend their reputations or appease their consciences on the worldwide stage."

"I've heard it said," Amanda professed, "that behind the official facade, those in authority have been dismantling the English foundation in favour of an internationalist agenda since we joined the EEC. Is that true, Mister Fraser?"

"Oh—" Breathing out noisily, he counselled, "the resolution of that enigma is extremely long and beyond the bounds of the business studies syllabus. Best we place the behemoth aside for your daytime economics and current affairs studies. What say you, Mister Bryant?"

"Quite correct, Mister Fraser. Let's stay spotlighted on business studies drivers."

"Er, where was I?" Roger appealed.

"Sycophantic hangers-on and appeasement," his daughter supplied.

"Oh yes. Thank you, Wendy." Regrouping his thoughts, he expressed, "such spending prodigality equates with a heavy price being paid by all taxpayers and the private business industries to underwrite government jamborees. The net aftermath is to lessen investment from financial services for fear of borrowers defaulting on loans. Consecutively, it leads to industry becoming uncompetitive engendering the downsizing of companies, unemployment rising and inevitably, the attendant social welfare cost escalating needing more taxation or…" He furrowed his brow, his disbelief tangible to the class. "…more government loans.

"Of course, when this economic paragon is moreover encumbered by out-of-control mass inward immigration procreating little if any net positive contribution to the economy, and thereby even less to the fiscal purse, once again government is confronted with either scaling-up taxation, or going cap in mitt to the World Bank or the IMF to guarantee their ill-thought-out policies."

Stepping into the centre of the class again, he spoke as he went. "And the cycle continues, the structural debt getting ever higher, the proportion of GDP rocketing year-on-year to secure the debt interest payments, let alone restore the capital.

"So there we have it, a thumbnail sketch encapsulating what most say are the irresponsible actions and disastrous policies of modern government. You young ladies will soon be joining the taxpayers club, your membership automatic and mandatory." Sure the girls had understood his message, he wandered to his lecturer station at the front of the class. "Now, as potential business people, how would you combat government spending negatively affecting the world of commerce?"

"What a humongous riddle, Mister Fraser," Gina retorted. "You're inviting us to grapple with a prodigy eluding, even outwitting, the finest minds in both government and the private sector."

"Yes I am, for two motives. One, such a matter might crop up in your A-level business studies examinations, and two, much more importantly, post-university, you will be matriculating into the workplace, and coming to terms with the costs of domesticity, meaning marriage, children, mortgages and the general cost of living. Your careers and privy lives will in part be impacted by the saddle of government taxation. You have to ask yourselves, am I going to be part of the problem or the solution."

A general discourse took place with the class tabling their thoughts and opinions venerating how to reign in public spending, Roger and Mister Bryant stunned by the girl's grasp of the thorny thesis and their cures to the pickle.

"I suspect all governments err towards conservatism to underpin their own status quo," Wendy postulated at the end of the debate, "and the difference between the public and private sectors is one is measured on activity, the other on results."

"Quite right, Wendy," her father applauded, glowing with delight. Perusing the class, he conferred, "well girls, that's it. The entire A-Level syllabus has now been screened with complementary examples from the real world of commerce."

"Any thoughts on examination technique, Mister Fraser?" Patricia polled.

"Oooh, being prescriptive is not in my brief. Any advice is down to the school and masters like Mister Bryant."

"Please, go on, Mister Fraser," Bryant encouraged.

"Well, throughout my A-Level days…" Abashed at the memory, he instinctively chortled. "…not as long ago as you might suppose." They obliged him with vicarious smiles. "Memorising information was fine, but it did not necessarily gain the top grade. Adjudicators then, like now, were trawling for a fresh aptitude to warrant acme marks against a given conundrum. Mathematics tends to require a singularity response to a puzzler, the answer being binary, the student's calculation either right or wrong." Waving a corroborating hand, he then designated, "business studies falls into a more visceral domain. Assuredly, interrogations posed require reiteration of the facts, but also in part, they beg for a considerate response in terms of how the student interprets the scrutiny. Realistically, such a riposte presupposes knowledge, perception and the ability to make judgements and conclusions from the files. It is this latter subset that uncovers the possibility for the student to make an individual assessment, and propose ideas maybe brand new to the examiners' experience, thus certifying if maximum marks can be attributed against the question."

"You're saying," Catherine purported, "there's little point in repeating parrot fashion, if you don't understand what it means, what its implications are, and what can be learnt from it."

"I do believe I am, "Roger confirmed.

"Okay, girls," Bryant began scrutinising his watch. "We're fast converging on the finish and I believe you have a surprise for Mister Fraser."

Startled, Roger developed an inquisitive face.

Reaching behind her chair, Zoey pulled up a package, stood up and beheld Roger. "We all clubbed together to get you a thank-you present in appreciation of the effort you've dedicated to the supplementary evening sessions over two terms."

Walking forward, she handed him the gift plus an envelope.

Near to emotionally overwhelmed, he unsealed the vessel containing a thank-you card signed by every student attending his classes. "Well girls…you really have caught me on the hop," he stuttered out. "I didn't envisage anything like this. I'm, I'm…" Bowing, his bedazzlement snowballed, a tear forming and sliding down his cheek.

"Let's have a round of applause for Mister Fraser," Zoey extolled.

Responding, the entire class and Mister Bryant stood and clapped wildly, Wendy rushing to embrace her awestruck father.

"Come on, Dad," she whispered in his ear, "they await a reply from you."

Gazing at her affectionately, he mouthed, *I love you.* Reciprocating, she then stood aside and joined in the applause.

Wheeling away from the class, he blew his nose then gathering control braved them with a jubilant beam.

"I can usually see things coming, but you young ladies have really floored me with your generous homage," he confessed as the adulation died down. "I didn't visualise anything like this. I…" Withdrawing into himself, his stupefaction became very apparent to his admirers.

"Open the package, Mister Fraser," Roxanne pleaded.

"Right." Twinkling at their still joyous faces he thought, *what superb generosity and tenderness these young women exhibit.*

Gently pulling away the package wrapping, he revealed a complete classic *When the Boat Comes In* TV series, twenty-four-DVD boxed set. "Oh, this is one of my favourite television series from when I was your age." Jerking up his noggin, he fondly voiced, "thank you so much, girls. I can't begin to tell you how inexpressibly impressed I am by your kind heartedness and your inspired selection."

"Being from the *far* North," Abigail opined, "we thought you'd like it."

"I was actually born in Middlewich, Cheshire," he daintily substantiated, "not Geordie land."

"Yes, Wendy told us, but we couldn't find any dramatic series based in Cheshire, so we thought a staging set on Tyneside was nearest."

"Good call. Once again, many thanks girls. It's been a privilege to give some guidance into the convoluted world of business and insight *vis-à-vis* how commerce is conducted in practice. I can confidently say, all of you will do very well in the A-Level business studies examinations, and I anticipate hearing from Wendy you have passed with flying colours, going on to university, then entering productive careers."

"Mister Bryant," Abigail called, "will you take some photographs of us with Mister Fraser, please?"

"Of course."

She handed him her iPhone replete with photographic facilities.

Darting helter-skelter for Roger, the girls gathered around him, Gina and Roxanne draping themselves around his torso and shoulders.

"Say cheese everybody," Bryant implored before initiating the camera function, its flash momentarily blinding the photographic group.

Surrounded by their brethren counting Wendy, all the girls took turns to hug Roger, Bryant obliging with rendered camera shutter workings to capture the moments.

Lastly, in her most beguiling Lolita pose, Zoey Dunbar encircled Roger's waist with her arm. Gauging Bryant was about to take the photograph, she kissed him on the cheek at the precise instant the classroom door unfastened, and headmistress Missus Greenwood entered, closely followed by Charlotte Fraser.

Dumbfounded by the pageant before them, their eyes sprung wide open and their jaws descended south.

Oh no, Roger thought, *the doghouse beckons yet again.*

Chapter 5: The Hanging Judge

With the exception of the Henry Fonda time-honoured film *Twelve Angry Men*, TV series and films centred on courtroom drama left Roger Fraser cold. His ambivalence towards the wig and gown brigade became heightened when he received a letter from M. E. Hutchings, Jury Summoning Officer, Maidstone Crown Court, stating he was required for jury duty 6th August through 7th September 2012 inclusive, at Judge J. P. Bartlett's pleasure.

"They *can't* do this to me," he bleated to Charlotte.

"Why ever not?"

"I *loathe* law courts and everything to do with them."

"It's a civic obligation, Roger. You have to attend."

"How about you go instead of me?" he optimistically nominated.

"That's not how it works. You can't delegate the requirement."

"But I'll make a lousy juror. I'll find everyone sent before the beak guilty on principle, and demand they are hung, drawn and quartered for the most inconsequential crimes, but most of all, for wasting my time." Halting his diatribe, he adopted a protruding bottom lip, puppy dog demeanour. "Besides, with my weak bladder, I'll be leaving the court every five minutes to relieve myself."

"You haven't *got* a weak bladder," she firmly amended then insisted, "I know you. You won't be objectionable, and you won't press for the death sentence to be applied to those found guilty of littering the streets. You'll be meek and mild in the presence of authority."

"*Don't* count on it," he rebuked. "You know I have a very low threshold of boredom. Becoming holed up for five weeks at a crown court will drive me stir crazy. Besides, my iPhone will be going off every few minutes with calls from irate clients, disgusted by the guttural squeaks, farts and pops made by The Firm's Essex boy traders during transactions."

"I think you'll find mobile devices and computers will be confiscated before you go into the court."

"*Oohhh,*" Roger twittered. "I can't afford to be out of contact with The Firm for five weeks. Sweeping business ventures can come and go over such a period, and I'd be helpless to participate in the sequent investment opportunity. Even harsher, my inbox will transpose into Elysian Fields, saturated with enough unresolved emails to keep a legion of staff juniors in work for a year." Grinding his teeth in frustration, he yelped, "hell, I'll probably get the sack for being out of touch with market trends."

"Rubbish," she condemned. "You're exaggerating. Lots of financial services personnel have been called for jury turnout, without receiving their P-45s."

"Well—" Curling his upper lip in disgust of his forthcoming incarceration at the pleasure of Judge Bartlett, he pressured, "you know what I'm driving at."

"I do, but you can't ignore this subpoena. It'd equate to contempt of court and you'd end up in the dock yourself." Lingering, she added, "just a tick."

She went to the study, backtracking with a copy of *Who's Who?* Flicking through it to the legal section, she found an entry for Judge Jasper Percival Bartlett.

"I'd be careful with this judge, if I were you, Roger. He was a member of the Labour Party before taking robes under Blair's administration and becoming a circuit judge. Unofficially, he has retained his support for the Labour Party and staunchly promotes State ownership of the banks."

"*Good grief.* He sounds more like an austere Stalinist-communist than a British judge."

She slammed the book shut, her amusement at his dilemma not lost on him.

"So," she began, her tone taunting, "how are you going to settle with this call?"

"How about if I send in a letter saying I have an incurable, transmittable disease and with one whiff of the Devil's breath emanating from my mouth, the undivided jury will be poleaxed?"

"Very inventive, Roger, but I think every get-out ploy you might table has been tried and debunked by court administrators in the past."

"Perhaps The Firm can send the court a letter saying, my absence could terminate in a worldwide economic downturn, with a knock-on catastrophic upshot on the nation?"

"From what I can gather, you can have your employer submit a letter on your behalf, lobbying the court to defer your jury duty."

"*Defer*!" Roger maddeningly repeated. "You mean, if I can somehow get out of this call, it will bite me again downline?"

"I do."

"Drat." Befogged he puckered his lips "That means, this infernal calling will be hanging over me *ad infinitum*."

"Best to get it out of the way, don't you think?"

"Maybe, but I'd rather do it later than sooner."

Undeterred, Fraser approached Jaclyn Hulme, The Firm's HR Director, requesting she wrote a letter along the lines of, 'Mister Fraser is scheduled to command the crucial implementation of a strategic campaign, aimed at compliance with both UK and international financial authorities stock trading requirements, during the period he has been summoned for jury duty. Under the circumstances, The Firm respectfully seeks he is excused from the bond.' Acquiescing to Fraser's desire, Hulme stipulated he sent The Firm's letter to Maidstone Crown Court with his own personal testimony.

Playing ball, Fraser composed a very deferential, business-like letter, supplementing The Firm's petition for deferment from the levy until at least August 2013, thus giving him the contingency to make the necessary arrangements for work cover.

As fate would have it, during his confab with Hulme she craved a complementary favour.

"Roger, as you know, The Firm likes to gain an independent view of applicants from non-connected third parties."

"Yes."

"I'd like you to interview a security guard candidate. He's already been seen by Chief Security Officer, Major Bling."

"It's an odd surname isn't it? The bullpen calls him Goldfinger or Colonel Blimp for obvious reasons. Anyway, being a team player, it will be my pleasure."

"He's waiting in the assessment room. Can you give him the once over? See if you think he has the necessary people skills and he'll fit into The Firm's culture."

Passing Fraser the candidate's CV, he made his way to the rendezvous.

After the usual introductory formalities, Fraser sat across a desk from Chad Gillis, the prospective security guard candidate, a mountain of a man nearing the size of a minor planet, examining his resumé.

"I see you are ex-British Army, Mister Gillis."

"Yes, mainly with the paras before transferring to the SAS."

Bemused, he accredited, "your CV also states you are a…trained killer."

"That is correct."

"Heavens." All at sea, Fraser spluttered, "I've not met a trained killer before. I suppose your specialty was drive-through shootings?"

"How could you possibly know that? It's classified."

"I was guessing." Fraser rejoindered, resting back in his chair and smiling.

"Oh, sorry."

"Tell me," Fraser tabled, "do you see an opportunity for using these acquired skills at The Firm?"

"Only if directed to do so."

"Mmmm, you'd be right for The Firm's executive level Praetorian Guard in Manhattan. There are quite a few ex-Special Forces jocks in their ranks."

"So I understand."

"How did you get on with Major Bling?"

"He's the kind of officer and a gentleman I've been serving in the armed forces for the past fifteen years."

"Good."

Closing his file, he peered at the ex-soldier. "I have no doubts you can handle yourself should the need arise. What I am trying to assess is if you have the necessary savvy to deal with the London operation's more irascible characters, and come to that, some of our crabby even cranky clients, without upsetting them."

"How do you mean?"

"Some can be cantankerous, startling, unorthodox. Others at times, worse for wear on alcohol after celebrating a mountainous win. We make allowances for such transitory behaviour. It's part and parcel of investment banking's high-pressure environment. Anyone getting too far out of line is disciplined, but that's a matter for line managers, not security staff. Your role is much more akin to a commissionaire or a bell captain than a physical enforcer. You understand my drift?"

"I do."

"Do you have any questions for me?"

"Do you think I'll fit in at The Firm?"

"I appreciate it's not required in the SAS rank and file, but you might try uplifting your cheek muscles a bit more. Remember, often security functionaries are the first people visitors see at The Firm. We want to project a warm, welcoming atmosphere for them."

Reporting back to Hulme, Fraser summarized, "being a trained killer with a drive-through shootings specialty, I have no qualms about his ability to handle trouble, but if you and Colonel Blimp, er Major Bling, do hire him, he'll need to go through The Firm's orientation induction."

"Yes, I came to the same conclusion. I suppose we can't expect stormtroopers to come pre-armed with civilian interpersonal and communication skills. There's a crossover required."

"True. I'd surmise the ideal security guard would be a mix of Terminator Schwarzenegger alloyed with TV presenter Holly Willoughby's effervescent credentials."

"*Hah*, you are a tease, Roger."

~ * ~

Jovially posting the Maidstone bound communications, he forecast an end to the juror bother. He could not have been more mistaken. A few days later, he received a reply from M. E. Hutchings, saying to be absolved from the summons, he'd have to appear before Judge Bartlett in a court chamber.

"What!" he spat out as he took in the letter's salient point during family dinner.

"Bad news is it?" Charlotte sarcastically checked, having seen the Maidstone post mark on the envelope before Roger arrived home from Canary Wharf.

"I've got to go to the county court."

"You've not been caught flaunting your private parts along the Queen's highway after a drunken celebration at Kappa Corinthians Rugby Club, have you?" Wendy swiped.

"Certainly not."

"Then you must have been done for abusing traffic wardens," James offered.

"A fair cop, but no." Making a disparaging face, he relayed, "I have to appear before Judge Bartlett, to make my plea to be acquitted from jury duty."

"Daddy," the ever-chastising Heather began, "it's your public duty to be a juror. I heard Adelaide Perrett's mother say that to another mum at Adelaide's house."

"Well, she should know," Roger rebutted. "Adelaide Perrett's mother is virtually a professional juror. She just loves condemning the innocent and nearly innocent to decades of imprisonment, or gigantic finds for the most trivial of crimes."

Not liking Adelaide Perrett's mother for her denouncement of left-of-centre political standpoints, Charlotte mentally venerated the notion.

"That's as maybe, Daddy, but you'll be able to lock up all those people who are cruel to animals and little children."

"Yes, but—"

She uplifted an authoritative hand. "I haven't finished yet, Daddy. You've always told me, it's very rude to interrupt someone when they're talking, so let me finish."

Exasperated, he breathed out noisily. "Very well. Go on."

"You shouldn't be weaselling out of your responsibilities to society, Daddy. If everyone did it, there'd be lots and lots of criminals roaming the streets, who couldn't be put in jail because there'd be no juries to find them guilty."

Withal riled, Roger's napper fell, nearly ending up in the beef bourguignon his wife had lovingly prepared. "God almighty."

"It's no good appealing to God, Daddy. He'd tell you the same thing as me, wouldn't he, Mummy?"

"Definitely, Heather."

"Now I know how Julius Caesar must have felt when Brutus and his other so-called best friends attacked him with daggers," Roger grumbled.

~ * ~

A few days later, having eventually parked his M3 a good half-mile away from Maidstone Crown Court, Fraser found himself in the unfamiliar surroundings of the legal system.

Presenting his letter from M. E. Hutchings at reception, he was told by a humourless female aide with a rather pronounced bill to report to the antechamber adjacent to court two, where Judge Bartlett finalised a trial.

Thinking he'd have the waiting room to himself, he was surprised to see three other men, milling around apprehensively. *I wonder what they've done*, Fraser deliberated. It soon became clear from the odd exchange between them, they were all begging for jury duty deferment from Judge Bartlett.

"He's got a reputation for intolerance," one worried man told Fraser.

"Oh. How do you know?"

"His trials are regularly in the Weald of Kent newspapers encircling The Kent Messenger. Invariably, he awards the maximum sentence allowable under the law to those found guilty."

"Bit of a hanging judge tyrant then?"

"Oh yes. Just last week he gave a two-year custodial sentence to someone refusing to pay their council tax to Kent County Council."

"*You're* kidding."

"No. The luckless pigeon concerned hadn't paid any council tax for three years and correspondingly been fined in the magistrates' court, but still hadn't paid a penny."

"Yuck, ridiculous. The prison costs of incarcerating the victim far outweighs the council tax loss."

"Ahh, the victim as you call him, had some previous with Judge Bartlett for persistent protesting, meaning haranguing and stalking the leader of Kent County Council in connection with no value for money council tax levies. He went before Bartlett when indictments were brought against him by KCC five years earlier. Bartlett gave him a heavy fine and a deferred custodial sentence on that occasion. The victim paid both the fine and the outstanding council tax, but recommenced non-payment and protests a year later."

"Jesus, this bastion of the law means business," Fraser heralded. "Tell me, are you here to plead for service deferment?"

"We all are." Scouring about defensively, he attested, "and Bartlett is just as intolerant of anyone seeking to get out of their civic duties."

When at length Fraser got toe to toe with Judge Bartlett, he found the unexpurgated proceedings incongruous. Called by a court attendant like a big-league witness for the defence, his name resounded up and down a connecting corridor before he was ushered into the number two court chamber. Apart from the judge sat on high at the zenith of the court architecture, a court recorder below him, and set in a much lower strata an auxiliary menial, the monumental space abided empty.

Not standing on ceremony, the *aide-de-camp* showed Fraser into the witness box, positioned to the judge's left and at an even lower tier compared to the recorder's station, then thrust a bible into his hand. Line by line, the not-want-to-be a juror duplicated the swearing-in avowal after him, Judge Bartlett peering down at Fraser from on high, and from behind thick-rimmed, bifocal spectacles, just like Velma's in *Scooby Doo*. In this age of anything goes sexual liberation, Fraser speculated if Judge J. P.

Bartlett was either a butch lesbian, a transgender or a tranny. Recollections of the Mister-Miss Lavery revelation and even Grayson Perry's alter ego Claire percolated the forefront of his mind.

Nevertheless, the thought evaporated when the judge's highly masculine voice reverberated through the court. "You are Roger Jon Fraser?" Bartlett enquired, speaking into a microphone, the inquisition echoing off the walls of the empty court through a cluster of wall mounted loudspeakers.

From what little Fraser could see of him, other than ropey sight, Bartlett embodied a late fifties manifestation with a crimped, long face and bony fingers. He pondered if the judge mollycoddled the traditional judiciary pastime of wearing stockings and suspenders beneath his robes during court sessions.

"Yes, Your Worship," Fraser replied, also speaking into a microphone.

"It's, Your Honour," Bartlett inflexibly corrected. "Better still, My Lord."

"Me Lord," Fraser readdressed.

Originating the hearing business, Bartlett picked up some papers, Fraser assuming to be the letters from Jaclyn Hulme and himself, craving the judge's kindness.

"I see from the letter you sent in from Miss Hulme, you are set to be aboard some driver to do with your employers, at the very time you have been subpoenaed for jury duty."

"Yes, Me Lord."

"Tell me, Mister Fraser—" Removing his spectacles, Bartlett released a contemptuous glower at the plaintiff. "Does this responsibility both Miss Hulme and you think is so critical to The Firm's future, encompass the same irresponsible actions and subsequent debacle culminating in the 2008 meltdown, and its knock-on effects to the all-embracing country?"

"Oh no, Me Lord. In 2008, the country suffered more through the irresponsible excesses of—" He was going to say, Gordon Brown and New Labour, before remembering Bartlett was a staunch Labour Party activist.

"Yes, Mister Fraser?"

"Yes, you are quite right, Me Lord. The country going down the tubes was down to the financial services sector."

"I'm glad we can agree on that. Now—" He perused the letter again. "Anent your application to have your liability deferred, you must realise, Mister Fraser, if the court assented to deferment for everyone summoned, the legal framework could grind to a standstill." Towering over his bench he probed, "or are you one of those misguided people, who think non-working people or god forbid professional jurors are needed to gauge evidence and make pronouncements as per a defendants' guilt or otherwise?"

"Well, er—" Hastily stopping, Fraser feared he might get himself into a worse situation.

"You were going to say?"

"No, Me Lord. I'm a keen champion of trial by the people for the people."

"Phooey," he blasted, "that's an Americanism, Mister Fraser. A term made popular during the American War of Independence. By implication, are you advocating revolution in England?"

"No, no, no, Me Lord, quite the contrary." Fraser's spiers unfolded to their extremities "Being a member of the investment banking brotherhood, we patronise the establishment status quo."

"I'm glad to hear it, Mister Fraser." Rifling through the letters for a third cycle, the judge then spelt out, "despite your unfortunate association with investment banking and your somewhat lackadaisical attitude to the due process of law, on balance, the court will defer your jury duty on this occasion."

Fraser's features lit up. "Many thanks, Me Lord."

Fleeing the witness box, he whispered a jubilant "yes" to himself.

"I've not dismissed you yet, Mister Fraser." Shooting an unsparing finger at him, Bartlett urged, "kindly return to the witness box."

Propping the mantle of a misbehaving choirboy, he did so.

"Let me be perfectly clear, Mister Fraser, I'm granting you a temporary deferment. Your statutory obligation still stands."

"Yes, Me Lord."

"And Mister Fraser," he thundered. "It's not, Me Lord. It's, My Lord. Only council are permitted that indulgence, and this courtroom is not the set for an episode of *Rumpole of the Bailey*, or any other of those unrealistic, somewhat fanciful television dramas, seeking to depict the judiciary as either rotund, flamboyant dignitaries or blithering buffoons." Pausing, he menacingly poured over Fraser. "Or do you think I'm the incarnation of Leo McKern playing Horace Rumpole?"

"Oh no, Me Lord, er My Lord. There's not the slightest resemblance. Leo's rendition of Rumpole was—" Suddenly shutting up, he realised he was about to say, *Doric, whereas you come across as a draconian enforcer*.

"Yes, Mister Fraser?" Bartlett murmured into his microphone, his hackles visibly rising.

"Nothing, My Lord."

~ * ~

Remarkably, just a week after his close encounter with the hanging judge, Trevor Evans, one of the least reprehensible of The Firm's Essex boy traders bounded into his office, greyed in countenance, panting and perspiring.

"Whatever's the matter, Trevor? You haven't been going out on a limb in the commodities markets again, have you?"

"No," he whimpered out.

"Your six-foot, stuffed brown bear mascot has not deserted you, and run off to Regent's Park Zoo, has it?"

"*No*," he snapped wringing his hands. "Biffo is at the dry cleaners, being fumigated."

"I give up. What *new* catastrophe has overtaken you?"

"I was stopped by the police for speeding on the M4, November 2011. Christmas week, I received a writ to attend Maidenhead Magistrates Court on an arraignment of driving over the speed limit."

"Oh, yeah." Fraser scintillated. "Doing your *Top Gear* Stig impersonation were you?"

"Hardly, but I'm extremely disquieted by it."

"Relax," Fraser entreated, raising his eyebrows. "Speeding is not too serious a crime."

"Roger, I've already got nine points on my licence. If I'm found guilty, I'll get another three points, making twelve in total, and I'll lose my driving licence!"

"*Aahh*!" Baring his teeth, he conceded, "puts a different complexion on it. If you get to the twelve, you'll lose your job at The Firm as well."

"Precisely. Sometimes I have to visit clients by car, and I can't see The Firm paying for taxis."

"No." Fraser became hesitant before tabling his thereafter reservation. "So why are you telling me all this, Trevor?"

"I need someone with gravitas and probity to plead my mitigating circumstances at the magistrate's court."

"Unequivocally a job for your boss, Ricky Henshaw."

"If Ricky knew my predicament, he'd fire me on the spot."

"Yep. They don't call Ricky the nemesis of delinquent dealers for nothing. He's slain more misfiring brokers than St. George has fiery dragons."

"I was actually thinking of you when I made the description."

"*Me*?"

"Yes. Come on, Roger, what with your new appointment and promotion, The Firm must think the proverbial shines out of your backside."

"Well, I'd not go as far as that." Taking in the nervy peddler, he fanned out his hands. "Regretfully, I don't think I can help you on this occasion, Trevor."

"But, but, but…but, but, but, but…" Evans began, perplexed to the point of being reduced to a single monosyllabic retort.

Amazed, Fraser howled, "you're clucking like a demented chicken."

Desperation overpowered Evans. Without Biffo to cling to, instead he clung to the door jamb hoping to relieve his anxiety. "Please, if there is anyone who can appeal to a magistrates' merciful side, it's you."

"I've said it before, and I'll probably have to say it again," Fraser reiterated, producing a wry aspect. "I'm not the patron saint of traders. I'm forever bailing you lot out of career threatening situations, and coming to your aid when you're not making your numbers."

"I know." Forlornly, Evans hung his head.

Reconsidering, and never one to refuse someone in acute distress, 'Chelski' fanatics apart, Fraser took pity on the dejected Evans.

"Okay—" He bit his lip, as if he knew what he was about to say led to anguish and heartache; his anguish and heartache. "I'll come to your rescue. But I'm not promising to contrive miracles with the magistrate. I'll give it my best shot, Trevor. Will that do?"

"Oh, thank you, Roger. You've taken a heavy load off my mind."

"Hold on, I've not done anything yet."

"You'll prevail. You always do."

Come the following week, a charged-up Fraser sat with a worried Evans in the Maidenhead Magistrates Court anteroom waiting for his case to be called. When the court usher eventually summoned Evans, he rose to his feet like a man about to prematurely meet his maker, the blood draining from his face as he edged his way to the courtroom. After taking the oath and identifying himself in the defendant's box, the main magistrate read out the indictment against him. When ticketed how he pleaded, Evans answered by claiming distraction during driving, work paradoxes the root punch behind his negligence, the declaration inadvertently making his over-the-speed-limit crime seem even more shocking.

Knowing he had to play his knight in shining armour saviour card quickly for the bench to gain a more rounded assessment of him, and his otherwise free-from-crime model citizen reputation, Evans requested his character witness take the stand.

Escorted by the court usher, a confident Fraser whirled into the magistrate's court, sure he could talk his colleague out of losing his license. Logging the accused holding onto the surround rail of the defendant's box like he rode the Alton Towers rollercoaster, he gave an encouraging wink to Evans. After going through the identification and oath affirmation in the witness box, Fraser pinpointed the lead magistrate, flanked by ancillary magistrates either side of him, one of them a lady.

"Mister Fraser," the lead magistrate initiated, "we understand you're acting as the defendant's character witness."

"Yes, My Lord."

"Ahem." Smirking, he whispered a few words to his fellow magistrates before reconvening with the witness. "The befitting form of address for a magistrate, Mister Fraser, is either Your Worship or Sir."

"My apologies, Your Worship. Lately, I had a tryst with a county court judge and used the term My Lord to address him."

"Nothing on the wrong side of the law, I hope?"

"No. I was just attempting to get out of—" Like at Maidstone, he stopped abruptly, cleared his throat and tattled, "I was arranging deferment for jury duty."

"Good. Being requisitioned for jury duty is synonymous with not having a criminal record. Mister Evans chose wisely when he selected you to be his character witness. Now, can you summarise your background?"

"My pleasure, Your Worship. I graduated from King's College Cambridge with a first degree in economics, and went to work for JP Morgan Chase and Merrill Lynch before joining The Firm in 1997, where I am currently director of market analysis, and also have a secondary commission as a trouble-shooter."

"Trouble-shooter," the magistrate repeated. "Surely such a calling makes you eminently qualified for the task before you." Dwelling, he took in Fraser. "How long have you known the defendant?"

"Since he joined The Firm in 2003."

"And how would you demarcate him?"

Beforehand, Fraser had decided to gild the lily, if not lie through his teeth at the court hearing. "Trevor Evans is a trustworthy, solid citizen and a significant contributor to The Firm's success. He is also a pre-imminent agent for various charities, including the Bembridge Foundation."

"The *Bembridge* Foundation," the inquisitor parroted. "Explain."

Fraser couldn't say a five-star retirement home for disabled, pox-ridden, brain-dead, gaga bankers. Instead, he chose to bullshit the magistrate.

"Your Worship, the Bembridge Foundation is a benevolent charity subsidised by members of the financial services sector, with the intention of donating comfort and companionship to both retired and battle-jaded members of our industry and their associates."

"Egad, sounds more like a five-star retirement home for disabled, pox-ridden, brain-dead, gaga bankers."

"How could you—" Stopping from saying, *possibly know that*? Fraser circulated the bench what he yearned to be a winning glitter and repulsed, "Your Worship, with the greatest of respect, you do an injustice to the banking industry. The Bembridge Foundation shelters everyone's needs, from those at the bottom of the pyramid, to those at its summit. All are treated with identical compassion."

"You don't say," he goaded. "Go on with your testament about the defendant."

"Your Worship, I have no reservation in saying Trevor Evans is a tip-top, ethical and honest chap. A man whose past professional performance guarantees him a brilliant future, that is—" He winced. "If you could possibly see your way clear to not taking away his driving license."

"I see." Picking up a file from his bench, the primary magistrate thumbed its contents. "It might interest you to know, the defendant has committed four speeding offences over the past forty-two months, the last one capping in his subpoena to this court, to decide his future as a driver, if in fact, he has one."

"Your Worship, I talked to Mister Evans about these offences prior to this hearing. On every occasion, he has only been marginally over the speed limit. It's my belief he didn't wilfully contravene the restriction. More likely, his mind became bewitched with business responsibilities, and his vehicle drifted over the speed limit without him noticing."

"Do you know what car the defendant drives, Mister Fraser?"

"Indeed I do, Your Worship, a Porsche 911 Carrera Cabriolet."

"A very powerful car."

"Yes, Your Worship."

"Don't you think with the bipartition between the defendant's inability to track the speedometer while cogitating on business affairs, he'd be better served driving a much less powerful car?"

"I do not wish to contradict you, Your Worship, but driving a less powerful car does not necessarily prevent the driver from exceeding the speed limit."

"*Really*?"

"If I might demonstrate by example?"

Pitching an irritated glimpse at his equally irritated co-magistrates, the principal magistrate then elevated an authorising hand. "Please, enlighten us, Mister Fraser."

"Often, when I've been driving my BMW M3, itself a powerful car, I've been flashed by 1.3 Escort and Astra van drivers, then gesticulated at to move out of the way for them to overtake me. During the exploit, they have broken the speed limit."

"That's all very well, Mister Fraser, but the bench is seeking justifiable pretexts why the defendant should not be awarded a fresh three points for exceeding the speed limit for a fourth time, and thereby forfeit his driving license."

"I believe the rationale for not applying the telling *coup de gras* is centred on both economic and social constituents."

Piqued by the possible content of Fraser's contention, the three magistrates exchanged chagrined pouts.

"Go on, Mister Fraser," the chief magistrate sanctioned.

"If he lost his driving license, losing his job inevitably supervenes at The Firm and he'd not find a job elsewhere in investment banking. Annually, he earns a substantial income, a large amount of which goes to the Exchequer to capitalise the public purse; hospitals, schools, and—" He made a guileless facial gesture. "Dare I say it, the judiciary. Compound the loss of tax revenue with Mister Evans becoming a life-long strain on State benefits, engendering drug dependency and alcohol abuse, his wife divorcing him, and his children going hungry, and you begin to realise from both an economic and social perspective, society in general would be the big loser."

"A very perspicacious observation, Mister Fraser," the master magistrate perceived before swapping a few words with his support team. "Undoubtedly, your argument is elegant," he grudgingly complimented, "but you do not necessarily persuade."

"Might it aid Mister Evan's situation," Fraser tabled, "if he were to make a commitment to engage his car cruise control, set to the appropriate speed limit enforcement whilst driving?"

"I must say, it's an inventive, somewhat novel strategy, but it does not excuse why the defendant has appeared before this court today."

"May I be frank, Your Worship?"

"Please." Rolling his blinkers, as if preparing to be moreover astonished by Fraser's plea, he assured, "I think I can speak for the bench and the entire court when I say, edify us with your latest dictum."

"Fine Mister Evans £1,000, £2,000 if necessary, and make him do a hundred hours of community service, but I beg, beseech and implore you, not to take away his driving license."

Forming a huddle, the magistrates weighed Fraser's defence, the court embodying onlookers and the local press transfixed with bated breath, Fraser registering Evans now hung onto the surround rail of the defendant's box so tightly, his knuckles glowed white.

"Mister Evans," the dominant magistrate began, "we have heard your evidence, and the character reference and recommended future path from your benefactor, Mister Fraser. Taking account of the interrelated factors ably pleaded by Mister Fraser, it is the decision of this court to fine you £2,000, and order you to supply 200-hours community service." Delaying, he rendered Evans a stern face. "Your license will not be accorded another three penalty points, which means you sustain the right to drive. However—" He lifted an admonitory finger. "If in the future, you are called before Maidenhead Magistrates Court, or any other magistrates court on driving offences, be warned, no clemency will be applied. Clear, Mister Evans?"

Gulping, Evans laboured to recover his ability to speak. "Absolutely, Your Worship."

"Oh yes, and make sure you use the car's cruise control, as Mister Fraser has suggested."

"I will, Your Worship."

Bringing his gavel sharply down on its hardwood sound block, the lead magistrate adjudicated, "case dismissed."

As the magistrates egressed the bench for lunch trailed by the court officials, a cheer went up from the gallery, and the local press commenced photographing the foremost players.

Grabbing Evans by the arm, Fraser petitioned, "come on, Trevor, let's get the flock out of here, as John Wayne said to the Welsh shepherds."

"Roger you were superb. I owe you everything."

Foreseeing new peccadilloes arising down line, Fraser issued the delinquent dealer a harsh glare. "I'll hold you to that. Think yourself lucky you weren't up before hanging judge J. P. Bartlett."

"Who's he?"

"Your gravest nightmare. Think Bembridge on speed with delegated dominion over all mankind."

"Wow, he must be implacable."

"Quite."

"By the way, Roger, I'm not married, and I don't have any children."

"I know. Let's hope the magistrates don't make any enquiries into your matrimonial status."

Negotiating a passageway merging towards the exit, Fraser and Evans were descended on by local press photographers snapping away as they departed.

They had only gone a few feet when they heard someone say, "Mister Fraser," in a commanding voice behind them.

Twirling about, the lady magistrate came into his sight line, shutting the magistrate's entrance door behind her. She beckoned them towards her. Mystified by the call, The Firm's men gawped at each other, then scurried to the rear of the passageway.

"Let me introduce myself. I'm Missus Juliana Shearwood."

She held out her hand, Fraser grasping it.

"Can we help you, Missus Shearwood."

"As it turns out, I might be able to do you a favour."

"Really?"

"I was very stirred by the way you conducted yourself on behalf of Mister Evans." Her manner becoming assertive, she sought, "tell me,

Mister Fraser, have you ever considered becoming a magistrate?"

"What, *me*?" Fraser near-to barked, his mouth remaining partially unsealed.

"I think you have the necessary poise, calm and calculated delivery to sit on a magistrate's bench."

"Oh, er—" Avalanching into a bashful deportment, he guaranteed, "I'm very flattered, Missus Shearwood, but I think my exhibition in a magistrate's court was a one off. There's far less to me than you might imagine. I was merely helping out a co-worker to the best of my ability." Blowing out his cheeks, he moderated, "I don't think I'd make a very good magistrate."

"We all think that before we're appointed, but once used to the charge, we discover we can do what is required of us. However, there's prodigious training and you'd get paid for the job."

Cajoled further, he smirked gregariously. "You make it sound very appealing, but—" He diplomatically quivered his brow. "It's not for me."

"At least let me have the Magistrates Service send you some details."

Contemplating, he then acquiesced. "Very well."

"Good, then you'll give it some deliberation?"

"Mmmm." He extended an investigating finger. "Can anyone who has a peerless social history apply to become a magistrate?"

"Yes."

"Then I think I know someone who might be interested."

"Oh. May I enquire who?"

"My wife, Charlotte. She exhibits all the necessary credentials needed to become a magistrate."

"How?"

"She's—" About to say, *got the same no-nonsense, uncompromising, unequivocal Witch Finder General attitude about her as the lead magistrate and hanging judge J. P. Bartlett*, instead he stopped abruptly for the nth time in his short exposure to the courts.

"Yes, Mister Fraser."

"Ha, ha...she's er—" Putting on his best artificial, glossy face, he earnestly praised, “she’s just like you.”

Chapter 6: Chav City

After taking up the violin at school, Heather pressured her father into purchasing her an instrument of her own, Mackenzies in Chatham High Street, exemplary for the purpose. Albeit both tutored on the piano, when Brother Colin and Roger were growing up in the 1970s, their parents took them to Mackenzies to buy guitars and guitar accessories. Whereas Colin did a pretty mean facsimile of Fleetwood Mac's Peter Green, Roger never paralleled that empyrean height, his playing more resembling a reject candidate from the Sex Pistols than the Mac maestro.

Forming the Medway towns along with Rochester, Strood and Gillingham, at the time, Chatham was still a Navel town, famous as the birthplace of Nelson's flagship the Victory, and home to many British Army regiments, incorporating a Gurkha brigade. Often, the Frasers saw the legendary Gurkhas off-duty, dressed in very smart blazers, slacks and regimental ties, walking along Chatham High Street. Taking pride in them, locals adjudged the brigade members to be good role models for young people. Though the Medway towns were invariably designated as a depressed area, commerce flourished, unemployment stayed low, and motorists were still able to drive along the High Street and easily navigate around the Medway conurbation. Workwise, the principal employers in Kent were Chatham Dockyard with its Royal Navy submarine base, and Marconi Avionics at Rochester where over 7,000 staff laboured to design and manufacture military equipment. Unspoilt by manmade organic progress, the North Downs tarried as a natural beauty setting, attracting local families after a hard weeks' graft. Likewise, just a few miles away from Chatham, the world-renowned Weald of Kent afforded opportunities for joyful pastimes, as did the River Medway.

Locally, the only demarcation divide centred on birthright either side of the River Medway, Kentish Men on the north side, Men of Kent to the south. Acting as a passive stimulator for inter-community competitive sports and thereby bragging rights, enacted in a good-natured, teasing guise, the traditional partition had been in place for centuries. Uniquely, the Kent-style dartboard and the game of bat-and-trap brought sports individuality to the county. Kent also boasted a long heritage of cricket success, seasoned England Test Match players Colin Cowdrey, Alan Knott and Derek Underwood forming the backbone of Kent's all-conquering county cricket club.

Since those Larkin-like days, Chatham had markedly deteriorated, the dockyard de-commissioned, and Marconi where Roger's Kappa Corinthians Rugby Club captain Martin Gayle was one of less than 1500 employees, acquired by BAE Systems. Many historical buildings had been torn down to make way for a poorly configured road traffic complex, and promised new developments never built. More grimly, in one of the poorest town planning schemes to be foisted on unsuspecting residents, the high street was closed-off to traffic, parking becoming an art form, commerce correspondingly suffering. It marked a downward spiral for Chatham into the abyss.

Disenfranchised by Harriet 'Harperson's' disastrous multicultural experiment, East End Londoners had flocked to and engrossed the Medway Towns. Rejecting the PC doctrine, they fled in an ever-growing wave of white flight, seeking to be amongst their own kind, to feel comfortable again. Compounding the overpopulation problem, Kent in general and the Medway towns in particular were additionally swamped beyond the means of overtaxed infrastructure and social services by an out-of-control influx of foreign interlopers, native Kent people forming an ever-decreasing minority. Just like carpetbaggers after the fall of Atlanta, Chatham was flooded by a multicultural assortment of opportunist dregs, imposed on England without consultation or consensus, out to make a quick illegal buck, and exploit the benefits system.

After Blair and Brown fabricated their perpetual underclass, Chatham also became oppressed by a brassy layer of migrating undesirables. Disparagingly known as 'Chav City', it got a reputation for attracting society's dross. Impervious to regular society canons, the Chavs were proud of their Channel 4 *Shameless* Frank Gallagher-like *modus vivendi*, low intellects, fake tans, ultra-cheap bling jewellery and an inability to speak English correctly. Most looked like flunked columbines from the cast of *Eastenders*; just too chavy even for that dysfunctional set of no-hopers, The Firm's Essex boy traders coming across like sophisticated aristocrats in comparison.

As the end of the twenty-first century's launching decade approached, Chav City took a third downward spiral into the cesspit, by becoming home to druggies, illegal immigrants, thwarted asylum seekers, down and outs and petty criminals from all points of the foreign compass. Trailer trash and tornado bait, to use Oklahoma terms, had descended on Chatham High Street, making it resemble a human zoo of extremely inelegant types fruiting in the thoroughfare, the town thereby gaining the uncouth moniker, 'lazoonland'.

If it could be avoided, Roger never went there. Even double-hard bastards like solicitor and rugby player extraordinaire Steve Hunt gave it second thoughts, Roger's pal naming it Dodge City, and championing Wyatt Earp and Doc Holiday might have had trouble keeping the streets cleansed of the human excrement, forever piling up with every in-coming tide of the River Medway.

Much to the shame of real locals, Chatham became the butt of the nation's didos. Satirists gibed, 'Channel 4 are making a new programme, where chavs cook meals for each other. They're calling it, Scum Dine with Me,' and 'The BBC will be broadcasting a variant on *Britain's Got Talent* called Chatham's Got Chavs.' Not remotely dignified, it only served to reinforce the public's impression of the stereotype infestation the once regal town of Chatham had to endure.

In spite of the mind-boggling negatives, Mackenzies rested as a terrific musical instruments shop, arguably the best in the South East, thereby making Roger's and Heather's visit mandatory.

~ * ~

On the day of the outing, as Roger drove the M3 along what little access prevailed on Chatham High Street, he discerned Heather gawking at the odd and often creepy array of human flotsam and jetsam meandering aimlessly along both sides of the street. Recurrently, she started to ask her predictable w-penetrations about the peculiar passers-by, but they drifted away as sketchy sentences, indicating even for an inquisitive little girl, what she saw, she found alarming.

Momentarily peeping away from the road forrad, her father pumped, "are you alright, Heather?"

She didn't reply.

"Heather," he persisted.

"Sorry, Daddy," she apologised, her mien signifying she had become even more dumbfounded by the incongruous curiosities drifting past the M3.

"You okay?"

"How long are we going to be here, Daddy?"

"Just long enough to buy you a violin."

Supposing she'd immediately respond, his daughter lingered unusually quiet. About to pry if some substance bothered her, he thought better of it, thinking she could table awkward explorations, his replies amplifying her dismay.

"The last time I came to Chatham," he reflected, deciding to distract her with an amusing incident, "Uncle Steve and myself went into a local pub for lunch. Whilst we sat at the bar, a man came up wanting to pay his bill. The barman told him the damage and the man reached into his inside pocket searching for a credit card, but realised he'd misplaced it. Embarrassed, he pulled out another item and optimistically mooted, 'I've got a Gillingham Football Club season ticket'. Steve and I had been clocking what was going on, and I couldn't help but jibe, 'well that's got no value, has it.'"

Chuckling at the remembrance, remarkably, Heather also let out a snigger.

"So, you understood my anecdote?"

"Oh, Daddy, I am eight years old. I do get your silly jokes."

"No, no, Heather. It really happened."

"You expect me to believe you?" She tutted. "Really, Daddy."

"But, but…oohh, molluscs." *She gets more like her mother with every passing day* Roger surmised.

After parking the beamer adjacent to Radio Kent's HQ at Sun Pier, he grabbed Heather's hand and they made the short walk to Mackenzies, an old-fashioned shop with a Dickensian pattern frontage, its real doorbell chiming as they entered. Festooned with all types of musical instruments, encompassing electric guitars and drum kits through to grand pianos and acoustic string instruments, walking into Mackenzies still equalled an Aladdin's cave for Roger, musky odours also giving it an air of antiquity and a bygone age ambience. Not changed in over fifty years, strip-lighting bathed the strategically placed displays in clear white light, bringing out hyperbolic curves in brass instruments, silver plated keys on clarinets and a sheen across the surfaces of Hammond organs, everything dust free and spotless. Judging by the gleaming 1950s lino-covered floor, unalloyed cleanliness still ruled. Marvelling at the shop's enchanting interior, he thought how sterile and functional modern department stores were in comparison.

An archetypal family run business, Mackenzies had been founded on the principles of prudent retailing practices, integrity of product knowledge and honesty of transaction. Hoping against hope Mister Mackenzie suddenly materialised from behind the counter, warmly greeting his clientele and enquired how he could be of assistance, in reality, a competent shop assistant bid them welcome and informed Roger, Mister McKenzie had retired many years ago, and his nephew Melvin now ran the business.

"Melvin is just taking delivery of some stock," announced the shop assistant, a mid-twenties man, tall and thin, with his hair brushed into a Gene Vincent curly quiff. *Probably a local musician* Roger mused, noticing he also wore a light brown shop coat of the variety Mister Mackenzie once used, just like BBC audio engineers donned at Lime Grove and Alexander Palace, before that once national treasure was kidnapped and held to guilt ransom by the ranks of the politically correct.

"Daddy, here's one I like," Heather trilled, her bright blue peepers sparkling with delight as they fell on a Hoffner violin, its price tag denoting the prestigious instrument retailed at £899.99.

Appreciating his daughter had inherited her mother's expensive tastes, he judiciously proposed, "maybe in a few years we could consider the Hoffner, if you are still playing."

"How about this one then?" she rebutted, pointing to a much more reasonably priced piece at £189.99.

"Ah, yes, a good incipient price-point," her father backed.

"Good morning, sir. May I be of assistance?"

Rotating, a man perhaps a few years older than Roger came into his view, like the shop assistant, dressed in a light brown shop coat. A receding hairline, deep russet-brown optics superficially possessing a personality all of their own, a craggy manifestation fingerprinting his face, an above average height and a medium build completed the picture. There before Roger stood his childhood remembrance of Mister Mackenzie.

"Hello," Roger cheerfully rejoindered. "You must be Melvin Mackenzie."

"Indeed I am, sir."

"My father," Roger fondly reminisced in a lilting voice, "used to bring my brother and I to Mackenzies at least thirty years ago."

"Must have been when Mister Mackenzie senior ran the business."

"Quite right. How is Mister Mackenzie?"

"Alas," Melvin reported, "my uncle retired to Eastbourne in the early 1990s. His son, my cousin Albert, inherited the business and we run the shop together."

"Do you know, you are the spit and image of your uncle."

"Yes, often people take Albert and myself for brothers."

Having indulged Roger in his yesteryear memories, Melvin became business-like. "Was there anything specific you're interested in, sir?"

Lazoonland might be a crap hole, Roger thought, *but Mackenzies is just as I remember from my youth*. Pleased it had retained old world charm, replete with pleasantries and courtesies, facets in the main dying out with the unstoppable rise of amalgamated retail conglomerates and supermarkets, both typified by lamebrain customer-facing staff with poor interpersonal skills, Roger looked forward to the balance of the procurement exertion.

Not long before the Chatham trip, he had gone into Boots at Orpington seeking a replacement shaver foil. Frigging around with her nails and chewing gum, the girl behind the counter abided deficient to registering his advance. When he dropped anchor, she carried on frigging, oblivious to the province Boots paid her to execute. Waving a rolled-up newspaper at her, Roger jabbered, 'Hello, purchaser here, hello.' Stopping frigging and chewing, she espied him and burbled, 'Ugh!' After he'd taught her rudimentary English, she gathered what he wanted. Checking the stock for a few minutes, she did not detect the article, Roger eventually telling her the shaver foil was right behind her, and they finally concluded the disjointed process.

"My youngest daughter," Roger explained, scintillating at Heather, "has taken up the violin at school. She now wants an instrument of her own."

"Ah, I see, sir," Melvin acknowledged, effulgent and clasping his hands together, fully cognizant with the sales opportunity. "I'd recommend your daughter starts off with a fairly inexpensive item. In a few years, if she is still going strong, trade in the first instrument, and invest in something with more tone and timbre."

This guy is on my wavelength Roger silently applauded. "My thoughts exactly," he approved.

Showing his clients a few student two-four, three-four and four-four alternates, Heather tried them out for size, then gave a tortured rendition of the intro into Bach's *Brandenburg Concertos* third movement to test them out.

After some debate with her habitual, 'are you sure no animals were harmed in the manufacturing of this violin?' and Melvin making the necessary assurances it was free from animal carcasses and cat's whiskers, she decided to select the student three-four. With the business finalised and Heather bubbling with joy, Roger decided to take the opportunity to talk to the shop proprietor about other matters.

"Tell me, Mister Mackenzie, how do you find business after so many, let's call them, changes in Chatham over the past ten to fifteen years?"

"Ahh, are you being prurient about our clientele," he poised, "or perhaps the high street inhabitants?"

"Both I reckon."

"Our consumers have tarried much the same," he confirmed. "Whether procuring string, wind or tympani instruments, all have reverence for a music shop. Some are dressed in suits like yourself, others more casually. Many rock instrument buyers dress in jeans and t-shirts. But in general, when they enter Mackenzies, it's like crossing into hallowed turf for them."

"You mean, like a place of worship?"

"Yes, I do, Mister Fraser," the studious proprietor sanctioned. "They become reverent and deferential to the staff." Clearly delighted, he appended, "and they're always pleased to be privileged to test our products before making a purchase."

"It's just as I remember," Roger advised before glinting towards the door. "What about outside, Mister Mackenzie? I mean, do you experience any anti-social problems?"

"Regrettably…that's not so good," he confessed, his joyful comportment down-shifting into sorrow. "We have to bring down metal shutters across all the windows and the front door after close of business. If we don't, they will be broken by unruly mobs wandering along the high street, either drunk or high on drugs, or by thieves out for a quick kill."

"What a shame," Roger accredited, with a wan expression. "To think, Chatham is where the Victory was built, Turner used it as a base for his paintings of the Medway estuary, and Dickens lived in this quarter."

"Quite right. Chatham has fallen a very long way from grace."

"It's not the town, Mister Mackenzie," Fraser disputed. "Bricks and mortar never hurt anybody. It's the new influxes inhabiting it. They're responsible for its demise and bad reputation."

"Incontrovertibly true."

Marking each other like two time-travellers revisiting past glories and knowing a new renaissance would never be seen on the horizon, they resigned themselves to the once renowned town of Chatham sliding further down the beckoning spiral into the maladjusted void.

"Well…I mustn't keep you chatting any longer," Roger affirmed in a faltering voice. "I'm sure you have things to see to, and we have to go."

"Many thanks for your custom, sir," Melvin graciously reciprocated. "We hope to see you and your daughter again."

"Good-day and thank you," he requited, shaking the shop owner's hand.

On the inverse foot walk to Sun Pier, Heather and Roger were passed by more examples of weird humans with accents originating thousands of miles away from Kent County. Some of the abnormal freaks and grubby, unkempt specimens made Ron Pearlman's enactment of Salvatore in *The Name of the Rose* arise as quite human and his stylisation fine-featured. Often, Roger heard Whoopi Goldberg would never win any beauty contests, but compared to some of the malformed and aberrant dross, trudging up and down Chatham High Street seeking out petty criminal opportunities to exploit, she was Miss World.

Staring at them agog, like she'd been caught in the web of a horror movie, or woken up to find herself at a monsters version of Madame Tussauds, Heather tightened her already firm grip on her father's hand and walked slightly behind him, as if trying to mask off the panorama to her front.

Usually when in new places, w-inquisitions poured out of her like a tidal wave. But as on the inbound journey to Mackenzies, she lasted question-less, even pensive for one so young. Normally, nothing fazed Fraser's youngest daughter, most adults easy prey for her above board, no-holds-barred routine, as Wendy's ex-boyfriend Sly had found to his cost. But Roger perceived she felt vulnerable, threatened, even targeted by the environment surrounding them. A far cry from when Colin and he were her age, they felt perfectly secure walking through Chatham with their parents.

What on Earth has happened to England, and where will it end? Roger cogitated. While he was heads-up and hungry for success at The Firm, tending to his family, scoring the odd try for Kappa Corinthians and generally engaging in light-hearted, carefree practices, untouched by the political and social stresses overarching it, gigantic and severe life-changing policies had been enacted in Parliament, under pressure from self-interested minority groups. Within the space of just two decades, the draconian changes in favour of the multiculturalism pluralists had resulted in the decline and fall of English society to the point whereby it would take several eons to recover, if at all.

Shamefully, the politicians' embracement of multiculturalism had seen England's population exponentially accelerate away through inward migration and booming immigrant child procreation. Taking the precedent to its logical conclusion, his life-long friend Gordon Anderson had voiced, if an English revolution didn't spring up and reverse the trend, economic disaster would set in, the welfare and health mechanisms collapsing under the ever-swelling encumbrance. Ubiquitous social unrest would befall, leading to riots and the indisputable approach of civil war. Being on the inside of the financial services community with access to world economic and demographic statistics, Roger endorsed his belief.

Effectively signalling the end of everything held dear by Christian societies, Gordon also predicted the same destructive behemoth happening concurrently in Western Europe and North America, forging a one-way passage back to the dark ages.

He also maintained English people stranded in the bedlam-like morass would migrate down under to Australia and New Zealand, abandoning twenty centuries of English heritage, history and accomplishment to be destroyed by the invading alien hordes, just like the Visigoths had sacked the Holy Roman Empire, bringing upwards civilisation to an end, until the rise of fifteenth century renaissance Europe.

Gordon's definitive chilling indictment appalled Roger. Even more injurious, after the old West comprising the Americas had been ravaged of all content, he forecast Australia and New Zealand to be in the sights of the marauding locust-like masses hereinafter. If chartered to happen, it equated to the equivalent of global thermo-nuclear war in terms of effect and finality, the last redoubt of a once great civilisation terminated through both passive and active genocide sponsored by the insufferable, liberal-fascist PC fraternity.

Taking place one evening when they were alone at the Fraser's house, the conversation had a dire corollary on Roger. After Gordon exited, he uncorked bottle after bottle of *Gevrey Chambertin*, his ingestion intended to blot out the abhorrent vision his friend had painted. Eventually, he fell asleep under the influence of deep intoxication. When he awoke the upcoming morning, after regaining his senses, Gordon's prediction came to the forefront of his mind. In terms of thought stencils, like a sore that won't exhaustively heal, it hovered in the milieu, never quite going away. Not wishing to alarm Charlotte, he didn't share the horrifying vision with her.

Such austere thoughts were alien to Roger, his natural constituency tarrying as the workplace, the home and the social environment, with all their fun-filled activities and occasional heartaches. Toiling to resolve a global threat hardly fitted within his frame of reference. He didn't want it to either. Apart from the obvious immigration reversing solution, the handicap remained just too gargantuan and insoluble.

Their parents Don and Angela had brought up Brother Colin and himself with the intention of giving them at least a commensurate, if not better lifestyle, than they were experiencing. Carrying the torch, Charlotte and Roger wanted to do the same for their children, the difference being, forty to fifty years ago, England was rock steady, but increasingly she now sailed on shifting quicksand, making their children's future, like that of the English nation, all the more unpredictable and uncertain.

When Roger and Gordon met at Kappa Corinthians Rugby Club a few days later, neither of them mentioned the thorny subject. It hadn't been discussed since, both men secretly knowing a time-bomb ticked away, and they were powerless to stop it exploding, apart from joining the English revolution.

As Roger walked along with his daughter, Chatham High Street's mixed bag of aliens from another world re-awakened the dark thoughts he had broached to Cousin Barry at Rievaulx Abbey, summer 2011. They had pondered the colossal social changes and demographic upheavals taking place in England, especially in the South-East, over the past twenty years. Despite rollercoaster economic compulsions and world wars constantly challenging society since the advent of the industrial revolution, England had steadily progressed in terms of nationwide social change for the better, complemented by excellence and high benchmarks in all walks of life, up until the early 1980s. Since, there had been a prominent falloff in moral behaviour, a sidelining of self-reliance and responsibility and a general downgrading of English institutions, values and traditions, crowning in the dysfunctional quagmire Heather and himself now found themselves passing through.

Seemingly, just as Gordon predicted, the trend appeared to be irreversible, its far-reaching, cataclysmic implications perturbing Roger more than ever. Ostensibly, the political and media classes determining the nation's future were accepting or more ominously, contributing to the fall into pandemonium. Shoddier still, they exhibited no essay to rectify the abject fiascos in ill-thought-out policies continuing to create the disorder.

All Roger could see about him during their walk represented more and more hard irrefutable evidence of the crunch intensifying, getting out of what little control currently constrained it, and English society imploding from within.

Although his mother-in-law, Lady Macbeth, could analyse what had, and perpetuated to be going pear-shaped, applying cause and effect criteria to apportion blame, and in her mind punishing those guilty of their heinous treachery, she had never expressed an over-the-horizon view apropos how it might end up. Whether cautious in the company of Charlotte and himself, not wanting to distress them, or she had not visioned out the probable end conclusion, Roger could only speculate about.

Surreptitiously, he had taken the sequence of events to their logical conclusion with Cousin Barry and one or two others within their inner circle of confidants, but never with Charlotte. Independent of the social calamity potentially crashing down destroying everything, the couple planned for their children's futures. Therein lay the bisection and the self-denial. Enacting their private lives in parallel with staggering social changes eating into the very fabric of Englishness with each passing day, they pretended, leastways Roger pretended, everything endured sweet in the Garden of England, but intrinsically, he could see uncontained events eventually bursting their idyllic bubble.

Painfully mindful his children might never fully experience the England Charlotte and he were a part of, and had helped sustain and grow, made him quail. But what could he do to ensure not only his children, but his grandchildren inherited the England he had known in his formative years? His trepidation growing, the spectre of a necessary English revolution loomed high in his mind again to depose the present set of duplicitous buffoons selling England by the pound, or he and tens of millions of other English people would have to go on deceiving themselves, all was hunky dory.

Suddenly, he felt a tug on his sleeve.

"Daddy, what are you thinking about?" Heather softly ventured. "I know you're thinking. I can always tell."

Laughing at his young daughter's ability to distinguish concern, merely by observing his body-language, he picked Heather up and hugged her. Normally, if he initiated the act in public, she reminded him she was in her eighth year, and not to embarrass her, because she wasn't a child anymore. On this occasion, Heather duplicated his affection, holding her father tightly. *Could it be, she has read my mind*, he considered? *No, but she did perceive something very awry*.

"It's nothing, darling," he assured her. "Come on, let's retreat to the beamer. On the way home, I'll buy you a pistachio cornet at the ice-cream parlour in Chelsfield."

When they were safely housed inside the M3, Roger revisited his thoughts about the future as he watched Heather persisting to be occupied by the passing freak pageant. With the M3 furnishing her safety blanket from lazoonland inhabitants, she relaxed, but again, Roger contemplated *what kind of England was she going to inherit*? His thoughts not positive, they lingered grim, foreboding, and very black.

Colin and he had built on their parent's generation outstanding post WW2 accomplishments, chiefly, driving society as a whole into upward mobility, with endless opportunity and freedoms. In retrospect, it peaked in his late teens. Instead of abiding in a halcyon, stable direction and sublime vein, English society had decayed into a burgeoning dystopia, the bottom of the pit still unseeable. Despite the Fraser family's superb circumstances, Roger worried about the children's future. Not their economic security, but in terms of becoming heirs of a country bereft of the Larkin-like innocence and well-being Colin and he had known, its nature and traditions irrevocably altered and devoured by external forces.

Without exception, when Roger had a lazoonland type experience, and they did happen in London as well, he thought Davina, his erudite mother-in-law, really was far-sighted in her appraisal of the world. Howbeit ensuring splendid entertainment, instead of baiting her to pour scorn on the guilty like Sally Bercow, Clegg and even Cameron, he deduced he must treat her opinions more seriously in the future.

~ * ~

At home, Roger hedged around Charlotte's interests about Chatham, diverting her along other paths and never mentioning his dark thoughts. A topic needing to be addressed with her one day, but *pro tem* he didn't intend to burden his wife. He hoped to god when they really did have to debate their children's long-term futures, there was still one to be had.

"You've been in *Chatham*?" James babbled, hearing the heel of the palaver as he entered the kitchen, incredulity dripping from his phiz.

"Yes, Mackenzies to buy Heather a violin."

"Geez, Dad, I didn't realise you were such a risk taker," James congratulated.

Startled, the inflammatory comment got Charlotte's immediate attention. "Risk taker," she repeated. "What do you mean, James?"

Breathing out heavily, as if his father and sister had dodged impending doom, he warned, "Chatham is strictly *Sin City*, Mum. It's full of vagrants and crims."

Tempted to say, 'it's almost as bad as Brighton,' the gravity of the discussion prevented any cracks at levity from Roger.

"It's a no-go realm for normal people," James alleged, progressing his bleak assessment, his pejorative tone suggesting his father had committed some terrible *faux pas*. "Why didn't you take Heather to

Protheroe's Music Store in Bromley?"

"Tradition," Roger justified. "Your grandfather Don and grandmother Angela took your Uncle Colin and me to Mackenzies when we were kids. I just wanted to retain the custom."

"What's all this about Chatham, Roger?" Charlotte interrogated, burgeoning solicitude conspicuous on her face.

"Well," he gently began struggling for soft words, "it's not quite the place you remember."

"*What*!" She recoiled, her features accumulating uneasiness. "How do you mean?"

"Let's just say, Chatham, preeminently Chatham High Street, could do with some cosmetic surgery."

"But why," she remonstrated. "It's only a hare's breath away from Rochester, and that's alright. Is James implying Chatham is now radically different?"

Before Roger could enunciate a measured response, so as not to panic her he'd taken their youngest to the back of beyond, James leapt in.

"Oh, Mum," he extolled, "where have you been? I thought you were aware."

"Aware…aware of what?" she demanded to know.

"Beirut, even Kabul is safer than Chatham town centre," he blurted. "Some year thirteen Chelsfield Grammar School for Boys students went there in the summer hols last year, returning home bloodied and robbed."

"*What*!" she exclaimed. "Are you quite sure of your facts, James?"

"Quite sure," he reiterated. "Though Chatham follows on from Rochester, geographically speaking, they've become worlds apart in social structure terms."

Still finding it difficult to trust the sentiment she had gained from her son, Charlotte quivered her brow. "I've not been to Chatham for many years," she admitted, "but it used to be a nice place. What has happened to it?"

Relaying on a sanitised version of what Heather and he had seen along Chatham High Street, Roger anticipated his daughter to jump in with the gory details, but she stayed quiet, reading one of her Brownie manuals. As his review unfolded, Charlotte's visage became progressively more rocked. Not even her recently acquired import of social inclusion prevented her obvious revulsion of his description.

Re-entering, James supplemented his father's account with harder material, Charlotte flustered beyond rational cognizance, her sensibilities agitated by disquiet.

"James," she blared, holding up a paw to cut off his vivid description, "I think we get the picture."

"But, Mother," he intoned, "there's more."

"No," she admonished, "that will do."

Just as the waves settled, Wendy came in from her hockey fixture.

"Hi, what's happening?" she tested.

"Dad and Heather have been in Chatham High Street." James gabbled, still drowning in disbelief.

"Golly…you're *joking*," Wendy trumpeted gawping at her father's vacant physiognomy. She twirled to gape at her brother. "You're not joking!"

"No."

"Dad," she sincerely began, "don't you know about Chatham's ghastly reputation these days?"

"Apparently not," Charlotte acrimoniously corroborated, and the undiminished hogwash restarted again.

Chapter 7: Holly Go-Everywhere

Playing squash, Fraser pulled a muscle above his pelvis, the sequent recurring pain motivating him to seek medical treatment when meditation failed as a cure-all remedy.

Calling the Hazelwood GP surgery to secure an audience with a doctor, the lady receptionist gave him a date two weeks into the future. Rarely having dealings with GP surgeries, the riposte flummoxed him. When he queried what patients did if they were in urgent need of treatment, she told him, 'phone on the day to get an emergency appointment between 9:00 to 17:30 hours, Monday through Friday'. Intrigued by the somewhat arbitrary procedure, he supplicated, 'when someone falls ill during out-of-hours surgery, notably at the weekends, does the GP come out to the patients' house?' The line went dead for a few ticks, then he swore he heard the receptionist laughing. When she eventually recovered control, she told him, 'GPs have not made house calls for epochs, and if someone falls ill during out-of-hours surgery, A&E is their only option.'

"Ridiculous," he flouted to Charlotte when recounting the colloquy. "What on Earth has happened to the NHS since I was a lad? In the seventies, patients could see a doctor the same day, and I recollect a GP coming out to my parent's house when brother Colin was stricken with scarlet fever. What do they do these days, just let them die?"

"Oh, Roger, your remembrance of the NHS carries no resemblance to todays' post code lottery."

"*Au contraire*. The NHS is always crying out for money, yet thirty to forty years ago, when it was run on a shoestring, it delivered a class act service." Abjectly he goggled at Charlotte. "Where does all the money go? Currently the NHS is the recipient of the lion's slice of the public purse from the world's fifth largest economy. It amounts to tens of billions of pounds!"

"By Jove," she wittered, as if he had just landed from Planet Claire. "You *are* out of touch. Patient groups have been posing the puzzlement for at least the past fifteen years."

"Huh, this is a prize exemplar of pouring money into a bottomless pit, within parallel, diminishing NHS standards to the patient." A critical angle coming to mind, he stopped. "What do we do, when one of the children is ill?"

"You mean, what do I do?"

"Yes, I suppose so."

"Well, your Bupa family plan paid for by The Firm shelters most things."

"You mean, I could have gone private with this pain?"

"Of course." She confronted him. "You're very lucky, Roger. Somehow, despite your gluttonous disposition, you've always managed to elude illness."

"It's because I exercise a lot."

"Bunkum," she castigated. "Apart from sporadic rugby training and match day outings for Kappa Corinthians, the only exercise you get is hoisting a beer glass to your mouth."

"Not fully authentic." Grimacing, he conceded, "well…it is."

Attending the surgery on the day given by the receptionist, he waited to see the quack, the surgery already full to the gills with patients, all fossilized, like they'd been waiting an eternity, Fraser swearing one chap had been there so long, he had died, and only a skeleton lasted, awaiting to be diagnosed for ailments. Casting his observation net most distant, the balance embodied a hibernation state, their metabolisms barely ticking over, boredom having set in after they had read every piece of condescending advisory literature in the waiting room, apart from one elderly man pacing up and down muttering, "I should have gone private, the Minister of Health needs to be tortured then disembowelled, and why did that fool Blair make GPs rich by awarding them £150,000 minimum pay packages?" Joining the unhappy band of patients, Fraser read all the condescending advisory literature, then hours after his meeting slot, like them, fell into a stupor.

Livening up when the receptionist came into the waiting vicinity, she moved in sync with the man pacing up and down so much a shoe repairer stood by to sole and heel his depleted footwear. Fraser awaited their confab.

Like an automaton from a futuristic SF fantasy, she aloofly informed him, "here are your tablets. You take them orally."

Angered by the interminable wait, he scrutinised her with overwhelming disdain. "Well, I didn't think you stuffed them up your *arse*."

Eventually, after Roger had developed a splashy moustache and a chin warmer thick enough to keep out an Arctic blizzard, the receptionist summoned him for his examination. Expecting to see a GP, instead he got a locum who could hardly speak English, and came over as bored with her job, as patients did waiting to see her.

Illuminating her *vis-à-vis* his ailment, the locum passed him on for physiotherapy treatment within a trifle. When he beseeched if she wanted to test him, he got a curt response along the lines of 'unless absolutely necessary, GPs don't touch patients these days.'

Remarkably, the adjoining day he received an invitation to the outpatient's fun day at Orpington Hospital physiotherapy department for the succeeding week.

Joining the session waiting for under starter's orders, he became subordinate to the same catatonic affliction he'd experienced at the GP's surgery.

Eventually, given the go signal by an administrator, he came toe to toe with a comely, curvy, blonde physiotherapist, he estimated to be no more than twenty-three and a half years old.

"How did you incur this squash injury, Roger?"

Rattled to be quizzed by his Christian name from the off, he later found out from Charlotte, the medical profession had dispensed with formality shortly after Florence Nightingale took office.

"Stretching whilst going for a low-ground shot," he related. "Got it as well, but when I straightened up, I felt a stabbing pain just above my right hip bone, and it wasn't my wife or my monster-in-law attacking me with a dagger."

His wit surfing over her napper, she perused him up and down, the spectacles she wore giving her the sagacity of authority, even domination. "Do you or have you ever suffered from premature ejaculation?"

"*What*!" he blurted, disconcerted by the inference. "Certainly *not*. What kind of an enquiry is that?"

"The body is a complex mechanism, the parts connected by life support systems and the bone structure," she neutrally explained. "PE can be caused by an over-excited nerve in the groin linked to the spinal column. That in turn is resultant from a weak vertebra."

"Are you suggesting I have a faulty vertebra?"

"Your stringent reply suggests you haven't. However, it had to be voiced to qualify out a latent weak back condition. Stand up and take off your shirt."

Beginning the supplication, he started to remove his suit jacket and tie.

"Slowly," she instructed.

Giving her a quizzical ogle, he still complied.

Walking all the way around him, she then prodded the small of his bare back with her finger tips, Fraser quailing with each thrust.

"Take off your shoes, socks, and trousers."

Again he gave her a sardonic gleam. "Slowly?" he tentatively reproduced.

"Yes."

Capping the undressing, he stood before her in his high-hipped y-fronts.

Making her way behind him, she enquired, "can you touch your toes?"

"I usually can, but this injury prevents me from extending all the way down to my toe tips."

"See how far you can get."

He did so, then assumed the vertical.

"And again," she decreed.

After several more attempts, she ordained him to stop. "Your backbone alignment is fine, but I'll double check. Lie on the couch face down. I'm going to manipulate your vertebrae to make sure they are aligned."

"Fine."

Pressing into the flesh cladding his vertebrae, she verified nothing had become twisted when the injury took place.

"Your bones are fine. What you're experiencing is muscle and maybe ligament strain, sparked when you overstretched. Sit on the side of the couch."

Complying, she then demonstrated some routines she wanted him to do twice daily.

"You're in pretty good condition, so the motions will relieve the trouble quickly. If it's still there after three to four days, make an appointment to see me. In the meantime, if the pain flares up, feel free to take pain killers."

"Oh, I'm used to pain. I also play rugby. Pain is part and parcel of the game. Besides, I don't like taking drugs of any kind."

"Very laudable." She twinkled at him. "You can get dressed now."

At the end of the session Fraser divulged, "I wasn't sure why you requisitioned me to take my clothes off, *slowly*, then it dawned on me."

"Yes."

"To prevent aggravating the injury through quick movement."

Gawking at him curiously she replied, "quite right. Why else might I petition you to do it slowly?"

"Erm, *hah—*" Glittering at her, he suddenly felt extremely self-conscious. "I thought you were, hah—"

"You thought what?"

Making to speak, he realised whatever he spouted could be interpreted as ridiculous. "Oh, it's nothing."

Placing her hands about her hips, she displayed a disapproving scowl. "You didn't think I told you to take your clothes off for my own gratification, did you?"

"No, no…well yes."

She tutted. "*Really*, Mister Fraser!"

What happened to calling me Roger, he was going to say, but fancied it'd only land him in hotter water.

~ * ~

As the curvaceous physiotherapist predicted, after four days of her prescribed exercising, his pelvis area became free from fatigue.

Joyfully working away analysing the latest Bank of England economic forecast at his desk without the distraction of pain, Fraser suddenly became conscious someone stood in his *sanctum sanctorum* doorway. Gaping up, his sight fell on Chief Analyst Henry Jacques, his demeanour somewhat forlorn for a normally optimistic and buoyant man.

"Henry."

"Do you have a moment, Roger?"

"I've always got a moment for you. What's up?"

Sauntering in, hands in his Rupert Bear-like cheque grey, black and red suit trouser pockets, his serious deportment weighed heavy on him. Parking himself opposite Fraser, he adjusted his customary kaleidoscope coloured bow-tie, not through necessity, but Fraser adjudged through nervousness.

"You remember the Gresham Harvey investment covenant with Parnell & Preston Holdings turning sour in the tsunami caused by the 2008 meltdown?"

"Indeed I do. It gave the New York folks a few brainteasers."

"Quite. Well—" He grimaced. "It's reared its ugly bonce again."

"You *mean*, our parent company wants to take on Gresham Harvey afresh?"

"Yes, and because of former history, I don't feel comfortable with it."

A conglomerate of industrial partnerships, mainly operating in the United States but with significant operations in the UK and to a lesser extent in southern Europe, Gresham Harvey had contacted The Firm's New York central command post in the autumn of 2007. Their investment banking requirement centred around mergers and acquisitions services and raising fifty per cent of the buyout price through investment capital, meaning stakeholder investment in a debenture preference shares scheme to part-fund their takeover of Parnell & Preston Holdings, a smaller sized industrial combine. Ostensibly, a substantial business model change for Gresham Harvey, they usually bankrolled purchases out of their own capital, or arranged some kind of shares-for-shares barter. However, Parnell & Preston Holdings represented their largest seizure to date, necessitating third-party investment to make the settlement fly.

Based on Fraser's foregoing experience of enterprise scale M&As from an analysts' perspective, Luther Bembridge had insisted Jacques assigned him to the UK end of the undertaking, Toby Chalcroft also annexing his weight to Fraser being a key player on The Firm's UK team. In all, The Firm assigned over forty staff to the business, ten from the UK. With the usual contract hiccups and tantrums from the principal players at Gresham Harvey and Parnell & Preston Holdings neutralised, all the financial instruments processing needed for a successful accord went reasonably well. However, when Lehman Brothers bellied up arousing widespread selling on stock exchanges worldwide, most of The Firm's investment players pulled out of the Gresham Harvey-Parnell & Preston Holdings opening. When the conquest collapsed, several executives at The Firm's New York HQ found themselves under the spotlight from the board of directors. Though impossible to plan for such a monumental reversal of fortunes, the affair left Gresham Harvey with a sour taste in their mouths and vowing never to become enmeshed with Wall Street financing ever again.

"I've just come out of a meeting with Bembridge and Chalcroft," Jacques uneasily advertised. "They want a slice of the action for Gresham Harvey's latest venture, and you are to partake in the negotiation."

"Who are they acquiring?"

"Roach & Randell."

"Gee, they're much smaller than Parnell & Preston Holdings."

"Yes, but they're UK based. Bembridge and Chalcroft want London to play a cardinal role, so an appreciable portion of the fees can be claimed for M&A services."

"So no third-party investment financing?"

"No, and in this exponent, it's good. However—" Jacques' sombre mood intensified. "In my experience, when business doesn't work out between dominant players, and the 2008 debacle took the biscuit in that respect, it's best they stay apart permanently."

Nodding in concordance, Fraser queried, "then why have Gresham Harvey reacquired The Firm for this acquisition?"

"I wanted to put forward the enigma, but Bembridge and Chalcroft were so euphoric about the opportunity, I differentiated if I tabled it, they'd pooh-pooh my reservations. You see, Gresham Harvey has other European quests in mind, and if London makes a success out of this particular business, Bembridge will have bragging rights in New York."

"Mmmm, but why has Gresham Harvey gravitated to The Firm? They could have liaised with at least a dozen comparable sized investment houses to provide M&A services."

"Precisely." Scratching his noggin he frowned, his discontent growing. "New York and London are skipping over the fact."

"We're not exactly short of business, but I surmise it's a case of never look a gift horse in the mouth, is it?"

"Yes, you're probably right, Roger. As many splendid legislators have commented, greed drives the financial services industry to the hilt."

"Did they happen to say which other European acquisitions Gresham Harvey has in mind?"

"New York asked, but the client refused to elucidate. They want this Roach & Randell procurement done and dusted before they open the emperor's kimono."

"I see. So, er, why do the Ayatollah and Top Cat want me involved?"

"Do you recall someone called Holly Kerrigan at Gresham Harvey from our 2007-8 clash?"

"Yes. Holly is their Global VP Industrial Futures." Settling into his chair, Fraser glowed. "She's also quite the fox, dripping in sexual innuendo to get the male of the species to do her bidding."

"Well, the fox has made a request for you to be part of The Firm's UK team. Bembridge thinks it will confer an ideal opportunity to really put some deep gloss on The Firm's London SBU from New York's standpoint."

"Fine. Let's just hope another unforeseen catastrophe doesn't crop up to dispirit Gresham Harvey."

With Fraser buying into the business, Jacques leaned towards him. "Initially, Gresham Harvey wants to meet with The Firm's M&A team at our New York premises," he stipulated, "but subsequently, because Roach & Randell are UK based, the residuum of the endeavour will largely be conducted in Blighty." Standing up, he renewed his quondam position in Fraser's doorway. "You're booked onto tomorrow's 08:30 flight from Heathrow Terminal Five to New York's JFK. April has your ticket details. Carter Wade from M&A has also been allotted to the undertaking. He'll be going with you."

Gaining a reputation for cutting some of the best deals The Firm's London setup had ever known, whilst keeping all participants tickled with his acidic quips and zany if not whimsical valuation of the world, Fraser had worked with Wade on several M&A business initiatives. Consequently, he looked forward to teaming with the comical yet highly professional operator again.

~ * ~

Having partied until three in the morning before going direct from the shindig to Heathrow, Wade caught some zees amid the early part of the flight, leaving Fraser to reflect on his genesis engagement with Holly Kerrigan. She didn't need any positive discrimination or quotas to get where she was going, the sheer coercion of her personality coupled with her mercurial talents propelling her inextricably upward. She believed in the meritocracy system and despised anyone employing PC dogma to compensate for their no-talent deficiencies to advance themselves. Patently a cross between fifties silver screen icons Lana Turner and Veronica Lake at their most alluring, naturally she drew some beat. She also possessed a fantabulous business mind and had graduated from Harvard with honours. Whereas men adored her, pug-ugly, uppity, jealous women invariable hissed at the very mention of her name. Too much woman for any man to cope with, she maintained men should be like Kleenex…soft, strong and disposable. Twice married and divorced, Fraser reckoned she'd be coming up to her forty-second birthday in 2012.

During her illustrious career, she had been everywhere and had met anybody worth knowing in the world of high finance. When a meeting of the minds took place with Fraser, he quipped she wasn't so much the Truman Capote creation, Holly Golightly from *Breakfast at Tiffany's*, more Holly Go-Everywhere, the girl most likely to steal your heart and eat your lunch.

Somewhere over the North Atlantic, Wade came out of his slumber.

Vision still sealed, he burbled, "ooohh, where am I?"

"You're on a flight to the Big Apple," Fraser advised.

"Oh, yes. Hello, Roger."

"You said hello, several hours ago when the stewardess poured you into the seat beside me. I didn't think you were going to make the flight."

"With the volume of booze I tucked away last night, I could have flown myself to New York under alcohol power."

"Right, who needs a 787 when liquor can liberate independence from the vagaries and petty frustrations of scheduled flights?"

"I take it you had a sticky encounter at Terminal 5?"

"Just some overzealous security man at hand luggage inspection. When the damned alarm went off as I passed through the metal detector, he wanted to strip search me."

"Yes, flying has become a major ordeal since nine-eleven. From the instant you enter an airport, to the thankful watershed when you exit arrivals, it requires a Teflon-coated constitution to survive the battleground."

"Normally, I don't mind the rigmarole, but this officious jobsworth had the dog breath of a Rottweiler and the sensitivity of a stormtrooper. I cringed when he frisked me for the presumed guns and grenades I carried."

"Strewth, you always have been good at composing highly graphic pictures, Roger."

"Well, I might have exaggerated a bit, but do they really think a well-dressed businessman with a business-class ticket is going to sully his Armani suit and Charles Tyrwhitt shirt with hardware?"

"A rag-head was it? They usually are at Heathrow these days."

"No, a Bin Laden, replete with a pube face. I hardly understood a word he mumbled."

"Phew, and no doubt he let all the Jihadists go through, without even checking them?"

"Probably."

"Just not right, is it?"

"No, but knowing when you finally get through the multi-layer security and being asked a thousand daft interrogations, you're just so grateful to find yourself in the tranquillity of BA's Executive Club lounge, you can't be bothered to make a fuss. I think obnoxious cretins like the Bin Laden know it, and it's why they harass non-Muslims, knowing they will get away with it."

"If it was an English security officer targeting sun-goblins and sand-scratchers, there'd be all hell to play, the mass ranks of the PC brigade, including the holier-than-thou BBC, marshalled to demand a public enquiry and the already draconian Race Relations Act beefed up to prevent thought crime!"

"*Whoa*, I see you haven't lost your acerbic humour."

"No." Sitting up, Wade licked his lips. "I need a coffee."

"I think you need a whole pot, Carter."

Beckoning a stewardess, Fraser explained his travelling companion had a few too many sherbets the preceding evening, and could she supply copious amounts of gourmet coffee to aid his recovery.

With a coffee intravenous drip directly connected to Wade's inner parts alcohol could not satisfy, Fraser probed him on his erstwhile night's nocturnal activities.

"Was the bash to celebrate anything in particular?"

"Wish it were, but I'm ashamed to say, since my divorce, of late, revelry has become my evening sport of choice. Unfailingly, it's with single swingers from The Firm, Credit Suisse, Barclays Capital, *et al*. You know, Hugo Morris, Oliver Stanton, and the residual of the in-crowd."

"Yeah, I know them. Different girl every night then?"

"Not quite, but the pastime does comprise a lot of one-night stands."

"How do you enlist them?"

"Depending on how much I've had to drink, which nightclub I'm at, or who's pad the blowout is being held in, I usually begin with an outlandish intro like, 'it'd give me the most enormous erection, er, I mean, it'd give me the most enormous pleasure if you…'" Circulating his right mitt in a pragmatic manner, he gave Fraser a knowing gander. "You can guess the rest. It's all configured to make them laugh."

"And it works?"

"Generally, but most of the dollies invited to these parties are up for it anyway, hoping to entrap a rich investment jockey into falling in love with them. There aren't many from Roedean or a Swiss finishing school in the clique, and if they are debutants, they disguise it by adopting a 'nothing will shock me' semblance. It's very disconcerting. We're meant to be the hunters, but they do the hunting."

"I've been out of the singles game for ages, Carter. Fundamentally, the rules of engagement seem to have changed."

"They have. Girls are stalking for a rich mate or a rich daddy, making it easy for their prey, me for example, to do the business." Caffeine taking hold, he slid down his seat. "It's an interesting phenomenon, Roger. I heard tell of a guy from Goldman Sachs, who'd had a one-night stand with one of these huntresses two years ago. She saw him in a night club Tuesday week, and behested he glided a twenty-three-carat jobby on her third finger."

"*Wow*, a real hostile takeover."

"Yeah. He told her to foxtrot-oscar, saying just because she'd let him slip her a length, it didn't mean she had any claim on him. Ahh—" Signalling accession to the situation, Wade upheld, "it's a jungle out there. You can never tell if a girl wants you for what you are and what she can see, or for what you're worth. I'll tell you, Roger, it came as a jolt to me, because I was off the market for twelve years."

A while later, after Wade felt a lot better with a gallon of coffee swilling inside him, Fraser enquired, "so besides carousing into the early hours, what else have you been up to?"

"Oh, you know…little bit of this, little bit of that, ducking and diving, questing to make good settlements for The Firm and fashioning a few privy investments."

"Anything tasty?"

"Just the usual run-of-the-mill goodies; better car, grander apartment at Saint Katharine Docks marina." Suddenly he burst into a cavernous glisten. "I'll tell you an amusing, if not amazing instance about my M&A colleague Cal Gimbert. You know him?"

"Yes. Nice chap, but despite his eminent perspicacity of M&A disciplines, he always reminds me of some of the dopier Essex boy traders in the bullpen."

"In what way?"

"He's not too tightly wrapped when it comes to making his way in the outside world. Huge brain but little savvy beyond financial instruments."

"Jeepers, for sure. Put it this way, he's already been nominated for the title, '2012 sucker of the year,' and we're barely into February."

"Yes, well, I don't mean to be unkind, but in some respects, he does come across as a fully qualified idiot. Having a Yosemite Sam likeness doesn't help. What's he done now?"

"He got stroked for seventy-five large on a bum car deal.

"*Seventy-five big ones*!" Fraser chimed.

"Yep."

"How?"

"He shelled out the trade price in folding stuff for a 1980 Maserati Khamsin advertised in Classic Cars. In principle, a good investment, because its value keeps on rising. He'd only had the vehicle for three days when plod came knocking, and told him he'd re-registered a stolen car with the DVLA."

"Didn't he evaluate the seller and the vehicle's provenance?"

"No, and the Maserati was restored to its legal owner. Not very clever, hey, for a guy who does multi-million pound transactions and is an apex earner at The Firm."

"Whatever was he thinking?"

"That's the point, Roger. He wasn't." Tapping Fraser's arm, he prattled, "persisting on the exposition of cars, you drive an M3 don't you?"

"Indeed I do," he affirmed, *amour-propre* ringing in his tone. "She's my pride and joy. Actually, she's my third M3."

"I'm staggered you don't drive a Porsche 911."

"Good god, no," he quacked. "They're so vulgar. Besides, it's the wet dream of choice for the Essex boy dealers, and I don't wish to be put into the same taste bag."

"How about a Merc?"

"We have a Mercedes Viano Sport MPV as our family car."

"I was actually thinking as a replacement for the M3, say the C-63 coupe from the AMG range."

"Again, far too vulgar for my tastes. Excessive chrome everywhere makes them resemble a mobile mirror. Besides, in a like-for-like division, the BMW M3 has always come out on top against its AMG equivalent in terms of price-performance. It resides as the definitive, four-seat, hot, sports, coupe-convertible market leader. Solicit Jeremy Clarkson, if you don't believe me."

"What about an M5?

"Dazzling performer, but the BMW 5-series is really for old men. M-saloons don't work for me. Cars have to be a coupe or a convertible to get my approbation."

"Sounds like you're stuck on the M3."

"I just adore its sleek, shark-like styling and shape combined with its power and handling. The only future replacement I might opt for is the M6 Coupe."

"And Porsche is definitely out?"

"Crikey—" Tittering, he rocked his skull against his seat headrest. "One of the brokers, I'm not going to tell you who, it'd be too cruel, came up to me and said, he was thinking about buying a Porsche, as in the word that rhymes with borsch. I squared, 'there's no such car. Do you mean, a Porsche, as in the girls' name?' He did, and went on to say, he fancied a Porsche, this time pronounced correctly, Boxster. Tongue in cheek, I told him a Boxster was a girls' car. Really deflated, he went away to rethink his car purchase options."

"Hah, and he *believed* you?"

"Well, it's at least partly factual. By the way, did you know

Porsche means small sausage in German and pig in Latin?"

"No."

"Surprising isn't it. All these quasi cool dudes and flash Harrys', cruising the square mile and the Isle of Dogs financial district in their Porsche 911s, and they don't realise they're driving a glorified sausage." Chuckling, he then canvassed, "what are you driving at present, Carter?"

"A Porsche 911 Turbo."

~ * ~

On arrival at JFK, Fraser and Wade took a taxi to The Firm's New York HQ in Pearl Street, Manhattan, its grandiose glass and steel facade indomitable like a Gotham City edifice, Avery Wexler, VP Global Mergers & Acquisitions and their main contact for the Gresham Harvey business, meeting them in reception.

"Roger," Wexler greeted with a genial gleam, grasping his hand. "How the devil are you?"

"I'm fine, Avery. May I introduce Carter Wade?"

Pressing the flesh, Wexler took Wade in. "Glad to meet you, Carter. I recognise your name from various M&A activity reports."

"An honour to be here, Avery," he responded, no trace of his previous night's debauchery residing in his being.

"Right. We have a meeting with Gresham Harvey at 09:00 tomorrow to go through their Roach & Randell procurement requirements. For the vestige of the afternoon, I'll introduce you to the balance of the designated team, and go over how we see this business. Oh—" Simpering, he clapped his hands. "Have you had lunch?"

"We had a meal on the flight," Fraser illuminated, "and our stomachs are still operating on London time, but thanks for your concern."

"By the way," Wexler guardedly informed, "Gresham Harvey are bringing in their lawyers with them for tomorrow's meeting."

"It's a bit premature, isn't it?" Wade inveighed.

"Absolutely," Fraser agreed. "Normally, the legal eagles are only brought in when we are getting down to the vinegar strokes of the barter.

Why now?"

"They're still ruffled after the Parnell & Preston Holdings fiasco, so they want to set the legal framework in place from the off. We'll have our attorneys in play as well."

After Fraser and Wade finished with their counterparts at Pearl Street, they were ready for a light dinner, followed by a good night's sleep at the Waldorf Astoria.

"I'm having a Vesper Martini, so I ordered one for you as well," Fraser announced as Wade joined him in the hotel's Peacock Alley restaurant.

"Thanks."

"Room okay?"

"Magnificent. Previously, The Firm booked me into The Roosevelt. It has plenty of ambience, quality and notable history, but I think I prefer the Waldorf Astoria."

"Me too. In 1999, I saw Jack Nicholson and Dennis Hopper having dinner here surrounded by a bevy of sensational starlets. They were joined by Martin Scorsese and Kim Basinger. Made me surmise, this hotel is a magnet for film people. You never know who we might see tonight."

"I'd be very happy if Anne Hathaway and Michele Williams wandered in seeking male company."

"Well don't let me stop you," Fraser sanctioned, amused by the prospect.

"You mean—" He sniggered. "If say, Michele was offering it to you on plate, you'd decline?"

Taking a pull on his cocktail, Fraser then divulged, "yes, despite her giving a sensitive portrayal as Monroe in *My Week with Marilyn*. As I told someone last year, I don't stray. It's bad form to cheat on your wife. Notwithstanding Charlotte can be a pain now and then, I love her dearly."

"Working overseas, there must have been plenty of opportunities for you?"

"There still are, and even in Blighty, but I don't take them. I don't even want to."

"Good heavens, Roger." He frowned. "You're making me feel

guilty about my one-night-stand dalliances, although I must say, when Glynis and I were married, like you, I didn't stray. Maybe all this fooling around now is a reaction to monogamy."

"Well, before Anne and Michelle whisk you away," Fraser implored, picking up the *ala carte* menu, "what do you fancy for dinner?"

"I've always wanted to do this." Gurning, a frolicsome aura enveloped his being. "I'm going to ask the waiter if the chef can fix me a Waldorf salad."

Giggling at the *Fawlty Towers* send up line, Fraser suggested, "if the waiter is plainly of Spanish origin and replies, *kay*, be sure to tell him what a Waldorf salad consists of in an irate Californian accent."

~ * ~

Along with Wexler's appointed team and The Firm's attorneys, the forthcoming morning, the two Englishmen awaited the advent of the Gresham Harvey contingent and their legal team at Pearl Street.

Promenading over to the edge of the expansive meeting room they occupied, Fraser and Wade stared out over the imposing grandeur of lower Manhattan from the intoxicating heights of the skyscraper's forty-ninth floor.

"Good grief, Roger," Wade whispered, "there are nearly twice as many of The Firm's lawyers compared to Avery's M&A brigade. Embracing us, I make the home team to be twenty-four. If Gresham Harvey adopts the same M&A to lawyers' ratio, forty-eight people will be milling around, all vying for a say."

"I don't think so," Fraser blocked, his pitch implying prior knowledge of the meeting's protocol. "The only mediator from the client side you will hear will be Holly Kerrigan, and Avery Wexler will steer for us. The rest of The Firm's M&A players numbering us, will watch, listen, and dwell on hot standby, ready to be called to the plate for batting action, if the need arises. Lawyers on both sides will not say anything unless they are called upon to make a legal judgment. I believe this is going to be a feeling out exercise. We'll learn more at the breaks through one-on-ones than across the table. If Gresham Harvey decamp with a confident vibe, the deal is ours."

"Yeah, you're right," Wade applauded, peering out of the immense periphery windows. "Some panorama."

"Assuredly. The Firm's Canary Wharf building bestows some all-round spectacular vistas, but I've always calculated the outlooks from Pearl Street outdo them."

"Have you boys seen the views from the zenith of the Gresham Harvey tower?" they heard someone say. "They will really take your breath away."

Twisting about, Fraser's gaze fell on a shimmering Holly Kerrigan. With her shoulder-length wavy blonde hair, large marine-blue eyes, delicately high-lighted high cheekbones, and crimson coated generous lips, she looked like she'd stepped straight off the cover of *The New Yorker*, her flamingo-pink blouse, tailored, two-piece Oxford-blue and black pinstriped suit, pale-crystal pantyhose, and black high-heel court shoes emphasising her ample height, and the curviness of her body and legs. To anyone not knowing Holly Kerrigan, they'd assume she was a supermodel.

"Holly," Fraser gushed, holding out his hand. "If anything is going to take away our breath around here, it's the sight of you. You look terrific."

Disregarding his outstretched hand, instead she embraced him, kissing either side of his face, Fraser replicating the greeting.

"Charming as ever, Roger, and how's your lovely wife and family?"

"Charlotte remains radiant, and since we last met in 2008, our brood have all grown five to six inches."

"And I hear you are now The Firm's trouble-shooter."

"Just for the London SBU," he modestly cooed.

"Well, we might just need a trouble-shooter to douse the flames, if our mutual business starts to go what you English people call, pear-shaped." She rendered him a wicked, sexually charged leer. "Or more properly, tits-up?"

"Ha, ha, ha," Fraser cackled. "I see you haven't changed, Holly. Still capable of delivering a semi-disguised rebuke with panache and grit."

"Well." She brushed a smudge of her lipstick off his cheek. "Behind the scenes, Roger, if this agreement gets done, I want you to carry the message, so no one at The Firm is under any illusions, there will be no scope for failure whatsoever."

"Message received loud and clear, Holly. Oh, I'm forgetting my manners." Swivelling, he smiled at Wade. "May I introduce Carter Wade, Industrials M&A Manager for The Firm's London operation."

"Hello, Carter," she acknowledged holding out her hand. "How's the Big Apple treating you?"

"I'd say developments have categorically taken an upward trajectory in the closing few moments," he expressed, gently taking her hand. "Roger described you as stunning, but I can see he underpraised you in the superlatives directorate."

"*Gosh*!" She beamed at him. "Another gallant and charming Englishman. You boys really put New York men in the shade when it comes to bolstering a lady's confidence."

Cheerily, Wexler strolled over from the imposing group beginning to form two circles around the meeting table, M&A players on the inside, lawyers in the outer circle. Like in a Rene Magritte painting, it was raining businessmen.

"Holly," he courteously enquired, "do you think we can begin?"

"Of course. My apologies for holding everyone up. I just had to reacquaint myself with my old friend Roger, and make his compatriot's acquaintance."

After fresh mutual introductions between the client's team and The Firm's cadre, the group got down to the Roach & Randell business, Holly at stage centre setting out the Gresham Harvey prerequisites and acquisition milestone requirements, Wexler responding to her demands on behalf of The Firm, and when needed, entreating Fraser or Wade to screen factors affecting The Firm's London SBU.

At the mid-morning break, Fraser took Holly aside.

"Tell me," he began, "why did you specifically request my involvement in this latest business? I mean, after what happened with Parnell & Preston Holdings, I assumed Gresham Harvey were none too keen to have anyone from The Firm associated with the debacle incorporated in future business dealings."

"True, but principally, The Firm's New York team came in for some harsh words. We didn't have a gripe against those from The Firm's London headquarters."

"I see."

"Regarding yourself," she elucidated, "I thought you did a good job from an analyst's standpoint. You uncovered some noteworthy components about Parnell & Preston, and proposed refinements central to honing our purchase bid. It didn't go unnoticed."

"After the cataclysm," Fraser recapped, "The Firm presaged Gresham Harvey would never do business with us again. All the same, I must say, there were extraordinary mitigating circumstances behind the investors pulling out."

"Undeniably, but you know how the business world works, Roger. Every catastrophe needs a scapegoat owner, whether warranted or not. The axe fell on many at Gresham Harvey, but politically speaking, we had to shift some of the blame onto The Firm. Otherwise, it looked like we were taking full responsibility for the flop. It's why in the immediate aftermath of the accord collapsing, Gresham Harvey made those carefully worded, non-liable proclamations to the press, anent our displeasure at what had happened. Our stockholders mandated it, so as to prevent the Gresham Harvey share price plummeting south."

"Oh yes, I'm familiar with how financial power politics works, and the need to find the guilty but pin the blame on the totally innocent."

"Quite," she conceded. "It's a game we all buy into and play, knowing we can end up as winners or losers. Let me assure you, Roger, I got my butt at least partially roasted."

Still in detective mode, he cast a sanguine facade at her. "Can I ask you something else?"

"You can, *but*," she cautioned, sensing another arresting item, "I can't guarantee to give you a reply."

"I'm told Gresham Harvey have other European acquisitions in mind, and if Roach & Randell goes off with no hitches, The Firm's London setup could be in line for more M&A business with Gresham

Harvey."

"Perfectly valid."

"But why The Firm, Holly?" Leaning into her, he emanated intense curiosity. "There are many investment houses capable of providing M&A services."

"You're the analyst." She fabricated a peaked visage morphing into a playful shine. "Why do you think?"

"I pondered that puzzler coming across the pond."

"And what did you deduce?"

"The Firm has a unique of some kind Gresham Harvey thinks will be beneficial to your future European M&A plans."

"Go on."

"Well, all things being equal, yes, we're pretty good at M&A services, hence Carter Wade's assignment. He's got an exceptional track record, you know."

"Yes, I've gained that impression," she cut in, "and essentially, he was not tarnished by the Parnell & Preston debacle, so he'll get the thumbs up from us. Sorry, I interrupted."

"I was going to say, however those capabilities are by no means unique."

"And what did it lead you to conclude?"

"Your future European targets already do business with The Firm at Canary Wharf." His dial lightening, he affixed, "there you have our unique."

Radiating at him, she upstretched her hands to one side and gently clapped. "You might think that, Roger, but I couldn't possibly confirm your supposition at this point."

~ * ~

After the two parties settled a frame of reference and a subsequent set of actions, Fraser and Wade took the BA redeye to Blighty in the evening.

Highly delighted with the meeting outcome Fraser surveyed, "what did you think of Holly?"

"Brave, clever, resourceful, and she's got exquisite legs."

"She's got exquisite everything. What a woman."

"But I distinguish too hot to handle permanently."

"Yep, unequivocally. She could take you to heaven in the bedroom bailiwick, but staying there…well, it'd be a temporary enchantment. Holly is destined for high office. She'll end up being CEO of Gresham Harvey, or some other like-sized corporation.

"When I first met her, I became astounded. Usually business brains and striking beauty are mutually exclusive. But once I got over her jaw-dropping attractiveness, I discovered she possessed more business acumen, people skills and charisma, than any man I've dealt with in the business arena. Holly is truly blessed in those domains, but I also know she feels defeated when it comes to making a successful marriage. When we were both high as a kite in 2008 through *Dom Perignon* overconsumption, she told me, having tried twice and floundered, she did not intend to try on the nuptials again.

"You'll have logged she asked about Charlotte and our children. It's the only part of my life she is envious about."

"Just goes to show," Wade perceived, "those we estimate to have everything, do in fact have some holes in their lives."

"Yep, a *bona fide* observation. Anyway, if I'm reading the signs accurately, we'll be seeing a lot more of Holly Kerrigan in Blighty. As the Gresham Harvey ensemble departed Pearl Street, she winked at me."

"And it means The Firm will be awarded the Roach & Randell takeover business?"

"I will be reporting a judicious, if not circumspect, *probably*, to the Ayatollah and Top Cat on our return to Londinium."

"Why so vigilant?"

"I never get optimistic until the ink has dried on the contract papers."

"Say, just changing the subject, Roger—" Wade's mug became a mass of mischievousness. "On the way over, you mentioned Cal Gimbert's unfortunate similarity to Yosemite Sam."

"Indeed I did."

"There are others at The Firm with cartoon character credentials."

"Such as."

"Alice Vaughan from HR is an obvious Betty Boop with her girly voice, curvy figure and next to nothing skirts."

"Yes, I can see the connection."

"I've often thought about giving her one."

"What, Betty Boop?" Fraser jested. "It'd have to be by proxy."

"Ha, ha, ha. No, Alice. And of course, Bembridge is flawless for Dick Dastardly."

"Or better still, Wile E Coyote, chasing all us roadrunners around Cabot Square."

"Of course, his playmate Toby Chalcroft is Top Cat, but he doesn't physically approximate or vocalise like the animated zoot suiter."

"No, I've always thought TC's inflection is more like Yosemite Sam's, especially when he gets hot and bothered under the collar."

"And the New York septic who came over to London summer 2011 to chivvy up the bullpen, ex-US-Army Lieutenant-General Benjamin Garrett Sygrove, VP Worldwide Sales Strategy, is the spit and image of Foghorn Leghorn. He actually enunciated like the irate rooster as well."

"What a splendid image," Fraser congratulated. "On a different note, when Dan Lebowski visited to go through the London's futures forecast, though I liked him tremendously, along with his forthright, latter-day Freddie Kruger-like tactic for redressing delinquent dealers, he exhibited an uncanny resemblance to the late, great Carroll O'Connor."

"The actor?"

"Yeah, particularly O'Conner playing Major General Colt in *Kelly's Heroes*. I kept on thinking Dan won't so much importune the data he needed from the traders, but order them to cough up on pain of fatigues punishment, or a long sojourn in the glasshouse."

"Yikes, all this talk of cartoon celebrities conjures up visions of watching *Looney Tunes* on television when I was a kid, and being entranced by Sylvester the Cat and Elmer Fud."

"My darlings were *Tom and Jerry* and *The Flintstones*, both Hanna-Barbera productions."

"Compared to the puerile pap foisted on the public today, in those days cartoons had a lot of depth and even gravitas."

"You must be talking about *American Dad*, *Family Guy* and the crowning turd in the pipeline, *The Simpsons*? My son James always banged on about how good they were, until I introduced him to *Loony Tunes* and *Tom and Jerry*. Now he's a convert and thinks modern cartoons are rubbish."

"I can't stand that twat, Homer Simpson. He's such a weak, feeble, little fucker, isn't he?"

"Couldn't agree with you more, Carter. You know—" He smirked as if about to share a hefty thought with his chum. "All those treasured cartoons we've tabled originated from the 1930s through to the 1960s. Between the laughs, they contained adult themes, counterpoint achieved by having goody-goody dignitaries do battle with menacing adversaries. In comparison, today's cartoon species are flat, boring, predictable, and terminally stupid. There's nothing lovable or admirable about them, whereas Tom and Jerry, Foghorn Leghorn, Popeye *et al* were clever, sparky and wonderfully evil."

"Of course," Wade lamented, "the prissy and priggish BBC won't screen *Tom and Jerry* and *Popeye* these days, because they are politically incorrect."

"How?"

"Occasionally *Tom and Jerry* have the archetypal big, black mamma in it, and *Popeye* those black head hunters with bones through their muzzles who eat white people."

"How's that politically incorrect? It's not fancy, it's factual. It's the real world. Why pretend otherwise?"

"Apparently, it stereotypes and pokes fun at black people."

"But every race, creed and colour gets to be the butt of cartoon roasts."

"Apart from Muslims," Wade shot in.

"Invariably. But why should blacks and Muslims be exempt from mickey taking? I don't hear other races or religions complaining, such as Jews and Third World nations like the Scots."

"Ah well, what you have to understand Roger is blacks and Muslims are the BBC's chosen people, the untouchables placed on a consecrated pedestal, far above mere mortals. Up there, they're immune from any criticism, and are positive discrimination recipients – the so-called minorities quota mechanism and, unprecedented arse-licking by BBC programme anchors and sports commentators, having woofters enraged with jealousy. They're always consigned to a favourable light. Any bad press, like Muslims grooming young English girls and blacks trafficking drugs to schoolchildren is swept under the carpet." Recoiling, he developed a disturbed face. "Surely you must have demarcated the BBC's entire broadcast schedule is centred on black and Muslim essays, comprising woe-is-me films about blacks and Muslims, comedies and dramas more or less singly populated with blacks and Muslims, and current affairs programmes founded on black and Muslim topics day in day out, week in week out?"

"Huh, I can't say I find television compelling, Carter. However, judging from what I read in the broadsheets and hear from other people, I'm sure you're right. It's the same with modern American sit-coms, like those total loads of old tosh, *Two & Half Men* and *The Big Bang Theory*. They're so bereft of cutting edge spiky humour, I can only deem some killjoy, halfway up her own arse, PC-programmed tsar has told the writers not to script anything remotely controversial or satirical. Capping the twaddle, the portrayals are gravely drab and mundane, forming the instant cure for insomnia. Unquestionably, none have a heartbeat. Twenty-five years ago, the US produced some very good sitcoms like *Frasier*, *The Larry Sanders Show* and *Married with Children*. They all had memorable luminaries, and the writers were allowed to send up any PC holy cow."

"Yes, *Married With Children* also had the sex-siren Kelly Bundy played by Christina Applegate, the source of many a wet dream."

"Distinctly, a very beguiling girl. Anyway—" He tapped Wade on the arm. "Enough bitching about the absurdities of the modern world. How do you see this Gresham Harvey opportunity from an M&A perspective."

"I have to say, it equates to being too impeccable."

"You mean, you can see unforeseen predicaments coming out of the woodwork?"

"Hhmm, it reminds me of a procurement we did a few years ago for KTZ Electric. In the early stages, that too was adjudged to be just as faultless."

"Oh yes, then target company Byman & Wolf were approached by another predator, and a bidding war began. Gee, it really put the cat amongst the pigeons." Grimacing, Fraser differentiated, "and you think Roach & Randall might go the same way?"

"The crux with super-sized conglomerates like Gresham Harvey is there's always someone who can't keep quiet about M&A intentions. Might be for stock option motives, or privy financial drivers whereby the guilty faction stands to gain via the transaction. Howbeit, I don't think anyone on our side of the fence might do it. Besides, we've all signed non-disclosure agreements. Any leak would probably be attributed to the client side, or Roach & Randall, once they're in play. Independent of Holly applying zip-lock fasteners to the deal, my reservation is the street becoming aware of the acquisition and the bid price accelerating away, leaving The Firm in an invidious position for a second time with Gresham Harvey. Plus—" He lifted his eyebrows in a show of disdain. "There's always an army of hacks surrounding our skyscraper entrance, waiting to harvest the odd morsel of commercially sensitive tidings and make it breaking news, the sect embodying Sidney Sartori."

"The flunky who broke the RBS derivatives scandal story for the unmentionable red top."

"Indeed. When it comes to ruthless, irresponsible reporting, Sartori is the king of all capricious, feckless and thoughtless bastards."

"Bit harsh, isn't it?

"Roger, if it looks like a prick, talks like a prick, and behaves like a prick, then it must be a prick."

"Yep, you're right. And you think if an inkling of Gresham Harvey's intention seeps out, Sartori or a similarly-sized prick will make hay on it?"

"It's a racing certainty."

"Yes…well—" Fraser became reticent. "We'll just need to keep our prick detectors on maximum sensitivity until the purchase is complete!"

~ * ~

Joining the throng of in-coming passengers arriving from worldwide destinations in the Heathrow baggage reclaim concourse, Fraser spied well-known socialite and man-magnet Nancy D, on-and-off girlfriend to a fallen with dishonours, ex-England football manager.

Nudging Wade, Fraser solicited, "you know who she is, don't you?"

"Oh, yes. I'd like to get close up and personal with her myself."

Still feeling in high spirits after the New York trip, Fraser collected his baggage and charged off after the celebrity.

"*Hey*, Nancy," he called.

She swung about.

"My dick is bigger than Sven's."

She scanned him up and down, then in a deep resonating, sour enunciation, bleated, "isn't *everybody's*?"

Chapter 8: Saint Paddy's Day Massacre

Hayden Wardell, player extraordinaire and social secretary at Kappa Corinthians Rugby Club had organised a Saint Patrick's Day celebration at their Farnborough clubhouse for members and their guests.

"I'm not sure you merit a pass out," Charlotte warned Roger when he proposed attending the festivity.

"But, why? I've carried out all your explicit instructions pertaining to domestic duties, and I've been home and in bed by 11 p.m. every night, workloads permitting since New Year's Eve."

"You're in bed every night by 11 p.m., driven by catalysts of a carnal nature."

"True, but nonetheless, I'm there by your side."

"I haven't forgiven you for your outburst at my parents on New Year's Eve."

"Which one do you mean? There were so many of them."

"The one when you aided and abetted my mother nagging me to make New Year's resolutions."

"Oh, Charlotte, it was *purely* for family entertainment. Nobody ever takes those promises seriously."

Unconvinced, her expression became fractious. "Hhmm, maybe."

"So," he tested, "have I your permission to chaperone Steve, Gordon and Charlie to the Saint Patrick's Day observance?"

"You're not even Irish, nor are any of your friends."

"You don't have to be Irish to celebrate Saint Paddy's Day. Besides, we also celebrate Saint Georges Day, and being good Christians and baptised by the Church of England, all four of us are well qualified."

"Either way, Roger, both anniversaries are used by your club as an excuse for getting inebriated."

"On the contrary, oh hostile wife of mine, I'll have you know we sanctify both saints in a tribute of reverence and homage."

"What you really mean is you and your gang of malcontents use these sacred days as an excuse to put away vast amounts of alcohol."

"No, no…well, yes," he admitted, "but's it's done in a ritualistic way, never contravening the rules of religious or social etiquette."

"Hhmm, when is it?"

"Saturday, which is good, because—" He stopped abruptly.

"Were you going to say, because it gives you a spell to recover on Sunday?"

"No. I was going to say it allows me to devote Sunday to continue with my allocated domestic chores, and care for you and the children."

He clocked her aspiringly, his best body language selling the proposal.

"Just make sure you come home relatively sober, or there will be a Saint Paddy's Day massacre greatly exceeding any doghouse penance you've experienced to date."

"Yes, my sweet."

~ * ~

Come the celebration day, James purloined his father to procure his take on climate change.

"I've been browsing the internet to find conclusive evidence corroborating the charge global warming is manmade," he told Roger as they entered the lounge.

"A homework assignment is it?"

"Yep, English report writing. We have to develop for and against propositions in a balanced review."

"And you can't find any solid evidence to verify the notion carbon emissions are responsible for the ice caps melting?"

"No, I can't." Tapping his laptop set up on the bureaux, James developed studious lineaments. "You see, the Arctic ice cap might be reducing nowadays, but since 1992 the Antarctic ice cap has been growing. If global warming affects the entire planet, then it's rational to expect both ice caps to be receding. Another factor is in the sixteenth century much of the Arctic ice cap melted, enabling sea voyages around North Canada between Baffin Bay and the Bering Sea all year round, well before the industrial revolution originating with the accompanying rise of carbon emissions into the atmosphere."

"So what have you concluded, son and heir?"

"Purely from a scientific perspective, the cause and effect elements are indeterminate. It's not like in a physics or chemistry experiment, where stimuli can be applied to a system and responses measured, culminating in the verification of universal laws. Climate change indexes, meaning stimulants are not linear in their impact. They don't even generate reproducible hyperbolic functions. The study of climate change lends itself much more to statistical analysis and probability paradigms. But there's a limitation in those models. They inherently contain error roots, because unlike arithmetic equations generating certainties, statistical and probability algorithms only render an educated guess, and dependent on how the variables are loaded, the results can vary widely."

"Very impressive. Your comprehension of the sciences needs no revisions from me."

"So, with my research in mind, Dad, how can a coherent argument be set forth for supporting or debunking carbon emissions as the pivotal germ behind climate change?"

"Well, it seems to me the science has been corrupted by politics."

"How?"

"World government organisations, national government ministries and QUANGOs in unison with a gargantuan host of wind farm and tidal device power generator manufacturers have a vested interest in advancing the idea that climate change is manmade, consequential from the burning of fossil fuels. The condemnation extends to all transport vehicles, predominantly cars, HGVs, aircraft and ships producing CO2 or greenhouse gases. This group promulgates global warming is provoked by these emissions, and the ice caps will melt, activating flooding, unless production of these by-products is stopped."

"But when much of the Arctic melted in the sixteenth century, there were no reports of excessive flooding."

"Hard evidence rather debunks the theory, doesn't it?"

"Yeah. So…this vested interest you mentioned, means jobs for some?"

"It does. The climate change industry not only inaugurates mercantile opportunities for manufacturers. It has also created jobs in the public sector. Civil servant careers in the Department of the Environment and undeniably higher education establishments have been forged on the basis of promoting global warming twisters. It's become an expansive business, and of course the politicians have stoked up the furore, all the primary parties officially capitulating to the theory of manmade greenhouse gases, and unjustly imposing disproportionate taxes. Climate change conferences held every few years are attended by most nations, enveloping legions of civil servants to back-up the politicos flying the Green flag. Treaties ensue from these conferences, apropos commitments to reduce carbon emissions. However—" Sceptically, he chuckled. "Apart from the gullible UK, most nations just give lip service to their hypothetical obligations."

"Why?"

"Because at the national level, applying Green taxation to fuels increases manufacturing costs, making countries less competitive in world markets. No government in their right minds is going to cripple their own economy. Those making no punitive taxation measures sweep up the business, whilst other countries whose governments apply the high tariffs have become uncompetitive to win."

"You used the word 'gullible', to describe the UK's Green policies. How about naive as equivalently appropriate?"

"Well, yes. Westminster knows their unilateral, some say kamikaze artifice, to reducing CO2 emissions is seen as both gullible and naïve by the ordinary man in the street, but remarkably, the politicos *do* know what the sequels of their draconian Green policies is doing to the UK economy. Albeit they think if the UK exhibits primacy, the rest of the world will follow. Of course, in practice, if it abides to the extent mandated by the Green lobby, the UK will be bankrupted. Whilst the

Westminster politicos claim the moral high *terra firma*, Johnny Foreigner laughs at them, the residuum of the world nurturing greenhouse gases handiwork and enjoying ever-growing economies."

"It's an absurd way for our politicians to act."

"Absurd, bordering on *criminal* treachery," Roger accused, his features crushed emphasising the reproach. "Besides, our planet is far more threatened by asteroids and comets. In terms of a global event, those beauties will put global warming in the shade if one hits the Earth."

"Yes, unless we tackle the danger, any measures taken to reduce CO2 emissions worldwide, will be in vain, if in actuality rising temperatures are derived from greenhouse gases."

"Have you considered sun spots as a source accountable for climate change, also rationalising why the Arctic ice cap melted in the sixteenth century?"

"Sun spots?" James echoed nonplussed at the suggestion.

"Look it up. You'll find sunspots and the solar wind are recognised as possible stimulants affecting the Earth's weather proclivities. They reach their solar zenith every eleven years. Some studies uncover sun spot activity has doubled over the past century. Viewed from Earth, the sun glows brighter by about point-one per cent than it did a hundred years ago. Some scientists say, it has been a significant constituent in the Earth heating up and producing widely varying weather patterns. I'm not intimating sun spots are altogether responsible for climate change, but they do have some connection with the phenomenon."

Confounded by the inexactitude, James frowned. "So, there's more possible spurs behind global warming, than we're led to believe."

"And being cynical about it, many think the Green-PC lobby have stirred up the issue in order to levy even more taxes, ending up subsidising their Third World vanity crusades, rather than buttressing the UK energy industry by investing in carbon-free power generation, in reality meaning both fission and fusion nuclear power." Dwelling, his air cascaded into catechism. "Tell me, James, what emissions data have you established?"

"From the sources I've studied, there is little convergence of the published statistics, but on average I've found currently, China, India, the

US, the Russian Federation and Japan yield fifty-eight point six-four per cent of worldwide CO2 emissions, China being the topmost at twenty-eight point zero-three per cent, whereas the UK scores less than two per cent."

"I see." Musing on the patent dichotomy, Roger peeked at Heather playing with her stuffed animals in the kitchen. "Heather." She glanced at him. "Can you help us please?"

Dumping Miss Piggy and Kermit the Frog by the side of a bowl of water she'd been using to baptise them, she wandered into the lounge.

"Heather," her father began, "observe what I'm drawing."

Taking a sheet of paper from James' notepad, he sketched a wall representing a dam defence. He then added a very large hole and a somewhat smaller hole in the wall, and depicted water coming through each of the holes. "Now, can you see what I've drawn?"

"Yes, Daddy."

"If the sea is on one side of the wall and land on the other side, which hole should be plugged first to stop the land from being flooded?"

"Oh, Daddy, it's obvious. The bigger hole."

"Why?"

"Because if the bigger hole is plugged, far less harm will be done to the land."

"So, you wouldn't start by plugging the small hole?"

"Of course not, Daddy. It wouldn't stop the sea water from flooding the land. Anyone plugging the small hole first, is stupid."

"Thank you, Heather."

Exiting to perfect her baptising ritual, she muttered, "I am old enough to work out sensible things."

"Now," Roger declared re-engaging James. "If an eight-years-old girl can see the bleeding obvious, why can't the PC-Green brigade and the Government?"

"You mean, there is no point in the UK reducing CO2 emissions, and in the process paralysing our economy, if the biggest CO2 producers, meaning China, India and the rest do not massively reduce their emissions first?"

"Exactly."

"I don't get this, Dad. Why does the Government impose these crippling green measures on our country?"

"That my dear James, is what many reasonably-minded people have been tabling for the past fifteen years. Some distrust the base motivations of the Green Party, because most of the old British Communist Party joined their ranks in the 1980s, thinking they could do more damage to the UK through the Green channel rather than plotting insurgence from within."

"And the Greens fell for it?"

"Well, yes, which means they also want to see our country brought to its knees. You see, the Green agenda has gone way beyond save the whale and the polar bear. When you hear their supremacists speak today, they spout the same ultra-leftist agenda the International Marxist Group adopted in the 1960s, spiced up with a bit of modernist PC rhetoric to appeal to so-called ethnic minorities."

"I agree, but what about the Government. Surely a Conservative-led coalition wants the UK to be the kingpin from an economic standpoint, because the unabbreviated country benefits from flourishing GDP and export sales?"

"Yes, like all the mainstream parties prop UK EU membership, those same stakeholders have some form of Green agenda, incorporating the Conservative Party. It begs the post-mortem, what's in it for the politicians? Unlike the EU, where politicos and civil servants can't wait to feast on the tax-payer bankrolled gravy train, the impulse for politicians to defend Green agendas is less obvious. Some pundits have papers indicating MPs and even members of the House of Lords are the recipients of immeasurable consultancy fees for Green lobbying in Parliament, moreover the opportunity to join the boards of companies contracted to supply these infernal wind farms destroying land and seascapes, and wave machines clogging up river estuaries." Pausing, his mannerism segued into a mishmash of bewilderment and sarcasm. "It's all part of the ubiquitous jobs for the boys industry."

"Jobs for the boys industry. How do you mean?"

"Hah, that explanation needs to be the object of another homework mindbender. Suffice to say, in government, it embraces literally thousands of QUANGOs and public enquiries, the latter, a forum whereby the enquiry chairman can string out the inquest for years, and thus become a millionaire through the public purse.

"In science, it encapsulates national and international academies spending trillions, working out when big-bang actually happened to the nearest light year, finding elusive subatomic particles, and establishing if we are alone or otherwise in the universe. They're tremendous fun for academics and of course some go on to earn worldwide notoriety and even the Nobel Prize for Physics. But these are super-sized vanity projects, irrelevant for any practical purposes and delivering no net, tangible product to be translated into a money-engendering asset to frame wealth."

Perturbed, James nominated, "there must have been some science projects that have harvested commercial exploitation."

"The one exception since WW2, was the US moon programme in the early-sixties, necessitating the genesis of micro-electronics, subsequently fostering the capacious I.T industry we see today. It cost US$ billions, but bred at least 10,000-fold on the investment in terms of export products coming out of Silicon Valley. Having said that, the incitement for the septics to beat the ruskis to the moon was political. Uncle Sam just happened to get fortuitous with the technology necessary to meet the mission requirement."

"More through luck than judgement then from a mercantile perspective?"

"Yes."

Briefly cogitating James concurred, "on the science front, I see what you're saying. Unlike applied scientific experiments, leading to the development of the internal combustion engine, aircraft, radio, television and telecommunications, these are pure science projects." He winced. "The world is not *always* the embodiment of the predictable, is it?"

"No."

"We accept things far too readily without qualifying if it is a good use of money and resources, and in the areas identified they all come out of the public purse. For example, clearly the world is astronomically overpopulated, and populations are confined to approximately fifteen per cent of the world's land masses, because the residue is too hostile to comfortably sustain human societies…"

"Go on," his father encouraged, "take the axiom to its logical conclusion."

"Undoubtedly, desert regions in Asia and Africa could be fertilised and irrigated to produce much more inhabitable environments, allowing densely populated societies in those continents to spread out." Gaping at his father, he sought, "how much would that cost?"

"A lot less than surfing the intergalactic airwaves, plodding to find a message from a source, trillions of lightyears from the Earth!"

~ * ~

"What did you tell Charlotte to get a pass out," Steve ticketed as the four jubilee caballeros sped through the night in a taxi bound for Farnborough.

"Oh, just some load of old bollocks I invented on the spot."

"And she *fell* for it?"

"No, my pass out only eventuated from pleading, begging and finally sobbing and wailing. I told her I'd be a social outcast at the club if I flunked attending."

"Yeah, I've found tears usually do the trick with Colette."

Withal, Q&A revealed both Gordon and Charlie had pulled identical flankers with their other halves.

Arriving at Kappa Corinthians clubhouse, Roger and his pals judged from the noisy rumpus and glinting lights emanating from the ajar doorway, the bash must already be in full swing. Strolling into the blessed den of good fortune for the beleaguered sex, they were confronted by a myriad of extremely jolly men, raising their glasses and gushing blithesome Saint Paddy's Day salutations, against a backdrop of Emerald green and the rustic country jangles of the Dubliners pouring from the PA.

Manning the members' desk in the foyer, on seeing the newcomers, burly lock forward Evan McGinley gibed, "well, bugger me with a fish fork, if it isn't Kappa Corinthians answer to the Three Stooges."

"You say that whenever you see us," Steve rebuked. "The joke is wearing a bit thin."

"Well, if you want to argue the point, Hunt, let's step outside for a moment."

"A *moment*?" Steve cryptically queried.

"Yes, it will only take me a moment to flatten you."

"Now, now, gentlemen," Roger intervened, "you both know fisticuffs are strictly verboten at the club. If there's any blood-letting to be done, let it be on the field of play."

"Quite right, Roger," Ewan authenticated. "I was only winding up Hunt the Happy Hooker."

"I know, but our esteemed vet's number two is easily aroused when he's constrained by repetition."

"I promise I won't call you lot The Three Stooges again," Ewan certified, "at least for the dregs of this evening."

Grunting and scowling, nevertheless Steve stayed tight-lipped.

"Right, I'll sign Charlie in," Roger obliged. "You two go to the bar and line them up."

A trice later, Roger and Charlie joined Steve and Gordon, the advanced clique still struggling to attract the barman's notice.

"What's happening?" Roger groused. "I'm dying of thirst here."

"There's only one barman on just now, and he's tending to a super large order from Dusty Maltman at the other end of the bar," Gordon explained. "The other one has gone down into the cellar to change one of the barrels."

"I see. Er—" He puckishly simpered. "Anyone like a drink while we're waiting?"

"Very funny, Fraser," Gordon rebuked.

Clocking Roger's contingent, Antipodean Dusty barked in a resonating Aussie brogue, "well stone me, it's the beer hunters."

"Hello, Dusty."

"Roger, you old limey bastard," he shouted above the din, glimmering with the usual jousting expectancy. "How the devil are you?"

"Fine, you underdeveloped Aussie excuse for a mobile dung heap."

"I see you've brought those other two donkeys with you."

Steve and Gordon glowered.

"Yep, you know we're all partial to a bit of throat charming. See you later, Dusty."

"Yeah, we'll sink a few together, Roger."

"I see the same acidic banter still takes place," Charlie observed, "just like on the previous occasions I've been invited to Kappa Corinthians shindigs."

"Oh, it's nothing hurtful," Roger argued furrowing his brow. "Just ruthlessly ripping the proverbial out of each other."

"Ahh!" Gordon whooped, "here comes the other barman."

"Yes gents?"

"We're after a cool and very refreshing commodity," Gordon stipulated.

"Well, we have Guinness or Guinness or Guinness, or for those not liking the blackest stout to come out of the Emerald Isle, Guinness."

"I guess we'd better make it Guinness all round then."

During the course of the thereafter few hours, between joining in singing traditional Irish folk songs comprising *Whiskey in the Jar*, *Captain Kelly's Kitchen* and *The Irish Rover*, and downing more of the black stuff, Roger, Steve, Gordon and their guest paid their respects to Club President Bob Westcott, Club Coach Milton Harvey, Club Captain Martin Gayle, and club toastmaster John 'the Revelator' Hillibrand.

"I must say, it is odd we commemorate Saint Paddy's Day every year," Gordon suggested, "when this club has no connection with Ireland whatsoever."

"I've often thought the same," Steve confessed, "but I'm only too happy to be part of the riotous festival."

"Aren't we all," Roger murmured, also stimulated by intrigue. "Maybe Geordie, number-five lock Terry Nicholson can shed some light on the matter. He's over by the club trophy cabinet, admiring his name on the player of the year trophy."

"Are you sure about that, Roger," Gordon cautioned. "He's still sore about us raking him over last summer."

"'He who dares', to quote Del Boy Trotter," Roger retorted.

"What do you three want?" Terry guardedly pumped seeing them loitering in his space. "And who's your gallybagger friend?"

Assuming a reassuring disposition, Roger entreated, "relax, we'll behave ourselves, and our friend is Charlie Farley." Swivelling about, he gawked at Charlie. "He's a social anthropologist, specialising in studying disturbed rugby players. And by the way, he's not a gallybagger. Moreover, he possesses intellectual physiognomy."

"No, I'm—" Before Charlie could go any further declaring his occupation as a materials research scientist, Steve gave him a jab in the ribs.

Standing to his full six-feet four-inch height, Terry began to brood. "Well he's not studying me," he snarled.

"No, no, no, Terry," Roger beseeched. "He's er…he's studying Hunt."

"*What*!" Steve blurted, drawing a dig in the ribs from Gordon. "Yes, er…that's right, Terry. Charlie is helping me keep my temper restrained for when I'm hooking."

"Cripes, a mammoth job," Terry vociferated staring at Charlie. "Hunt is the most psychopathic player we've ever had at the club."

"*What*!" Steve exclaimed, clenching his fists before Roger dug him in the ribs. "Yeah…okay, I must admit, sporadically, I do lose it on the field of play."

"So, Terry," Roger reconnected, "we want to ask for your guidance."

"If this is another one of your windups, Fraser, I promise you I will be merciless with my retribution."

"It isn't."

"Or if just one of you disrespects Geordie culture, encompassing your intellectual mate, I'll fettle the lot of you. I haven't forgotten your piss-take at Christian Bowcott's stag night last summer. If Martin Gayle hadn't been with us, you'd all be pushing up the daisies."

"You have our solemn oath, we will not impugn the mighty Geordie nation."

"Well, what is it?"

"Correct me if I'm wrong, Terry," Roger began, "but right now, we don't have any Irishmen in the club."

"The final Irish player was second row Lochlann O'Shaughnessy. He returned home to Dublin in 2009. You might also call up Diamaid McGuire, who emigrated with his family to New Zealand in 2006, and Mainchin MacNamara who took a job in the West Country, and played for Penzance for a while."

"Yes, I recall Mainchin MacNamara in particular, because often his name got misspelt on the team sheet, and it came out as 'Munchkin' MacNamara."

"Yeah," Steve upheld. "He was a feisty sort as well. Didn't take kindly to his name being taken in vain, but he did have savage acceleration and blistering perpetual pace. Once he was away, not even a Bugatti Veyron could catch him."

"Without a single Irish player, Terry," Gordon pointed out, "why do we celebrate Saint Paddy's Day?"

"Tradition, reverting to before when any of us were born," he acquainted. "Bob Westcott told me a few years ago, the practice had been going since the late 1920s."

"I see," Roger acknowledged. "Nothing more to it then?"

"No. What were you anticipating?"

"Oh, perhaps an association with an Irish rugby club, like we have with Carmarthen in Wales and Bayonne in France."

"Hey," Steve began grabbing their attention, "do you recall the trip we made to Biarritz in 1996?"

"Categorically," Roger verified.

He referred to a short tour, Kappa Corinthians made of the Bordeaux region, when Roger, Gordon and himself were in their prime, and played for the senior first-fifteen. After bruising fixtures against Libourne, Mont-de-Marsan and Bayonne, the gallant Kentish men finished up in nearby Biarritz on the Bay of Biscay with Bayonne Rugby Club players. After cruising the wine bars, they ended up at Red Café, a brasserie in the town centre popular with rugby enthusiasts. As soon as word went around the Englishmen in their midst were a rugby union team, the Kappa Corinthians were treated with almost heroic reverence, tray after tray of Bordeaux's finest wines presented to them by the adoring locals.

Howbeit, the evening became memorable because after the Red Café exodus for their hotel, as drunk as a lord, giant of a man, openside flanker Clayton Moorhouse somehow got detached from the group, and ended up joining a bunch of people heading for the Esplanade du Port Vieux, en route for a night cruise. Overwhelmed by *vin* over-consumption, Moorhouse went aboard the cruiser, and pronto passed out. When he came to his senses, he found himself with other similarly inebriated people sitting on a bench rubbernecking a seascape he supposed to be the Bay of Biscay from Biarritz. After finding no fellow Kappa Corinthians amongst their number, he stopped a passerby and investigated in French where he was. The answer came back in Spanish. Indeed he was staring at the Bay of Biscay, but from the quayside in San Sebastian!

Troubled by his predicament, he called Steve Hunt's mobile, telling the hooker his location. Also feeling the aftereffects of too much *Pomerol* and *Saint Emilion*, Steve responded saying it was too early in the morning for razzes, promptly terminated the call, switched off his mobile, and caught more zee's.

It was only when the Kappa Corinthians were assembling in their hotel foyer for a coach to take them to Biarritz Pays Basque Airport, a count exposed they were one player short, the subsequent rollcall uncovering Clayton Moorhouse's absence. Putting two and two together, Steve switched on his mobile to find a barrage of messages from the openside flanker dominating his inbox.

"Moorhouse was none too pleased when he eventually touched down in Blighty," Gordon reminded Steve. "Fancy advising him to travel by parcel post."

"Yeah, he didn't take too kindly to the suggestion, when I requited his messages."

"*Too kindly*," Roger repeated. "As I recall it, when he got to the club, he was all for stoving your cranium in. Only Bob Westcott's intervention prevented Colette from becoming a young widow."

"Yeeesssss," Steve hesitantly accepted.

Ending their yesteryear discussion with Terry Nicholson, they resisted the temptation to make condescending remarks about his Geordie heritage, mainly through the indisputable knowledge, despite there being four of them, the oversized number-five lock really could fettle all of them. Thanking him for his assistance, Roger & co then procured another round of Guinness, and the group moved away into a relatively quieter part of the clubhouse.

Settling down in four easy chairs, the funsters scanned the bawdy and boisterous gathering, as the music changed from Irish to English.

"Bless my soul," Roger uttered. "*Bushes and Briars*. That's unexpected."

"What?" Steve interrogated.

"It's an old English country folk song. The version being played was arranged by Vaughn Williams."

"Heavens," Gordon castigated, "whoever is in charge of record selection, can't tell his Irish traditional from his English choral."

"Actually, *Bushes and Briars* come from the eighteenth century," Roger confided. "It became popularised again in the 1960s by folk-rock bands like Fairport Convention, and Julie Christie gave a warm rendition in the film *Far From the Madding Crowd*."

With the music talk taking root, they slid into an old chestnut; great and cool bands, and even greater and cooler concert experiences.

"Seeing Blondie and Television at the Hammersmith Odeon, then Tom Petty & The Heartbreakers and Nils Lofgren at the Rainbow were unforgettable events," Charlie advocated.

"Sure, but we only got in," Steve qualified, "because we were escorted by our elder brothers and sisters."

"Indubitably," Gordon confirmed.

"Debbie Harry," Roger drooled, a joyful mien encasing his face. "Caramba, she had a monumental awakening on my sexuality appreciation."

"Arguably, she was the most stunning woman on the entire planet then," Charlie praised. "A rebirth of Marilyn Monroe incarnate."

"For sure," Steve approved. "But weren't Television fantastic. They really stole the show, twin guitar players Tom Verlaine and Richard Lloyd setting the gold standard for the New York *avant garde* new wave."

"Couldn't agree with you more," Roger ratified. "The upcoming day I bought *Marquee Moon*, well, my mother bought it for me as a birthday gift. Since, I've acquired it twice more on CD releases. If I compiled a top-hundred derivative rock albums chart, I'd place *Marquee Moon* in my top-twenty."

"We never did get to see the Sex Pistols, did we?" griped John Lydon fan Steve.

"No," Gordon corroborated, "we were just a little too young to become deeply embroiled."

"The Sex Pistols are still one of my favourite bands," Steve endorsed. "I could get my rocks of to—"

"I'll tell you what," Charlie interrupted. "What's the name of Cameron Webb's sister? She was a few years downstream the track than us."

"Abbey?" Gordon offered.

"Yes, that's her. I had a conversation with Abbey at a shindy Cameron held at their parent's house. I sought what music and bands she was into and she elucidated, 'I like Throbbing Gristle.'" Charlie's listeners readily began to giggle. "'Oh yeah,' I cajoled. 'What's so special about Throbbing Gristle?' She told me, 'I've always liked meaty members, and the male members of Throbbing Gristle are really meaty.' So I petitioned, 'Is there any clear-cut part of them you especially like?' thinking she'd submit a girly notion like, 'Oh, I like their faces.' She shrugged her shoulders and gibbered, 'I just really like their male members.'"

"Oh *god*!" Roger bellowed chuckling. "Talk about innocence. How old was she then?"

"She must have been about sixteen."

"I wonder if she still likes, *Throbbing Gristle*?" Gordon posed, leering at the prospect.

"Well, she had dozens of boyfriends, and has been married for the past twenty years," Charlie reviewed, "so she must have seen plenty of throbbing gristle."

With sexual innuendo an axiomatic mainstay of their blokey banter when away from the regulating and policing disciplines of family and professional life, the four funsters broke into raucous laughter.

"Persevering with Steve's affection for the Sex Pistols," Gordon impishly taunted. "Can we presuppose they're the *de facto* band of choice for all solicitors?" Purposely ceasing for effect, he winked at Charlie and Roger. "I mean to say," he vaunted getting into his stride, "there's a cross-over in terms of commonality of purpose, singular attitude and philistine etiquette."

Charlie and Roger began to teehee.

"Bollocks, Anderson," retaliated the easily offended bastion of the law. "Being a solicitor and liking the Sex Pistols are not mutually exclusive."

"Yes, I'll give you that," Roger granted. "In retrospect, the Sex Pistols, Public Image Limited and substantively the whole English punk scene was the necessary antidote to the stifling and bombastic, po-faced mush rock music had got into."

"You must mean the excesses of prog-rock bands like Yes and ELP?" Charlie chastised.

"Absolutely."

"I always thought ELP stood for, extremely large penis," Gordon ascribed tongue-in-cheek.

"Quite, but lodging on the punk theme," Roger prescribed. "When Johnny and his mates came along and dealt the rock scene an enema, it was long overdue. Punk revitalised rock music with raw energy in two and half minute gems." He halted as if smitten by a revelatory thought. "By the way, as a front man, I'd put Lydon right up there with Jagger, Iggy Pop, Daltrey and Percy Plant. There's no one like him around today. They're all dreary, sulky saddos, like that Boy George copycat…oh, what's his name?"

"You must mean Anthony Hegarty," Charlie professed.

"Yeah, that's him. I still can't work out its gender."

"Me either," Steve cited. "I used to think it was male. Now I'm not so sure." Cringing, he espoused, "there's some strange creatures on the current rock scene who've got under the radar. Some are more vegetable and mineral than animal."

"Quite."

"Most of what has come out since the millennium," Gordon bickered, "such as Kasabian, the Kaiser Chiefs and the Arctic Monkeys play like under-rehearsed high school bands, and they're so *passé*, without attaching anything original to the lore. Worst of all, they're boring and lack weaponry. You're right, Roger, there's no larger-than-life virtuosos in rock these days, no John Lydons."

"I regret having to say it, but I think we're witnessing the finalising spits of the rock and roll movement, but as you say, effectively, it's been in decline since the millennium. The unknown is, what will be the son and heir of the primary rock and roll wave, circa 1955 to 2000, if anything?"

"A vexing enigma," Steve proclaimed. "There's a massive gap in progressing the genre, giving rise to the prodigious accumulation of tribute acts. Many of the younger generation are hunting for bands more stimulating and exciting than fifth-rate rockers like Muse, the Stokes and Arcade Fire, explicating why they backtrack to discover Zep, the Stones and the Stooges. More aggravatingly, wanna-get-rich-quick-with-no-talent numpties have flocked to that paragon of mediocrity promotion, Simon Cowell."

"Yes," Roger sustained, his articulation tinged with sadness. "Cowell has won the hearts and minds of voluminous legions of young people, who have had their rock and roll instincts surgically removed. Hey—" He squinted appreciatively. "Do you guys remember Andy Durham?"

"Him with the Bromley twang?" Steve stipulated.

"Yep. Andy was a real music aficionado. He had a room solely devoted to his vinyl and CD collection and his Bang & Olufsen set up. He once told me it meant so much to him, he used to hug and kiss his vinyl collection every night before going to bed."

"Real dedication," Gordon applauded. "What happened to Andy?"

"He quit his job at IBM, sold up and buggered off to downtown France with Dominique, his French wife. They have a fifty-acre farm at La Rouquette, about eighty clicks north of Toulouse."

"Does he still hug his vinyl before retiring?"

"Assuredly. Dominique thinks he loves the plastic bendy stuff more than he loves her. Several years ago, after concluding some business in Toulouse, I stayed at his farm for a few days. He took me out on his tractor to survey his kingdom." Glistening at the recollection, he relayed, "it became an odd if not funny experience. All the locals working the land doffed their caps to him, and greeted, '*bonjour Monsieur* Durham,' in a sublime French accent. Andy beheld them like he was Henry V after Agincourt, and flippantly dispensed in his Bromley twang, albeit not meaning to be obnoxious, 'Morning peasant.' It did make me laugh."

"Yeah, Andy always did have a touch of the *Basil Fawlty's* about him," Charlie remarked.

"Lenny Corran was another two-ounces-of-plastic-with-a-hole-in-the-middle fan," Steve interposed. "He used to raid the second hand vinyl shops in West London, trawling for rare gems."

"Lenny Corran," Roger parroted. "Would you Adam and Eve it. There's another name from the past. I've not seen him for eons. Do you know what he's up to, Steve?"

"Last I heard, he ran a couple of girls at King's Cross, then moved into heavier things south of the river."

"You mean…"

"Yeah," Steve broke in, "Lenny boy is a fully paid up member of the Brixton brothers pimp club."

"*Wow*, who'd have thought it!" Charlie gabbled. "He was a choirboy, wasn't he?"

"Yep," Roger rejoindered, "and in the same year at the Grammar as Colin. My brother used to tell me, Lenny got callously ribbed for his choirboy, butter-wouldn't-melt, goody-two-shoes image."

"Can't beat it, can you," Charlie insisted. "Perfect Christian up-bringing, a grammar school education, and he still ends up on the felonious side of the trail. Puts a thumping void in all this disadvantaged up-bringing crap being responsible for a life of crime, doesn't it?"

"*Jesus*," Steve spouted, "talk about all our yesterdays."

"I know, but it does seem like all this happened yesterday," Gordon admitted. "I can't believe over thirty years have gone by."

"We really must be getting old," Roger bemoaned. "We never

used to talk about what happened to us from just a few years ago, let alone in our early teens."

More enamoured by teenage recollections than the passage of time and thereby age recognition, Roger's remark went unregistered by his pals.

"What about sons of Joy Division, New Order?" Charlie broached.

"Hhmm," Steve blustered, curling his upper lip. "Not so sure about them. A bit suspect. What do you say, Roger?"

"If you are intimating they lost the rock plot, I agree. I went to see New Order at the Forum Ballroom Kentish Town with Bill Lowe and his girlfriend. Came away thinking I'd been short changed. You know Bill, don't you?"

"Of course," Steve cordially inveterated.

"Then you'll summon up the lads holiday we had in Malta after the A-levels examinations?"

"Of course, again, I was there," he specified before turning to Gordon. "You weren't on the Malta trip, were you?"

"No. I went trekking in the Outer Hebrides. Nearly froze my dangly bits off."

"What about you, Charlie?" Roger debated. "I'm sure you were part of the Malta crazy gang."

"No," Charlie replied. "Keep in mind, I was a year in advance of you three, and already at university."

"Of course. Now I think about it, it was Charlie Sissons."

"Oh yes, good lad, healthy outlook on life, superb story teller," Steve complimented. "He liked to be called Charles, didn't he?"

"Quite. Anyway," Roger perpetuated, "I'm bringing up Bill's name because one night when the six of us—" He delayed. "There were six, weren't there, Steve?"

"Let me count them off…you, me, Bill, Charles, Bob Gee and the Big Fish."

"*The Big Fish*!" Charlie aped, astounded at the name.

"He means Ian Sturgess," Roger validated.

"Oh, I get it," Charlie chirped, "Sturgess, sturgeon…big fish."

"Spot on," Steve acknowledged.

"Sounds very like that puritanical, bolshie bitch, Führer Nicola Sturgeon, the charmless Celtic nerk from the SNP."

"You're completely right there, Charlie," Gordon vouched. "She really is Adolf Hitler and Joe Stalin rolled into one. If you listen to her rhetoric, what she and that other nauseous, fishy specimen Alex Salmon want, is—"

"You mean, the Flying Scotsman," Roger interjected.

"What?"

"He used to be called 'the Flying Scotsman' because he was always high on narcotics. Sorry, I cut you off."

"After all his exposed falsehoods shouldn't it be, 'The lying Scotsman'?" Steve proposed.

"Erm…yes," Gordon okayed. "Where was I?"

"Berating the fishy specimens," Roger provided.

"Yes, they want full independence for Jockland underwritten by English taxpayers via the Barnett formula, whilst retaining Scottish seats in the House of Commons to vote on English legislation." Fuming, he trilled, "the nerve of it, and that silly bastard Cameron is opening his legs wide and taking it. For goodness sake, why is it the English are perpetually fucked by petty tyrants like those two Celtic wankers, and the fucking EU?"

"That's easy," Steve proclaimed. "No one is batting for England in Westminster. Food banks and vagrancy are on the rise, but the politicians are more concerned about giving our hard-earned taxes to the ODA and the EU, rather than helping English people. To my mind, when every English person is living in the lap of luxury, like—" He sneered. "'Cherry' Blair, then and only then, can the do-badders seek our permission to spend our taxes on their do-badder vanity projects."

"Here, here," chimed-in Steve's compatriots.

"Anyway, regarding Malta," Roger re-engaged. "One night, we all got mortal on cheap Maltese plonk at a St. George's Bay *al fresco* dinner. When we returned to Sliema, where we were quartered, Bill and I somehow got separated from the other merry men, and made our way down to Roscoe's, a bar we'd been frequenting for the best part of the antecedent week and a half. We'd got to know Roscoe very well, a giant Geordie, unquestionably as gargantuan as Terry Nicholson. But unlike Terry, he could speak English. We also got to know his Maltese girlfriend. I think her name was Krista."

"Kristina," Steve redressed. "Picture-postcard girl, very shapely."

"Yes, Kristina. On this occasion, Bill and I sat at the bar and Kristina served us up a couple of Maltese beers. We'd just about began slurping, when all at once, Bill came over all volatile, like he was about to throw up and the *Alien* explode through his stomach. Before I could get him away to the gents, he'd honked-up most of what he'd eaten and drank during the previous four hours over the bar. Other customers drew away from the foul smelling, green and purple slime spreading across the bar surface towards them. Little did Bill realise, just before he gushed, Kristina had crouched down on the other side of the bar to get some Maltese savouries. She got up *ala* Sissy Spacek fashion in *Carrie* saturated in blood, except she'd been mantled in a ghastly concoction of regurgitated shellfish and cheap plonk. Bill wiped his mouth, stared at the sick-encrusted girl, and wittered, 'I don't remember eating you!'"

Charlie and Gordon broke into fits of laughter, their imaginations running wild about Kristina's unanticipated sick bath.

"I'd forgotten about the episode," Steve conveyed between chortles.

"It got predatory," Roger affixed. "Roscoe didn't see the funny side of it. To be rigorous, he went ballistic, raging like a wild buffalo. Bill and I made a hasty exit, with Bill still in the act of secondary spewing over anyone within honking distance. Needless to say, we haven't been Malta bound since!"

"Yeah," Steve favoured, "we were lucky Roscoe didn't massacre the lot of us."

"Speaking of massacres," Roger echoed, "Charlotte has warned me I will be subjected to a Saint Paddy's Day massacre, if I show up at home drunk."

"Well, we'd better not disappoint her then," Gordon proposed. "*Barman*," he shouted, "another round of the black stuff."

Chapter 9: The Man from Uncle

About to trot off to Canary Wharf tube station after 'a hard day's graft' to misquote the famous Beatles ditty, Fraser got a call from Luther Bembridge's PA, entreating if he could spare Mister Bembridge a few minutes. Decoded, it connoted as, 'get your rear end up to the executive floor, *tout de suite*.'

Materialising in the Ayatollah's inner sanctum, Fraser saw they were not going to be alone. A sprightly, lofty dude, well groomed, and attired in a 1950s style city gent suit came into his view.

"Roger," the VP Investment Banking piped up, his intonation even more serious than usual. "Glad you could join us."

His spider senses on max sensitivity, Fraser espied all was not well in the wonderfully wise and witty world of investment banking.

"Roger, this is Raif Fallows-Northcott." Stopping abruptly, he grimaced as if nettled, heightening Fraser's suspicions. "He's, er…he's with the Government."

"Good to meet you, Mister Fallows-Northcott," Fraser gingerly expressed, shaking his hand.

"Mister Fraser," the government man reciprocated, examining the stock analyst with a searching demeanour.

He must be a new and presumably very important overseer, Fraser guessed, *but why am I here*?

A short awkward silence ensued, before Bembridge got on the intercom to his PA. "Miss Knight, I won't need you for anything else this evening. You can go home now."

Settling down in Bembridge's leather bound, deep pile, executive suite chairs, Fallows-Northcott continued to direct his gaze at Fraser, the

Ayatollah following suit. Speculating what he might have possibly done, headmaster's study syndrome came over Fraser. He hadn't 'buggered the bursar' to use a Michael Caine term, or been caught *in flagrante delicto* with analysts department PA April Harrington, not that he had any interest in her. So what was it?

"Roger," Bembridge inaugurated, "we've got a tricky situation to discuss with you." Goggling at the mysterious Fallows-Northcott, he begged, "Raif, perhaps you could put Roger in the picture."

"Certainly, Luther, but first—" He targeted the stock analyst. "Have you signed the Official Secrets Act 1989, Mister Fraser?"

"No…I haven't." Sucking in breath, a daze came over him. Twisting to address the Ayatollah, he queried, "what's going on here, Mister Bembridge?"

Like he'd been stabbed with a stiletto, the VP shakily bared his teeth. "The Firm might be in a bit of a tangle, Roger," he explained, beholding Fallows-Northcott.

"We'll disclose more," the outsider cut in, pushing a set of papers towards Fraser across a reinforced glass-top table, "after you've signed this document."

Picking up the instrument, he clocked the front sheet had the HMG crest embossed at the top and was entitled 'Official Secrets Act 1989'. Taking a fleeting gander at his companions, neither reacting, their stony dispositions abiding solid, a million qualms crossed Fraser's mind. After scan reading the main text and two sets of supplementary schedules, he dialled Bembridge again, as if seeking advice.

"Please sign it, Roger," Bembridge genially requested. "Don't worry, it's quite alright. I've already signed the Act."

Retaining prudence, nevertheless Fraser scribbled his full name across three acceptance signature boxes, then propelled the paperwork pack back across the glass table.

"Thank you, Mister Fraser," the enigmatic stranger mellifluously imparted, as if he had secured his skills for an as yet to be delineated chore.

"May I ask," Fraser began, "exactly who are you, Mister Fallows-Northcott?"

"Let's just say, I'm here on behalf of HM Treasury," The Firm's visitor informed, parading an authoritative mould like he'd made the same reply on multiple occasions.

"I see. And why am I here?"

"Because what we're about to tell you," Bembridge rationalised, "falls within your trouble-shooter remit."

"Sounds more like black-ops than commercial trouble-shooting," Fraser postulated. "Does Toby Chalcroft know about it?"

"No. And right now, no one else is to know outside these four walls."

Scouring Fraser intently, Fallows-Northcott tarried unsure if he'd play ball. "Mister Fraser, how much do you know about money laundering?"

"Enough to know it carries a jail sentence."

"Good, then you're under no illusions." Thinking the trouble-shooter had softened, he got up and walked over to the window array exposing the dimly-lit central London skyline, then onerously cocked his head at him. "Tell me more about your discernment."

"It's the practice of concealing the source of money obtained by illicit means. As an example, in 1996 the International Monetary Fund estimated two to five percent of the worldwide global economy involved laundered money. A titanic underestimate, more recently the Financial Action Task Force on money laundering has stated overall, it is impossible to produce a reliable estimate of the amount of money laundered, and they refuse to produce published figures. Other academic commentators and government agencies have likewise adopted the FATF standpoint. Today, money laundering loiters as a complex dilemma, its scale still to be accurately defined."

"Quite right. So you assent it's a significant tribulation?"

"Yes."

Bowing his head as if preparing Fraser for bad news, Fallows-Northcott enlightened, "it appears The Firm, as it's euphemistically known in financial circles, has unwittingly become used by a third-party to launder money."

Staggered at the declaration, Fraser's lips parted involuntary. "I see. Do we know who the middleman is?"

Directing his scrutiny at Bembridge, Fallow-Northcott corroborated, "yes, we do." *Good god, it's not the Ayatollah, is it?* Fraser thought to himself. "But, if this distinctive somebody and the cartel he represents are to be brought to justice, they have to be caught in the act." Letting his words sink in, he then particularised, "we must have hard, irrefutable evidence, or it will be thrown out of court as entrapment."

"Who is this individual?"

"You tell him, Luther."

"Does the name Victor Carville, mean anything to you, Roger?"

"No…nothing at all."

"His real name is—" The Ayatollah coughed to clear the tension in his throat. "Sir Anthony Summerson."

"But…he's Chairman of the Dryden Group, the UK's primary civil engineering conglomerate, and one of our major clients." Astonished, Fraser fell back in his seat.

"Entirely correct," Bembridge uneasily concurred, for once, his usual, ultra-high gloss, confident body language visibly dissolving.

"Are you sure you have the right man? Sir Anthony is a much-respected business maven, well-connected throughout commerce and the Establishment. He has friends in the current administration and…he's a billionaire." Resting to collect more thoughts, Fraser grilled, "how do you know it's him and not another Dryden Group executive, or even a lower echelon officer?"

"Because—" Fallows-Northcott deliberated. "Let's just say, we have an operative in his syndicate."

"You mean a sleeper, a mole?" Fraser hypothesized.

"If you like."

Sniggering at the incredulity of the proposition, he then became flummoxed. "But…why is such a public dignitary risking everything to launder money?"

Thinking, *this guy is smarter than I fancied him to be*, Fallows-Northcott peered at Fraser. "Unequivocally, he is our man and we do have some evidence to that effect."

"You mean, you have a paper trail ending in identifying him

through stock trading governance procedures?"

"Yes, a full audit trail."

"With a provable connection this Victor Carville is, in truth to tell, Sir Anthony Summerson?"

"Something like that," awkwardly undersigned the cagey visitor.

Monitoring the incomer, Fraser asserted, "you're being very obtuse, Mister Fallows-Northcott." Noting the Treasury man possessed a practised stealthy aura about him, coupled with impassivity and ambiguous body language making him difficult to fathom, he appended, "evidently you have some kind of proof, so what's stopping you from arresting Sir Anthony?"

Abashed, Fallows-Northcott became reticent in his manner. Had Fraser been indiscreet beyond the confines of the document he'd just signed? Warily, he advised almost as a throwaway explanation, "wheels within wheels. This is a complex business." Glowering at Fraser, as if about to tear a strip of him to bring the incisive stock analyst to heel, he changed his mind, the indignation subsiding. Reconvening with Bembridge, he submitted, "I think we're going to have to tell Mister Fraser more."

Casting an admonishing smirk at his quick-witted trouble-shooter, the VP conceded, "yes, Roger tends to qualify until he feels comfortable with situations," the tribute enunciated with a hint of annoyance.

"There's more to this intrigue than Summerson," Fallows-Northcott divulged. "It could unravel why he is risking everything."

"Go on," Fraser encouraged.

"He's tangled in other activities interconnected with money laundering. Initiatives, shall we say, of more significance on the world stage."

"You're still being obtuse, but neglecting your reticence to come clean, what's his motivation? I assume the monetary volumes are vast, so he can't be using Dryden Group accounts. It'd be quickly peeled, and indisputably he has enough yachts to water ski behind for life, so—" Fraser leaned forward. "Why is he doing this?"

Not used to being on the receiving end of an interrogation, Fallows-Northcott's discomfort mushroomed. "Sometimes, rich men also want to be muscular men, muscular in the sense of controlling world events," he broached in a testy voice. "Summerson belongs to an undercover secret society called 'One World'. Their aim is to confront elected government policy and bring it in line with their vision of how the world, meaning the world economy, should be run."

"So why the money laundering? It's still not clear."

"You're quite right about Dryden Group money. Their accounts are clean. Let me see if I can position this, so you will gather what's going on." Reversing from the window array, Fallows-Northcott sat opposite Fraser. "One World needs funds, very large funds, untraceable in their origin, so as to avoid an audit trail to registered companies like the Dryden Group. Hence, Summerson cannot use the Dryden Group or his personal resources to bankroll One World."

"Not without it being detected very quickly," Fraser interjected.

"Definitely. So they acquire rich pickings from other sources, and then launder them through financial services investments into off-shore accounts. Eventually, the currency ends up in holding companies used to pay for One World schemes."

"Where does this undetectable wealth come from?"

"Huh—" All at sea, he wrinkled his snout. "You must have formulated a theory already, Mister Fraser."

"Illegal pursuits?"

"Quite."

"And?"

"Our American counterparts at the US Department of the Treasury tell us One World revenues primarily comes from drug trafficking. It's a multi-billion dollar, worldwide criminal business."

"Well, if you know for sure," Fraser quibbled, "why don't you terminate the surveillance and arrest Summerson on drug trafficking indictments?"

"Because, he is not directly implicated in the narcotics part of One World. Other members of the guild are responsible for the drugs business. His segment makes provision for the laundering scam."

"So, if I'm reading you rightly, you're waiting on the hereinafter instance of a laundering transaction taking place to snare him in the act?"

"You catch on well. Yes."

"I see." Staring down at his reflection in the glass table, he opined, "so what are you expecting me to do?"

"Clean the stables, Roger," Bembridge boldly proclaimed, getting to his feet and pacing by his cherished trophy cabinet. "Summerson's deception is being orchestrated through The Firm's London operation. If this ever got out into the clear light of day, it'd be catastrophic for The Firm, the market losing faith in our integrity, and as you know, integrity is the single most valuable asset an investment house relies on for business sustainability."

"Are our New York brethren up-to-date with the situation?"

"No…and they have to remain out of the picture."

"Mister Fraser," Fallows-Northcott took over again, "we want you to help us trap Summerson in the act."

"You mean, help set up a sting?"

"Yes."

"But such a ploy is tantamount to entrapment, and if Summerson is brought to trial, it could uncover the accountability of the Government in this blueprint. Surely you want to avert such a circumstance arising?"

"You might well think that, Mister Fraser," the Treasury man icily licensed, "but I couldn't possibly confirm or deny it."

He verbalises just like Ian Richardson playing the conniving Francis Urquhart in House of Cards, Fraser recognised. *I wonder if Fallows-Northcott is just as ruthless.*

"Is it what you *really* want?" Fraser tested. Then the penny dropped, and he self-answered. "No…that's not what you want, is it? In fact, it's the last thing you want. A trial would unveil everything, and everybody, including The Firm." Blinking at the stranger, he voiced, "you don't want to put Summerson on trial…do you?" Dwelling, he then closed the allegation. "You want to barter a deal with him after he's been caught red-handed, don't you?"

"As I say, Mister Fraser, you might well think that, I couldn't possibly confirm or deny it."

"Nonetheless, that's it," Fraser pressed. "You want the bigger fish in this insipid pool. What did you call it?"

"The One World confederation."

"You want to put the whole thing to bed without the public glare of a trial, don't you?" Fraser evoked, perceiving no forthcoming admission. "*Ipso facto*, you and whoever you represent, don't want this matter to ever see daylight."

"Mister Fraser, you've just signed the Official Secrets Act," Fallows-Northcott crisply reminded him, indicating unassailable authority. "Whatever we do has national security repercussions enacted in the national interest. Those even remotely connected with this endeavour, such as yourself, are bound by the conditions of the Act."

"You mean, keep their mouths shut?"

"Precisely, Roger," Bembridge emphatically articulated. "It's best for The Firm as well. All I'm bothered about, is stopping this practice, and making sure The Firm is washed squeaky clean, with no one apart from ourselves and Raif's team mindful of what's gone on."

Dawning on Fraser, by being allied to the salacious criminal info, his entanglement with its resolution came within the Act's territory, he began to appreciate the ramifications, whatever they might be, were just around the adjoining corner for him.

"Okay," he heedfully commenced, "so how is Summerson, aka Victor Carville, pulling the con? How does it work?"

"All the drug loot is channelled into a numbered Swiss Bank account," Fallows-Northcott cleared up. "Carville uses this account to make investments through The Firm as a private investor. Instructions are made to buy certain stocks during the course of a working day, knowing up front their value will rise. When the stock reaches its peak measure, directives are given to sell, then the original capital investment plus the return are deposited into a separate off-shore account."

"How do you know this Swiss numbered account is operated by Victor Carville?" Fraser probed. "Banks, above all Swiss Banks, do not give away client details, even to government organisations."

"They do to my agency," the stranger warranted.

"And how does your mole in Summerson's Dryden Group know it's him making the transactions under a different name?"

"Pillow-talk, Mister Fraser. High calibre execs can never resist inflating their egos by telling at least one confidant about how they are pulling a stroke."

By the by, Fraser noticed the Ayatollah gaped towards the window, when the Treasury man made the comment about execs inflated egos. He meditated if Bembridge was rerunning the Zicon General-Dwight Armstrong contretemps in his mind.

Twenty minutes later, Fallows-Northcott withdrew to report to his taskmasters, leaving Bembridge and Fraser to work out a plan of campaign at The Firm.

"Mister Bembridge," Fraser began.

"Luther, Roger," Bembridge allowed. "You may call me Luther during this offensive when we're by ourselves."

"Luther, am I right in thinking you knew Mister Fallows-Northcott before this affair?"

"Yes…very perceptive of you. I met Raif Fallows-Northcott at Oxford, though until a few days ago, I hadn't seen him for nearly thirty-seven years."

"He's not really with HM Treasury, is he?"

"Depends upon what construct you apply, but please don't ask me to certify who he really works for, howbeit, I'm sure you can guess."

"Snagging Summerson in the act will result from applying an audit trail to the governance of his transaction source and tracking the booty to its ultimate destination. There, someone will either send it on to a holding company account, or en-cash the trade." Bembridge didn't argue the point. "But I still don't see what merit I can add to the procedure. The frame-up will be handled by a trader in Ricky's team."

"It will."

"Who manages the Victor Carville account?"

"I checked before you joined us." Frowning, Bembridge confided, "it's Trevor Evans."

"Nervous Trevor. *Ouch*," Fraser bawled, thinking only latterly he'd been instrumental in Evans keeping his driving licence. "He'll be blissfully unaware his remuneration is predicated on money laundering."

"Indeed, he will."

"I can monitor transactions through the trade-watch application,"

Fraser spelt out, "but Trevor will be suspicious when trade payment is not made, and he doesn't get his commission."

"You mean, when Summerson aka Carville, is arrested?"

"I do."

"Yes, I elucidated such an occurrence to Fallows-Northcott, but I think we can rely on Trevor's nervous nature to swallow any official line we give him. Trades have been stopped before for all kinds of compulsions, so I will invent a highly plausible reason to keep him on-side."

"And Ricky and Toby too?" Fraser annexed.

"Yes."

"Well, er…to en-cash the laundered truck," Fraser interpolated on the spot, "Summerson has to empower an intermediary with an account number and-or a dummy name, along with bank deposit details, in say Switzerland, the Channel Islands, or some other offshore financial haven. If he's clever, there'll be a series of nested accounts all over the world into which the spoils can hedge-hop in an attempt to elude traceability. When they finally come to rest, a third-party can flash the account number, and with some kind of pin and Q&A security, withdraw the money and discontinue the account."

"Once again, you've rocketed to the nub of the demand," Bembridge acknowledged. "If the act of money laundering can be proved against whoever withdraws the swag from such an account, then the audit trail will connect that accomplice with Victor Carville. It's up to Fallows-Northcott to then play his cards with Summerson and broker whatever covenant legitimises the UK Government and the Americans to wind up this One World plunderbund."

"And in the process," Fraser favourably supplemented, "insulate The Firm from aspersion."

~ * ~

Several days passed without any word from Fallows-Northcott. Servicing his normal stock analyst workload, Fraser put the meeting with the man fronting for HMT to the rear of his mind. He began to think the

Summerson episode had fizzled out until he got a call from the Ayatollah's PA, saying the VP wanted to see him.

Hotfooting it to the executive suite, Bembridge told him the situation had changed. They'd had a break. It transpired his ex-Oxford pal's mole in Sir Anthony Summerson's executive staff team had provided timing details for the contiguous money laundering racket.

"We even know the crowning terminus of the ill-gotten gains," Bembridge enthused. "You're going to Grand Cayman, Roger."

"To do what exactly?"

"We're going to tag the transaction with a code for identifying trail onward from London. Fallows-Northcott needs an authorised officer from The Firm at the Royal Bank of Cayman HQ in Grand Cayman, to both verify the code source and witness the arrest by his people, making Summerson play ball in Blighty."

"I see," he guardedly declared. "Who will do the transaction encoding?"

"I've had to take Marcus Greenaway into my limited confidence."

Another Oxford man, and a dependable friend to Bembridge, Greenaway occupied The Firm's director of governance and compliance post for the London setup. Fraser and other analysts worked with his team on a regular basis, Greenaway's resource advising them on overarching legislative cruxes buffeting investment opportunities before the analysts assigned them to someone in Trading Floor Sales Manager Ricky Henshaw's team.

"What have you told him?"

"As little as I could get away with, so as not to necessitate him signing the Official Secrets Act, and opening another can of worms. Don't be perturbed, Marcus will be judicious."

"Have you informed *The Man from Uncle*?"

"What?"

"The MI5 London central spook."

Responding with a jumpy glimmer, Bembridge reported, "Fallows-Northcott is fully in the picture."

"So," Fraser reviewed, "Trevor Evans will perform Victor Carville's stock transactions for the day. When he is instructed to transfer the accumulated funds to the Royal Bank of Cayman, Marcus will intercept the payment transaction, adding the tag code. In parallel, I will oversee the money transfer with my trade-watch application."

"Affirmative," The Ayatollah authenticated. "You'll stand by at the Royal Bank of Cayman with Raif's people, ready to nab Summerson's, aka Carville's bagman. Marcus will email you the tag code. When the bagman is detained, you will breach the account containing the transferred laundered money, and compare the tag-coded transaction with the accounts content. As you pointed out the other evening, the bagman will have to give an authorization code to the bank for the collateral to be encashed. The account access security file will contain the same code. By implication, it will belt and brace the bag carrier into illegality."

"When do I hit Heathrow?"

"Saturday," Bembridge specified. "The fraud will take place Monday. You'll be lodged at the Ritz-Carlton. One of Raif's staff will contact you. Miss Knight has your flight and hotel reservation details."

Like a shot, Fraser beheld Bembridge differently. He saw Ian Fleming's M character played by Bernard Lee prepping him, with Marcia Knight in the Miss Moneypenny role, the scene making him 007! Bringing himself into a reality regime, he investigated, "how do you want me to play this, Luther. I mean, what is the aspiration?"

"As I say, Roger," Bembridge reprised, emitting a Dutch uncle goggle, "Raif's man will give you the briefing over the weekend at the Ritz Carlton."

Discussing the sortie in more detail, Fraser verified timings, the VP filling in his knowledge gaps. With all the bases covered, the trouble-shooter made his culminating remarks and launched into scooting out of Bembridge's inner sanctum.

"*Roger*," The Ayatollah yowled before he opened the door. Twisting to the call, he noted Bembridge wanted to speak, but whenever he neared forming his words, he gawped away, as if unsure what to say.

"Is there something else, Luther?"

"Just..." he juddered out, his carriage restless, his usual *de facto* businessman's impassive guise replaced with a considerate shaping.

"Just…take care, Roger."

Smiling in acknowledgment, Fraser exited, unable to decipher Bembridge's twitchy behaviour.

Outwardly counting not why, all the same he began to feel apprehensive. Seemingly the challenge amounted to a simple audit trail undertaking, remotely tracing Trevor Evans transactions with a trade-watch application on his laptop. What could possibly go awry?

By the time Fraser sat down in his own refuge, feelings of uneasiness had snowballed. The hairs on the back of his neck usually told him when a situation was going pear-shaped. At that moment, they stood out at the perpendicular. What hadn't he seen sticking out like a sore thumb staring him in the face? What was missing from Fallows-Northcott's and Bembridge's disclosure? His mission had surfaced as over-simple for the embodiment of a multi-dimensional conundrum, the trouble-shooting content minimal. It was really a compliance and governance function, much more suited to Marcus Greenaway. So why him?

Slicing and dicing *ad infinitum*, Fraser went through the dichotomy, but nothing obvious came to mind, Bembridge's parting, 'Just…take care, Roger,' ringing with no particular gravity. Usually, the Ayatollah dispensed his edicts dispassionately, independent of the contest severity for The Firm's appointed representative, Toby Chalcroft employing the same clinical technique. It seemed to be customary executive sphere methodology. Issue the command, don't give any encouragement, and anticipate the outcome to be achieved post haste. He had accepted other trouble-shooting allotments under the same provisos, but they were mainstream investment banking duties, whereas the Summerson conflict was radically different. The more Fraser thought about it, the more he fingered the Cayman Islands caper could not be as simple as Bembridge signified.

~ * ~

So as not to alarm Charlotte, Roger told her he had a trouble-shooter obligation necessitating travel and local preparation over the weekend.

"You do get to some obscure places with this new directive," she cited, testing the trip's veracity.

"Yes, but the Cayman Islands are a major offshore financial centre. The Firm does a lot of business in the Caribbean, especially with private investors. Invariably, they use the Cayman Islands banking facilities to hold investment funds."

"You mean, to eschew paying taxes?" she cryptically submitted.

"Yes, just like British expats such as Lewis Hamilton taking up residence in Monaco or Switzerland to shirk paying higher-rate and capital gains taxes," Roger sketched. "I don't approve of them, but it's not illegal."

"Just morally reprehensible," Charlotte criticised, "I mean, the man you mentioned…"

"Lewis Hamilton."

"Yes," Charlotte acknowledged, narrowing her blinkers in a token of disapproval. "He's had all the advantages of being brought up in England, his education and health provision paid for by the State, and when he has the opportunity to express his gratitude by reimbursing the taxpayer, he jumps ship." Sombrely, she condemned, "pure greed is what I call it."

"Yes, I agree, but as I say, it's legal."

Fettered to do anything about the scurrilous conduct, she crabbily uttered, "mmmm," then switching moods supplicated in a cherishing voice, "how long will you be away, darling?"

Radiating rosily, he embraced his wife and kissed her. "Oh, just a few days."

She poured over his face, her feminine instincts alerted by her husband's not-quite-right comportment. "Roger, you haven't the same enthusiasm for this trouble-shooting task, as you did for say the Guatemala trip. Why?"

Straightaway, he realised she had discerned out of the ordinary tremors in his body-language, even his vocalisation. Striving to comfort her, he laughed and held her close to him. "Sorry, I think the working week has caught up with me. I'm just feeling a bit tired."

"Strewth, and they take it for granted you'll be up early tomorrow to go to Heathrow, as well." She surveyed her husband's aspect more rigorously. "I know you think you're invincible and will live forever, but…everybody needs rest. You don't look like your normal self." Hesitating, she searched further for signs of unrest. "Is anything amiss, Roger?" She pushed herself away from him. "You are telling me everything about this trip, aren't you?"

He beamed at her. "I adore you so much," he glorified. "You can always tell if I am bothered, but—" He blew out his cheeks. "I just need to get some sleep. There's nothing more to it."

"Periodically, I might give you heat." She wrapped herself around him. "But I love you just as much as the day we got married."

"Oohh, Charlotte." He melted, his demeanour dreamy.

Chapter 10: I'm not Adam Carter

En route to Grand Cayman, Fraser encountered the usual array of oddballs and eccentric luminaries rich enough to travel business or first-class in the Heathrow T5 BA Executive Club lounge, the ensemble embodying an Ethiopian wearing a Haile Selassie style, multi-coloured coat and Elton John-sized mega sunglasses, with a portable CD-player hitched to his side, earphones strapped around his lugholes, and a tea cosy on his napper. *A Bob Marley tribute act,* Fraser assessed. His casual inspection also revealed a tall, gaunt gent, straight out of Chav City's lexicon of lazoonland-like creatures, only this critter sported a Hugo Boss suit and a top-of-the-range Rolex. However, it was his somewhat curious gait, a cross between a long-legged schoolgirl running after a netball and a giraffe on wacky backy that fascinated Fraser. *Clearly a refugee from the Ministry of Silly Walks*, he concluded. More flaky and freakish beings came into Fraser's view, some mirroring extras from a David Lynch movie, one a dead ringer for Frank Booth, the psychopath played by Dennis Hopper in *Blue Velvet,* but paradoxically, all of them exuding wealth or status. Then a familiar and somewhat more regular sight crossed Fraser's gaze, Kappa Corinthians Rugby Club Captain, Martin Gayle.

"Martin," Fraser near-to yelped, startled to see a normal person.

"Hello, Roger. I'm surprised to see you here on a Saturday."

"Yes, a call beyond routine duty takes me to sunnier climes, and yourself?"

"West Coast bound for the umpteenth time."

"BAE Systems making extra demands on you?"

"We're chasing a hush-hush project with Lockheed-Martin at the Palmdale Skunk Works." Kindling a jaundiced countenance, he lamented, "it's not all beer and skittles, you know."

"I'm sure it's not," he endorsed, yawning resultant from interrupted sleep.

Perusing his associate more intimately, Gayle remarked, "you don't quite look the ticket today, Roger."

"No, I'm a light sleeper, and I was awoken in the early hours of the morning by Woody Woodpecker hammering on the cowling of a street lamp at the bottom of our driveway."

"Woody Woodpecker?"

"You know, the cartoon character drilling at anything made of wood with his beak."

"Aahh."

"Well for the past week, some bird of unknown origin has taken to doing a Woody Woodpecker simulation, the reverberation from its schnoz vibrating against the cowling like a power drill. If it's still hammering in the early hours when I'm home again, the Purdey will be coming out to dispatch the pest to hell."

"Ha, ha, ha," Gayle jabbered out before his light-heartedness dissipated to a solemn disposition. "Have er…have you heard about Eugene Gilson on your travels?"

"Our esteemed 2IC to Coach Mason Harvey?" he prudently queried.

"The very same. He's had a run in with the law."

"Is that why he wasn't at the Saint Paddy's night celebration?"

"Yes. Eugene came to the assistance of an old dear being turned over by some Brixton brothers. Intervening, he decked three of them, and was instantly arrested by plod."

"But *why*?" Fraser screeched, appalled by the injustice. "He was acting as a good public citizen. Did the old dear a favour."

"London's finest materialised JIT to see Eugene planting the scum. They said he'd used undue force to quell the mugging attack, quite a lot of claret flowing out of the aggressors. Eugene fended, attesting the muggers used knives. The cops validated the claim, but still apprehended the Brixton brothers, and Eugene."

"So, what's happening?"

"The incident has gone to the director of public prosecutions. If they think there's a case to answer, Eugene will be brought before a magistrate, and if found guilty, he could lose his project manager job with Fereby Construction for having a criminal record."

"*Ridiculous*," Fraser savagely denounced. "It's indistinguishable from saying to the public, if you see a gang of thugs attacking an old lady, do not intervene." Producing horrified physiognomy, he divulged, "I'm shocked."

"Me too. Eugene is as tough as goat's meat, but this has hit him for six. It's principally why he didn't attend the Saint Paddy's Night event."

"Eugene is one of the most affable and trustworthy blokes I've ever known. To use a term from my world, he's as steady as The Bank of England. Society is flawed, even rotten, if a knight in shining armour comes to the rescue, and gets *fucked* for being a good guy."

"It's the price we pay for political correctness."

Exasperated, Fraser blared, "don't get me launched on the relentless downside of PC, Martin."

"Do you think Steve Hunt might represent him in court?"

"Steve will do it for free, and he'll win. Just give him a call. He'll don himself in anti-PC robes and have Eugene off the hook before you can say, Shami Chakrabarti."

"Who the hell is that?"

"Some PC zealot I was told about in the autumn who runs Liberty."

"Good." Blowing out, Gayle released tension. "I'm relieved." His mood changing to buoyant, he originated, "on a brighter note, though its yet to be officially sanctioned, you'll be receiving a letter from the Kappa Corinthians board of directors, inviting you to become a club mentor to the juniors."

"What, *me*?" Staggered, Fraser reacted, "I'd have thought Dusty Maltman, Gordon Anderson or even Damien Chapple are far more qualified than me. Their performances on the field of play are legendary. Besides, I'm already a member of the 1932 Committee. I'd hate my Kappa Corinthians brethren to think an undue amount of gift was coming my way."

"*Hah*!" He rippled his brow. "Modest as usual, Roger. Rest assured, you have the full support of members. In a straw poll, those approached thought you'd make an excellent mentor."

"What does the task entail?"

"Oh, the usual inspirational advice and stories from a seasoned vet." He nudged Fraser's arm. "Even some demonstrations of your fabled body swerve."

"If I ever had a fabled body swerve, it's long past its sell-by date."

"I don't think so," he sturdily upheld. "A few weeks ago, I beheld your hippy, hippy shake during the vets' match against Harrietsham Hawkers. It still came across as pretty effective to me."

"Huh, maybe." Fraser twinkled. "Well, I must say, Martin, I'm inexpressibly energised by your news. It will be a great honour to bear the appointment."

"Bob Westcott and the other board directors also thought with your financial services backcloth, you might be able to offer our younger players some money matters advice."

"It'd be my pleasure."

"*Good god*," Gayle bellowed out of the blue. "What on Earth is that?"

He'd seen the gaunt gent, straight out of Chav City's lexicon of lazoonland-like caricatures loping across the lounge.

"I clocked the varmint a while ago. I'm not sure what it is, but it has the same pondlife semblance as a failed contestant from one of those 'Dawn of the Dumb', chavy, reality shows."

"He's got such a pained expression," Gayle bewailed. "Do you think he takes it up the chutney?"

"Possibly, you never can tell these days. Often within the confines of anonymity, the Mister Clean types are raving poofters, whereas those popping up as not too tightly wrapped are as straight as a die. Objects like that refugee from the Ministry of Silly Walks are par for the course in jet-set circles."

"Yes, I've indexed over the many years I've been frequenting first-class and business-class air lounges, they are often a kind of *The*

Wizard of Oz zoo for adults, a concoction of half-man, half-indeterminate species representing Scarecrow and Tin Man, interspersed with normal emulations like Dorothy."

"What an excellent, expressive depiction," Fraser praised. "And I must say, using another film metaphor, some of the lounge inhabitants I've lamped conjure up a Fellini epic, cinematique in tenor, the cast reminiscent of his distinct blending of fantasy with the baroque. I'm often encumbered with the feeling a clown or an opera singer will emerge from stage left, to join an already unlikely association of well-heeled, hedonistic time-travellers and their Pre-Raphaelite acolytes."

"Changing the subject, Roger, what are your observations on the Greek debt crisis?"

"Ahh. Uniformly, it generates polarized discrimination and consumes even more fruitless cycles than an out-of-control spin dryer." Halting, he pressed his lips together as if the enigma fermented his loathing of insoluble afflictions. "To prolifically handle what's going on, the politics have to be decoupled from financial indices. Trouble is - the politics are the problem causing the Greek debt crisis. So long as the staunch Europhile politicians prop up a lame duck currency, no worthwhile solution is possible, other than pouring in more good money after bad, and-or cancelling the debt, German taxpayers picking up the tab. It's synonymous with defending the indefensible. Even a sixth-form business studies student would quickly form the opinion, imposing a common currency and fiscal discipline across nineteen countries, widely differing in their culture, work ethic and capability to compete on the global stage, will not work. It's a recipe for consummate disaster. Politics and finance simply do not mix. They're oil and water when it comes to facing realities, and will never coalesce into a creditable fusion." He paused. "Why do you ask?"

"Oh, Claudette and I were thinking of taking the kids to Athens this summer."

"Well, unconditionally, you'd get a lot of bang for your buck, but inflation is raging. Who knows what things will cost in downtown Greece by Q3."

"I thought you might say that."

"The main perplexity *vis-à-vis* a resolution to the Greek debt crisis is there's no workable quorum meeting the criteria constraints of a rugged financial cure. Any interim or eventual measure will be half-baked, and will never have legs as far as the financial services industry is concerned. Albeit there is a comical slant to it." Punching out a paw and scrawling into thin air, he recapped, "the logline read, 'Greek economy doomed'," then augmented tongue-in-cheek, "it was in the *Sun*, so it must be true."

"Ha, ha. With that in mind, we'd better re-think our holiday plans."

~ * ~

During the London to Grand Cayman flight, Fraser pondered again about the Summerson affair. He had touched on irregular if not borderline legal transactions in the past, but nothing on the scale of money laundering.

In the intervening period between when he met the mysterious Fallows-Northcott to Friday's Bembridge meeting, he had not devoted much bandwidth to rationalising the riddle. Now those parting words from the Ayatollah, coupled with his own neck hair reaction amplified his deductive convictions. He'd missed a clue, a component for some inexplicable reason Bembridge couldn't find within himself to share with the trouble-shooter.

Dissecting the brainteaser, Fraser discriminated the Ayatollah's prime solicitude had to be The Firm, because any of the nasty stuff coming down sequent from a money laundering exposure could be very bad for him. Unlike the Zicon General-Dwight Armstrong situation where Bembridge could bale out clean if need be, and plummet into one of The Firm's competitors to uphold his VP career, if tarnished with the scandal brush, he might find himself dismissed from The Firm and with no place to soft-parachute into. Knowing the natural ruthlessness of the beast, Fraser hypothesized, possibly on instruction from Fallows-Northcott, Bembridge had been selective with the full facts, probably rationalising if he had come clean, Fraser could have vetoed the mission. But was it that bad? What set of circumstances might arise in him refusing a trouble-shooting venture, knowing its probable implications might sternly limit his own future at The Firm?

Weighing the dilemma, Fraser guesstimated the unknown factor had a severe measure of risk and most probably, a life-threatening segment. Invocating the image of Bembridge in his mind, he cogitated, *bastard, swaggering, big bastard with pox and warts*.

~ * ~

Clearing customs and baggage-check at Owen Roberts International Airport, Fraser spied into the arrivals concourse, searching to see someone holding up a sign with his name on it, but no one came into sight. Navigating to the centre of the concourse, his search still came up short. Deducing he was not being met, he ambled towards the taxi rank way out.

Just about to go through the concourse exit's revolving glass doors, he heard someone behind him say, "Mister Fraser."

Rotating, he came toe to toe with a woman, perhaps no older than thirty, willowy and sophisticated, wearing a light floral dress with pink, high-heel court shoes.

"I'm Tiffany Fallows with Raif Fallows-Northcott's team." She dipped her sunglasses and glittered as if wanting to reassure him. "Were you expecting a man?"

"I don't know what I was expecting," Fraser accredited, fully taking her in. The dipped sunglasses had unveiled playful, hazel-blue eyes set in a paradigmatic, Greek goddess-like face with high cheekbones, a narrow button nose and generous lips, sixties Jean Shrimpton coiffured hair completing the picture. "You must be related to Fallows-Northcott."

"He's my uncle."

"I see. So…you're the niece of *The Man from Uncle*?"

"What?"

"Nothing. It's just a private joke." Cultivating an inquisitive gaze, he ticketed, "so what happens now, Tiffany? Do you need to see some identification, my passport perhaps?"

"I know you're Roger Fraser." Her toothy facet reignited. "We've had your photograph for a few days, and Heathrow passport control vouched you were on the outbound flight to Grand Cayman."

"I see. So how do I know, you are, who you say you are?"

"You don't." Her countenance became a bedevilling squint. "Come on," she commanded, "I'll take you to the Ritz Carlton."

Scrutinising his chauffeur's dynamic as they perambulated to the car park, Fraser appreciated Tiffany was in lovely condition. Her mass of dark wavy hair bounced as she walked along, and based on her trim figure and deportment, she'd been to finishing school, the deduction fortifying his *ala mode* Jean Shrimpton estimation. Topped off with a lofty air of confidence, she gave off a worldly aura, like she had graduated from the international play-girl set, and now engaged in more meaningful pursuits. He mused, *she probably dodges bullets like Uma Thurman in Kill Bill, and has a string of ex-lovers with broken hearts, willingly trailing in her wake.*

Making him wince with trepidation, the short journey to the Ritz Carlton in her Alfa Romeo ARC8-Competizione sports car became eventful. Judging by her ludicrous road user etiquette, he presumed Tiffany graduated from the same driving school as his bluff and crusty with other road users Italian pal, the uncompromising Alfredo Bachelli. Unmistakably, red lights meant go for her, and overtaking with a string of traffic coming the other way, mandatory.

"You're not Italian, are you?"

"No, seventh generation English." She sniggered. "Why do you ask?"

"Oh, it's just you appear to come from the same school of reckless and daring driving as an Italian friend of mine living in Rome."

"Does he drive fast?"

"Put it this way, he actualised a keen impression of Stirling Moss when we initially met."

"Maybe if we meet again, my driving will be more to your liking?"

Mutually goggling at each other, when Fraser looked forrad again, he saw a hulking lorry coming across their path. "*Watch out*!" he cried.

Neatly skirting around the obstacle, like a prima ballerina

negotiating a stage set, Tiffany then floored the gas pedal again.

"Well, we missed it," she smoothly proclaimed, glancing at her white-as-snow passenger.

~ * ~

After Fraser registered at reception and deposited his luggage in his room, he joined Tiffany at the bar.

"I've got us some Margaritas," she announced from her Caribbean raffia chair. "Sit down and make yourself comfortable."

"Heavens," the trouble-shooter yammered, "I can't remember the last time a girl bought me a drink."

"Make the most of it, Roger," she advocated, "Kirkley Neaverson will be joining us soon."

"Who's he?"

"Let's just say, he runs our bureau here in the Cayman Islands."

Leaning frontwards, his beforehand playful banter with her replaced by a more direct offensive, he queried, "who do you actually work for, Tiffany?"

"My uncle."

"No, I mean what federation?"

Like *déjà vu*, the inevitable serene but inscrutable dial he'd seen on her uncle's face, blossomed in hers. Sipping on her Margarita, she then coldly solicited, "don't ask questions you know I can't answer, Roger."

Progressing their tennis fixture for a few more minutes, whenever Fraser played what he thought to be a winning volley, Tiffany returned it with interest. Ruminating he'd learn nothing about the 'Mata Hari' or her organisation she didn't want him to know, he changed the conversation to air travel versus train travel, Tiffany willingly joining in. Then Neaverson showed up.

Similar in presentation to Fallows-Northcott in terms of a poker face, Oxbridge accent and impeccable decorum, the only vital difference was instead of city gent attire, Kirkley Neaverson blended in with other Europeans resident in the Caymans by virtue of his casual whites and sea captains' blazer.

After quickly making his introduction, he got down to the business in hand, explaining the caper.

"We have a bit more work to do tomorrow," he warned, "before the sting on Monday."

"Oh," Fraser gingerly bandied. "What exactly?"

"The mark jets in on Sunday morning."

"You mean, Summerson's bagman?"

"Yes," Neaverson candidly inveterated, his lineaments stretching with faint praise. "I see you're *au fait* with the terminology. He's billeted at the Marriott on West Bay Road, just a few blocks from the Ritz Carlton. We need access to his laptop to get a memory dump of the other money laundering deceits he's enacted on behalf of Summerson. When Fallows-Northcott confronts him, it will help convince Summerson to guide us into the inner sanctum of the One World group."

"It will be an encrypted password, protected file," Fraser mindfully specified.

"Yes," Neaverson affirmed, "and that's where you come in."

"*Me*!" he squealed, jack-knifing forward.

"Yes. Your boss, Mister Bembridge, told us with your investment banking credentials, you might be able to crack the password code."

"*What*!" Fraser shrieked. Finally, he began to see why the Ayatollah had projected a Dutch uncle goggle at him, and why an odd feeling of apprehension permeated his being the day he departed Bembridge's executive suite.

"Well, you've probably got more intuition for the encryption code than we have," Neaverson dogmatically complimented.

"Mister Neaverson." Feeling the distinct need to go formal, Fraser rose from his chair. "I signed up to play The Firm's witness when you arrest the bag carrier, not play Adam Carter to your Harry Pearce in *Spooks*." He pursed his lips. "Carter got killed in the end!"

"You are confusing fiction with reality. We are real. Adam Carter is a figment of screen craft imagination."

"From my perspective, there's no difference."

"Yes, well, we can't compel you to help us, but er—" He lingered, as if he'd been put in a difficult situation not of his own making. "Mister

Bembridge told us you are also The Firm's trouble-shooter. As such, he felt this task came within your remit."

"He did, did he?" Fraser spat out, imagining himself throttling the Lizard King-like VP Investment Banking, his scaly tail coming to a standstill, as he squeezed the final breath from the reptile's body.

"Yeessss." Awkwardly shuffling around in his seat, Neaverson cheerlessly articulated, "our Mister Fallows-Northcott got the unmistakable imprint your Mister Bembridge does not like being let down."

"Yeah, I could tell you why," Fraser frostily snapped out, "but I'd speculate you've already worked it out." Boring at Neaverson he cascaded into actuality. "So you're inferring Bembridge implied I'd cooperate?"

"I believe it was along those lines," Neaverson corroborated in as soft a voice as he could muster.

"And if I didn't?"

"Well—" Lobbying for her support, he attracted Tiffany's attention, the chanteuse fixing Fraser intensely. "I can only envision there are other candidates at The Firm, who could carry out your trouble-shooter mandate."

"I see…a *fait accompli,*" Fraser angrily countercharged, resuming his seat and thinking, *the Ayatollah is a bigger, king-sized twat than Toby Chalcroft in his most cryptic incarnation.* Having been charged with draining the swamp, TC hadn't given Fraser the full SP on the Guatemalan tumult until he was up to his arse in alligators. Bembridge had taken the liberty several steps upstream.

"I'd not go as far as that, Roger," Neaverson contended. "But I'd suggest, it's in your long-term interests to help us."

"Just a minute…if you're going to arrest the felon at the bank, you can also recover his laptop from his hotel room."

"True."

"So why the need for the cloak and dagger?"

"It's insurance, just in case anything goes wrong."

"I see. Are there any risks?" he pumped, slogging to stop his inner volcano from erupting. "I mean, does this mark as you call him, carry a gun?"

"Possibly. We won't know until we arrest him."

Gawking at Tiffany, Fraser hoped she'd bring some sanity into play. She spread her optics wide at him in response, as if to say, got you.

"This has all the hallmarks of an entrapment exercise," Fraser indignantly designated, folding his arms. "Call me a bluff, old traditionalist if you like, but I come from descendants synonymous with doing battle out in the open with the adversary, not sneaking up behind him and plunging a dagger between his ribs."

"Very laudable, Roger," Neaverson felicitated, "but the type we are going up against don't play by Marquis of Queensbury rules. They do whatever is requisite to achieve their objectives, without auditing for contravention of any civilised code."

Acquiescing to his predicament and thinking ahead, Fraser voiced, "I understand the Americans are your partners in this endeavour."

"Indeed."

"Well, if you can't get this guy to confess and implicate Summerson, a good lawyer would claim circumstantial evidence in an American court."

"Maybe, but we happen to know the mark is short on guts. In your model, what's he going to do anyway? Plead the Fifth Amendment, and somehow the Constitution will come to his rescue when he's obviously hiding a monumental screamer?"

~ * ~

Early on the Sunday morning, Tiffany, Neaverson and Fraser were at Owen Roberts International awaiting the bag carrier's entry, Neaverson's Chevrolet Tahoe SUV parked-up so they could see the arrivals concourse exit.

After Neaverson had dropped his bombshell, Fraser countlessly went through the mark's dossier, one Cornelius Omar Montez, toiling to find an article hinting at the access code to unlock the money laundering hustle quantities on Montez's laptop. According to his new playmates, Bembridge thought because of Fraser's stock market analyst qualifications, somehow it gave him an insight into the vagaries of password selection for the criminal sorority! *Some indictment,* Fraser had brooded as he derived the possibles.

Moulded from Montez's background details, he came up with twelve feasible passwords. Incredibly, most I.T users' worldwide instigated passwords having some sort of intimate significance, Fraser being just as guilty of the elemental security flaw as anyone else. Ancillary to family and pet names, typical passwords enshrined house names, car names or registrations and the sports team the owner favoured or played for. Additionally, a whole host of other permutations unearthed themselves by pouring over someone's confidential file. Much broader and deeper than visceral details held in a typical employer's HR files, the portfolio compiled by Neaverson's employers contained so much data, password possibilities were extensive.

Wanting to bottom out risk, the foregoing night Fraser had enquired as to how the caper was going to be played out, Neaverson telling him it couldn't be simpler. He'd laid-on a honey hook for the mark, not the delightful Tiffany because she was Uncle Raif's cute niece, but an all-together more sordid lure. While Fraser undertook the laptop chore, a local part-time operative had been selected for the purpose. Professedly, Montez batted both ways. Not averse to a little rent boy action, this would be the nature of the decoy. Whilst the disgusting interlude took place, Neaverson intended to monitor the mark, enabling Tiffany to get Fraser into Montez's room with the aid of a special electronic device, to execute his crucial part of the sortie.

Replaying the scheme in his mind, Fraser petitioned, "what happens if the mark always keeps the laptop with him?"

"He never does," Neaverson submitted. "Our Mister Montez is not a stickler for security, and has no motive to suspect he is under surveillance. Going on the erstwhile occasions he's made this trip, he'll be hunting for rent boys immediately after he's checked-in and scrubbed up."

"That's how you know about his sexual habits?"

"Yes, but as his record reveals, he goes for anything with a pulse. He comes across as placid in social company, but an aggressive side unmasks itself in one-on-one sexual clashes. He's capable of hurting people."

"Sounds just like Hannibal Lector."

"*Ah-ha*," Tiffany whooped. "Here he comes."

An inconspicuous man with pale black, near-to olive skin, a short Afro and slender build emerged through the same revolving doors Fraser passed through less than twenty-four hours earlier, his presence easily overlooked without registering on anyone, making him optimal for his assignment. So ordinary and nondescript, just about any witness description of his facial features and physique canopied the possibilities, the facet ensuring his universal anonymity.

"*That's him*?" doubted an astonished Roger Fraser.

"Yes."

"He doesn't look much like his dossier photograph."

"No," Neaverson conceded. "It was taken several years ago. There are more up-to-date images in our photo library, but he hardly stands out as an arch-villain, does he?"

"Not what is envisaged for a member of an international criminal cartel." Making him think about the ordinary people he did business with daily, he deliberated how many of them were clandestine law breakers, rapt in subterfuge and furtive goings-on beyond the realms of stock-trading?

"For sure," Neaverson concurred. "They don't tend to come in black hats *ala* Jimmy Cagney or George Raft, with badass emblazoned across their foreheads. Montez is typical."

"And this guy is dangerous?" Fraser tested, his consternation enlarging.

"As I said Saturday night, we don't know yet. People react differently when alongside law enforcement officers. His apparent repose in business circles might be retained. Alternatively, a different side to his identity could pop up."

"Sometimes," Tiffany appended, "even the most innocuous mark can be a trained killer."

"Well, that's done wonders for my confidence," Fraser bleated.

Jumping into his hired car, Montez drove at a leisurely pace towards Seven Mile Beach, splashy location of all the capacious hotels and casinos. Driving the Chevy, Tiffany adopted an ultra-conservative attitude for the pursuit, staying at least 300 yards behind the mark's Pontiac G8 sports sedan. She had previously distinguished his ultimate destination anyway, so no point in getting too close and alarming him.

Knowing the mark would be scoping for a surreptitious liaison, Neaverson had arranged for the rent boy jailbait to be handy for business in the Marriott's bar when Montez checked-in. Pulling up outside the hotel entrance, the Chevy's occupants surveyed him. Trotting away from reception for his room, stereotypically, he dialled the rent boy's coded body language message inviting contact.

Taking up discreet stations in the lobby, less than ten minutes later, the appraisers observed Montez casually sauntering over to the bar to begin his engrossment with the rent boy. While reconnoitering them, Neaverson and Tiffany inserted ear-housed R-T devices. Ticks later, Neaverson gave her and Fraser the go-signal, and they made their way up to Montez's fifth floor room, Neaverson having already arranged Montez's specific habitation with the Marriott.

Using her magic door unlocking device, Tiffany gained entry to room 513, the pair cladding their hands with thin rubber gloves before searching for the mark's laptop. As Neaverson denoted, Montez had not been security conscious. Within seconds Tiffany found the laptop in the wardrobe, Fraser setting it on a table and powering it up.

"Now," he initiated, "let's see if any of these possible passwords work."

After applying the ninth candidate without success, Fraser surmised he must have misread Montez's profile. By the twelfth and concluding option, also coming up short, he cerebrated he'd been totally on the wrong track.

"How about a combination of two possibles?" Tiffany suggested.

"Yes, of course. Sometimes users create a hyphenated password, or a string of two words and two numerics."

Renewed with the possibility, he busily began on combinations of the twelve baseline options, Tiffany noting down those found wanting. After a further quick-fire fifteen attempts, no amalgam had been successful. Then Tiffany got a call from Neaverson on her R-T device. Montez and the rent boy were on their way up to room 513.

By the time Fraser had powered down the laptop and carefully replaced it in the wardrobe, they couldn't vacate without the mark seeing them in the connecting corridor between the elevator doors and his room. To sustain the burden's security, Neaverson insisted they hid on the balcony, until Montez and his playtime mate had gone.

Instants after they'd concealed themselves on the veranda, sealing its sliding door behind them, they heard the room door snap free and the rumble of muffled voices, followed by the chink-chink of glasses and some laughter. Then suddenly the balcony door slithered open, and they heard the clear voices of Montez and the rent boy, Fraser cogitating, *if the mark comes out onto the veranda, the ruse is blown.*

Devoured by his desires, Montez swiftly got familiar with the rent boy, the intonation of voices replaced by the noise of clothes being taken off. Already feeling nauseous about what was about to take place, Fraser grimaced at Tiffany and stuck his tongue out. Unabashed by proceedings, she indicated for him to keep still. Moments later, they heard moaning and grunting noises, Fraser covering his ears to blot out the clamour of the sickening depravity occurring a few feet away, and thinking, *the things I do for The Firm*, and even graver, *if the caper ever got out*, *I will never be able to hold my noggin high at Kappa Corinthians Rugby Club ever again.* By the same token excommunication would befall for witnessing a heinous act of degeneracy, the triple x-certificate lechery bringing an unforgettable new meaning to the phrase, 'going outside for a fag.' Despite shielding his hearing and sealing his vision, his inventiveness took over. Vomiting approached. Fraser found the funny side of most things in life, but he didn't need to peek around the balcony sliding door to authenticate his stomach-churning revulsion. Those introductory rackets alone were enough to stimulate craven images formulating disgust and loathing. Though he tarried sure Tiffany had witnessed many distasteful melodramas beyond most people's experience, she peeked away from him, and the perverted indulgence. Then it all went quiet.

Shortly after, the hiders heard muted conversation and the rustle of clothes being put on before the mark and the rent boy took off after shutting and locking the veranda door, imprisoning Tiffany and Fraser. She got on the R-T to her partner. He also had a magic key to undo the door to room 513, and soon they were released from their temporary prison.

"Where's Montez?" Tiffany canvassed.

"It's okay," Neaverson responded. "He's gone off with the rent boy. I have an operative trailing them. Did you get the figures?"

"No." Peeping at The Firm's man, she uttered, "we haven't cracked the password yet."

"Damn," Neaverson blasted.

"Sometimes, people inverse passwords," Fraser pointed out. "Come on, I'll take another gander at the laptop."

"I thought you were reluctant to help us, Roger," Neaverson recounted.

"I did have pangs of conscience about Montez," he admitted, then facing Tiffany qualified, "but after hearing what's just been transpiring in this room, I have no qualms about nailing him."

Agog, Neaverson gazed at Tiffany, the spy enchantress coughing and making a licentious notation.

"Oh…I see," Neaverson appreciated, "Montez got down to—"

"Yes," Fraser interrupted, his disgust welling up again.

"Ahh, right," he spluttered, realising what had gone on must have been horrific for the unschooled. "Well," he optimistically supplemented, "let's see if Roger can perform some of his sorcery."

After firing up the laptop again, Fraser began on a series of antithetical letter passwords based on the original twelve baseline options, without success. He then tried inversing the word-numeric combinations began before Tiffany and himself were interrupted. Bingo, the term nwotegdirb03071960 unlocked the laptop's front door security, and they were in. Breaching the file management system, he found the folder containing the money laundering transactions Fallow-Northcott needed, and downloaded them onto a memory stick. Game over.

~ * ~

At 3:00 a.m., local time on the Monday morning, Tiffany and Fraser were busy inside the Royal Bank of Cayman HQ. Using his stock-watch application, Fraser monitored Victor Carville's investments made through Trevor Evans from commencement of trading on the London Stock Exchange at 08:00 GMT.

On standby from mid-morning, Neaverson and other members of his team waited to shadow Montez journeying from the Marriott to the bank, Tiffany receiving a message from Neaverson on her ear-mounted R-T at 11:20 a.m. to say Montez was on his way.

Having logged Carville's trades, at 11:30 a.m. local time, the London Stock Exchange closed, Fraser acclaiming, "this is going to be immense."

"How much?" Tiffany beseeched.

"I've recorded an investment aggregation of £72million, comprising the incipient £60million investment capital. Not bad for a days' trading. Indubitably, Carville knows where to invest. In itself, it reeks of insider dealing."

"Yes," she warranted. "That's our contingency position if all else fails. It's minor compared to the money laundering scam, but all these illegal acts boost the canon of evidence my Uncle Raif needs to affront Sir Anthony Summerson aka Victor Carville with."

Within a few minutes after closing, Carville instructed Trevor Evans to make the accumulated money transfer to the Far Eastern Bank, Singapore, Marcus Greenaway intercepting the money transfer, annexing the tag code, and sending it on its way, before emailing the label to Fraser.

"Here comes the tag code," he informed Tiffany, seeing a new message in his in-box.

"Good. Montez will be here very soon."

"We have a green light," Fraser heralded. "The money transfer is in flight,"

Zinging from London across two continents, with bated breath Tiffany and he observed the transaction on the world map part of the trade-watch application. Touching down in Singapore for re-routing to Sidney, Hong Kong, Frankfurt, Sao Paulo and San Francisco, ultimately it came to rest in Grand Cayman.

Logging the transmission, Fraser then advised, "the contraband has been received by the Royal Bank of Cayman clearing network and deposited into Carville's numbered account ready for bag carrier Montez to withdraw."

"Right, we have a go situation," Tiffany approved. "Stand by Roger—" She slung an authoritative mien at him. "And don't move until I tell you."

Spying from their concealed refuge as Montez impassively strolled into the bank carrying a large, ruggedized case with integrated security locks, they saw him make for a bank clerk and inaugurate the security clearance procedure for en-cashing the £72million, just over 95million Cayman Island dollars minus transfer levies.

Acting as a cardinal financial transactions centre for worldwide business, the Cayman Islands' banks regularly dealt with sums in excess of one billion Cayman Island dollars every working day. Not massive by these standards, the Carville enterprise only necessitated perfunctory security audits.

A well-practised routine, Montez nonchalantly rendered the account number and access code for withdrawing monies, the clerk keying the details into the bank's investment transfers application. Accepting the transferral, the clerk then invited Montez into a private room, Fraser reckoning he'd wait inside the chamber until the clerk had withdrawn the banknotes from the vault, and backtracked to the room with the booty, the bagman counting the money and signing off the transfer, before putting the stash in the case.

While they waited for Montez to re-emerge, Neaverson entered the Royal Bank of Cayman with the remnants of his team, placing them around the foyer, ready to intercept their quarry.

Caught up in the intrigue, several tension-filled minutes elapsed for Fraser before the door to the private room unfastened, and Montez reappeared with the case.

Receiving the go signal from Neaverson over her RT, Tiffany instructed, "come on, Roger, it's showtime."

Smartly moving from their concealment place, they intercepted the bag carrier face-on at the centre of the foyer, Fraser one step behind Tiffany.

"Cornelius Omar Montez," she checked, flashing a badge Fraser had not seen before.

Startled by Tiffany's impetus, the bag carrier stopped in his footfalls. Not replying, he perused about sensing she didn't act alone. On cue, Neaverson's team advanced on the mark, other bank clientele craning their necks in the direction of the encounter.

"Cornelius Montez," she continued, "in connection with money laundering schemes, I'm arresting you under the terms of the United Kingdom's Proceeds of Crime Act 2002. You are not obliged to say anything, but—"

Before she could go on with the arresting protocol, Montez pulled a handgun from his inside pocket, directing it at Tiffany, then Fraser, then again at her. Several patrons gasped, one lady letting out a petty scream fleetingly drawing the bag carrier's awareness before he refocused on Tiffany and Fraser, his outlook expressionless, his gun hand steady.

Never having had a gun pointed at him before, Fraser felt a distinct loosening feeling in his bowels. *My god*, he thought, *this guy is going to shoot us*. Then he heard Neaverson's voice.

"Mister Montez."

Attracted to the source of the elicitation voice, the bag carrier glimpsed to where Neaverson stood.

"There is no possibility of escape. Please put the gun down."

Neaverson's team had drawn their handguns, pointing them at the mark. Slowly oncoming to stand between Tiffany and Montez, Neaverson never lost contact with the mark's mince pies. Holding out his hand, the gesture betokened Montez to surrender his gun. Searching around to substantiate his bleak situation, Montez complied.

Staring at Neaverson, whilst battling to extinguish the butterfly parade ravaging his stomach, Fraser thought, *cool son of a bitch, isn't he?*

Pocketing the gun, Neaverson then took the case and nodded to his team. Collaring Montez, they handcuffed him as Tiffany completed the arresting protocol, also telling Montez The Firm's representative could verify the illegal transaction he had just made. Under supervision from the bank's own security contingent, Neaverson's team then escorted the mark away to a back-office, just as another Neaverson team member entered the bank carrying Montez's laptop seized from Room 513 at the Marriott, its memory contents a supplementary piece of evidence to indict Summerson by association.

Matching Montez's Royal Bank of Cayman transaction against the tag code supplied by Marcus Greenaway for source corroboration, as The Firm's authorised officer, Fraser verified the money transfer had been inducted by Victor Carville, thus irrevocably validating the end-to-end money laundering racket with Cornelius Montez.

"Splendid," Tiffany pealed. "My uncle can now confront Sir Anthony Summerson, and we can make inroads into One World."

Taking Fraser aside, Neaverson gently slapped his upper arm. "Thanks for your help in nailing Summerson, Roger, and…" He grinned. "…residing cool when Montez pulled his gun."

"*Cool*!" Fraser blurted. "More like frozen to the spot."

Chuckling at the poignant remark, Neaverson declared as if Fraser might reprise the happening, "well, there's a first time for everybody."

Detecting the come-on, the trouble-shooter assured him, "it'll be the last for me."

~ * ~

Subsequent to crossing the pond on an overnight flight, Tiffany having driven him to the airport and pecked him on the cheek for his invaluable service to Queen and Country as she called it, Roger Fraser landed at Hazelwood mid-morning the succeeding day.

After blanketing her husband in kisses and telling him the children were at school, Charlotte gabbed with the entire house to themselves, they had an opportunity to play doctors and nurses, husband and wife enacting an extended session of daylight love-making, an infrequent but most welcome interlude of prolonged physical release, enjoyed to the full.

Regardless of her acquired feminist, Green and left-of-centre addictions, when out of the public glare and within the confines of their love nest, Charlotte remained the inventive and passionate lover Roger had fell for at Cambridge. Constantly amazed by her transformation from strident convention to empress of sexual oblivion in the bedroom, Roger enjoyed both their regular and impulse excited sessions. Embroiled in endless role play, much of it at Charlotte's instigation to the point of his exhaustion, Roger loved every juice-filled instant of the elation.

When they had *ab initio* fallen in love and were exploring each other's bodies, Charlotte had confided she had a penchant for cameos, meaning dressing up. Kinky, Roger called it, but he became a willing participant in their one-on-one theatre. Beyond the titillation of Charlotte dressing up as a French Maid, a naughty nurse, or his best-loved fantasy, a schoolmistress, knowing Roger was a leg man, her rigs always included spike high-heels to flaunt her pins to optimum effect. Additional to her exceptional facial features, those particular parts of her glorious anatomy had snared him from the onset of their relationship. Venerating her side of the fantasy threshold, he knew Charlotte had explicit adornments and bedroom games in mind to maximise their delight. She wasn't a nymphomaniac, but she did sexually attach herself to her man like a limpet, often driving Roger into sheer heaven with her appetite for experimental sex.

By his early twenties, Roger's body had become a finely-honed piece of man flesh, designed to pump with the best of them. A seven-times-a-night man, his legendary staying prowess and capacity to pleasure gave him the name 'Full-on Fraser' at Kappa Corinthians, notwithstanding the nickname had seldom been used of late.

One of the earliest romping desires Charlotte got her partner to enact, involved her being rescued by courageous and dashing woodsman Roger from a ferocious grizzly bear attack. Dressed in one of her scantily clad outfits, she called for help, Roger coming to her rescue attired in fur boots, a fur hat, and carrying an axe, the rig making him approximate Brezhnev taking the annual October Revolution presidium salute from the Kremlin balcony overlooking Red Square, rather than the intended Davy Crockett Doppelganger. Quite how the grizzly bear became nullified abided a conundrum for Roger, but in the mechanism of deliverance from rapier claws and crushing jaws, the inevitable horizontal samba occurred with her.

On one occasion at a five-star country hotel, he slipped on the bedroom's polished floor and went headlong, jamming the fur hat over his bill, as his bounce connected with a four-poster bed frame, Charlotte sent into fits of laughter. Taking her nearly twenty minutes to remove the offending skull piece, Roger squawked she was ripping off his hooter. A hard knock-knock on the room door, and an irate male voice demanding they kept the noise down, or he'd call for the vice squad to arrest the bawdy pair, quietened their stunt.

"How did the business trip go?" Charlotte polled after their fun and games were over.

"Eventful is the overarching word to describe what happened."

~ * ~

As he anticipated, the upcoming day at Canary Wharf, the Ayatollah's PA Marcia Knight summoned the trouble-shooter to his executive suite where Bembridge and Fallows-Northcott awaited.

"Come in, Roger," Bembridge invited as Miss Knight opened the double-door to his executive lair.

"Mister Bembridge, Mister Fallows-Northcott," Fraser acknowledged.

"Ah, Mister Fraser, or may I call you Roger?" the spook requested.

"Certainly."

"We're very pleased with your attainment in the Caymans, Roger," Fallows-Northcott extolled. "Kirkley Neaverson and my niece Tiffany Fallows report you did everything expected of you."

"Mmmm, I don't know what was more harrowing," Fraser peevishly quipped. "Having a gun pulled on me, or listening to the disgusting honks and bellows made by a couple of bum-boys."

Not foreshadowing a forthright response, Fallows-Northcott cleared his throat whilst blinking at Bembridge. "Yes, er…I heard there were some unforeseen incidents," he confessed, before developing a rosy aspect. "But never mind, the important thing is the proof we needed to nail Summerson has been accomplished."

"And," Bembridge supplemented, "the unmitigated occurrence has not seen the light of day, so The Firm has been insulated from controversy and bad publicity."

"What happens thereafter, Mister Fallows-Northcott?" Fraser emphatically wooed.

"Raif, please."

Fraser obliged him. "Raif."

"Well," he sheepishly began, "I don't think we need to burden you with that."

"Oh, *why*?" Fraser waspishly interrogated.

"It's a matter of State now. We've been talking to Sir Anthony—"

"About this One World alliance?" Fraser interjected.

"Yeessss," Fallows-Northcott uneasily ratified.

"Well, by virtue of the risks I've taken, are you going to enlighten me?" he near-to bawled. As at their preliminary meeting, he realised he was being dead-pan, even truculent with Fallows-Northcott, but flopped fathoming as to why. Maybe the double-barrel surname annoyed him or his supercilious, superior attitude, but whatever the source, Fraser couldn't rationalise his obvious dislike of Raif Fallows-Northcott. Normally, he gravitated to those speaking the Queen's English properly, and conducting themselves according to the situation they found themselves in. Doubtless of that select breed, and maybe there were other sides to Fallows-Northcott the trouble-shooter may well like, but the one he had presented still brought out an unsympathetic, confrontational retort from Fraser.

Locking onto the aggression, Fallows-Northcott gaped pleadingly at the Ayatollah.

"I don't think we need to concern ourselves with that, Roger," Bembridge asserted taking the initiative. "The important thing is, The Firm has been saved from scandal."

Recasting the press, Fraser coaxed, "in view of what happened in Grand Cayman, and my participation in making the ambush a success, I'd like to know it's not been in vain, and what's in store for Sir Anthony Summerson, aka Victor Carville."

Shooting another beseeching squint at Bembridge, the spook's redeeming features decayed into exasperation.

"Roger," Bembridge breezily began, "we're aware of your pivotal contribution in bringing Summerson under restraint, and preserving The Firm's integrity, but—" As if unconvinced of his own words, he radiated a grimace at Fallows-Northcott. "It's best if we now leave Raif to carry the torch. Your work is done."

Grasping he had permeated the career limiting zone, Fraser abated thinking if *The Man from Uncle* was true to his word, Summerson's demise would quickly become public knowledge.

A few days later, the Dryden Group called a press conference announcing Sir Anthony Summerson had stepped down from his company chairman appointment, and relinquished his board membership of a raft of other companies, to pursue precipitous family burdens. Moreover, the *Financial Times* reported at least a score of premier industrialists, media magnets and politicians had gone the same way throughout the world, and a multitude of arrests had been made on arraignments of conspiracy against the national interest, with more to come.

When Roger returned home that evening, he found Charlotte absorbed by the Channel 4 seven o'clock news on the lounge television. PC, liberal-elitist faction member Jon Snow, put an anti-capitalist slant and spin angle on the revelation, suggesting the mass resignations and arrests were connected by an international conspiracy, not named because of legal constraints. As part of the review, Summerson's dealings in the Cayman Islands were mentioned.

Aghast, Charlotte twirled to challenge her husband, her complexion befuddled, her mouth unlatching involuntary. "Was this why you were in the Caymans?" Her astonishment mushrooming at the incredulity of her query, she stood up and studied him intensely. "Is this down to your trouble-shooting escapade?"

Clearing his throat, Roger adopted his best Francis Urquhart semblance and voice. "You may think that, my dear. I couldn't possibly comment, confirm or deny it."

Chapter 11: Dog with Tourette's

During a Saturday lunchtime session of the Hazelwood & District Gentlemen's Club held at local pub The Cricketers, with associate drinking pals Steve Hunt, Gordon Anderson and Charlie Farley, Roger acquainted, "I was told this story the other day by one of the bullpen traders about a dog with Tourette's."

Having demolished a hearty pub lunch and on their third round of Shepherd and Neame Master Brew, their inhibitions, not that they ever had any, had melted away on the feast and sherbet concoction, bawdy joke telling, improbable stories and unsuitable polemics for mixed company, replacing earlier exchanges about their families and working lives.

"A dog with *Tourette's*!" Steve cryptically repeated, almost spilling some of his precious hops and yeast-based elixir. "Is this going to be one of your larger-than-life anecdotes from the crazed world of investment banking?"

"No…well yes, but it's authentic…I think."

"Go on," Charlie encouraged. "Get it off your chest, or you'll be dying to tell us all afternoon."

"Right. Do you all know what Tourette's is?"

"It's an inherited neuropsychiatric disorder with onset in childhood," Gordon stipulated, "or I should say in this instance, puppyhood, defined by multiple physical, meaning motor tics and at least one phonic, meaning vocal tic."

"Quite correct," Roger applauded. "Well, reportedly, this dog, a Staffordshire bull terrier developed a Tourette's vocal tic."

Wrinkling his beak, Gordon grilled, "they're quite aggressive dogs anyway, aren't they?"

"Assuredly," Roger endorsed. "Devil dogs of the highest degree. Thirty-five pounds of robust, knurled and knotty body, on stubby, solid legs supporting a gigantic head, mainly comprising a mouth of bone-crunching teeth that *Jaws,* the murderous great white, would be proud to own."

"Blimey," Charlie trumpeted, "sounds just like Steve."

"*Bollocks*, Farley," Steve snapped. "Watch it, or you'll be feeling my displeasure about your personage."

Tickled by the riposte, Roger and Gordon burst into laughter.

"Don't wind him up, Charlie," Gordon warned, "he's got a terrible temper, and if he carries out his threat, he'll kiss you to death."

"What!" Steve roared. "Don't you start, Anderson, or I'll have my revenge on you at the forthcoming rugby practice. We hookers have a way of dishing out fist-to-snout strikes in rolling mauls to those irritating us referees never spot."

"They're only kidding, Steve," Roger implored, tapping the irate hooker on his arm. "Well, I think they're only kidding. Calm down, or you'll burst a blood vessel." Snickering, he quailed at Gordon and Charlie. "He does so externalise his feelings."

Mystified, Gordon murmured, "what the hell does that mean?"

"I have no idea, but it jangles as good."

"Very well," Steve grouchily consented, "I'll desist, but I'm very sensitive about my appearance."

"Quite," Roger commiserated. "Moving on, the Staffordshire's owner, one Rod Merrifield, Barnsley lad with a pronounced Yorkshire accent, furnished me a photo of the fiend. It looked like it could take your mitt off with one bite of its massive, sharp-teeth-lined jaws. Even animal lover Heather wouldn't care for it. Anyway—" Resting, he assumed an imperious face, accruing extra gravitas to the tale. "When devil dog Muttley, named after the 'rasom-fasom' hound in *Wacky Races*, got angry and began to snarl, perceivable words came forth."

"Such as?" Steve quizzed.

"Rod told me, if Muttley sees someone he doesn't like, he gets crotchety, his growls transforming into perceptible words and phrases like 'rollicks' and 'bugger off.'

"Bollocks, Fraser," Steve denounced. "This is another of your fanciful tales configured to draw us in, before we suddenly twig you're being highly economical with the truth."

"No, no, no," Roger blared. "I'm speaking with a straight tongue."

"A devil dog that *woofs* out obscenities?"

"Growls out actually."

"In theory," Gordon began, "it's possible."

"There's more. You know how owners often mirror-image their pets?"

"Yes," Charlie seconded.

"Well, perusing the photo again, I suddenly noticed Rod bore an uncanny resemblance to Muttley. He's an ugly brute as well."

"What, Rod or Muttley?"

"Both of them."

"Yikes, not the kind of pet to take any liberties with then?" Charlie proposed.

"No. Entertainingly, Muttley demonstrates affection by stalking his owner from behind, then leaping up and snapping his jaws onto his rear end. Rod's had the arse-end of over ten pairs of trousers ripped away before he squirmed free, or the devil dog released its grip."

Persuaded, they all chuckled at Roger's colourful description.

"Rod gave me a book to read as well, written by one of his mates."

"Jeepers, a big ask for someone with supposedly limited intellectual equipment, isn't it?" Steve mocked.

"That's one of my lines, Hunt," Roger chastised. "I really need to patent my extensive compendium of catchy one-liners. Whatever, you're right apropos most dealers, indisputably those hailing from Essex are short of grey matter, but Rod is quite discerning. Besides, it's his mate who wrote the book, and he's an anthropologist."

"So, what's this book about?" Gordon investigated.

"I'll begin at the beginning."

"Oh, it's an Irish book, is it?" Charlie tested.

"Certainly not. It's entitled, *Lama Shagging in the Andes* by M. J Royal."

"*Oohhh*! Fuck off, Fraser," Steve shot back. "You really are grafting to mug us with your singular stabs at gratuitous satire."

"*Au contraire*, my fine-feathered, disbelieving friend. I'll have you know, I've read and inwardly digested Mister Royal's narratives of his sexual activities up the Amazon, in the swamps of Patagonia, on the limitless plains of the Atacama Desert and in the loftier spheres of the Andes." Dwelling, he leaned towards Steve emanating a knowledgeable phiz. "Without the company of women, a man can become desperate in these isolated places."

"Bollocks," Steve inevitably grunted with gusto.

"Actually, Fraser might be right," Gordon averred. "I've read about herdsmen in the Middle-East affianced in protracted love affairs with goats and donkeys."

"Then there's always the fabled Welsh shepherds," Charlie tabled. "After days of tending to their flocks on Snowdonia slopes, suddenly they see a ewe winking at them, and cannot resist a bit of the old in and out, Monica Lewinski style."

"Monica Lewinski style," Steve reproduced. "What's that?"

"Oh, I can elucidate," Roger volunteered. "He means, the shepherd did the business kneeling down, reputedly just as Monica did it with President Clinton."

"Rubbish," Steve contradicted. "It's all folklore, and wishful thinking."

"Ahh, not quite right," Charlie argued. "There's much medical evidence to ratify AIDS came about in humans through woofter herdsmen up in the plains of central-west Africa relieving their libido by slamming the ham into bovines, then doing it with sailor poofs in West African ports."

"*What*!" Steve yelped.

"Ostensibly, it's how it went viral in the 1980s, spreading like wildfire in Western, backdoor bandit communities. Then it got into normal heterosexuals through sexual relations with bisexuals."

Amazed, Steve goggled.

"It's genuine, Steve," Gordon bonded.

"So, all this old fanny about Africans getting the virus from chimpanzees is not the whole story."

"Well," Charlie rejoindered, "over the past thirty-odd years, the science has been subjugated to political pressures from poofter colonies seeking to distance themselves from their incontestable participation in spreading AIDS, especially in the United States. But the crucial certitude is initially AIDS became manifest in gay communities with a proliferation of well-known celebrity shirt-lifters like Freddie Mercury, Rock Hudson and Liberace admitting they had the disease."

"No smoke without fire, hey," Steve postulated. "But how?"

"Evidently, the virus does exist in chimpanzees, and African tribesmen slay them for food. If the tribesman is cut whilst hunting, and receives an infected slash of chimpanzee body juices into his bloodstream, the HIV enters his entire system incorporating his reproductive glands. If the tribesman is also a herdsman and a butt pirate, when he has his evil way with a bovine, the object of his lust acts as a carrier and incubator for the AIDS virus. If the unfortunate beast is also raped by another butt pirate herdsman, the rapist is then injected with the virus, and so the chain reaction proceeds."

"All the way down to the ports, and across the oceans?"

"No quibble, Steve. Contagion into normal people through sexual acts, blood transfusions and infected needles followed. Most people can't stand woofters because they deny they're responsible for the worldwide epidemic."

"Well, that settles it," Steve affirmed. "I won't be taking the family to the monkey house at Chessington Zoo again."

His companions burst into hysterical cackling.

"Steve…" Roger stammered out between laughs. "You're priceless."

"Well," he grumpily bayed. "No point in taking any chances," the refrain making them laugh even more.

Coming down from merriment, Charlie exposed with authority, "seriously though, AIDS should not be underestimated. Though it has faded from its news height of the 1990s, it hasn't gone away. The pity is, prominent gay men still refuse to take responsibility for its unbridled spread, and don't advise their brethren to take precautions. And of course, rear gunners have gained a voice through positive discrimination, guaranteeing woofters are awarded paramount standings, notably in the media, so their axiomatic role in the spread of AIDS is never broached."

"Yes, positive discrimination and quotas always results in the warts being hidden," Gordon professed, "and the truth locked away."

"Definitely," Steve bolstered. "Albeit, I don't mind shirt lifters, so long as they're discreet about it, and don't ram it down our throats like those twats Graham Norton and Alan Carr, but I do—"

"You wouldn't be tolerant, if you'd seen or heard what I experienced in the Caymans," Roger precipitously raged, cutting Steve off, the Montez-rent boy incident still fresh in his memory. Straightaway, he realised he shouldn't have let the cat out of the bag.

"What, Roger?" frisked a fascinated Gordon.

"Oh…nothing…forget it," he pleaded.

"One of your trouble-shooter escapades got out of hand, did it?" Charlie posed.

"You know I can't talk about those dealings," Roger repulsed. "Please—" He made an anguished face. "Just do me a favour, and forget it."

Steve, Gordon and Charlie glinted at each other.

"Okay, young Fraser, we'll desist," Steve complied, "but—" He scintillated wickedly at Gordon and Charlie. "You're not going all ambidextrous on us, are you, batting both ways?"

"*Absolutely fucking not*, Hunt," Roger quacked with vitriol. "I am, always have been, and always will be, a red-blooded alpha male porking nothing but female flesh."

"Roger, Hunt is only winding you up" Gordon deftly pledged. "He didn't mean anything by it."

Acknowledging he had overreacted, Roger conceded, "my sincere apologies gentlemen. Sorry, Steve, you just hit a raw nerve. You see—" Deciding to come partially clean, he licked his drying lips. "I saw…rather I heard something, when I was on business in Grand Cayman, nearly bringing me to the point of throwing up like Freddie sick-as-a-parrot face Davies. I can't tell you anymore about it, because of company confidentiality. Besides, I don't want to handicap my best friends with what I heard." Stopping, he traversed around his comrades for succour. "I'm sure from the inference, you can work it out, but it's not a juncture I'd care to replay. I just find the thought of it sickening, let alone having to describe what I heard."

"Message received and understood, good buddy" Steve reciprocated. "Now, where were we?"

"Talking about devil dogs and lama shagging in the Andes," Charlie recollected.

"Hey, talking about shag-meisters, I forgot to tell you guys," began a glistening Gordon, "I bumped into the Biter the other day."

"You mean, Michael Swerving?" Roger queried.

"The very same."

"I've not seen Swerving since an incident comprising a feather duster, whipped cream and a dolly with huge sweater stretchers." Jolted by his recall content, Roger's companions bred circumspect bores. Registering their perplexity, he caveated, "don't ask…it'd take too long to explicate, other than to say, he needed a bit of Fergie time."

"*Fergie time*," Charlie recapitulated, fazed by the unfamiliar term.

"You know, Alex Ferguson, the charmless Celtic nerk managing Newton Heath, aka, Manchester United."

"And so?" Charlie persisted.

"Fergie time is the period added on after injury time, enabling Newton Heath to either draw or win a match. Fergie time goes on until either outcome occurs. Similarly, Swerving employed Fergie time to wind-up his lurid predilection."

"Wasn't Swerving also known as 'Bald Buster'?" Steve advanced.

"Yeah, came about when Bob Tumen—"

"You mean, he who liked his conquests to have a wet schnozzle, preferably be on four legs, exude a penchant for Winalot, and above all, exhibit floppy ears to facilitate his fellatio requirements?"

"Yes."

"Wasn't he once caught with a cocker spaniel on the end of his hampton?"

"Yes again."

"He once told me, Deep Purple's *Black Night* was on ode to a nodder manufacturer."

"In what way?"

"Apparently, the lyrics convey the theme of a reckless seducer wearing a 'Black Night' branded nodder to prevent his seed from spreading far and wide."

"And you *believed* him?"

"Seemed feasible at the time."

"Right." Depleted by abject disbelief, Roger shook his bonce. "Anyway, Bob kept on teasing him about his non-existent receding hairline," Roger defined. "He'd hoist a paw to shade his sight and say to the Biter, 'the light reflecting off your bald spot is blinding me.' I knew Michael before I met Bob, and when I originally witnessed him winding up the Biter, I thought, this guy is either very brave, or very stupid."

"Why?" Charlie sought.

"Because the Biter was, and probably still is, a black belt karate grandmaster. He has the proficiency to kill with a single stroke of his knife-like hand."

"I can't remember," Gordon testified, "why was he called the Biter."

"Ahh, I can shed some light as to why," Roger upheld. "Michael always had a gargantuan sexual appetite. According to Bob, he was constantly picking out pubic hair from between his teeth after marathon sessions of cunnilingus."

"*Yuck*," Gordon howled, "I've never been keen on oral copulation. Pussies are strictly for poking, not making inspections at extremely close quarters."

"Damien Chapple said the exact same thing to me when Corinthians played Crusaders last autumn."

Grinning, Gordon explored, "wasn't Michael also known as 'Headboard Swerving'?"

"Yes," Roger articulated. "Bob suspected Michael had got his mythical bald patch from slamming his crown against the bed headboard during rampant acts of hiding the bishop, hence 'Headboard Swerving.'"

Steve giggled. "So, how's the Biter doing, Gordon?"

"Just fine, he's got a lovely wife, two offspring, and has become a retailer of FMCG and domestic goods."

"You mean, he's a shopkeeper?" Charlie drawled.

"Yep. I bumped into him in Barclays Bank Maidstone, making a cash deposit of his takings from his business in Harrietsham."

"How did he look?" Roger petitioned.

"Well, the legendary bald spot is still non-existent, and judging by his finely-honed physique, he's still a black-belt grandmaster."

"Still a double-hard bastard then."

"Yeah, bullets would bounce off him. I think *Iron Man* was modelled on the Biter's impregnable exterior."

"Just returning to Bob, I'm thinking with his fondness for dogs, you'd better put him in touch with your mate Rod," Steve advised. "See if he fancies a blowjob session with Muttley's jaws fastened about his tallywhacker!"

~ * ~

Mid-afternoon, Roger went home feeling pleased with the Hazelwood & District Gentlemen's Club outing, particularly the general reinforcement of camaraderie with his friends.

"Roger," Charlotte called as she heard the front door shutting.

"Yes, dear," he light heartedly replied, still feeling high on sherbet over-ingestion and the stimulating if not controversial parley.

"BT is trying to fleece us again," she announced.

Charlotte referred to the Frasers annual broadband service contract renewal falling between quarterly billing tolls, BT's billing division presupposing because the contract had not been revived, the special discount no longer applied, and thus exerted the full whack for the supply. If refreshed, a rebate accrued for broadband consumables on the hereinafter quarterly bill.

Not significant, the cost delta amounted to twenty-pounds, but multiplied by the tens of millions of BT consumers pirated by the same irregularity, the accumulated sum tallied to perhaps a £200million tax-free loan per quarter, BT choosing to either invest in short term placements or to featherbed their running costs, before repatriating the overburden to punters.

Deciding the practice was wholly unacceptable, verging on illegal, for the past six years Roger had an annual dialogue with BT, along the lines of syncing the broadband renewal contract with the billing application, so users were not fleeced. He argued every other business embracing other telco providers could manage this extremely simple act, so what was BT's excuse for not being able to do it?

Without exception, BT certified it'd not happen again, but Charlotte's announcement signalled for the seventh year in a row BT had reneged on its promise.

"Oh, no," Roger jabbered, his hackles rising. "*Ridiculous*. If The Firm behaved in such a way, and our clients complained about us making unjustified upfront charges, we'd soon come under the beady-eye of the SEC."

"Quite, but BT think they can get away with it."

"What makes it even harsher," Roger bleated, "is they levy a five pound billing processing fee, when the cost of handling each payment is less than a penny, and every other utility builds billing costs into fixed charges. I've always been a BT advocate, but maybe we ought to pour over some other telco vendors, like Richard Branson's Virgin."

Clearly frustrated, Charlotte conveyed, "I called the BT customer care centre, but they couldn't wait to hand me off to the complaints department, rather than taking responsibility for operational failings."

"What compounds it, is the telco ombudsman must surely know about this underhand practice, and condones it."

"So, what do you intend to do about it?" she menacingly demanded, arms folded and tapping her foot.

Before he could answer, Heather parachuted into the scene. "Is Daddy going to get into a fight with BT again?"

"Yes, my little darling," he validated. "Your father will have to strap on his suit of armour and take on the mighty British Telecom leviathan."

"Daddy, when you last did that, you ended up screaming down the phone line."

"Yes, I know, darling, but as your mother will agree, there is a principle at stake here."

"What does that mean?"

"It means, Heather," her mother began, "I'll have to get the tranquilizers out for your father after he's done battle with BT."

"So, Daddy will become a drug taker?" Heather pushed.

Puzzled, Roger discharged a curious puss at his daughter. "No…what makes you think I'd become a drug taker, if Mummy dispensed a few tranquilizer pills for me?"

"Well, I overheard Mummy talking to one of her friends who loses her temper, and she takes lots of tranquilizers, and one of Mummy's other friends said she was heading for the funny farm." Staring at her mother blankly, she augmented, "will Daddy also be heading for the funny farm?"

Withal nonplussed, Roger hit his wife with a blank pout.

"She's talking about Penelope Packard," Charlotte clarified. "Francine Mallory thinks she is close to the edge."

Another of Charlotte's zany friends from the local tech's arts & crafts class, Penelope Packard had been re-christened Penelope Pitstop by Roger after the *Wacky Races* racer, because she was always excusing herself to go to the bathroom as she put it. Whether to take a leak, drop a few PCP pills or devour a line of coc, people could only speculate, but on several occasions Charlotte had pointed to her honker indicating Penelope needed to wipe her own nasal appendage.

At one social event, James had debated why she needed a bath every five minutes, only to be told by his mother, the term implied Penelope was going to the ladies' room. 'To powder her nose?' James devilishly promoted, much to his father's exhilaration. Convinced Penelope had a throng of drug dependencies, and some form of recreational white powder had become her enduring need, Roger had tarried sure of a price being paid eventually.

Knowing it presented a major ordeal to her sensibilities, inducing her to spend hours in the bathroom, Penelope had declined her invitation to the Fraser's 2011 summer garden fete. Accommodating her, Charlotte had not investigated as to the specific compulsion, but assumed Miss Pitstop would find the cut and thrust of some of her husband's friends just too taxing. She'd also been invited to the Woodrow's Halloween horror show, but again refused on the reckoning coming *mano a mano* with ghosts and goblins could send her completely Tonto.

Converse to popular opinion, Alan Mallory, husband to Francine and one of Roger's best friends, suggested Penelope Pitstop just might be a faker, and the elephantine intake of drugs she apparently polished off was a facade to cover up her social interaction inhibitions. 'It's not angel dust traces around her snoot,' he had insisted on more than one occasion, 'it's baking powder.' His dictum had some credibility. For someone making so many trips to the bathroom, Miss Pitstop had none of the usual heavy drug user tell-tale signs, such as sallow skin, overly dilated pupils, sudden mood changes and a proclivity for non-stop sex. Roger thought she either had the constitution of Keith Richards, her body virtually immune to drug ravages, or indeed as Alan maintained, she feigned it to conceal her social exchange short-comings.

"Ahh, Penelope has indulged in too much angel dust?" Roger postulated.

"Roger," his wife admonished. "Not in front of Heather."

Wait for it, thought Roger to himself, *here it comes*.

"Daddy…what's angel dust?"

"It's erm…"

"Is it bad?"

"Yes, it's almost as bad as a dog with Tourette's."

Chapter 12: Nedstock

Delegated to attend a meeting with chemical company giant A. B. Garwood plc at their Carlisle HQ, Fraser and pension fund manager Oscar Giddins had elected to travel by train. Garwood were expanding their business in both the UK and abroad with a series of new developments and acquisitions. Like for private equity investors, chemical companies were also particularly attractive to pension fund clients, because their relative stability insured longevity on both investment capital and returns, hence Giddins appropriation for the trip.

Fraser's enmeshment was a little less clear, at least to him. Unequivocally, from an analysts' perspective, his wide portfolio of verticals did encompass some chemical companies, and over the years he had gained some inside knowledge via Brother Colin's career in the chemical industry, and to a lesser extent from his cousin Barry, a stalwart of the biotech's and pharmaceuticals. However, the foremost radix why Fraser became assigned laid in the verity usual A. B. Garwood analyst and MCC life-long member Dennis Passmore had to perform PR duty, taking a prominent member of the Dutch Embassy around the hallowed halls of Lord's Cricket Ground.

"Do you know, this journey takes three hours and twenty minutes," Giddins remarked as The Firm's team took their allocated-in-advance seats in first-class.

"I do. And your point?"

"In the same period, we could fly to Bucharest or Sofia."

"If you're intimating rail travel is slow in the UK, I concur. We could have flown to Manchester Ringway and hired a car to get to Carlisle, but the end-to-end duration would be more than three hours and twenty minutes, preeminently because of all the check-in and deplaning rigmarole at Heathrow and Ringway."

"True."

Focusing on the business, Fraser commented, "this A. B. Garwood plc requirement seems pretty straight forward. Call me a counterfeit doubter if I'm wrong, Oscar, but after examining the investment profile, I can't see any show stoppers or bear traps."

"Yes, it does look like a banker without warts," Giddins concurred, withdrawing the investment file from his briefcase. "However, we both know face to face meetings often bring out unforeseen quandaries, so let's not count our chickens. Oh—" Lingering, he lowered the papers he thumbed through. "I take it Mitch Mansfield will be providing investment assessor amenities, Roger?"

"No. I requested his participation based on his knowledge of the chemical industry from Roslyn Joyce, but he's incapacitated right now?"

"How?"

"He's suffering from temporary tennis elbow."

"Too much racket sport?"

"Too much self-abuse," Fraser established, raising his eyebrows. "Roslyn is fielding Robin Asquith."

Astounded, Giddins threw him a skewed sulk. "I thought Asquith suffered from permanent tennis elbow."

"He did, but now he's got a girlfriend to exercise his prerogative, if you take my meaning, the impediment has waned."

Just before the train pulled out of Euston, a man dressed like a 1950s spiv, replete with snazzy moustache, *Signal*-white teeth and wearing a wide pinstripe, two-piece suit, two-tone crocodile shoes and a Homburg, took his seat opposite Fraser and Giddins.

"Mornin' gents," he trilled in a broad cockney accent. "Larry Leggett's the name. Beautiful day for feedin' the ducks, innit. Think I'll get meself somethin' from the dining car. I 'aven't had brekkie yet. Back in a jiffy."

"Yes, good morning, Mister Leggett," Fraser convivially interchanged, smirking as the verbose traveller made his way along the aisle.

"Good grief," Giddins exclaimed. "What was that?"

"If I didn't know better, I'd swear Boycie from *Only Fools and Horses* will be joining us for the journey north."

"I've not seen anything like that out in public since I was a boy," Giddins brought to mind. "And it was in *Dad's Army*."

"Actually, I've just remembered another Boycie incarnation juncture."

"Go on."

"Three summers ago, Charlotte and I rented the *Villa da Como de Grande* with friends at Lake Como while we toured the Italian lakes. We'd hired a Mercedes Benz Viano MPV, not dissimilar to the one we own, from Europcar at Milan Malpensa Airport to ferry us around. I was tasked with returning the vehicle to Europcar on return to Malpensa. I'd finished my transaction when the doors to the Europcar branch burst open and in walked a family of six led by a spit and image replica of Boycie. He wanders up to the customer counter and says to the attendant in a broad South London accent, 'oi mate, got a mota?' Wobbling his pate he replies, '*mi scusi.*' 'Got a mota, mate?' Boycie repeats holding an imaginary steering wheel in both hands and manoeuvring it, 'you, know, brumm, brumm?' The *aide-de-camp* dropped into a perplexed condition, so I decided to play the Christian and help him out. I said in my broken Italian, '*mi scusi signore, il signore vuole noleggiare un'automobile.*' Boysie looks at me all indignant and says, 'yeah that's what I said, a mota!"

"Jesus, I can just imagine it. Wonderful stuff, Roger."

"Oh, by the way, before I forget," Fraser pressured, becoming serious, "what's your opinion of Miranda Payton?"

"Our illustrious female dealer? Well, one of them."

"Yes."

"I muster from sources in the know, she's a sublime shag, but in terms of business savvy, for a trader, she's a little short of instinct, and—" Derisively, he curled his upper lip. "She gets on my tits!"

"Hah! Prove the theory and disclose the evidence."

"Very funny, Roger."

"Come on, why?"

"Every time I see her, she's either faffing about applying

cosmetics or quaffing up her hair, when she should be rampaging through the business A to Z looking for new clients."

"Yes, that has not gone unnoticed in other quarters."

"Anyway, why do you ask?"

"Henry Jacques has pressed me to recommend someone to take on the Buchanan-Elston account before he goes to Ricky and suggests the candidate."

"Oh I see. What about Lance Brisket? He always strikes me as being astute."

"He ingests too much Columbian marching powder."

"What?

"Coc."

"Ah, yes. He does seem hypnotised by white line fever."

"I agree he's perspicacious and in this contemporary age of less than Einstein-like bullpen inhabitants, even intelligent, but running off to the gents every five minutes and reappearing ersatz he's had an accident with a tin of talcum powder equates with a no-no for interfacing with the Mister Cleans' at Buchanan-Elston."

"Alright, how about Austin Franks?"

Fraser sucked in breath. "Bit too ponsified. He even makes sisters Beavis and Butthead appear masculine in comparison. I know it's unintentional, but the odd way he dresses, walks and even talks, could soon incur the indignation of Buchanan-Elston. I've mulled over advocating other old-school candidates, but most are maxed-out already, or for various reasons I don't think the client would be comfortable with them."

"Phew, a Catch-22 then."

"Yes." He grimaced. "Now I'm thinking, I'll have to give sincere consideration to the Essex barrow boy fraternity."

"That's really scraping the barrel. I mean, if Miranda, Lance and Austin don't fit the bill, what would Buchanan-Elston make of the likes of Lawrence Springs and Brendan Kirkman?"

"Good point. Only recently, someone requisitioned me to label the Essex brigade traders. The best I came up with was rough, blurry, fast, dark. Some of them might be capable of delivering on the client's prerequisites in terms of nous coupled with presentation, but invariably as a subsection of mainstream society, they always feel inclined to live up to their own mythology. It'd scare the client."

"So who are you going to endorse?"

"I'll give it more thought. You see, despite Henry and I being close, I think he's handed me a poison chalice. Buchanan-Elston is going to be an important account for The Firm, and if whoever I commend as the designated dealer fuck's it up, it will rebound on me."

"I must say, setting aside Henry's charm and obvious business talents, he can be a sly old fox, if need be."

After gaping down the carriage aisle, Fraser tapped Giddins arm. "Watch out, Flash Harry's approaching."

"That's betta," Leggett announced, patting his stomach. "I can't function prop'ly in the mornins', until I've 'ad an injection of caffeine an' a bacon roll."

"What's taking you north, Mister Leggett?" Fraser enquired.

"You can call me Larry."

"What's taking you north, Larry?"

"Well, it's like this. I'm an impresario and a rock band manager. I'm goin' to Glasgow to bash out a bargain for my band Fanny's Aunt on the Nedstock roster."

"*Nedstock*!" Giddins cackled. "What on Earth is that?"

"You remember Woodstock?"

"Vaguely, I was taking my embryonic steps at the time."

"Well, Nedstock is the Glaswegian equivalent of Woodstock, only with local Ned bands and a few outsiders, like my Fanny's Aunt."

Confounded by the term, Giddins echoed, "*ned*?".

"Allow me to enlighten you, Oscar," Fraser submitted. "A Ned is what older Glaswegians call a young Glaswegian tearaway."

"You mean, yobs?"

"Yes, yobs is the nearest facsimile."

"And presumably, Mister Leggett, er Larry," Giddins qualified, "the people frequenting Nedstock are also Neds."

"Got it in one, guv'nor. Fanny's Aunt 'ave done very well in Jockland over many years, ever since their singer, Butch Bollocks—"

"*Butch Bollocks*!" Giddins interceded, goggling at Fraser. "With such an outlandish stage name, he must make Kenny Everett's Sid Snot come across as highbrow."

"Nice of you to say so, but 'e's not that sophisticated, and by the way, it's his real name. Anyway, as I wos about to say, Butch got done for grand theft auto, so I'm hopin' to negotiate a very lucrative contract with the Nedstock management."

Glowering with mystification, Fraser prompted, "do I take you to mean, the Neds see car stealing as a feather in the cap of those tangled in the entertainment industry?"

"Oh yeah, theft and Neds go 'and in glove, specially when it comes to half-inchin' a tasty set of wheels."

"And can we surmise," Giddins propositioned, "the female variety of the species is a Nedette?"

"Quite right, guv'nor. 'ere—" Leggett leered, his moustache stretching to form a coyote-like kisser. "Why doesn't a Nedette use a vibrator?" Bemused, The Firm's men negatively quivered their heads. "Because it'd chip her teeth. Hah…hah, ha, ha…hah." Appalled, The Firm's men exchanged disgusted mannerisms. "'ere's another. How do you confuse a Ned?" Flustered, Giddins and Fraser exchanged bewildered visages. "Put 'im in a round room and tell 'im to piss in the corner. Hah…hah, ha, ha. I got hundreds of them."

"That's quite enough. Mister Leggett, er Larry," Fraser entreated. "We get the picture."

"Nedstock will be full of Neds and Nedettes, all wantin' to get their clammy, nicotine stained mitts on my Butch Bollocks." Gloating gleefully, he predicted, "it means Fanny's Aunt are gonna sell a lot of copies of their new album, *Pussy Squirt Death Mask*. It comes out just before Nedstock."

Simpering, Fraser then mis-quoted, "by the time we got to Nedstock, we were half a million strong."

"Wot?" Leggett bawled, mouth agape, tongue flopping out and evidently mystified.

"It's an adaptation of a Joni Mitchell lyric."

"Oh, yeah."

"Forgive my unambiguous ignorance, Larry," Fraser begged, "but I've never heard of Fanny's Aunt."

"You must 'ave done, guv'nor," Leggett refuted as if his act were a national treasure. "Their name wos splashed all over the front and centre pages of the *Sun*, the *Mirror* and the *Daily Sport*, summer 2011, when the band wos arrested with a bunch of groupies having it away in the Trafalgar Square fountains." Pausing, he developed a smug expression. "I put 'em up to the ruse, as a publicity stunt."

"Sorry to disappoint you, Larry, but the occurrence never infiltrated the culture section of the *Telegraph*." Leaning frontwards, Fraser puckishly snooped, "tell me, do you see yourself as a latter-day Malcolm Maclaren?"

"I used to know Malcolm in the 1970s, but he went all up-market, so I lost contact with him. Shame."

"What type of music does this act of yours play?" Giddins supplicated, already shuddering at the prospective answer.

"It's a little bit of D-beat, mixed in with rap-metal, an' a smidgen of Ghettotech."

"I'm not going to investigate what those terms mean, because I know I won't understand, or like the clarification."

His vocal chords ringing with pride and neglecting the obvious put-down, Leggett furnished, "I can get you gents a couple of Nedstock complimentary tickets. Then you'd get to see Fanny's Aunt. They were 'eadliners on their 2010 US tour. Played every venue between New York and Los Angeles, and for top dollar too. If I play my cards right with the Nedstock promoter, my band will be 'eadlining alongside Kojock, a local bunch of right nutters from Gorbals."

"Appealing though it sounds, Larry," Fraser restrained, "I think we will pass on your kind offer. By the way, are Kojock a kind of Celtic take on *Kojak*?"

"Dang, well…" Consumed in concentration, he scratched his hooter. "They're follicle challenged like the Telly Savalas character, but it's because they've 'ad their 'eads shaved and tattooed with erect muff marauder images."

"Dickheads then?" Giddins concluded, his latest slight sailing over the impresario's "ead'.

"'ere, I'll give you gents some free advice. If ever you do end up in Glasgow, mind your jam jar. I caught a couple of urchins in the Gorbals with their paws all over my vintage '59 caddie. Had to give them a seeing-to. I mean, touching a man's mota is as bad as touching his dick! It's written in *The Bible*, one of the commandments; 'Thou shalt not touch another man's mota, on pain of excruciating death.'"

"Irrefutably," Fraser capriciously backed whilst gurning at Giddins.

As the train thundered through the Midlands, Leggett's iPhone went off so often the guard pointed to a sign stating SWITCH OFF MOBILE PHONES and politely solicited him to take the calls in the connecting corridor between carriages, enabling the businessmen to discuss topics other than Nedstock and Fanny's Aunt.

"Egad," Giddins let slip, ogling the English language-deficient auteur vanishing out of the carriage, "if we ever ventured as far as Glasgow, these Neds and Nedettes would be our *bête noire*."

"Oh, I've been to Glasgow," Fraser confided.

"*Really*!"

"Do you recall the Clydebank development project, The Firm financed in 2001?"

"Vaguely."

"All the meetings with developer Mcfadden Holdings took place in their central Glasgow building. I went up for a few days with Howard Jenner, Ricky Henshaw's predecessor, to finalise the brokerage and discuss a possible IPO, subsequent to the Clydebank project taking off."

"And what were your impressions of Glasgow?"

"It was more the wonderment hatched by the Mcfadden Holdings folks that has persisted with me. Fundamentally, their board were brickies made good, and they thought every investment riddle could be solved with brute force, a bit like Jeremy Clarkson's solution to every car maintenance and repair stumper is to hit it with a hammer." Reposing in his seat, Fraser twinkled. "Rufus Mcgilloway, their director of projects, wore a toupee. Howard and I christened him, Rufus the Rug, his crown warmer moving around his cranium like an inquisitive rat labouring to find a comfortable foxhole to take a nap. It mesmerised us to the point whereby we'd have to call for a break, go outside, howl with laughter, recompose ourselves and re-enter in the hope the mobile hairpiece resided in one place. Huh—" His features broadened. "They also had us going from site to site, inspecting development land. It became a peripatetic adventure, Howard and I never differentiating from one minute to the next where we might end up. Some sites were in existing residential precincts and small to medium sized industrial parks. Others were out in the glens at Milngavie and Dougalston. Green field sites were extremely unlikely to be granted planning permission by Glasgow City Council, but Mcfadden Holdings assured us they could get around the issue."

"How?"

"We never explored because it translated as suspiciously illegal, and knowledge is tantamount to being part of the crime. Besides, it didn't affect the financing from our angle because the requirement was forged in such a way as to render rolling funding dependent on the fruits from early developments, and those were all in brownfield sites."

"Hhmm, I'm surprised The Firm got into bed with such an iffy outfit."

"Oh, in the end, common sense prevailed, and much of their, shall we call it, barely legal ambitions, faded away." Evanescently ceasing, he then erupted again. "Jesum crow—" Beaming, Fraser shared, "Mungo Mcgreevy, memorable name hey, their CFO, became a constant source of amusement for Howard and me. We could never quite make out if he was eccentric or just a blithering idiot."

"Why?"

"He'd table a contentious item for discussion permanently not having legs, and after playing bat and ball with other board members while we observed impassively, as a rule it went full circle, Mcgreevy ending up decimating his own proposal. He'd go from hubris, to nemesis, and finally redemption." Stopping fleetingly, Fraser then attached, "here's another one to confound you. During the flight to Glasgow, the guy in the window seat adjoining me was clearly a jock. When I exchanged a few words with him, I was imbued with a vague feeling I'd said yes when I ought to have said no, and vice versa, because I hadn't understood him. He told me he worked for, and I quote, 'Scottish poor.' So I queried, 'you're involved in charity work?' He bug-eyed at me like I was touched, and reiterated, 'no, Scottish poor.' After pulling a mien suggesting I didn't comprehend, he slowly enunciated the words again, and I realised he was saying, 'Scottish Power.'"

"Dear me, Roger," Giddins sympathised. "Could only happen to you."

"Quite. Oh, and by the way, on the esoteric stratum, I found Glasgow to be fascinating."

"In what respect?"

"It's very different from fashionable London but has a pizzazz all of its own. The people are lively, spry to use a Scottish word. They're a composite of pluckiness and potency, and its people that make places. I mean—" He sparked like a lecturer making a salient point to a student. "Take the people out of Canary Wharf and what remains is a hollow edifice, a monument of glass and steel to the financial services industry. Have you ever been there at the weekend?"

"Occasionally, when The Firm calls me in, but like during the week, the architecture is translucent to me, as are passers-by or the lack of them. I'm usually rapt in thinking about whatever it is, needing my attention. If the Lord Mayor of London skated by in his horse-drawn carriage, I wouldn't notice."

"The point I'm making is at the weekend, our work habitat is a ghost town, the structures matrix acting as canyons echoing the slightest sound. Without the hubbub of workers and traffic, it loses ambience. That's what I mean by people make places."

"You were saying about Glasgow," Giddins stimulated.

"It's a little-known fact, but there's no women in Glasgow. There's only hens, and when the men procreate with the hens, they don't produce children, they produce a curious Glaswegian species, called weans. It's similar to Newcastle. There are no women there either. Everyone is called, 'man', and when the men get together, and one of them drops a sprog, it's called a burn."

"Hey, erm, resuming your Buchanan-Elston enigma, what about Jayson Keighley?"

"Mmmm...yes. He could be my recommendation if I can't see another trader being equitable to the client. All that public school, apartment in Mayfair and knowledge of the opera stuff he has on his CV is ideal. However, in his drive to land the big enchilada, sometimes he forgets to dot the i's, and cross the t's. And...he's notorious for overlooking his email. Ricky had I.T Support rig up his email application to announce, 'mail, motherfucker.' Then after ten prompts without him acting, it up-rates to, 'hey motherfucker, open your mail.' But on the favourable side, he's a ruthless seller, targeting the vulnerable, those with limited cognitive ability, the intellectually bereft, lamebrains—" Fraser made a woeful face. "And people from Essex."

"Okay, what about Dorsey Deakins then?"

"What, the author of those essential boy's companions, 'How to Pork Pretty Girls' and 'Doing it Your Way'? The winner in the abstract of the synchronised shagging event at the Sex Olympics, when in reality he's a Jaffa, firing more blanks than the Territorial Army?"

"All factual, but surely he's a contender?"

"Afraid not." Fraser quivered his brow. "He's still waiting on a spine donor."

"Oh, Roger, ha, ha, ha. Bit unkind, isn't it?"

"Deakins is fine for well-defined investment trading, where he can make a packet of wonga without going out on a limb, but when it comes to hedging his bets, even in a bulls market, he's more conservative than an Amish preacher." Projecting an astounded aspect, he attested, "you must have heard, the Essex barrow boy fellowship christened him chicken-shit Deakins?"

"No."

"Whenever one of them goes past his trading workstation, they fold their arms up under their sides to form wings, flap like a Cornish large fowl, and cluck. Plainly, Buchanan-Elston doesn't want their money to be put at risk, but they do count on a substantial yield on investment. With the greatest of esteem for Dorsey, he's not their man."

"I wish I hadn't put his name forward now."

"No problem, Oscar. I've been through all the possibles, and I've still come up short with a definitive candidate."

His facets lighting up, Giddins prodded Fraser's arm. "I've got one for you. How about our new-found friend, Larry Leggett? He looks like he'd go out on a limb to acquire a can of Heinz Baked Beans."

Laughing at the notion, Fraser joked, "yes, we could always get him to sell Buchanan-Elston on Nedstock and Fanny's Aunt!"

Starting to titter, Giddins saw the Boycie clone regressing to his seat. "Ohh, here he comes again."

"*Blimey*!" Leggett squealed as if his ever-active mouth had been deep-fried in linseed oil. "I've just bin talkin' to this bloke up in Glasgow, a councillor, about gettin' some readies for Nedstock from the council. Anyone would fink I wos asking the Earth for Fanny's Aunt appearance fee. Wot they don't get is fixed costs have to be met before my boys earn a penny." Becoming sullen, he moaned, "that's the trouble with politicians, they're out of touch with reality. Huh, you try to 'elp out these fledgling Third World nations, and all you get is a load of old fanny in return."

"Presumably, as in, Fanny's Aunt," Fraser ironically intimated.

"Wot?" Baffled, he then caught on. "Oh yeah, old fanny, Fanny's Aunt, hah…hah, ha, ha, ha. I must tell the boys that one. Seriously though, politicians are always sayin' they'll embrace initiatives bringing in knock-on business, but when somethin' like Nedstock comes up, they promise they'll 'elp, but then do nothin'." Miffed, he folded his arms in disgust. "I don't know why I bother to vote."

"Who do you vote for in elections?" Fraser canvassed.

"Monster Raving Loony Party."

"*Oh*," he mischievously chirped, "you vote for the Lib Dems."

Chapter 13: Mary Jane

On the subject of illegal substances, *vis-à-vis* Penelope Packard and numerous Firm practitioners, Roger and Charlotte got a humongous shock when they attended a riotous soiree given by Darrell and Elaine Horton at their plush mansion set in five acres south of Betchworth, in deepest Surrey.

Employed by Citigroup for over twenty years, Darrell Horton currently held the VP Mutual Funds position for their London operation at Canada Square, adjacent to The Firm's glass and steel high-rise. Fraser regularly bumped into him at investment banking conferences and industry confabs, the two men developing a mutual veneration and liking for each other, both professionally and on a personal basis.

Unlike stalwart Establishment VPs such as Luther Bembridge, others at The Firm and the industry in general, Horton did not slide into the same conformist glove, either business wise or in the social environment. Exhibiting a cavalier inclination to the often stifling and inhibiting investment banking backdrop created by generation upon generation of status quo brass elevated to high office, instead of assuming the *de facto* orthodoxy mantle of blue-chip autocracy and absolutism, Horton adopted an experimental and egalitarian stratagem to maximise the throughput of his mutual fund's division. Some maintained he was a visionary blessed with foresight. Others argued he represented an anathema to the tenets of investment banking traditionalism and conservatism. Whatever the truth, Horton's province changelessly topped Citicorp's SBUs in terms of revenue gains, and he had made a fortune through graduated and bonus salary earnings combined with astute investments, reportedly in excess of £50million.

Fraser deemed Horton to be a breath of fresh air, and a soul mate in terms of *modus operandi* and business execution protocol. Consequently, he felt a kinship with him, often fantasising about Horton joining The Firm with an executive rank and challenging the ongoing schema with his brand of business methodology. Of course, irrespective of how good as a profit provider, it could never happen at The Firm. Responding to prevalent market conditions by employing quick-buck artists like the Essex boy guild in the bullpen got the green light, but it was entirely different to rock the myriad eons of old guard, cast in stone, structure and disciplines permanence at the executive level, by taking a maverick onboard. Independent of the palpable financial benefit, super-enterprise scale investment houses like The Firm always veered away from fundamental change in the hierarchy upper echelons. Fraser believed the only rationale pertaining as to why Horton survived at the Citigroup behemoth lay in the certainty as he moved onward, his doctrine evolved. Joining Citigroup in 1992 from Société Générale S.A. as an equities and debt manager, better known as stocks and bonds, he came across as a model business manager, nothing leftfield in his system to alarm his new employer.

Over the intervening years, he found pickings' income success, the only critical measure of accomplishment in investment banking, often maxed out using conventional business methodologies. To take his spoils potential to higher standings, he took the precepts of lateral thinking coupled with his own inventions to surge into uncharted waters, previously either disregarded or avoided by orthodox investment banking wisdom. When he attained VP status in 2003, his go-to-market inventiveness accelerated, resulting in the mutual funds resources always topping the pile in terms of Citigroup's London setup lucre. Nobody in their right mind on the Citigroup board was ever going to kill the goose consistently laying golden eggs. However, insomuch as never mentioned by his superiors, Horton rated because of his offbeat business slant, he'd never be installed to the corporate board. Having tremendous fun and becoming mega-rich, to him it didn't matter. Contentment and Darrell Horton were synonymous.

Fraser had been to his mansion once before, when invited to a clay pigeon shoot, The Firm's man breaking out his trusty Purdey for the purpose. Arriving, he spied the bonnet of a Bugatti Veyron sticking out from the side of the mansion. Stimulated by the find, Horton led him to a large garage at the rear of the mansion containing a McLaren F1, an Aston Martin DB9 and a Ferrari F430, all glorious and gorgeous supercars admired by Fraser. He also identified a BMW 750i tucked away in the corner, Horton explaining it was the family car, mainly driven by his wife. Fraser could have spent all day marvelling at the array of petrol-powered magnificence before him, but Purdey duty called.

~ * ~

"Do I take it the guest list will be mainly populated by members of the investment banking community?" Charlotte tendered as the M3 sped along the A25, west of Reigate.

"Not necessarily. Like myself, Darrell has a wide circle of friends outside of the industry, and his wife Elaine will have invited her set of friends."

"Have other people from The Firm been invited?"

"Some, encompassing Ricky Henshaw. You met him at Bembridge's Cheney Walk charity fundraiser last summer."

"Yes, I remember him. What's Elaine like?"

"Five-seven, curvy, brunette. Elegant and well spoken. She's very friendly and larger than life."

"Oh, how do you mean?"

"When I formerly met her, she was wearing a figure-hugging, full-length, crimson gown, split to the thigh, *ala* Jessica Rabbit, but equally she could have come straight off the set of *Gone With the Wind.* She has the same aura about her as Vivien Leigh playing Scarlett O'Hara."

"Does she work?"

"No. Like you, she gave up her career to concentrate on rearing a family. They have two boys and a girl, aged between seventeen to twenty-two. Why the third degree?"

"I'm just trying to get a feel for what to expect."

"Don't think of her as being competition," he promoted, sensing her concern. "You'll love Elaine."

"What about Darrell?"

"One of the most erudite and congenial people I have ever known," Roger glorified. "If you saw him in a crowd of investment banking players, demeanour wise, he'd look no different from the rest, apart from his Colin Firth-like pulchritude. But if you had the good fortune to engage him in conversation, you'd quickly find yourself entranced by his rhetoric and how he delivered it. He's a natural born salesman. He can sell anything."

"You're a natural born salesman," she emphatically commended. "You can sell anything."

"Maybe, but I'd concede the crown to Darrell."

"As usual, you're being modest, my love."

"Realistic, darling. Ah—" Roger peered into the short distance. "We're coming up to the turn off for Betchworth."

"If you like," Charlotte generously imparted, "I'll drive us home, so you can drink."

"*What*!" he whooped, terror etched in his aghast countenance. "You want to get behind the wheel of my baby?"

"It's a ruggedised car, built to the highest standards in Munich, as you keep on telling me, not a fragile piece of porcelain."

"But, but, but, I've seen the way you treat the MPV, and I wince. If you did the same thing to my baby, I'd have a Connery."

"You mean a *coronary*."

"Whatever." Breathing out heavily, he flamed an anguished ogle. "You will treat her gently, won't you?"

"No. I'll floor the gas pedal, and have your baby as you call her, going around corners on opposite lock, tyres screeching and scaring the living daylights out of the local badgers." She scowled at him. "Of *course* I'll treat her gently."

"You're not just saying that, so I let my guard down, have a skinful, allowing you to drive us home like a psychotic rallycross driver, and tomorrow morning I wake up to the smell of burning rubber, and my baby looking extremely woeful?"

"*Of course not*," she barked. "I'll be good."

Glaring at her, he examined for signs of a double bluff, but she persevered as sanguine. "Alright, I'll have a few sherbets, so—" He bared his teeth. "You can drive us home."

After meandering through the village and crossing over the River Mole on Snowerhill Road, the M3 took a side road then sashayed into a tree-lined driveway uniting the Horton's Georgian-fabricated mansion, bathed in light from spotlights placed strategically around the gardens, its extensive gravel covered forecourt littered with guest cars.

"Wow, some pile," Charlotte praised as the M3 came to a standstill.

"Eight bedrooms, five reception rooms and all the habitual utility and leisure rooms in 22,000 sq. ft."

"You sound like an estate agent. What else?"

"Twenty-metre indoor pool with sauna and steam rooms. Tennis courts and a croquet lawn within landscaped gardens, filled with a profusion of trees, shrubs, flowers, hedgerows, water features and manicured lawns."

"How much?"

"Darrell bought it for £9.5million in 2005. Now it's worth approximately fourteen."

Arm in arm, the Frasers made their way to the mansion's Greco-Roman entrance, its oak and frosted glass double-doors set yawning, and through an inner set of shut glass doors, the muffled reverberation of the Rolling Stones' pulse-raising *Jumpin' Jack Flash* surged from somewhere deep within the bowels of the mansion. Packed with jovial partygoers, many on the verge of hysterical laughter in response to the most unfunny of anecdotes, the hall beyond vibrated with excitement. Permeating the throng, Roger and Charlotte exchanged a few 'good evenings' and moved on, Roger scrutinising for their hosts. Coming into his line of sight, he outstretched a mitt to attract Elaine. Seeing him, she scintillated and edged her way through the assembly to meet her latest invitees.

"Roger, darling." She pecked him on both cheeks. "So glad you could make it." She gazed at Charlotte admiringly. "And this must be your dazzling wife. Hello Charlotte, I'm Elaine Horton."

"I'm glad to meet you, Elaine. Your revelry is certainly going off with a bang."

"It's absolutely fabulous, darling. Everyone is having a wonderful time. Now—" Smiling gregariously, she set out, "some basic information to get you through the night. We brought in caterers, and they've set up a food and drinks hall in the conservatory. Just ask them for your heart's desire. I promise you, we have everything from beluga caviar to quail's eggs, *Veuve Clicquot* champagne through to *Jose Cuervo* tequila. If you want harder stimulation, you'll find some goodies in the kitchen."

Searching about, Roger queried, "where's Darrell, Elaine?".

"He's in the games room, playing snooker with someone from Citigroup and others from your industry. Do you want me to fetch him out?"

"No, no, no. I'm sure we'll bump into him during the course of the evening."

Seeing new revellers in the hallway, Elaine extended an arm. "Melinda, darling—" She simpered at Roger and Charlotte. "Got to go. See you later."

"Just as you painted," Charlotte remarked, as the hostess evaporated into the pasticcio, "she's quite the larger-than-life extrovert, more like an intelligent version of Patsy Stone from 'Ab Fab' rather than Jessica Rabbit, but I like her."

"Hhmm, you might be right. Come on, let's make for the food hall."

During their trek, they slithered through more groups of very merry patrons, many grinning like Cheshire cats or guffawing like demented hyenas.

"Gosh, I wonder what they've been drinking?" Charlotte supplicated.

"Probably tequila slammers or Long Island ice teas. They're both pure rocket fuel, guaranteed to unlock the most socially challenged, shrinking violets' unfathomed depths."

After Charlotte had nibbled some baked zucchini sticks complemented with rum punch, and Roger had gobbled down enough mini spinach artichoke dip bites, buffalo chicken meatballs and cranberry feta pinwheels, washed down with *Hawaiian Redneck* to temporarily expand his waistline by six inches, they were all set to seek out Darrell in the games room on the south side of the mansion.

Taking a couple of glasses of *Veuve Clicquot* with them, and after negotiating a congregation of people gyrating away like monkeys on speed to The Pixies *Where is My Mind* in the morning room's converted dance floor, they passed through an interconnecting door into the games room.

"Roger," Darrell greeted as they closed the door behind them. Quickly making his way around a full-size snooker table, he took Roger's hand. "How the devil are you?"

"Fine, Darrell. May I introduce—"

"Charlotte," Darrell completed. "You're as lovely as your husband has described you." Radiating like the sun, he gently took her hand. "You're a lucky man, Roger. I think you underestimated how exquisite your wife is."

"You'll make me blush," Charlotte graciously burbled. "But thank you so much for the tribute."

"You're very welcome." Glowing at Roger, he informed, "well, since another member of The Firm has materialised in our midst, how about Corky and me from Citigroup take on you and Ricky in a best of three frames?"

Scanning the gathering, Roger acknowledged Ricky Henshaw, Citigroup's Bill 'Corky' Corcoran, Merrill Lynch stalwarts Floyd Ingleby and Preston Gilchrist, Roman Styles from Deutsche Bank, plus a few unknown faces, and their wives and girlfriends.

"How about it, Ricky?" Roger posed.

"Rack 'em up. Let's do battle for The Firm."

Already knowing her through Roger's association with Merrill Lynch, Charlotte joined Jane Gilchrist and the rest of the 'First Wives Club', Vivian Karlsson introducing herself to Charlotte as Ricky's latest girlfriend.

"To bring out the best in the players, I propose we each commit ourselves to a £1,000 levy, the winners to give the pot to a charity of their choice," Darrell extravagantly proposed, his winning lineaments gaining nods in harmony from those surrounding the snooker table. "It will also bring a measure of altruism to balance our daily commercial considerations."

"Assuredly," Fraser permitted. "I suppose Bembridge's foundation for disabled, pox-ridden, brain-dead, gaga bankers could do with a recharge. Alright with you, Ricky?"

"Either that, or we could use the pot to do some missionary work in London's East End."

Perplexed, Roger joshed, "you're having me on."

"No, if we win, I'll tell you about my proposal at the ranch."

"How about you and Corky," Roger ticketed. "What's the Citigroup charity of choice?"

Darrell and Corky exchanged glances.

"Well," Darrell began, "I was going to suggest one of the High Street charities. However, Bembridge's foundation seems pretty good to me."

"Does Bembridge accept candidates from outside of The Firm for his banker's funny farm," Corky enquired.

"Yes, it's industry wide," Roger verified.

"Right, gents," chivvied a gleaming Darrell. "Let's get on with it."

Regrettably, frame one didn't quite go as foreseen by The Firm's team. Having not played snooker for over a year, when Roger conclusively got his eye in, and had mastered the rub of the table, the Citigroup duo were forty-two-eighteen up, with only the colours to go. Ricky cleared the table after Corky messed up the brown, but still eight points short of a winning score.

Parity became restored in frame two, albeit after a trifling lapse, Ricky making an opening break of thirty-two before misjudging his forthcoming red depositing it over the right side pocket, Darrell easily potting it. He went on to score fourteen, before a series of minor mistakes by both sides led to a forty-two-thirty-three score in favour of The Firm's team. Coming into his own with a break of twenty-one, Roger left the colours apart from yellow and green up for grabs with the score at sixty-one-thirty-three with twenty-two points still on the table. Needing snookers to cover the points deficit and clear the residual colours to win the frame, Corky's attempt at a cue ball snooker behind the black boomeranged, affording Ricky scope to polish off the frame.

"So, honours even," Darrell proclaimed, snickering at Roger, "and we have a decider."

"It's been good recreation so far," he rejoiced. "Let's see who can go the extra mile for a win."

"That will be down to taking risks," Corky guardedly suggested.

"Gee whiz," Ricky extolled. "It's what we do every day of our working lives, so we should be good at it."

Breaking for Citigroup, after disturbing a single red from the pack, stopping invitingly over the top right pocket, Darrell's shot brought the cue ball into baulk.

Coming to the table, Roger weighed up his options. He could play safe off the pack and bring the cue ball into baulk, or go for the lone red.

"What do you think, Ricky?"

"You are really on the ball now, so be bold."

"My thoughts exactly."

Taking up his cueing stance, Roger poured over the cue ball, then the target red. If he balls-up this shot, the cue ball could rebound off the top cushion, canon into the pack and spread the reds, making a good opportunity for the opposition to take an unassailable lead. Carefully lining up the cue, he stroked the cue ball into momentum, taking an eternity to reach the top end of the table before striking the lone red, the target ball bouncing to and fro between the pocket jaws before dropping into the pocket.

"*Yes*," Ricky jubilantly whispered.

Unfortunately, or fortunately, depending on player sentiment, the cue ball ended up dislodging a couple more reds from the larboard top corner of the pack, before coming to rest on the left side cushion, leaving the black snookered by the pack remnants and the pink non potable. With no choice but to play a safety shot off the brown, Roger made sure the cue ball ended up in baulk.

Progressing with the audience on tenterhooks, the frame edged on with both teams rendering risky shots, but neither succeeding. Then Corky constructed a break of twenty-four, taking the score to forty-two-twenty-six championing the Citigroup team. Undeterred, Roger and Ricky rallied with small breaks. With only the colours unused, the score stood at fifty-one-thirty-nine, both teams chipping away at the remainder, until the score hovered at fifty-six-fifty-three.

"Black ball game then," Darrell quipped with him to play next, the cue ball in baulk's right side, and the black ball a few inches off its spot.

Retiringly, Roger and Ricky nodded, whilst smelling victory Corky sparkled.

Carefully lining up the shot, Darrell deftly knocked the cue ball, everybody in the games room absorbed by its trajectory towards the target. When it struck, the black ball moved in the direction of the top left pocket, but caught the top cushion before bouncing against the pocket jaws' sides. It finished up about fourteen inches from the pocket, the cue ball having travelled down the table, not quite into baulk as Darrell had intended, but just outside the safety zone on the right side of the table.

Ricky leaned into Roger. "Time for glory, Mister trouble-shooter."

"Yeesss," Roger edgily emitted.

Giving him a heartening slap on the shoulder, he commanded, "off you go."

Suddenly, Roger discriminated that the watchers had moved a little nearer to the table. Clocking Charlotte, she glistened at him and mouthed, *you can do it*.

Clearing his throat, he settled into a location behind the cue ball making ready for his shot. Like for Darrell's last shot, when he connected with the cue ball, paradoxically, it behaved as if moving through glue, before connecting with its target, the black ball slowly trekking towards the top left pocket before caressing its right-side jaw and toppling in.

Resuming the vertical, Roger couldn't help but crack, Ricky lauding, "well done, partner."

"I think it's called a skin of the teeth victory," he credited.

Shaking hands, Darrell and Corky offered their congratulations to The Firm's team.

"I'm thinking you must have had a misspent youth, Roger,"

Darrell gibed.

"Well, I must admit, I once told my father, 'Dad, when I grow up, I want to be a snooker player'. He educated, 'Son, you can't have it both ways.'"

"Ha, ha, hah, oh dear me, I must store that one away."

Promenading into the games room, acutely jolly, Elaine cajoled, "I hate to break up your little cabal, Darrell, but I'd like to show Charlotte the residuum of the house."

"Your timing is immaculate," her husband congratulated. "We've just consummated the mother of all snooker matches."

"I'd like the grand tour as well," Roger hinted. "May I join you and Charlotte?"

"Of course," Elaine replied.

~ * ~

Starting on the uppermost floor, Elaine unveiled the mansion's multitude of lavish bedrooms and deluxe bathrooms to the Frasers.

"We've also got some stuff in the loft," Elaine advised. "Darrell and our sons, Spencer and Wyatt have a massive train set and a Scalextric running side by side taking up over half the loft, and our daughter Alexis and I have the rest for girly things."

"Geez," Charlotte lamented, "demonstrates men never grow up."

"Yes. What do you say, Roger?"

"Oh, I couldn't agree with you more. As David Bowie once wrote, 'we're just taller and older children.'"

Negotiating paths between joyful invitees at the ground floor level, Elaine pointed out the salient features of the opulent reception rooms, vast conservatory, kitchen and utility facilities, Roger and Charlotte picking up fresh glasses of *Veuve Clicquot* as they steered through the conservatory.

Retracing steps towards the hall, Elaine enlightened, "we've also got a cellar. Come and see."

After inspecting row after row of quality vintage wines and spirits cradled in racks and gathering value with each passing minute, Elaine alerted, "I've got one more item I'd like to show you."

Taking them to what they presumed to be the far end of the cellar, she stretched behind a very large wine rack, pressed a button, and the rack pivoted about its vertical axis to reveal a hidden door.

Facing the baffled Frasers, she glimmered teasingly. Unlatching the door, the glimmer bloomed into a full beam as intense light poured out from a secret room, causing her confidantes to shield their vision.

"Come through," she invited.

Inside, the Frasers were confronted by what looked like a subset of escaped exotic plants from the Royal Botanical Gardens hot house at Kew Gardens forming a potted twenty by twenty matrix. Bathed in artificial light from a complex of ceiling mounted fluorescent strip lights, the eighteen to twenty-four-inch tall specimens had lime green leaves drooping from whitish stalks.

Then bingo, it dawned on Roger what they were studying. "Are these what I think they are?"

"What do you think they are?" Elaine playfully pumped.

"I think I'm gazing at a weed farm."

"*What*?" Charlotte yelped.

"Ganga, Panama Gold…Mary Jane—" Sensing she had not caught on, he leaned towards her. "Marijuana."

"Oh…I see."

"Well, Elaine," Roger began, "you have floored me. I never took you and Darrell for cannabis aficionados. I take it, you don't deal?"

"Ha, ha, ha. Of course not, darling," she confirmed. "It's purely used as a relaxant, and for parties."

"Parties," Charlotte repeated.

"Yes, when you arrived, I said, if you want anything harder, you'll find some goodies in the kitchen."

"*Goodies*," she echoed.

"We slice and dice the marijuana adding it into hors d'oeuvres, such as jalapenos crammed with sausage, mini crab cakes and stuffed mushrooms. I've even baked some giant skillet brownies, banana nut scones and cinnamon roll brioche, marijuana forming part of the ingredients."

"*Ahh*!" Roger gushed. "So that's why so many of your guests range from very happy to thoroughly zonked?"

"Precisely, darling. We've always found to aid people to lose their inhibitions and make the function go with a swing, a light sprinkling of Mary Jane as you call it, always does the trick."

"I think I picked up and ate one of those banana nut scones when you took us into the kitchen," Charlotte warily recounted. "And I must say—" She adopted an appreciative expression and giggled. "I am feeling a little more fuzzy than usual."

"Oh, how absolutely fabulous, darling," Elaine crooned. "Soon you'll be feeling like you're having the time of your life."

Immediately, Roger put his glass of *Veuve Clicquot* down then gave his wife an overpowering gawp. "I think I'll be driving the M3 back to Hazelwood."

Chapter 14: Made in Japan

Gratified for the respite from rapacious dealers pumping him for leads and corporate managers setting him life-threatening tasks, Fraser's working day had been going splendidly, until the 'bat phone' rang. From the caller identification display, he saw Toby Chalcroft was calling, not his PA, Miss Chadderton. Usually, it meant Fraser was required to go into *Mission Impossible* mode and become Jim Phelps.

"Toby, what can I do for you?"

"Come up to my executive suite, Roger. I want to discuss a matter with you."

The line went dead.

"*Damn*, just when I thought I was in clear blue water," Fraser muttered to himself.

Ambling into Top Cat's domain, Fraser took his usual station in the *Mastermind* seat opposite Chalcroft's capacious executive desk, ready to be grilled by the equities director from his seated position.

"We've had a behest from New York regarding your trouble-shooting capabilities."

"Oh yes."

"Bembridge has agreed with the folks at HQ, you can be used under secondment to settle a dispute in Japan."

"Was a transfer fee involved?" Fraser taunted. Clocking Chalcroft scrutinising him with bad intent, straightaway he perceived making light of the mandate equated to a *faux pas*.

"I'm not pleased about this, Roger," he stipulated. "It sets a precedent. I'm half inclined to suggest you flunk this assignment to ensure the begging bowl is not brought out again, but such a measure is irresponsible."

"Surely New York has people who can take care of tricky situations, or better still, The Firm's agency in Japan."

"Yes, you'd think so, but your name has become synonymous with solving tricky situations at Pearl Street. As an example of how efficiently and effectively he runs his part of the London SBU, Bembridge is always promoting your successes with the New York hierarchy. Along with Gresham Harvey's Holly Kerrigan specifically beseeching for your inclusion in the Roach & Randell acquisition, your currency is riding very high."

"May I enquire as to the nature of the Japanese puzzlement?"

"It centres on Hikaru Matsumoto, Vice President Global Manufacturing for Fujimoto Industries. Currently held by Nomura Holdings and the Mitsubishi Tokyo Financial Group, lately, our Tokyo combine has made a proposal to Fujimoto Industries to use The Firm for their future investments and M&A requirements in Asia-Pacific. Of course, they don't aspire to take the whole cake, just a portion of it. Despite approval from other Fujimoto executives, the staunchly Japanese Matsumoto is blocking the accord. Shiro Akiyama, the Fujimoto Industries CEO won't sanction the business without Matsumoto's say so. New York wants the impasse unblocked. The board then surmises success will then evolve from our Tokyo resources."

"Comes across much more like a selling exercise than a trouble-shooting perplexity."

"It does, but there is more. As you know, Fujimoto Industries have plants throughout the Americas and Europe, and they're planning to build more in both continents. Nomura and Mitsubishi have little footprint in these spheres compared to The Firm. With our credentials and experience, we can help overcome any planning difficulties with governments, and cobble together a beauty parade of local investors to finance the plants."

"So, it's a *quid pro quo*. The Firm's Tokyo operation gets a fair crack at Fujimoto's Asia-Pacific business, and The Firm's SBUs in the Americas and Europe smooth the way for Fujimoto's business expansion in those global regions."

"Exactly."

"Still equates to a selling job for one of those New York based, high-powered shakers and movers like Dan Lebowski."

"New York feel their big hitters, embodying Lebowski, are shall we say, a bit too forthright with their selling craft. They think someone with diplomatic skills coupled with business acumen is much more likely to succeed. Principally, it's why you've been put in the frame. It needs a sprinkling of your stardust."

"So, to cut to the chase, you want me to get Matsumoto on side, and barter a resolution with Fujimoto Industries across the board."

"On the dot, Roger, and if it comes off, intrinsically there will be business for our practice downline, the one justification I have for supporting Pearl Street's request for your services."

"Of course, if it doesn't come off," Fraser light-heartedly kidded, "our man in Tokyo will have to commit *hara-kiri* for the shortcoming."

Unimpassioned, in his usual entirely tactless way under such grim circumstances, TC professed, "it's that brand of self-indulgent, woe is me, let's all sit around in a circle, hold hands and cry rubbish, that has marked the downfall of the alpha-male." Peeved, he fixed Fraser uncompromisingly. "There are casualties in all business transactions. Whoever is responsible for the Fujimoto Industries account, will have to take their chances."

"Quite," Fraser upheld, recognising while he had made a pithy joke, Chalcroft abided deadly serious, no leeway in his humanities palate for a deficient Japanese.

Backtracking to the analyst's department, Fraser bumped into Mutual Fund Manager Leonard 'Tubby' Noakes in the connecting corridor with the bullpen.

"Hello, Roger."

"Tubby—" He shone at the rotund figure. "I haven't seen you for a while. How the devil are you?"

"Fair to middling. I've just been sorting some Parnaby Brothers investments with Ricky Henshaw's man Pierce Finlay." Making a defamatory face, like he'd been close to throwing up during the meeting, he groused, "of all the Essex boy traders, I'm convinced Finlay is the least intelligent. Just when we need a didactic approach to overcome some challenges at Parnaby Brothers, all you get out of him is an incomprehensible drivel, most of it mumbled in guttural shrieks and squawks."

"Doesn't jolt me. You'd get more conversation in a wax works."

"For sure. Hardly endowed with intellectual brio, is he?"

"Huh, reputedly—" He twinkled. "He suffers from pogonophobia."

"What's that?" Jarred by the unfamiliar term, Noakes scrunched up his lineaments.

"Fear of beards."

"You're kidding me, Fraser. *Rubbish*."

"No, it's perfectly true." Inserting a finger in his mouth and wiping it on his lapel he made a convincing mien. "See this wet see this dry."

"Fear of beards!" Noakes parroted, his jarring transforming into a facade of incredulity. "Omigosh, he's weirder than I thought."

"The bigger the beard, the more severe the ricochet, Captain Birdseye-like embodiments bringing out the uttermost rebound. Ricky told me, one night when Finlay was celebrating exceeding the 2010 half-yearly yardstick with the bullpen team at Brodies, some chap came into the bar sporting a chin warmer putting W. G. Grace's magnificent specimen in the shade, and large enough to hide a badger. When Finlay saw him, he came over all quaking and sweating, like he was being tortured. Allegedly, he said he had to go, because he'd always had an aversion bordering on a psychotic reaction to excessive facial fuzz."

"Holy kamoly, holy fuck, and every *other* mama mia shock response!"

"Since, there's been widespread speculation that as a lad, Finlay was rear-ended by a toy shop Father Christmas with a ginormous admiral's pennant, and that explains his chronic pogonophobia." Pausing, Fraser heightened Noakes' tremors. "I'm told, eventually he had to go see a trick-cyclist about it."

"A what?"

"Psychiatrist."

"*Ye gods*." Gawking towards the bullpen, Noakes articulated, "just goes to show, even the most hardened of barrow boys have quirks and weaknesses. Dang—" He simpered. "I heard he's a bit kinky as well. His latest relationship is with a sheep."

"It's a goat actually."

"Sweet Jesus, even worse."

"Maybe. I'm led to believe it depends on whether you have a predilection for wool or leather. Ostensibly, Finlay likes leather as part of an inclusive *ménage a trois* with his girlfriend."

"You mean—" Unlocking his jaws very wide, Noakes made his bewilderment plain. "He does the business with both the goat and the girl?"

"Apparently so, though 'more honoured in the breach than the observance,' to quote from Shakespeare."

"Oh, dear me. The things some people are attracted to, to satisfy their perverted sex life never fails to amaze me. Say—" His astonished demeanour gave way to a more clinical face. "Before I forget, have you heard Rosemary Harlow is on her way out?

"Her with the Hollywood complexion who works for Herschel Ventura in trust funds management?"

"Yes."

"Get away." Startled by the news, he stepped forward. "Why?"

"Put it this way, she's always on transmit, never on receive. The first bit of her anatomy to wear out will be her vocal chords. She's salubrious at giving advice, but not so good at betting on winners. She's slipped from grace. Her quarterlies don't bear examination. They're so far adrift from her goal, not even a life raft can save her."

Discomposed, Fraser made a diffident face. "Oops, inaugural casualty of the year. Indubitably, you can actualise like a million dollars and have a sultry voice that could coax the Pope's redundant equipment to attention, but if you're not cutting the cake and making the numbers, it counts for nought."

"Whereas you can project like an archetypal degenerate and have the spit-and-sawdust voice of Brick Top from *Snatch*, just like those pesky Essex boy brokers, but if you're hitting the bullseye, you're fireproof."

"Absolutely."

"Oh, by the way, with reference to the Vanguard equity income fund investment you're dissecting for private investors, I've fielded several calls from Vanguard's legal team, appealing for access to the corporate structure. What do you think?"

"Tell Vanguard if they want to get closer to The Firm to dial direct. Going through their lawyers only puts barriers in developing the relationship." Fraser lifted a cautionary finger. "But be careful who you give the privilege to at Vanguard. If I were you, I'd evade granting access to Arron Ingermann, Director of Mutual Funds."

"*Good grief*, he's the one who has been pushing most through the legal route."

"Ingermann has history with Chalcroft. Top Cat doesn't care for him for reasons shall we say, lasting indeterminate. When Vanguard originally came knocking, TC told me to avoid encouraging Ingermann into The Firm's inner sanctum. He's happy to do business with Vanguard, but he doesn't care to court a cosy relationship, and in much the same way I get unwanted calls from my son pleading for money, unqualifiedly, he won't take unsolicited calls from Ingermann on the subject of finance. Their relationship, if ever they had one, is totally terminated."

"I wonder why?"

"*Phooey*," Fraser boomed. "I hear that waving refrain whenever the phone rings these days. Suffice to say, when it's either Toby or the Ayatollah hoisting a potential red flag, I've got into the habit of checking out the object of their disdain via third parties external to The Firm." Hesitating, his review became edifying. "I'm reliably apprised, given enough latitude, Ingermann is capable of pulling a flanker. He's a high flyer at Vanguard, but he got there by slashing and burning as he went. He has more hooks than in a fisherman's tackle box. You'll find his team lives in fear of him. Our darling Ricky, the terror of the bullpen, is a pussy cat in comparison."

"I must say, when I met him, I didn't peg him for the empathetic type, when it comes to deals going sour. He's more likely to tear you another arsehole than wipe your tears away."

~ * ~

Knowing Japanese business protocols were very different to their Western equivalents, when Fraser conducted business in Japan during his Merrill Lynch tenure, he had genned up on Japanese business practices and etiquette in preparation for the visit.

During the eleven and a half hour flight from Heathrow to Tokyo, he revisited the data he had compiled and transferred to his Firm laptop, reviewing the dos and don’ts to seal the business, without contravening Japanese protocol and incurring disfavour.

Landing at 6:15 am, after clearing immigration and customs, Bonds Manager Genzo Shimizu from The Firm’s Tokyo setup whisked him to their ivory tower in Tokyo’s financial enclave for a briefing with his boss, VP Securities Atsuto Ishikawa.

“Were you able to sleep during your flight, Mister Fraser?” Ishikawa delved.

“Unfortunately, Mister Ishikawa, I find it near to impossible to sleep on flights. However, I’m fresh and ready to help you in any way I can with the Fujimoto endeavour.”

“Are you conversant with Japanese business introductions protocol?”

“If you mean, have I bought a memento for Mister Matsumoto, then yes. I also know how to make the exchange of business cards at our meeting into a ritualistic ceremony.”

“Excellent. Let me acquaint you with the current situation and Mister Matsumoto’s profile.”

Going into chapter and verse about the scope of the Fujimoto Industries business for The Firm in the Asia-Pacific geography, and Matsumoto’s particular foibles and idiosyncrasies beyond his published CV, Ishikawa then outlined the business potential for the Americas and EMEA territories, Fraser noting all the pertinent points.

“Very helpful, Mister Ishikawa. Thank you.” Lingering, he assembled his thoughts on the critique. “During the flight, I perused the sales plan your 2IC kindly emailed to me earlier. You have all the angles covered in terms of timescales, revenue projections, champions and primary decision makers at Fujimoto Industries. The only outstanding task is to bring Mister Matsumoto onside."

"How do you think it might be accomplished?"

"Well, we will need to identify a singularity beyond the usual business-to-business horse trading uniquely provided by The Firm to form our key selling point."

"Yes, but what?"

"Reading Mister Matsumoto's file, I see he's a football fan."

"Yes. He's a FC Tokyo disciple and has a hospitality box at the Ajinomoto Stadium, but it is well known he is a huge Liverpool FC fan."

Fraser glittered. "So am I."

"Ahh. Perhaps you can play the LFC card when you meet him?"

"Yep. I also noted, he was a keen rugby union player until his mid-thirties."

"Indeed."

"I still play rugby for my local club," Fraser divulged, chortling.

"Two things in common. Let us hope Mister Matsumoto takes to you."

Standing outside the Fujimoto Industries epicentre of mightiness, Fraser and Ishikawa stared up to where the skyscraper vanished into a low-hanging fog bank.

"On a clear day," Ishikawa elucidated, "in the abstract, the summit of this building goes on to infinity."

"Sixty-plus floors, is it?"

"Sixty-two, actually."

"It's taller than 1 Canada Square at Canary Wharf." Facing Ishikawa, he postulated, "I take it Matsumoto is resident on the sixty-second floor?"

"Yes, the sixty-second is exclusively for corporate executives."

"Figures."

In typical Japanese business vogue, The Firm's representatives were met by Kenshin Watanabe, one of Matsumoto's lieutenants, secretaries and PAs rarely used to receive foreign guests.

Ushered into the board room, they had barely accustomed themselves to their surroundings when Matsumoto materialised, dismissed Watanabe, and murmured in Japanese to Ishikawa, the two men bowing to each other as part of the Japanese greeting tradition.

"Mister Matsumoto," Ishikawa voiced, indicating at Fraser, "may I introduce Mister Roger Fraser from The Firm's London organisation."

Fraser bowed, Matsumoto duplicating the felicitation. "I am very glad to meet you, Mister Matsumoto," he celebrated, offering him his business card.

"Welcome to Fujimoto Industries, Mister Fraser." Carefully scrutinising every detail on Fraser's business card, he then flipped it over to read the equivalent message in Japanese, Fraser having had special cards made for the visit beforehand. Nodding and blazing with approval, Matsumoto handed Fraser his business card, The Firm's envoy following suit, surveying both the Japanese and English details.

"It's my pleasure to be here, Mister Matsumoto." Diving into his briefcase, Fraser pulled out a package. "On behalf of The Firm's London operation, may I present you with this gift?"

Again, Matsumoto nodded and blazed. "Your knowledge of Japanese business protocol is excellent, Mister Fraser."

Unravelling the blue-ribbon outer packaging and boxing, Matsumoto revealed a bottle of Glen Garioch 1797 Founders Reserve single malt whisky. "A distinguished keepsake, Mister Fraser, and one I suspect chosen with meticulous care."

"Indeed, Mister Matsumoto, the Glen Garioch distillery is operated by Morrison Bowmore Distillers owned by Japanese company, Suntory."

"Please, gentlemen," Matsumoto began, indicating at the boardroom table, "let us sit." Calling in Japanese, Watanabe re-entered the boardroom in riposte to his voice. After studying the Englishman, Matsumoto enquired, "may I offer you some refreshment?"

"Japanese green tea, please," Fraser replied. "Fukujuen, if you have it."

Matsumoto gurgled a few Japanese words to Watanabe, and he shuffled out to arrange the nourishment.

Initiating the meeting, Fraser qualified the motives behind Matsumoto's reticence to contract with The Firm, the Vice President

Global Manufacturing replying, as a loyal Japanese, he was duty bound to want to stay with Nomura Holdings and the Mitsubishi Tokyo Financial Group. Responding, Fraser said he admired his loyalty to nationalism, but in this age of globalisation, on some occasions there might be benefits in using a non-Japanese investment house, if that house possessed a set of business uniques. When Matsumoto queried the claim, Fraser sketched how The Firm could aid Fujimoto Industries business ambitions in the Americas and EMEA. Howbeit conceding the point and admitting both Nomura Holdings and the Mitsubishi Tokyo Financial Group had little reach in those regions compared to The Firm, he still needed a distinction to brace The Firm being adopted for Fujimoto Industries investment banking needs in Asia-Pacific.

Playing his LFC card, Matsumoto's features lit up at the prospect of watching the mighty Reds at Anfield Road with Fraser. As an adjunct to furthering UK business for Fujimoto Industries, the astute trouble-shooter also casually threw in he'd be happy to entertain the dutiful Japanese gent at Kappa Corinthians Rugby Club.

After Fraser made a few adjustments to finesse the transaction, and Matsumoto committed not to block The Firm as an investment house when Fujimoto Industries CEO Shiro Akiyama tabled the proposal at the upcoming board session, the meeting concluded.

Exiting the Fujimoto Industries HQ, Atsuto Ishikawa effervesced with excitement.

"Lodger-san, er, I may call you, Lodger?"

"Certainly, but it's Roger."

"Yes, that's what I said. Lodger-san, it would do me incalculable honour, if you consented to be my companion for dinner this evening."

"My privilege, Mister Ishikawa."

"Please, call me Atsuto when we are not in a straight-laced conference."

"Fine. I'm all for informality if the occasion permits. What do you have in mind?"

"We'll go to the Budokan to see a martial arts event, comprising kendo and karate, then on to Kyubey for dinner. Do you like traditional Japanese food?"

"I adore traditional Japanese food. In London, I often take business associates or my family to Benihana on the Kings Road or Wagamama at Covent Garden."

"Excellent, Lodger-san."

Reflecting on his confabulation with Toby Chalcroft, Fraser supplicated, "tell me, Atsuto, who is responsible for the Fujimoto Industries account?"

"Genzo Shimizu, but as VP Securities, ultimately it is my responsibility as far as New York is concerned."

"I see." Bashfully, the Englishman intoned, "well, it's been my supreme delight to help you resolve the problem with Mister Matsumoto."

"Don't worry, Lodger-san," Ishikawa counselled, profoundly probing Fraser's relieved face, "not all Japanese commit *hara-kiri* after defaulting."

"Glad to hear that."

"Besides, we have success."

"Yes."

~ * ~

Back in Londinium, Fraser notified Chalcroft about his visit to Fujimoto Industries.

"So how did the meeting go with Hikaru Matsumoto?"

"He was not quite what I envisioned, Toby."

"Oh."

"Atsuto Ishikawa, our main man in Tokyo, didn't warn me Matsumoto has a physical impediment."

"What kind of impediment?"

"He has a glass eye. When we went through the formal Japanese introduction protocol, it took me a short while to realise one of his blinkers swivelled as normal, whilst the other tarried static."

"How did you cope with it?" he ticketed, fearing an indiscretion might have occurred.

"To shun peering at just the good eye, and on the footing he's sensitive about the handicap, I focused on the apex of his nose."

"Goodness, well there you go, Roger. Your diplomatic caché prevailed. If it had been Lebowski, he'd have committed a blooper, saying something like, 'do you take out your glass eye to polish it?' Holy moly—" He cringed. "Now and again, the New York division can be about as subtle as an air raid." Pulling a defamatory face, his aversion to controversy became clear to Fraser. "Anyway, apart from Mister Matsumoto's defect, how did you find him?"

"Staunchly traditional but open to a coherent business proposition, the devil being in the detail, as they say."

"Yes, I gathered that from the status report you emailed me while you were still in Tokyo. What I'm more interested in is does he have any peculiarities, even weaknesses we can exploit?"

"He has a single chink in his armour."

"What?"

"He adores Liverpool Football Club, as much as I do."

"Ahh—" Chalcroft's face ignited. "So you played on the commonality?"

"Put it this way, Toby, when Mister Matsumoto comes to London to explore financing for Fujimoto Industries business development ambitions in EMEA, I will be requisitioning you to license a package of corporate entertainment at Liverpool FC."

"Well, I credit your trouble-shooter mandate inherently embodies the role of chief entertainments officer as well?"

"Quite," Fraser happily warranted, craftily thinking how he could milk Chalcroft's sanction to get more corporate festivity at his beloved Liverpool FC.

"Anyway, whilst you were performing your loaves and fishes trick—"

"What?"

"Performing miracles."

"Ahh," Fraser acknowledged, near to blushing.

"Perhaps I should say, when you were away, we got word from Pearl Street concerning an imminent change in the stock market landscape caused by the US fiscal cliff debate. Apparently, House of Representatives Speaker Boehner's indecisiveness regarding tackling the national debt is giving the market the jitters. Worse still, rumour has it, in making a play for power, that total imbecile Nancy Pelosi could scupper any proposals made by Boehner."

"Recently I heard something about her demonstrating her complete lack of statesmanship and global appreciation."

"Go on."

"A noted psychiatrist was a guest speaker at an academic function where House Minority Leader Nancy Pelosi happened to appear. Ms. Pelosi took the opportunity to schmooze the good doctor. 'Would you mind telling me,' she asked, 'how you detect a mental deficiency in somebody who appears completely normal?' 'Nothing is easier,' he replied. 'You ask a simple question which anyone should answer with no trouble. If the person hesitates, that puts you on the track.' 'What sort of question?' asked Pelosi. 'Well, you might table, Captain Cook made three trips around the world and died during one of them. Which one?' Pelosi thought for a moment, and then said with a nervous laugh, 'You wouldn't happen to have another example, would you? I must confess I don't know much about history.'"

"*Godfrey Daniel.* Sadly, they walk among us! And, more sadly, hold high offices!" Shaking his noodle at the recognition, TC then continued. "Anyway, Roger, I want you to assess all the feeds coming into the London SBU. See if there is anything substantiating Pearls Street's worry."

Returning to his analyst duties, Fraser embroiled himself in the US fiscal cliff maze, examining the latest World Bank and Bank of England stock market quarterly forecasts and comparing them against The Firm's own accumulated and aggregated records. Absorbed in highlighting the exceptions on his laptop, he didn't notice Brendan Kirkman, unofficial principal clansman of the Essex boy trader brigade, had breezed into his hideaway, like he was visiting his local library to take out some choice quality fiction, not that his reading capabilities extended much beyond picture books and *The Beano*.

Grunting to snag Fraser's note, the analyst became mindful his sacrosanct space had been invaded.

"Is it a quick one, Brendan?" Fraser investigated, gawping up from his work.

"Wot?" he blundered out, as if he'd been petitioned to give a state-of-the-union address on The Firm's future.

Oh, brother, thought Fraser. "Why are you in my sacred shrine?"

"Oh, yeah—" He squinted. "It'll cum to me in a minute."

Sitting up, the put-upon analyst scoured at the intruder. "The clock's ticking, Brendan. Do you want to phone a friend?"

"Oh, yeah. I got it." He stopped abruptly.

"Well…get it off your chest."

"Er…ha." Discombobulated, his mien became devoured by confusion.

"You haven't leveraged The Firm to the hilt with some dodgy derivatives, have you?"

"No…not this week. I nearly did last week when a derivatives stock ran amok and then 'eaded south. Ha, hah…" He made a leery visage at Fraser. "…Only kiddin', Rog."

"Then can you get to the point?"

"Wot?"

Twisting away, he faintly agonised, "god preserve us." Refacing Kirkman, he tacitly gushed, "what do you want?"

"Oh yeah. I've got some commodities stocks I'd like you to audit," he illuminated pushing a printout forward, Fraser browsing it as his phone rang.

"Roger Fraser…"

Kirkman continued to hold the printout at arm's length.

"…Yes, I'm sure it's possible, Mister Jennings…" Fraser convinced, on the telephone.

Becoming impatient, Kirkman rustled the printout catching Fraser's heed.

"…we can do it within the contiguous forty-eight hours…"

Not deterred, Kirkman rustled the printout again, Fraser digesting the statistics as he listened to Mister Jennings requirement.

Alarmed at what he read, Fraser blurted, "*that's a load of crap*." Then realising Jennings might have thought he was talking to him, babbled into the phone receiver, "…oh, not you, sir," whilst scowling at

Kirkman.

Terminating the call, he glared at Kirkman. “Do you know who that was?”

“Yeah, Andy Jennings.”

“Yes. One of our most important private investors.” Fuming, Fraser bleated, “when I see him Thursday week, I’ll have to make a full apology.”

“Yeah.” Kirkman sneered. “Hah, hah, ha, ha.”

“It’s not funny, Brendan.”

“It is, from where I’m standin’.”

Provoked, Fraser breathed out noisily. “Show me the printout again.”

Kirkman complied.

“This exceeds a piece of crap,” Fraser growled, screwing up his lineaments in disbelief. “It’s undiluted, unadulterated rubbish, the kind of stuff coming out of a lucky bag. It’s so counterfeit, it could have been made in Japan.” Stopping, he recognised despite his appreciation of Japanese culture and very good experience in Tokyo, like for most Westerners, Japan remained the sovereign source of technology bad copyists in his mind, inventing nothing but innovating on everything, some of it so tinny, like Japanese cars, their bodywork folded easier than a cheap tin of soap.

“Wot?”

“It doesn’t matter. Where did you get this data from?”

“It was given to me.”

“By whom?”

“Someone I know in Dublin.”

“Not, Kieran Kavanagh from Whately & Waterson?”

“Yeah.”

“If you did but know it, Kieran is always taking the piss out of you Essex boy, stock market jockeys. It’s in his nature, and if you were smart enough to deduce your chain was being pulled, we wouldn’t be having this unnecessary parley.” Blazing at Kirkman like a headmaster admonishing a negligent schoolboy, he censured, “did it never occur to you, the indicators could have been doctored to steer you into the cabbage patch?"

"No," he lamely confessed.

Contemplating the only solution to improve Kirkman's nous centred on a brain transplant, he chastised, "before coming to see me, you could have verified its validity. I mean, why do you think the personal computer was invented?"

"To access internet porn."

"Yes—" Fraser frowned at how readily he had affirmed the contention. "That, and other things. Predominantly, in our world of investment banking, to corroborate evidence from secondary sources before acting on it."

"He's a bastard that Kieran. When he cums to London again, I'll give him some GBH of the inner ear."

"Right, well, I'd suggest you categorically disregard Kieran's little subterfuge. If you want to know the state of play in the worldwide market, come to me or one of the other analysts."

"It's why I'm 'ere, Rog," he plaintively submitted.

"No, that's not what I *mean*…er—" Staring down at his desk, he crinkled his features like he'd been directed to solve the Gordian knot. "Nevermind, Brendan. Instead of me trying to imbue you with some common sense, an undertaking possibly subsuming an eternity, just tell me what you want, and I'll sort it for you." Prospecting away he groaned, "that's my eternal fate in life," then appended, "I need to do some meditation."

"Wot?" Kirkman retorted yet again, his countenance emitting a signal confirming less than average wit and intelligence lay in the lofty spheres of his cranium.

"Ohh—" Fraser vigorously curled his upper lip. "*Molluscs*!"

Chapter 15: Charlotte's Drama Teacher

Roger and Charlotte busied themselves preparing for a short Easter break in Paris with long term friends, Alan and Francine Mallory, Roger's Aunt Jemina volunteering to take care of the Fraser children during the four-day jaunt.

"Are we going to need suntan lotion?" Charlotte polled.

"Sun tan lotion!" Roger repeated, arching up from packing his meditation books in his suitcase. "We've only just come into April. I don't think your tender skin will be at risk from extreme ultraviolet light."

"Forget it. I had an evanescent mental aberration."

Amused at his wife's over-cautiousness, he grinned, but decided not to rib her for fear of suspension of conjugal rights.

"By the way," she alerted, "don't forget we have an invite to my drama teacher's soiree next weekend."

"*Crikey*, judging on how frequently the teaching profession moan they're not paid enough," Roger derided, "I'm surprised he can afford an ice-lolly, let alone indulge in a blowout for his students."

"Mister Emmerich is very passionate about his drama classes," she rebutted, her hackles beginning to rise, "and he believes the best way to bring out good performances in players is to form a deep relationship with them."

"Didn't work at Tania Woodrow's somewhat farcical production of *The Rake's Progress* last Halloween, and I don't believe your Mister Emmerich attended the rendition."

"Roger, I've told you not to raise the item ever again. Tania is still struggling to live it down and I abide unconvinced you weren't part-responsible for what occurred."

"As I said at the shindig, dearest, I was just an innocent bystander."

"I'm still not convinced." She glowered at him. "The unscheduled turn of events had all the hallmarks of one of your sabotage sorties."

"Now you're being paranoid." Self-assured of his unblemished innocence, he cockily stood up from packing his suitcase. "Anyway, so why didn't Mister Emmerich show up?"

"He had already committed to another social function at the tech when Tania broadcast the invitation," Charlotte enlightened as she made some adjustments to her hair in her dressing table mirror.

"Boy, the social life for academic staff at Orpington Technical College must be a joy to behold," he jeered. "Puts my investment banking socials in the shade."

"Don't be sarcastic, Roger. It doesn't become you."

Pushing out his tongue at her, he quickly reeled it in as she rotated to blaze at him. "I saw you in the mirror. That little misdemeanour will cost you extra domestic duties when we blow in from Paris."

"*Nnnrrgghhh*," he griped.

~ * ~

Having negotiated the tumult of check-in at Heathrow's saturated with holiday makers Terminal 5, in itself necessitating Roger to mentally recite some mantras to calm his inner being as prescribed in *Teach Yourself to Meditate*, and then assuming battle assault mode to get through passport control and security, the foursome emerged into the relative tranquillity of the duty-free shopping mall.

"Francine and I are going to buy a few things," Charlotte announced.

"Let's take a seat while we wait for them," Roger tipped Alan.

After scrummaging around like David Livingstone slogging to find the source of the Nile in the jungles of central Africa, they spotted two spare seats in the mall concourse.

"Whilst the girls are away," Roger began, "let's talk a little bit of mutual business. How's life at Standard Chartered?"

"My stars, Roger," He pursed his lips. "It's a colossal topic to give a simple answer to. In my line of wholesale banking treasury and cash management work, the possibilities of both good fortune and disappointment come in identical measure. Sometimes, life can be pleasing, even wondrous, or alternatively, it can be dark and shabby."

"Resonates with familiarity, yet perceived from the outside, in general the financial services industry always has a shine putting other industries in the shade."

"For sure. When the media and the politicians bandy around trillion-dollar numbers, the general public get the impression we're drowning in money, but it's not authentic. Money in itself is a commodity and on the stock markets most of it is in flight as highly inflated currency, not really existing in real terms. On any day, if the great trader in the skies were to call a halt to trading and freeze assets at their current monetary value, over two thirds of the stock in play would be worthless. We spin illusions, pull rabbits out of hats, effectuate monetary miracles and institute marvels out of near-to nothing every day of our working lives, but…" He twinkled. "…both of us know it's largely smoke and mirrors, built on human emotions of risk versus confidence. One moment everybody rides high on the zeal of a bull's market, then the thereafter day some unforeseen disaster happens on the other side of the world, and we're scrambling about in a bear's market."

"Doubtless, Alan," Roger praised. "Do you know, I often envy you fellows who still work in the Square Mile."

"You mean, as opposed to the Isle of Dogs financial district?"

"I do. There's a vibe of permanence about the area bounded by Middlesex Street, Charterhouse Street, Chancery Lane, and Lower Thames Street, whereas the edifices at Canary Wharf would come crashing down with the dawning tsunami to roll up the Thames."

"*Whoa*!" Alan trumpeted, glittering at the catastrophic vision. "You do paint some very eloquent pictures. Anyway, you were talking about some mutual business?"

"Oh yes. Like The Firm, I know Standard Chartered are interested in bank rolling the new skyscraper developments in Vauxhall and Lambeth. I've been urged to test the temperature of the water with you apropos fabricating a teaming approach for developer Apollo & Lancaster's financing requirement."

"Too much for the mighty Firm to handle all by itself then?"

"No. Owing to the volatile construction market conditions projected over the hereinafter five years, it's much more induced by the need to share the financial risk."

"Yes, I was only kidding. We've come to a similar conclusion."

"So, can I get our Mister Bembridge to contact your Mister Masterson about discussing the possibility of teaming for the Apollo & Lancaster business?"

"By all means, Roger." Nudging his friend he warned, "watch out, the wives are returning, and you know they don't like us discussing work drivers."

"Quite."

"What have you two been up to?" Francine enquired.

"Oh, just chewing the cud in general," Alan crisply depicted.

"How about we retire to the BA first-class lounge?" Roger suggested. "I can get us all in with my BA gold card."

"Oh, that's wonderful, Roger," Francine lauded. "Anything to get out of this human zoo for a while. It's very exhausting."

Having grabbed refreshments from the lounge catering bailiwick, the four travellers found a couple of couches with a panorama exposing Heathrow's two runways. Awaiting the Paris flight to be called, they chilled out and chatted about nothing in particular whilst gazing at the air traffic, the metronomic aircraft landings and take-offs near to hypnotic.

Bored with the wide-bodied jets' graceful ground and air display, Roger searched around the lounge, his observance coming to rest on a pair of tall slim gents, one with a full noggin of silver hair, the other donning Buddy Holly genre spectacles.

"You know who those guys are, don't you?" Tapping Charlotte on the arm, he then pointed.

Collapsing the magazine she read, she took a cursory glance. "No."

"You *must* do," he assertively claimed. "They're mega-musicians."

She assayed again. “Bros.”

“*Bros*!” Roger shrieked. “Really, Charlotte. Wash your mouth out with soapy water.” He scowled. “Bros indeed. You’re beholding half of the finest instrumental combo the world has ever seen. Along with Tony Meehan and Jet Harris, those giants over there formed the Shadows.”

“Oh, I know who they are. They’re, erm—” She pouted. “It’s right on the tip of my tongue.”

“Bruce Welch and Hank B. Marvin,” Roger accredited.

“Oh yes. Holy cow,” she mocked. “Rock stars in our midst.”

“I hope you’re not going to be facetious and say, ‘we are not worthy’ and make bowing motions at them.”

“Hardly, Roger.”

“The Shadows,” he bayed, with enough reverence to give any listening passerby the notion he hailed the band with august adoration and deference. “I recall Colin playing the Shadows on his Dansette when I was very young. He’d got into the Beatles and the Rolling Stones and scouted to find their influences.” Jabbing her again, he deflected her concentration from reading a BA High Life magazine. “Do you know,” he began in an above average Michael Caine accent, “the Shadows were instrumental in the development of the early 1960s British rock scene. In their formative years, Lennon and McCartney and Jagger and Richards paid tribute to the Shadows. George Harrison, Eric Clapton, Pete Townshend, Tony Iommi and scores of other lead guitarists were all influenced by Hank B. Marvin.” His Caine twang heightening, he voiced, “not a lot of people know that.”

She flapped, flowering disquiet distilling into her features. “I trust you’re not going to go over and wet yourself in adulation, like you did with Jeff Beck at Ronnie Scotts?”

“Cheeky girl.” Miffed, he rivetted her with a stern grimace. “No, my frothing over with unbridled exuberance fan days are over. I shall admire them from afar.” Tapping her arm yet again, he informed, “when The Shadows formed, bass player Jet Harris was one of the coolest dudes around. Sometimes he played a six-string bass guitar, a feat the peerless Jack Bruce caught onto playing with Cream.” Again, he tapped her arm. “Tony Meehan was merited as the most ingenious drummer of the burgeoning British rock scene, and even today, Bruce Welch is recognised by those in the know, to be the best rhythm guitarist ever."

"Roger, will you please stop poking my arm. It's not a pin cushion. And will you kindly quit your Michael Caine parody, and stop pestering me with your Shadows rock history lesson, while I'm endeavouring to read BA High Life."

Knowing he'd driven as far as matrimonial bliss allowed, he pulled an imaginary zip across his mouth.

~ * ~

Come the succeeding Saturday, Charlotte and Roger ventured over to Mister Emmerich's West Wickham abode, the place teeming with his admiring students and their less than enthusiastic other halves.

"Charlotte, so glad you could make it," Emmerich jabbered, greeting the new partygoers in the hallway, "and this must be your boyfriend Cedric."

"I'm her husband actually, and it's Roger," he flatly redressed, peeved by the obvious attempt at malarkey humour.

"My Charlotte," Emmerich wailed, his tone dripping in mischief, "you are being conventional bringing your husband in place of your boyfriend."

Whilst she giggled at the playful remark, not finding it remotely funny Roger hit Emmerich with a cold, icy visage. Already he appraised the evening would not be enjoyable from his standpoint.

"And what is it you do for a crust, Cedric, oh sorry." He smirked spitefully. "Roger."

"I work in investment banking," he proudly rejoindered, then under his breath added, "though right now, I'm thinking of becoming an instant vivisectionist."

"Oh, dear, what an unfortunate dispensation," Emmerich denounced, smirking at Charlotte, "what with all the corruption and mismanagement in that despicable industry."

Moreover riled, Roger ground his teeth but did not make a rebuttal.

“Now, Charlotte,” Emmerich trilled, “you really must get more involved in the acting side of the drama course. I know you’re a terrific director, but I’d like to see how you deliver Hamlet’s monologue.”

“That’s a *male* role,” Roger stipulated.

“Oh, Cedric—” He tutted. “You’re strictly *passé*. Women have been taking on Shakespearean male identities for decades.”

“Why?”

Affronted, he fixed the doubter with an intimidating stare. “Are you against females taking on leads?”

“Not when they are Shakespeare’s conceived female leads, such as Viola in *Twelfth Night*, Desdemona in *Othello* and Cordelia in *King Lear*.” Wishing to bide serious, he neglected Lady Macbeth in *Macbeth* as a comical reference to Charlotte’s mother Davina. “But having females as male characters is one of the acme PC absurdities of the modern age.”

“*Crumbs*!” Emmerich blustered ignoring Roger’s comment. “An investment banker with knowledge of the great bard. Must be an infrequent occurrence in the Square Mile.”

“Oh yes, it’s become my immortal credo,” he superficially parodied. “However, with so-called progressives like you making a travesty of Shakespeare with inverse gender roles, the patina is damaged and rendered vulgar.”

“Well,” the drama teacher nimbly retorted, “no need to take offence, Cedric.”

Fuming, Roger clenched his fists but refrained from retaliation.

Re-engaging Charlotte, the pair exchanged supplementary lovey-dovey niceties, in tandem Roger gauging their host’s manifestation. Dressed in a dapper, multi-coloured, striped jacket, white slacks and shirt, with a cravat eagerly flying from his neck, he reminded Roger of a 1930s Henley Regatta rowing entrant. *He’s probably younger than me*, Roger adjudged, an immediate black mark, *but nowhere as fine-featured.* Scrutinising deeper, he deduced Emmerich had the same menacing disposition about him associated with dotty film directors and men of obscure and irrelevant letters, his angular phizog topped by eyebrows near to meeting in the middle, a bonce adorned with lobe less ears, always a sign of insanity, and a mass of black hair brushed away from his forehead and splayed about his shoulders, cementing the manic stamp.

Much as Roger considered himself to be intellectually sound, the hifalutin rap emanating from Emmerich bordered on chronic boredom, its content so pregnant with platitudes and pomposity, it seemed explicitly detached from its owner, on automatic, and in a world of its own making.

Amazed his wife even gave Emmerich a few ticks of airtime before moving on, she resided fixated by his discourse, like she'd been mesmerised by a snake charmer. As to why, Roger could only guess. Could be her natural sense of courtesy and good manners prevented her from calling him a supercilious agent of the hyper-pumped up ego guild. Alternatively, perhaps she wanted to stick in his good books, to ensure gaining good coursework and examination marks. But he speculated.

"Well, my dear," Emmerich bombastically espoused, "do have a delightful evening with Cedric."

"*Roger*," her husband corrected again.

"Nice to have met you, Cedric," Emmerich ill-naturedly tattled before floating away to greet new guests.

"What a complete all the way up his own rectum prick," Roger vociferously condemned.

"Oh, he's not that bad," Charlotte argued. "He was just travailing to break the ice with you."

"You think?" His countenance blackened. "I got the feeling he declared all-out war."

"You're being over-sensitive, darling," she mildly reproached, kissing him on the cheek. "You can usually take a joke from people."

"I've only just met this guy, and he begins by getting my name wrong on purpose. Roger is nothing like Cedric. I'm all for making light of peoples' foibles and idiosyncrasies, but not in an initial meeting. It's more than over the top. It's downright insulting."

"And of course." She brushed his lapel and glistened provocatively. "You never insult anybody."

"Only when they deserve it. Here I am, accompanying my lovely wife to one of her highbrow do's, and the host comes across like an attack dog on ecstasy during introductions."

"Don't take on." Aspiring to defuse his strop, she gleamed at him.

"I'm sure he won't call you Cedric again."

"If he does," he spat out, "Orpington Technical College will need to find a new drama teacher because your Mister Emmerich will be pushing up daisies."

Startled, she professed, "he really has got under your skin, hasn't he?"

"*Yes*, and I'm annoyed with myself for letting him."

"Why don't you slink off into a corner, and do a bit of meditation to calm your nerves?"

"Nuts, meditation is too lightweight. Without delay I need a stiff drink."

"Cripes." She kissed him on the cheek again. "You are funny."

Calming down, he pitched a rueful stare at her. "Anyway, is there a Missus Emmerich?"

"There was, but they parted company many moons ago."

"Why?"

"Irrevocable differences."

"How?"

"She caught him philandering."

"Hah-ha," Roger scoffed, "so he's not so virtuous and perfect then."

"I never said he was."

"You implied it the evening you delineated our, meaning my, social calendar for the month." Frowning, he beefed, "you used words to the effect, he is highly regarded."

"I was talking about his teaching abilities at the tech, not his private life." Still desiring to tranquillise his dander, she kissed his cheek for a third time. "Come on, let's get a drink."

After visiting the kitchen and picking up two large glasses of *Chateau Mouton Rothschild*, the Frasers made their way to the lounge, where a congregation of neo-intellectuals debated drama subjects with enough fervour to spontaneously generate electricity.

"Not a bad pad for a supposedly underpaid teacher," Roger remarked.

"Yes, I must admit I was anticipating a modest habitat."

"Perhaps when he's not bewitching students at the tech, Emmerich is a jewel thief?"

"I'm sure you'd like the hypothesis to be right, but I fancy his wealth comes from another source."

"Go on."

"He let it slip, I think on purpose, he's related to the Duke of Robertsbridge, and is the recipient of a monthly allowance."

"So he's a fifth-rate aristocrat."

"Don't be so outraged, Roger. You're hardly one for advocating a presidential-style government based on the precepts of federalism."

"It's not the point."

"Ahh," Charlotte chimed peeking into the hallway, "Brigit has just moseyed in. Come on, let's join her."

"Ohh *no*," Roger quietly groused, "I don't need another jousting session with Cruella de Ville."

"What?"

"Yes, lets," he forced out.

Making their way through invitees getting intimate like packaged sardines, all discussing the finer points of dramatic art between slurping drinks, Charlotte waved to her friend.

"Charlotte, darling," Brigit unfolded for starters, her usual high handedness drizzling in her intonation. "How are you?"

"Fine, Brigit, and yourself?"

Furrowing her brow, as if God almighty had charged her with owning all the world's problems, she whined, "overloaded with perpetually subduing life's difficulties."

Nothing trivial I hope, Roger mused.

Facing him, Brigit's gregarious smile fell into a condescending register. "Roger," she acknowledged before spying away and waving to a confederate drama student.

"Cruella," Roger muttered. "Just parked your broomstick, have you?"

"What?" she cried, swiftly surveying him again.

"Hello, Brigit," he remedied.

Wafting at a tiny moth making circles above her napper, she

launched a laser beam of vitriol at the infringing insect. "I can't abide anything that buzzes."

"Does that include vibrators?" Roger murmured.

"What?" she hissed. "Stop muttering, Roger."

Growling, he curled his top lip at her in an act of defiance but refrained from further verbals.

Straining her neck, Brigit peered over the throng surrounding her. "Have you seen Mister Emmerich yet, Charlotte?"

"Yes, he greeted us when we arrived."

"Extraordinary man, isn't he. Refined, articulate and witty."

"*What*!" Roger faintly burbled prying elsewhere. "The bloke is a king-sized twat."

"Well, he is decidedly stimulating," Charlotte diplomatically countersigned, hoping Brigit had not picked up on her husband's debasing assessment.

"Incidentally, how did your Paris trip go?"

"Divinely. While Roger and Alan chilled out at the Hotel Vernet, wine tasting as they called it, Francine and I took in the shops on the Champs Elysee and waltzed around The Louvre."

"Bunkum, tasting wine in Paris is sacrilege," Brigit insisted. "Here you were in arguably Europe's most cultural city, and all your husband could do was get drunk."

"I did *not* get drunk," Roger strenuously denied, glaring at Cruella. "Alan and I sampled some of the more superior and sophisticated creations from the Loire Valley, at a wine event held in the Hotel Vernet's *Salon Signature*. We did not gobble it down by the vat load, as *you're* erroneously implying."

Brigit spun to address Charlotte. "I see your husband still needs a leash to control him, and he definitely has to frequent some temper control sessions."

"My temper is arrested, Brigit," Roger resolutely defended, "and the only person needing psycho-babble therapy around here, is *you*. Actually no—" Gaining verve, he stepped forward. "I'll update that. What you really need is surgery to remove the bug permanently trapped up your arse, since the day you were born."

Recoiling, Brigit's mouth slackened. Shook up, she placed her right hand across her chest.

"*Roger*," Charlotte scolded.

"Well, she's been asking for the truth ever since the fateful day when she rose from hell to impact our lives."

"*Roger*," Charlotte scolded again.

"If you'll excuse me, Charlotte," Brigit begged, "I've just seen a couple of friends I must say hello to."

Sheepishly, she meandered away, tail between her legs and licking her gaping wound.

Not expecting her husband's vehement attack, Charlotte looked disconcerted. "What's come over you this evening?" she drilled. "I know Brigit always has a go at you, but what you voiced to her was unforgivable. Under all the bluster, she's very sensitive. You hurt her."

Culpable of excessive veracity, he remained silent regaining his poise. "I will apologise to Brigit later on in the evening, albeit what I advanced is flawless and needed to be said." Restlessly shuffling around on his feet, he alleged, "I think your Mister Emmerich is the source of my discontent, and unfortunately I took it out on Brigit."

"He got under your skin that much?"

"He did, but it's not just him. It's the accumulation of insults, and the build-up of derision and disdain. I don't know why people from your social group think I'm fair game to ridicule and make fun of, just because I come from the real world and I'll continue to open my legs wide and take it without reacting." Pausing, a sheen of validation pervaded his phiz. "These meditation exercises I've been doing have made me realise just how much built-up tension resides inside of me in response to their constant digs and slights." Puckering his lips, he moderated, "okay, on occasion I've got a blast in before I'm blasted, but it's nothing hurtful. Fundamentally I'm a nice guy and some members of your playset see the facet as a weakness to be exploited. Usually I can take it, but tonight…" He hesitated. "…it just became too much, and my volcano finally erupted. It won't happen again. I'll bite my lip in the future."

"Roger," she gently whispered, holding him close. "You silly boy."

~ * ~

Putting aside his out-of-joint outburst and confession, Roger resumed his normal good ol' boy, *de facto* individuality, as the Frasers met more people from Charlotte's tech set, incorporating Virginia Loos-Smyth and her husband Ronald, revellers at the Fraser's summer reception, Alfonso Allgood, a clay specialist at the tech taking over from shotgun-marriage bound Pablo Pringle, the ubiquitous Hattie Harriman, another arts & crafts lecturer Charlotte had introduced her family to during their visit to the Detling antiques fair the preceding autumn, and Freda Fortescue, whom Roger liked, and her husband Greg, who he liked even more. Then appearing out of nowhere, Steve and Colette Hunt joined them as they chatted to Freda and Greg.

"*Steve*," Roger heartily welcomed, like he'd met a long-lost friend. "I didn't know you were coming to this do."

"I didn't know myself until earlier this evening."

"Yes you did," Colette chastised. "I told you about it weeks ago, only you chose to park it in the recesses of your mind."

Steve pivoted his gaze at Roger. "I wonder why?"

"Are Gordon and Rachel coming?" Roger enquired of Charlotte.

"No, they're away at Rachel's parents this weekend."

"Shame, if Gordon were here to support Steve and myself, I'd feel a whole lot more…"

"Yes, Roger?" Charlotte stirred.

"I was going to say, more secure." Making an uncertain kisser he then defensively fanned out his hands. "There's strength in numbers."

"Oh, Roger," Freda empathetically proclaimed. "Anyone would think you were under attack."

"Funny you saying that."

Taking the initiative, Charlotte drove the colloquy away from her husband's persecution complex into general topics, culminating in a controversial quodlibet shocking the men, especially Roger.

"What are you reading these days, Freda?" Charlotte canvassed.

"Some chick-lit, some romance. Out of curiosity, I've even been tempted to go for the more risqué, like the LBGTQ genre Farrah Ullman and Coral Kelly read."

"What on Earth is LGBTQ?" Roger tentatively cross-examined, confident of being rattled by the reply.

"Lesbian, gay, bisexual, transgender and queer."

Shrinking at the explanation, all the men took in sharp intakes of breath. Going into recollection overdrive, Roger's mind conjured up visions of the gut-wrenching clamour he heard in Grand Cayman, and the revelatory news *vis-à-vis* Lionel Lavery becoming Laura Lavery at Gravesend Grammar. "Yuk," he whimpered to himself.

"And who are Farrah Ullman and Coral Kelly?" Greg probed.

"They're a couple on the drama course," Freda explained.

"A couple of what?"

"Well, Farrah is a lesbian. Coral started out as a heterosexual, became a bisexual, and is now exclusively a lesbian."

"Strewth," Steve exclaimed, "there must be more weirdos running around Scott-free, than Teresa May has us believe."

"*Steve*!" Colette rebuked, giving her husband a decimating glare.

"Did, er," Roger began whilst staring at Charlotte, "Farrah and Coral attend our garden party last summer?"

"Yes, I introduced them to you."

"What do they look like?"

"Much the same. They are both blonde, well bottle-blonde and tallish."

"Ahh…yes." Making a puzzled frontage he spilled, "I thought they were twins, not—" He faltered.

"Lesbians," Charlotte provided.

"Are they here tonight?"

"Yes, that's who Brigit went off to talk to, after you'd abused her."

Putting two and two together, Roger's jaw dropped. "Does it mean, Cruella, er Brigit, is also a rug-muncher?"

"What do you think?" Charlotte sought with a thoroughly straight face.

"Good…god," Roger slowly verbalised. "I always suspected but thought it to be sheer daydream." He developed a sober expression. "So that's why she is so anti-man?"

"Well, I'll grant you, she's anti-you."

"So, these muff divers, er lesbians, are here tonight?" Greg queried.

"Yes," Charlotte established. "They're on the other side of the room engrossed in each other."

Everyone swung in the given direction to observe the objects of their fascination, kissing and canoodling on a couch.

"Which one is the bulldyke?" Steve asked.

"*Steve*!" Colette berated yet again, jabbing her husband in the ribs.

Disconcerted by his wife's unforeseen admission, Greg rotated to query Freda. "I thought you girls read Danielle Steel and crap, erm…and er, other fluffy romance stuff?" He frowned. "Not lurid tales of gender-benders and back door bandits."

Sidling up to her husband, she disarmingly admitted, "well darling, maybe I'm on the turn."

All the men's faces went ghostly white.

~ * ~

A little later, Felicity Raeburn, another arts & crafts and latter-day drama student, and her husband Judson joined the group. Roger had met them at the Woodrow's Halloween bash.

"Mister Emmerich is on crowning form this evening," Felicity gushed. "He imparted some very witty things to Judson." She glimpsed at her husband. "Didn't he, darling?"

"I'd *not* go as far as that," he judiciously snapped, his lineaments awash with contempt.

Whilst Charlotte and the other members of the Emmerich appreciation society poured more praise on the drama teacher, Roger uttered to Judson, "took some liberties with you, did he?"

"I'll say." Leaning in towards Roger, he yapped, "if it hadn't been for Felicity, I'd have given the unnerving Mister Emmerich a piece of my mind, if not a bunch of fives."

"Tiresome, arrogant, bastard, isn't he?"

"None worse, but he'll get his comeuppance. Despite my placid nature, I don't forgive and forget easily. When that arsehole is least foreshadowing it, I will take my revenge."

"What did he actually say to you?"

"Oh, he kept on getting my name wrong, and implying anyone working in commercial enterprises is an exploitative capitalist, needing to be taxed to the hilt to carry the public sector."

"Yes, he did the same with me."

Jarred by the onslaught, Judson explored, "what do you think provokes it?"

"Probably an alter ego desire to be the alpha dog in the presence of his students."

"But it can be achieved without having to resort to snide remarks and putdowns."

"Unconditionally it can, but being an unmitigated Cuthbert Ulysses Norman Trollope, usually goes mitt in glove with those lacking real confidence and inner strength."

"Are you saying, the man is a megalomaniac?"

Roger brooded. "He's a teacher, isn't he!"

As the various conversations in the group ensued, glass levels got lower and mouths drier.

"Anyone care for a refill?" Roger solicited.

Without exception, everyone replied in the affirmative.

"Can you give me a hand, Steve," Roger requested.

"Of course."

Making their way to the kitchen, Roger interrogated, "have you met Mister Extraordinary yet?"

"You mean, Emmerich?"

"Yes."

"I have."

"And your impressions?"

"My dear Roger, my impressions are so forthright, even the *Sun* wouldn't print them. He's a Cuthbert Ulysses Norman Trollope of the first-order."

"Yes, I said the same to Judson. He purposely got my name wrong when he met Charlotte and me."

"What did he call you?"

"Nevermind what he called me. Did he get your name wrong?"

"I didn't give him the chance. I took one gander at the guy, concluded he was not a gentleman, and expeditiously gave him my hooker's stare."

"The one you use before a scrum down when your opposite number has offended you?"

"The very same."

"Ha, ha…so he took fright?"

"Let's just say, he never tested my patience!"

Chapter 16: Missionary work in Tower Hamlets

Taking a respite from whipping his dealer team to new heights of success, Ricky Henshaw travelled the short distance from the bullpen to the analyst's department.

Knocking on Fraser's eternally open door he ticketed, "Roger, you remember I mentioned at the Horton's gala, the snooker pot we won could be used to do some missionary work in London's East End?"

"Indeed I do. Sounded intriguing."

"Well, here's what I propose. The Firm is always being buttonholed by the less doctrinaire, more receptive East End councillors and council officials to sponsor what they see as good causes."

"Such as?"

"Compensating for the failings of local schools by giving pupils a foundation in subjects useful to them, instead of the namby-pamby, social engineering they've been indoctrinated with. Introduce them to the real world of competition, where there are winners and losers, not the bogus shades of attainment they have been told is socially fair. You follow?"

"I see," he responded, his interest waxing. "So, what are you proposing?"

"We hire a boat, pick up some of these unfortunates from North Woolwich Pier, and cruise up river to Westminster Bridge, taking in London's major features as seen from the Thames."

"And what's to be done with these unfortunates, as you call them, onboard the boat?"

"As well as feeding and watering them, tell them about the Isle of Dogs financial district on their doorstep, and how it has brought prosperity to the East End."

"Huh, it's brought prosperity to some," Fraser murmured, "but little to most, apart from subsidising drop out hostels, daytime centres and social misfit rehabilitation sanctuaries from Canary Wharf's astronomical business rates, all going to the London Borough of Tower Hamlets."

"True, and from what we can gather," Henshaw supplemented, "as well as becoming intoxicated by shady council contract practices, a lot of councillors are living the life of riley on that plunder, voting themselves massive salary increases, jetting off to their native countries of Bangladesh, Jamaica and Sudan on fact-finding tours, and bringing their unqualified family members and friends into key council positions, just like the Kinnocks did with their offspring at the EU."

"Don't get me enveloped on dissecting Neil and Glenys Kinnock's tawdry track record," Fraser remonstrated. "I read in one 2009 Sunday newspaper they'd received more than £10million in pay, subsidies and pension entitlements working with the EU in Brussels. And these are the same preaching, hypocritical, mendacious, sanctimonious do-badders who don't believe in privilege!" Incensed, he got into his stride. "Labourites say its contemptible, even criminal for bankers to be greedy, but it's quite alright for a floundering ex-leader of the Labour Party and his wife to abuse the public purse." Maddened by the double-standard, he scowled. "The same report outlined MEPs received £270 each day they sign a register at the European Parliament, capping their other perks. However, it's abused. Austrian MEP Hans-Peter Martin has filmed MEPs ambling in early in the morning, only to sprint straight to the airport without doing any work. He documented Glenys Kinnock scooting from the Parliament stronghold within an hour of signing-in on twenty-six occasions during his two-year reconnaissance." Contemptuously leaning forward in his chair, Fraser twirled a pen between his fingers. "Now tell me if I'm inaccurate, Ricky, but if you or I were tangled in such a practice at The Firm, we'd be sacked and end up in prison for fraud."

"Quite correct."

"So how come this great nation of ours, has been hoodwinked into backstopping the EU, when UK taxpayers are being fleeced silly by the Kinnocks and their ilk?"

"For many, out-and-out stupidity, a couldn't care less so long as I'm getting my State benefits attitude, and an undying belief, the EU super-state is somehow good for them."

"But it's patently fake," Fraser maintained. "Along with Germany, the UK are the only net contributors to the EU. We're capitalising the lavish treadmills of other EU countries, and all this hogwash about the EU being the UK's biggest market is simply counterfeit. The UK imports ten times more from the EU, than we export across the channel. We're endlessly in deficit, and have been since that total arse Heath foxed our parents' generation into voting for EEC entry in 1973. My mother-in-law, Lady Macbeth, can quote chapter and verse on this oppressive con. Worse still, the duplicitous Kinnocks intemperance is just the tip of the breathtaking abuse of public money by MEPs and EU officials, dipping their snouts in the EU gravy train trough, financed through both streetwise taxpayers and simpleton, brainless nincompoops and halfwits. No—" He grimaced. "I'll rephrase that, quarter-wits, having no idea about the misdeed."

"We've drifted off the primacy, Roger. Let's focus on Tower Hamlets."

Frowning, Fraser stared north-east out of his den window, towards an ultra-modern, shining white, four-story structure in the regenerated East India Docks complex, less than a mile away. "Strange how Tower Hamlets' Mulberry Place Town Hall is the most palatial council complex in England, yet the council whines their borough is the poorest in London."

"It's also one of the nation's most corrupt councils," Henshaw acrimoniously specified. "You might recall television and newspaper explorations into multiple electoral frauds and corruption offences, during councillor political careers defined by playing the race card to secure power. I've also heard via a contact in the City of London Police, Tower Hamlets will soon face allegations of cronyism, corruption and religious extremism. Professedly, in the 2010 local government elections, Lutfur Rahman—"

"*Who*!" Fraser interrupted. "What kind of a half-assed name is that?"

"He's a Muzzie Bangladeshi immigrant. Don't be coy, Roger, you know there's no English people left in the East End. They all took flight to Essex and Kent after the invasion."

"Go on."

"Well, Rahman was elected mayor, but a swarm of the borough's residents alleged Rahman and his Labour Party workers, filled out other people's ballot papers, and smeared his opponents as racist."

"Surprise, surprise, the routine weapon of choice for every immigrant politician."

"Quite. Well, a sufficient rumpus has been evoked in numerous locales for the police to probe Rahman and his dilettantes, many of them Bangladeshi born Labour Party councillors on Tower Hamlets council."

"Again, surprise, surprise. I bet the police wrung their hands for an eternity for fear of being branded racist before biting the bullet."

"My contact says the City of London Police are building up irrefutable evidence. When it reaches critical mass, suspects will be arrested."

"But it won't change anything, will it? Rahman might get deposed, but his successor will come from the same breed, so the practice will endure." Fraser sniffed as if a bad smell had come to mind. "I did read in the *Telegraph*, the Rotherham Muslim gang child-grooming lawsuit is starting to unfold. Ostensibly, over fifty English schoolgirls have been systematically exploited for sex by this gang since the late 1980s, but Rotherham Council has paid no heed to the practice, and the police have dismissed multiple claims of child abuse, for fear of being accused of racism."

"Yes, I read it as well. Beggars belief. Somebody needs to be shot for allowing it to go on for so long. And still the authorities have taken no action." Crushing his dial in disgust, he harangued, "irresponsible PC bastards."

Wincing, Fraser thought, *there for the grace of god, go Wendy and Heather*.

"Apparently," Henshaw shared, "what has come to light through press investigation, is just the tip of the iceberg. It demonstrates officialdom has become politically correct to the point of absurdity, and as a consequence, schoolgirls' lives have been irrevocably destroyed."

"Makes you wonder," Fraser began, "who is our real enemy?"

"Quite. Anyway, we have four thousand for the egalitarian purpose, and I've already spoken to Top Cat about any overspend being sheltered by the slush fund."

"And Toby has *sanctioned* it?" he delved, his vocal chords chiming with amazement.

"Yes, reputedly, more developments are set for the London docks by several wholesale banking companies. Acme investment players like The Firm are devoting a portion of profits to local philanthropic campaigns, so as to build up brownie points when the plans come before the Tower Hamlets council planning panel."

"What's in it for The Firm? I mean, we don't have ambitions to erect auxiliary edifices to house the London operation, do we?"

"No, but The Firm might be the beneficiary of investment capital for bankrolling the new developments."

"Ahh, got it. We have a very large thumbprint in the London real estate market, so anything helping smooth the way for future developments will aid that revenue stream."

"Anyway, whatever we need for our missionary work, will be a pittance in the grand scheme of things. TC thought about it for all of a millisecond before giving his approval."

"Right. So, how do you propose to make this river excursion work?"

"Just leave it with me, Roger. I'll fix the unreserved thing up."

~ * ~

A few weeks later, Henshaw and Fraser stood on North Woolwich pier, awaiting the advent of schoolchildren accompanied by a few teachers from local Tower Hamlets schools and a local councillor, the river boat they had hired replete with crew tied up to the jetty, gently bobbing up and down on the incoming tide.

"Who's our main contact regulating the rabble?" Fraser grilled.

"Well, it was meant to be a Missus Alamieyeseigha—"

"You're kidding me," Fraser interrupted. "What kind of a goddamn name is that?" Swivelling to place his weight on his larboard leg, he charged, "you've just made it up to throw me and give me the heebie-jeebies."

"No, it's a real name. She's from Trinidad via the Central African Republic."

"*Golly*! Is there going to be an interpreter with her?"

"If you let me finish, I was going to say, Missus Alamieyeseigha has been called away on urgent business with UK Black Pride, and Missus Igbinedion will be taking her place."

"Will she need an interpreter?"

"Possibly. Interpreters form a sizable part of the population around here. It's big business for translator companies."

"Who picks up the interpreter amenities tab?"

"The taxpayer of course. Who did you think, *Robert Mugabe*?"

Fraser checked his Louis Cartier chronometer. "They're late."

"Only to be expected," Henshaw merited. "Herding together a bunch of excitable schoolchildren, and transporting them through the juggernaut and bus packed streets of East London, can pull apart any schedule."

Movement in the distance caught Fraser's observance. "Oh, here they come."

"Where?"

"Just emerging from behind the Dunkin' Donuts billboard." he informed, pointing.

"Oh yes." Scrutinising forrad, Henshaw hollered, "holy fuck, there's more of them then I presumed."

At least a hundred children of various shapes and ages came into sight with more popping up from behind the billboard.

"We're going to need a bigger boat," Fraser yawped.

"That's a line from *Jaws*."

"Spot on."

Coming down the gangway linking to the jetty, making it oscillate under heavy footsteps, Henshaw and Fraser counted enough bodies to sink a battleship.

"Need a bigger boat…" Gulping, Henshaw goggled at Fraser. "…we're going to need a fully-fledged fleet of them."

"Good god," Fraser spurted, "is that bolshie Labour MP Diane Abbott in their midst?"

"No, no, no," Henshaw disagreed. "That's Missus Igbinedion."

"Ig-bin-ed-ion," Fraser echoed. "How the hell did you manage to pronounce her name?"

"I've been practicing."

Unconvinced, Fraser stared at the entourage again. "Are you sure it's not Diane Abbott?"

"Roger, I'm telling you, it's Missus Igbinedion. I met her at Mulberry Place when I was organising this jamboree, er educational outing with the local education committee."

"Did any of them speak English?"

"Some. Anyway, Missus Igbinedion is the principal teacher at Jomo Kenyatta Academy, formally Blair Street Secondary Modern, a flopped school put under the Department for Education Inspectorate administration before gaining academy status."

"Have educational benchmarks improved?"

"Don't be silly, Roger, of course not, but don't mention it to Missus Igbinedion, or any of the other teachers."

"Why?"

"Just let's say, our job is to father a favourable footprint of the financial services industry in general and The Firm in particular, so Missus Igbinedion and her affiliate teachers take a positive indent to Tower Hamlets Council."

"And airing reality is counterproductive to the aim?"

"Yes. We know the schools are crap. They know the schools are crap. Even Tower Hamlets Council know the schools are crap. But saying it in public is an absolute no, no."

"You know, all this let's lower the bar so as not to make the untalented feel like numpties doesn't do anyone any favours. Dialectical prognosis reveals it's a sociological absurdity. Dragging standards down to the lowest common denominator just makes England more susceptible to being run over and smothered by the off-shore competition. South

Korea and other South-Eastern Asian countries are forging ahead in terms of *raising* the boom in their educational systems. Consequently, they are begetting the forthcoming groundswell of young scientists and business entrepreneurs."

"Bingo, but don't mention the growing attainment gap."

"I see. So, we're going to play the role of diplomats and ignore the truth."

"Yes."

"Okay," he acquiesced. "Well as you know, Ricky, I can play The Firm's ambassador as good as anybody, so I will turn a blind eye, play dumb, endorse manifestly false testimonies, and in general, lick arse as good as that arch PC doyenne, John Motson, to bring Missus Ig-bin-ed-ion the shiniest smile she's ever known."

"Good. Incidentally, you'll get the hang of pronouncing her name. I managed it after about nine-hours practice."

"Nine hours! I haven't even got nine seconds."

"Quiet, it's showtime." Sprightly stepping forward to evince courtesy, Henshaw felicitated, "Missus Igbinedion. Good to see you again."

"Good morning, Mister Henshaw," she trilled in a pronounced West Indian accent, as the schoolchildren surged past her, past The Firm's contingent, past the crew, and onto the boat like locusts about to devour a harvest.

"May I introduce you to my colleague, Mister Fraser, also from The Firm."

"What is it you do at The Firm, Mister Fraser?"

"Oh—" Producing an impassive phiz he hunched his shoulders. "I just keep the wheels of investment banking well oiled, and the business pointing in the right direction."

Reciprocating, Missus Igbinedion introduced The Firm's team to the other teachers, all women, all vastly overweight, all spouting West Indian accents, and all with unpronounceable surnames, plus Tower Hamlets councillor, Mister Akhand-Khandoker.

With the boat bursting at the seams with exuberant schoolchildren, and the crew taking refuge in the steering house, the grownups made their way down the jetty, The Firm's gallant men bringing up the rear.

"I've just about got my mind around pronouncing Ig-bin-ed-ion, Ricky," Fraser whispered. "However, I'm not sure I can cope with Bab-ang-ida, O-kad-ig-bo, Ani-kul-apo-Kuti, and the rest."

"Yes, they're giving me trouble as well. Mister Akhand-Khandoker is child's play in comparison."

Slipping her moorings, the boat journeyed up river at a leisurely pace, the din made by the schoolchildren drowning out the putt-putt rumble of her diesel-motor.

Approaching the tip of The Isle of Dogs, Henshaw prepared to draw everyone's notice to the splendid vista of Canary Wharf, especially The Firm's towering edifice, but Missus Igbinedion had other ideas.

Grabbing a loudhailer from him, she barked, "pay attention children. On the southside of the river, you will see the crest of the National Maritime Museum, behind The University of Greenwich in the foreground. There's an exhibition in the museum dedicated to the enslavement of black Africans by the white man." She loured at Fraser and Henshaw, the Firm's men exchanging raised eyebrows and pouts in response. "English slave traders sold black slaves to the North American colonists in the eighteenth and nineteenth centuries. This terrible practice saw an incalculable multitude of negros shipped across the Atlantic from West Africa to the American east coast and to the West Indies…"

Scanning about, Fraser and Henshaw recorded the other teachers nodding their approval of Missus Igbinedion's rhetoric. Arms folded and adopting airs of moral superiority, they too glared at The Firm's men.

After consummating her diatribe, Henshaw disputed in the most accommodating verbalisation, "excuse me, Missus Igbinedion, but aren't you giving a somewhat narrow perspective of slavery?"

Scowling, she brusquely retorted, "what do you mean?"

"Didn't slavery originate in Africa over 4,000 years ago, and isn't slavery still practiced in Africa today?"

Growling her disapproval, she wrinkled her already flat schnozzle at him to the point whereby self-suffocation began to make her cough.

"He's right, Missus Igbinedion," Fraser bonded. "You also need to balance the atrocity you so ably described, by telling the children

European ports were raided by black Muslims, and white Christians were taken as slaves for their Barbary Coast regime in North Africa. It happened between the fifteenth and twentieth centuries, until European troops ended the white slave trade in 1911—" Mimicking the teachers, he folded his arms in an act of reverse denigration. "forty-six years after slavery was abolished in the Americas."

"Faultless appraisal," Henshaw complimented before Missus Igbinedion could react. "Before that, 2.5 million Eastern European and Black Sea region White Christians were taken by the Ottomans from 1450 to 1700, and an additional one and a quarter million Western Europeans were enslaved in North Africa, between the sixteenth to the beginnings of the twentieth century." Dwelling, he gazed to the west. "The Barbary Coast slavers used to raid Cornwall and Devon ports. Lord Exmouth led a combined Anglo-Dutch battalion, freeing over 3,000 White Christians from enslavement from the Dey of Algiers in 1816."

Her scowl transforming into a fierce grimace, Missus Igbinedion curled her upper lip, as if sparked by a nervous twitch or burgeoning anger. "Those issues are irrelevant, and have nothing to do with black history." Her rage swelling, she perpetuated her unbridled and highly selective evaluation of slavery, the indoctrination hitting home with the schoolchildren.

After passing more riverside landmarks embracing the Tower of London, the Globe Theatre, and the Houses of Parliament, Missus Igbinedion or one of the other teachers somehow using each monument to illustrate England's exploitation of blacks, the river boat moored adjacent to Embankment and opposite the London Eye for lunch.

As the schoolchildren and their supervisors tucked away everything the crew placed before them, Fraser and Henshaw reviewed the morning's events.

"I'm sorry, Roger," Henshaw began. "If I'd known this river sojourn was going to be used by 'Winnie Mandela' and her black sisters for indoctrination purposes, I wouldn't have advocated missionary work in London's East end as a suitable candidate for our charitable benevolence."

"That's quite alright, Ricky. You weren't to know."

"No, retrospectively," he upheld, still pouring out regret, "the plan was highly ambitious, and totally unworkable."

"Well, in the abstract, maybe," Fraser appraised, attempting to lighten the usually double-hard bastard, trading floor sales manager's misgivings.

"I could half see the connection between some London monuments and so-called black oppression, but when Missus Ani-kul-apo-Kuti banged on about Somerset House being an archive expunging black history from the development of the UK, and The London Dungeon is a jail for black activists, it really took the biscuit. I mean, do these kids really think she vents the truth?"

"Well, none of them are English. Most are black or Muslim or both. They're hard-wired to believe the bullshit theretofore. The teachers' jaundiced sentiments just fortify the doctrine."

"Wowzers, and that liberal idiot Cameron wonders why there's an entire army of Muslim terrorists in every Muslim ghetto in England."

Glancing towards the bows, where the Tower Hamlets councillor shielded his peepers from the sun gazing at the Houses of Parliament, Fraser commented, "Mister Akhand-Khandoker doesn't say much, does he?"

"No, he's only here for the photo-opportunity and to facilitate an official quote to East London journalists. His mind is firmly set on stepping up from local into national government as a Labour Party candidate."

"Evidently. From the way he's peering at Big Ben and licking his lips, you're right."

Yammering indecipherably, one of the schoolchildren sauntered up to The Firm's men, Fraser giving his associate a bewildered gape.

"He's actually addressing you, Roger."

"Is he? I thought he was talking to you."

"When you have to deal with the guttural modulations spurting from the mouths of my Essex boy trader's limited vocabularies, every shake of the working day, you develop a skill to interpret sentence intention, if not precise content. He wants to know if we'll be dropping in at Tate Modern on the way to North Woolwich."

Considering for a trice, Fraser instructed, "tell him, I've been to Tate Modern, and its contents have little, if anything, to do with art, and if he wants to see some real art, his teacher should take him to the National or the real Tate on Millbank."

~ * ~

As the outing lengthened, Missus Igbinedion or one of the other teachers, conducted a running commentary through Henshaw's loudhailer, detailing more Thames landmarks and their function in oppressing blacks, The Firm's men refraining from making further challenges to the highly biased and invariably invalid rhetoric.

"It's hard to tell if the schoolchildren are taking in this dribble," Henshaw remarked. "I haven't seen one paw upstretched to voice a question."

"Maybe the teachers are going for a subliminal stratagem to implant their messages. Incontrovertibly, it works for television advertisers."

Nearing South Dock on the inbound journey, Henshaw and Fraser took the opportunity to give a thumbnail sketch of the investment banking companies resident in the skyscrapers looming large above the riverboat, incorporating HSBC, Barclays Capital, Credit Suisse and of course, The Firm. Stimulated by their eloquence, many of the schoolchildren asked about the money markets and The Firm, much to the frowning teachers' displeasure.

Prior to the outing, The Firm's men had arranged gift packs for the schoolchildren, April Harrington flanked by tactless Essex boy broker Landon Boyce arriving at the quayside, just as the Q&A session concluded. Boarding the vessel ladened with a multiplicity of marketing giveaways such as belt buckles, T-shirts and executive play toys, all embossed with The Firm's prestigious marque, the schoolchildren descended on them, grabbing the souvenirs and making merry by howling and hollering at their newly acquired possessions.

"My, they're an excitable bunch," April proclaimed, disentangling herself from the fray.

"Yes," Fraser backed. "Ricky and I feared for our lives earlier in the day."

"What!"

"Only kidding, April."

"Has the event been a success?"

"Hard to judge. Unmistakably, the kids were excited by what Ricky and I told them about The Firm, but I'm not so sure they were enamoured with the political indoctrination masquerading under a history lesson banner the teachers were pontificating." Hearing a high-pitched shriek, he twisted to see Boyce disappearing under a mountain of schoolchildren rummaging through the freebie bags he carried before he could even allocate them. "I see Landon is communicating with the natives."

"I'd better give him a hand," April extended. "Looks like he's about to suffocate."

"Yes," Fraser nonchalantly corroborated. "He's turning a very pretty shade of purple."

Once the furore died down, The Firm's representatives gathered together.

"I think if it had been up to the kids," Henshaw remarked, "they'd have been highly delighted to have cruised around Canary Wharf, instead of going up river."

"Yes, it's the most content we've seen them all day," Fraser consigned.

"I think one of them half-inched my Parker pen when they were raiding me for the gratuities," Boyce announced.

"Ah, don't worry about it, Landon," Fraser petitioned, "I'm sure with your jumbo remuneration package, you could afford to buy at least a thousand replacements without impacting your champagne and truffles walk of life."

"Just remind me," April investigated, "what's in this act of philanthropy for The Firm?"

"Mainly PR collateral," Henshaw enlightened. "It's why Mister Chalcroft authorised the venture."

They were still talking when a schoolboy tugged at Fraser's suit jacket and mumbled a few words to him, the usually erudite stock analyst fetching up nonplussed in response. Facing his co-workers, he acknowledged, "I thought I had a hang-up toiling to understand the Geordie and Glaswegian accents, but they're a doddle compared to the current brand of Tower Hamlets inflection. Landon, you originate from the East End's lazoonland. What's this urchin saying?"

Imploring the kid to repeat what he emitted, Boyce then tuned in Fraser. "He wants to know if he and his pals can visit The Firm's London headquarters."

"Tell him, ohhh—" Ogling Henshaw, his physiognomy fell into forlorn reality. "Do I take it, Missus Ig-bin-ed-ion and the other teachers would not like the schoolchildren to visit our workplace?"

"Ye gods, Roger, they'd see such a visit as a sell out to the forces of imperialism and black subjugation."

"Shame." He wheeled to direct Boyce. "Tell him—" Glistening at the kid, he reciprocated. "We'll try our best."

Shortly thereafter, April and Landon waved the riverboat goodbye as it eased away and navigated out of South Dock rejoining the Thames opposite the O2.

"I feel bad about not being able to guarantee a visit to The Firm for that kid," Fraser confessed. "When he smiled at me, I got the distinct hint he knew what was going on and his mug hid probable disappointment."

"Well," Henshaw joshed, "I suppose we could deposit the schoolchildren at North Woolwich Pier, then press on to Tilbury with the teachers and Mister Akhand-Khandoker, pull the riverboat sea plugs and let her sink with them still aboard, while we and the crew jump onto a passing launch."

"Yes, categorically it'd bring scope to invite the kid and his pals to The Firm, and in the process accord us enormous satisfaction." Quailing, he substantiated, "until the contiguous set of politicos replace them."

"Yes."

"Dear me." Mopping his brow, Fraser avowed, "this has been one of the most exhausting days in my entire career. I think I'll do a bit of meditation when we return to The Firm."

"Hhmmm, I think I'll hit Brodies, see if alcohol can restore my zest."

"Yeessss…" Ambivalently, he gawked at the boisterous fracas gathering steam behind him and scratched his chin. "On reflection, I think I'll join you, Ricky. Alcohol reaches those parts of the body meditation seems to bypass."

Chapter 17: Quiz Night

Out of the blue, Charlotte pressurised Roger into participating in a quiz night at Hazelwood Community Centre. Unwilling to buy into the jaunt, in his usual inimitable way, he threw up excuse after excuse as to why he couldn't go, all scuppered and rejected by his persistent wife.

"Anyway, Saturday I'm playing golf with the boys," he finally tendered.

"Yes, but the quiz is in the evening, and you'll be back way before then." She dwelt developing a frisky grin. "Your friend, the Right Reverend Reddick will be there."

"Blimey, hardly a justification to attend. Though we parted on good terms at Christmas, I'm not sure he'd be keen to see me again in a social situation."

"I saw the good reverend last week. He enquired about your health and frothed he enjoyed the spiky banter he had with you."

"*What*!" Roger blurted. "He threatened to have me excommunicated at one point."

"No, he didn't." Wandering up to him, she wrapped her curvy body around him and kissed him on the lips, sex always the ultimate weapon in her armoury to get what she wanted. "Rachel and Gordon will be there."

"Really?"

"Yes." She kissed him again and jostled her right thigh into his groin area, Roger moaning under the caress.

"I guess we'd better go then."

~ * ~

Come the day, Roger, Steve, Gordon and Charlie travelled to Leeds Castle to play golf. Set in landscaped rolling hills, ponds and forest, Leeds boasted one of the prettiest, if not the least difficult of golf courses in the British Isles.

Perennially misty over the lake surrounding the castle in the early morning, the welcoming prospect served to enthuse golfers with a spirit of awe and pageantry, sharpening their competitive faculties like mediaeval knights preparing for a jousting event.

After paying their green fees at the professional's clubhouse, the four intrepid golfers made their way to the course, all of them observing flutes of fog rising from the lake's surface, and the mist-covered rolling fairways in the distance.

"Bit parky this morning," Roger observed, preparing to tee-off at the first with his driver, its fairway and green running parallel to and literally only yards from the lake.

"Forget the travelling meteorologist report, Fraser," Steve raspingly preached. "Just get on with it."

When it came to golf, Roger had stacked up more centuries than Geoff Boycott had playing cricket. Rarely taking part in The Firm's golf events, it normally took him a few holes to get his swing going. At a Firm end-of-financial-year celebration golf event in Barbados, he had drawn a tee-shot so much the ball cleared the fifty-foot fence around the course he and his companions played, flew over into an adjacent golf club territory bouncing along its driveway, crashed through its yawning clubhouse front doors, straight into the members' bar and smashed a pile of glasses on the bar, scaring the living daylights out of the members sipping their piña coladas. Afterwards, Roger had to pay a visit to the adjoining clubhouse to make grovelling apologies to the club captain for his less-than pure golf swing, and to cover the cost of damages, comprising therapy bills for distraught members.

"Bear with me," Roger appealed, "I don't want to end up in the lake."

A few moments later, the four golfers gaped as his ball rocketed into the wild blue yonder, eventually coming to rest 175 yards down the fairway.

"*Perfect*," he proudly hailed.

"It's the only hole-one tee shot you've ever cleanly connected with," Gordon observed.

"No, I won't have that," he castigated, "there was one at Deangate Ridge in 1999."

"That was on the practice pitch and putt course," Charlie prompted.

"Whatever," he retorted hoping to deflect supplementary contention.

Smirking at Roger's awkwardness, the others teed off, Gordon and Charlie hitting the fairway, Steve's pulled shot ending up in the rough, narrowly avoiding going into the lake, hole one becoming completed when Gordon putted to achieve par, Roger and Charlie bogeying, and Steve double bogeying.

Strolling to the hole-two tee-shot belt alongside the lake, already the player's club grips had a layer of moisture on them resultant from mist condensation. Closing the tee-off, Steve lost his grip on his driver during his follow-through, the club sailing up into the air and doing several cartwheels before plunging into the lake.

"*Fuck*," he snarled.

"Looks like a goner," Gordon gauged, riveting his lips together aiming not to laugh.

Whirling away, Roger and Charlie struggled to control the mirth building up in their stomachs.

"You'll have to use your fairway wood for teeing off," Gordon decreed.

"Sod that," Steve blistered. "The driver cost nearly £300."

Emanating fortitude, he peeled off his clothes.

"What are you going to do?" Charlie beseeched.

"This lake is not very deep. It's really a moat around this side of the castle. I'm going to wade in and recover my driver."

Amused at his intention, Steve's companions laughed.

"You'll get sucked down by the vegetation and drown," Roger foretold.

"Well, if I do, tell Colette and the kids, I died for a good cause."

Frozen by his resolve, Roger entreated, "Steve, mate, it's just a club. A solicitor's half hour will net you more than £300, so it's easily replaced."

"I'm going in," he unerringly pledged.

"You can't," Gordon objected, "there's a four-ball just behind us."

"Well, they're in for an early morning treat."

Stark bollock naked, Steve stepped over the lake bank between some reeds, and began wading towards where the wayward driver had ended up, mist shrouding his upper body. Just about to fumble where he thought the club could be found, miraculously, the lake's muddy bottom released its implanted head and its synthetic rubber grip followed by its shaft rose up like Excalibur being given to King Arthur by the Lady of the Lake, Steve firmly grasping the shaft.

Retreating to the bank, he received a ripple of applause from his mates, and the four-ball behind them, now bearing down on the green. Drying himself off with a golf towel, he then redressed and proceeded up the second fairway, as if he had enacted an everyday occurrence.

Phenomenally, the round went on without further dips into the lake or pond pitfalls, until the four-ball hit the sixteenth, Roger already voyaging for his usual cricket score, Steve not far behind him, Gordon and Charlie both fifteen over par. After playing their subsequent shots towards the green, they walked up the fairway line-abreast, pulling their golf trolleys behind them, the spring sun blazing down above. Advancing to the edge of the green, they heard a few sighs and grunts coming out of a sand trap bunker to the forefront of the green.

"What's going on there?" Charlie whined.

Steve and Gordon exchanged wary kissers.

"I'll take a gander," Roger volunteered.

Abandoning his trolley, he walked in the direction of the murmur's source. Gawking down into the bunker, to his amazement he saw a couple of late teenagers indulging in a bit of the old in and out. So enraptured in their carnal partiality, Roger abided transparent to their wits.

Beckoning to his golfing companions, all four of them beheld the entwined couple in the throes of ecstasy and still oblivious to their audience.

"What the hell do you think you're doing?" Roger posed. "Haven't you read the signs around the golf course? No swimming, no diving, no fishing, and incontestably, *no shagging*."

Maintaining his pumping action, the male in the duo gawped up, the girl just too far gone into the act to care less. "I'll be done in a minute," he assured.

"Bollocks!" Steve exclaimed in his customary no-nonsense manner. "You'll be done right now. Come on, let's have you out of there. What do you think this is, an outdoor knocking shop?"

"Just getting down to the vinegar strokes," he bragged.

"Nevermind the vinegar strokes," Roger opposed. "Come on, let's have you out of there."

"Aaaahhh…finished," the male announced, a big, leery, satisfied shimmer developing on his pimply face.

"If you don't move *now*," Steve threatened, "I'm going to come down there, and shove a nine-iron up where the sun don't shine."

"Alright, alright," the male bellyached. "We're done."

Thereupon, whilst still pulling up their underwear, the amorous couple sneaked away into the woods abutting the green.

"Well, I'll be blowed," Gordon babbled, still reconciling what had taken place.

"Unbelievable," Charlie spat out. "The nerve of those people. Fancy using a bunker to get their rocks off. It's, it's…"

"Illegal?" Roger judiciously enunciated.

"Yes, illegal," Steve validated. "Shagging in a public place contravenes the Indecent Exposure Act, and more latterly, the Sexual Offences Act 2003 section 66 clearly states unmasking genitalia for the purposes of coupling in public is a hanging offence, well…a heavy fine, and for recurring offenders, a custodial sentence."

"The nerve of the guy," Gordon lambasted, "'I'll be done in a minute', 'just getting down to the vinegar strokes.' If we'd behaved like that at his age, we'd have been ostracised and put in the stocks."

"*Bunkum*," Roger cut in, "we got up to shoddier things."

"What!" Steve prattled. "What are you on about, Fraser?"

"It might have been lost in your limitless catalogue of social misdemeanours, Steve, but during our final A-Level year at Chelsfield Grammar, you were hauled out of assembly by the headmaster on an impeachment of inappropriate behaviour with Lorene Keeley from the girl's grammar school."

"Oh, yes, you're right," Gordon corroborated. "Weren't you caught giving Lorene a dose of your chief of staff behind the bike sheds at the girl's grammar?"

"Poppycock," Steve bawled. "It was nothing, an incident amplified out of all proportions."

"The way I heard it," Gordon substantiated, "was the only thing amplified out of all proportions was your Dr. Feelgood."

"I can also pinpoint," Roger argued, "Gordon and Charlie were no strangers to the horizontal samba in their late teens."

"Well, you're a fine one to talk," Gordon decried. "In the upper sixth, weren't you once known as *Martini* Fraser, the anytime, anyplace, anywhere man, capable of seven-times-a-night performance with anything having a heartbeat."

"Rubbish, I was always very discerning with my conquests." Faltering, he sheepishly verified, "notwithstanding, the introductory part might hold water."

~ * ~

After the eighteen-hole marathon - marathon as far as the occasional golfers were concerned - they retired to the Park Gate Inn for lunch.

Seizing his glass, Steve elevated it to his mouth as a passing dolly bird distracted his concentration.

"Do you enjoy a pint with body in it, Steve?" Roger surveyed.

"Of course."

"Good, because there's a wasp doing the backstroke in your Master Brew."

"Huh!" Gazing into his glass, he howled, "good god, it's ploughing up and down like its competing in the insect Olympics."

Carefully removing the Olympic swimmer with a beer mat, the wasp fluttered its wings freeing itself of Shepherd & Neame's finest, before taking flight and landing on the bare neck of a very large, rugged farm boy. Moving his arm to take a swig of his beverage, the wasp stung him. Yelping, his beer flew up into the air, coming down on a group of German tourists sitting beside him, gobbling down their lunch. Springing up, they reprimanded the farm boy in graphic German.

"He must have mentioned the war," Roger quipped.

"Did you see the girl who just glided by?" Steve supplicated.

"The tall shapely blonde in the tight sweater and tight jeans?" Roger tabled.

"Yeah."

"No."

"Yes, you did."

"I think we all did, Steve," Gordon attested. "We wouldn't be men, if we hadn't noticed."

"Explicitly right," Charlie certified. "It's hard wired into the male psyche to be attuned to goodly members of the opposite sex." Leaning towards Steve, he educated, "it's why you didn't see the wasp in your beer."

"Yeah, you're right," he conceded. "Puts me in mind of Shannon Spencer from my youth. She was blonde and curvy."

"I remember her," Gordon tattled. "Congenial girl. I'd clean forgot you persuaded her to go out with you."

Steve blew out as if favourably reminiscing. "Yowzah—" Producing a cagey puss, he shared, "once I got her loosened up, with her guard down—"

"Don't tell me," Roger interrupted levitating his eyebrows. "You went for her left breast."

"Yes." Astonished, he nearly dropped his beer. "How did you know?"

"Because you always did, when we were still at the grammar. You've had a left breast fixation since we were kids reading James Bond."

"What?"

"Fleming always had Bond go for his conquests' left breast. You were pretending to be 007."

"Was I?"

"It was probably subliminal," Charlie vouched. "You read it, it got locked into your mind and re-emerged when the opportunity arose to play Don Juan. It was the same with your 'large' and 'portion' fascination at the Isle of Man."

Charlie referred to a trip the four merry compatriots made in 2007, after managing to negotiate week-long passes from their other halves to attend the Isle of Man Centenary TT. During the Superbike race won by the legendary John McGuinness, the tourists were befriended by a local man they assessed to be in his early fifties. Inviting them to his nearby house in Douglas for tea and to meet his wife, Roger & co envisaged the wife to be a similar age, but were confronted by a ravishing, comely charmer, estimating her to be no more than thirty. When she offered them tea, she logged Steve licking his lips and gaping at an appetising Dundee Cake on the kitchen table.

Forwardly requesting, 'Could I take a portion?', she quizzed, 'Large portion is it?'. 'Of course,' Steve cooed. 'Large is the only size I do.' Entertained by his gameness, she urged him to help himself. About to cut into the Dundee Cake, he suddenly recognised his boldness might have been a bit needle-like, and more importantly, he'd forgotten his manners. 'Oh, excuse me,' he begged, 'can I give you one?' the query engendering Roger, Gordon and Charlie to pirouette away, trying not to guffaw hysterically at the blunder. 'Yes,' she commissioned, 'I'll take a large slice.'

When they'd made their farewells to the local couple and walked a few yards down the street, Roger, Gordon and Charlie couldn't hold their mirth in any longer. Bursting into laughter they critiqued the tea interlude, pointing out to Steve his use of the words, 'large' and 'portion' could have been construed as having alternative meanings of a sexual disposition, and the confab could just as well have been about his genitalia and his fondness for sex, as about his appetite for Dundee cake. Of course, he roared 'bollocks' to the accusation, but later, having thought over the incident, concurred with his companion's synopsis.

"You make my use of the words large and portion seem like an addiction," Steve moaned.

"They are," Charlie insisted.

"Meeting Giacomo Agostini was the highlight of the trip," Roger affirmed.

On the fourth day of the TT tournament, the funsters were in the Glencrutchery Road grandstand glued to the Senior TT event, again won by John McGuinness, when they spied someone familiar, Italian Grand Prix multi-world champion motorcycle road racer, Giacomo Agostini. Admirers of the renowned man since they began to walk and talk, the four enthusiasts were unable to resist closing in on Agostini and striking up a conversation with him, all of them feeling the warm glow of being in the company of motorcycle royalty, until Agostini had to go to meet Ian Hutchinson, winner of the Supersport Junior TT.

"For sure," Steve assented. "I couldn't believe how friendly and accommodating *Signori* Agostini was with us."

"Well, he's a natural PR man," Gordon acclaimed. "Most of the matchless sportsmen the world has ever known have all been outstanding communicators with their fans and the media. Pele, Roger Federer, Ian Botham, Johan Cruyff and Bobby Moore readily come to mind. They're imbued not only with supreme talent, but also the ability to make people adore them through the sheer magnetism of their personalities."

"Valentino Rossi is also a member of that valiant group," Roger proposed. "I briefly met him in the Heathrow Terminal Four BA first-class lounge in 2007. I was with Henry Jacques, a colleague from The Firm, and the lounge was near to fully occupied. When we sat down, I dialed a curly haired man talking to a more elderly man a few yards away from where we sat. I canvassed Henry, 'Do you know who that is?' Dazed he replied, 'no'. I told him it was four-time, Moto-GP world champion Valentino Rossi, known as the Doctor, and adored by tens of millions of motor sport enthusiasts worldwide. Searching about the lounge, I suddenly realised I was the only onlooker to recognise Rossi. By Jupiter, if it had been at Silverstone, he'd have been mobbed by his adoring fans."

"And you went over to say hello?" Gordon ventured.

"Of course, I did. I waited for an opportune juncture when Rossi went to the bar to order some refreshments. On his return, I intercepted him in mid-flight, donating my congratulations for his fantastic win at the Portuguese GP in Estoril the foregoing weekend. We shook hands as he gleamed his trademark clock at me, thanked me for my praise, then told me he was Japan-bound for the upcoming Moto-GP."

"So, I speculate," Charlie cryptically suggested, "you haven't washed your right hand since?"

"Of course not," Roger crowed with pride. "Since 2007, the Doctor has taken two more MotoGP world titles, and in many quarters, mine included, is esteemed to be the greatest ever motorcycle champion."

"Hey, Roger," Steve prompted, "backtracking to our Isle of Man expedition, there was that incident in the dimly-lit Manxman Arms outhouse in Douglas."

"You mean, when we went to the gents, and saw a whopping-sized biker guy taking the mother of all pisses, like his bladder housed a sturdy electric motor pummelling out his slash like a fireman's hosepipe?"

"Not that, though I do recall even after we'd taken our slashes, he was still blasting the urinal, the splash-back shrouding adjacent bikers, also taking a piss. He must have had a bladder the size of a fish tank."

"What then?"

"It was the night after, when again you and I were taking a slash, and someone burst into the gents desperate to throw up but all the other urinals were in use. He banged on the trap doors, finding one not locked, rushed in, and proceeded to honk on some biker taking a dump."

"Oh *yes*," Roger endorsed laughing. "Even when he apologised, the guy taking a dump he'd honked on was none too pleased. With relish, he extracted retribution by making the honker sit on the throne while he pissed on him. The undivided incident was hilarious."

"Then there was the guy in the Manxman Arms tapping out his pipe debris on a Hell's Angel's stormtrooper helmet," Gordon brought to mind, "the spent Saint Bruno ended up in the Hell's Angel's beard."

"Yeah, he got eased for his impudence, as well," Steve recollected. "I didn't think it was possible to squeeze a man's bonce into a microwave oven, but the Hell's Angel managed it."

~ * ~

"Why am I here, Charlotte?" Roger restlessly catechized as they entered the quiz night venue.

"You're here to support the local community."

"Upon my soul, the local community is hardly in need of a boost. This is one of Kent's richest locales."

"I mean by way of commonality of purpose…neighbourliness, comradeship, a feeling of mutuality."

"Yikes, you echo the shtick of an over-enthusiastic pension fund manager."

Out of the corner of his eye, he saw the Andersons on the far side of the very large room.

"Can we team with Gordon and Rachel?"

"No. Everybody has been pre-allocated into teams."

Catching Gordon's awareness, the put-upon nominee lifted up his trouser leg to reveal a metaphorical ball and chain, Roger scintillating at his friend.

"Come on," Charlotte nagged, "we're in Vera's team."

"Who's Vera?"

"You know Vera…short, late fifties, gregarious smile."

Rebutting the assertion, Roger aired a perplexed phiz.

Narked, his wife narrowed her peepers. "She's the one who sent a letter to Doris Johnson objecting to him wanting to build an airport in her back garden."

"Oh, yes, of course." He grimaced. "She got that line of complaint off me. I used the same phrase in the challenge I sent into Doris. Cheeky woman."

"Oh, Roger," she griped. "Authentically, you composed a letter, you read out at the Hazelwood and District Residents Association meeting in this very hall, pushing everybody to use it as a template for their remonstrating letters."

"Ahh, I'd clean forgotten."

"Oh, there's the Right Reverend Reddick," Charlotte identified. "We'd better pay our respects."

"Must we."

"*Yes*."

Strolling over to a quiz team incorporating the Vicar of Saint Giles Parish Church, she opened, "good evening, Vicar."

"Ahh, good evening, Missus Fraser," he reciprocated, looking up from examining the quiz forms. Clocking Roger, he added, "I see you've got your husband with you. And how is the wonderous, if not wacky world of financial services, Mister Fraser?"

"Fine, Vicar," Roger interchanged, responding to the barely disguised gibe. "Still going to 'Chelski' matches, baptizing and burial duties permitting?"

"Hah, I see you're sustaining your sledgehammer wit from our previous encounter on Christmas Day night."

"Well, as it says in the bible, do unto others, as you would have them do unto you…but do it first."

"Can I have your attention," the quiz contestants heard booming from the PA.

Facing the reverberation source, Roger saw a man Charlotte reliably informed him was the quiz master, dressed in the fashion of a 1940s comedian, embodying a boater and a bow tie, reminding him of Tommy Trinder, assisted by, again according to Charlotte, Rudolf, an equally weird concoction in the mould of clown Charlie Cairoli. He mused if Tommy's exotic wardrobe subsumed spats and tails, and whether Rudolf had a predilection for jumbo red noses and black eye makeup.

"I thank you, ladies and gentlemen, boys and girls, you lucky people," the quiz master cackled, bouncing his boater about his dome.

It is Tommy Trinder, Roger concluded.

"Come on," Charlotte directed, "time to leave the Vicar to enjoy his quizzing and join Vera and the rest of our team. Good evening, vicar."

"Good evening, Missus Fraser."

Striding away, she poked her husband's arm. "*Really*, Roger!"

"What?"

"If you're not hell-bound already in the afterlife, subsequent to your latest unwarranted attack on the Right Reverend Reddick, you're definitely flirting with Hades halls."

"I was just taking the initiative, before the Right Reverend big dick roasted me again about the shortcomings of the banking industry."

"Whatever. Come on."

Scurrying over to their quiz colleagues, Vera introduced Charlotte and Roger to her sister Kitty, Kitty's husband Wilf, Wilf's younger brother Aubrey, a shy girl in her early twenties called Darlena, and Herman, a gent even taller than Roger and resembling Nosferatu the Vampyre as played by Max Schreck in the 1922 film *noir*. Unlike relative newcomers the Frasers, they all descended from Hazelwood families over numerous generations, in Herman's case Roger thought from the dawn of time.

"We're about to get underway," Tommy announced, "and the opening round is geography and history."

"Yuck, an aggregate of only partially related subjects," Roger censured. "What's the succeeding round; particle physics and cordon bleu cooking?"

"Shush, Roger," Charlotte blistered.

"Does any team wish to play the joker?" Tommy enquired.

"How does he mean?" Roger explored.

"Playing the joker doubles a teams' score for the round," she explained, just as someone piped up on the other side of the room producing the joker. "But it can only be played once."

"Right, we're off and running," Tommy gabbled, flashing a toothy glimmer. "What is the capital of Mongolia?"

"Ulaanbaatar," Roger imparted before anyone else on Vera's team had engaged their brains. "The Firm almost installed a branch there," he casually appended, "but our negotiator got encased in yak crap, so we were put off the idea."

Appalled by the course remark, Charlotte gave him a dig in the ribs. "Roger!"

"U-lan-bat-tar," Team Captain Vera phonetically enunciated, scribbling the incorrect spelling on the geography and history round sheet.

"Question two," Tommy snapped. "Where was the battle fought between the Houses of Lancaster and York on 22nd August 1485?"

"Bosworth Field," Roger instantly shot out, Vera noting down the answer.

"Question three. What are the names of the islands off the tip of India?"

"The Maldives," Roger served up without hesitation.

"No, it's Sri Lanka," Kitty pressed.

"He said islands, not island," Roger amended.

"He's right," Wilf bolstered. "Put down the Maldives, Vera."

"Question four. In what year did Winston Churchill first become Prime Minister?"

"1940," Roger responded. "In fact, 10th May 1940."

Vera wrote down the feedback.

"Question five. What is the name of the deepest hypersaline lake in the world?"

"The Dead Sea," Roger whispered, leaning frontwards.

"Are you certain?" Kitty cross-examined. "What about the Caspian Sea?"

"It's far larger in terms of surface area, but not as deep," he characterised. "The Dead Sea is also the saltiest sea. It's so buoyant, you don't so much as swim in it, you bounce off it."

"You've done that?" Aubrey polled.

"Yep. During a business visit to Israel. You're only authorised to swim in designated locations, but I couldn't find them, so I timed the Israeli patrols going past a point of the road parallel to the Dead Sea I'd stopped at, waited for the thereafter patrol to pass, then took a dip. While swimming, I saw an appointed realm around the cove. After reversing to the shore, I jogged to my hire car just as the thereupon patrol went past, and then drove to the zone to shower off the salt."

Laconically drumming the table, Wilf governed, "put down the Dead Sea, Vera."

"Question six. Who was on the throne when William Pitt the Younger became Prime Minister for a second time?"

"George III," Roger propounded.

"I thought it was George IV," Kitty contradicted.

"No, Pitt's second tenure was from 1804 to 1806. George IV didn't accede to the throne until 1820."

"Put down George III, Vera," Wilf instructed, before nudging Kitty and murmuring, "silly mare."

"Question seven. What is the largest county in England?"

"North Yorkshire," Roger expounded without vacillation, Vera busily writing down the answer.

"Question eight. Who was the third president of the United States?"

"Thomas Jefferson," Roger stipulated, Vera doing her end of the business.

"Question nine. What are the names of the world's five cool grasslands?" Tommy pumped. "And I will need all five to get a point."

Roger counted them off as he named them, Vera hurriedly taking the information down. "The Prairie in North America, the Steppes in Central Russia, the Veld in South and Central Africa, the Pampas in South America, and the Downlands in Southern Australia."

"And finally, question ten. What was the name of the commanding officer whose forces stormed the heights of Quebec in 1759?"

"Wolfe," Roger advised. "Major-General James Wolfe."

"Are you a teacher, Roger?" Aubrey asked.

"*A teacher*!" he shrieked looking highly insulted, the gesture making his fellow team players smirk, apart from Charlotte, her complexion abiding neutral.

"Well, decidedly you know a lot."

"Most modern teachers don't know anything, apart from how to indoctrinate the gullible young with fanciful PC rhetoric." Casting his noggin to one side, he jovially tested, "do I resemble a god-damn teacher?"

Aubrey blinked. "No."

"You're having a very exciting life, Roger," Vera praised. "Not many people can have evaded Israeli security militia to swim in the Dead Sea."

"True but the stunt was just youthful exuberance, moreover, I was in my early twenties. Gosh—" Roger twinkled.

"What?" Aubrey queried.

"Driving to Tel Aviv, I got stopped at an Israeli control point by a couple of girl soldiers, south of Hebron. In those days, the Israelis' patrolled the plenary West Bank. I'd been stopped before and despite me obviously being English subordinated to the full rigour of security checks by sombre soldiers. I was determined to make them chuckle, so I made one or two funnies when they were inspecting my passport, and the girl soldier's staunch demeanours relaxed. They couldn't have been more than age twenty, and their intrinsic girliness came out when we chatted. Then we heard the roar of another vehicle emerging from the south, and they resumed their uncompromising miens, and sent me on my way.

"In my Tel Aviv hotel, I suddenly realised what it must be like to be surrounded on all four sides by enemies, who but for Western influence would obliterate Israel. Those girl soldiers had been born into virtual captivity, their only way out of Israel by sea or air."

After some *tête-è-tête* hustle and bustle in the room, Vera swapped her team's history and geography answers sheet with the neighbouring team, everybody probing the opposition's declarations.

"Good grief," Roger denounced, "judging by these responses, there aren't many history and geography scholars on their team."

"Right," Tommy rumbled out, "time to verify the answers."

Reeling off the Encyclopaedia Britannica returns for each puzzler, Vera awarded a tick or a cross on the opposition's geography and history sheet.

"Question seven. The largest county in England is…Shropshire."

"*What*!" Roger yapped. "Point of order, Mister quiz master, I think you'll find the legitimate provenance is North Yorkshire."

"Yes, North Yorkshire," an insistent man blared from the other side of the room.

"It's Scotland, isn't it?" someone else impishly shouted, flowering in widespread hilarity from the gathering, apart from a man with ginger hair, a ginger beard, a ginger moustache, and sporting a tam-o'-shanter on his napper, who tarried deadpan.

Doubtful about the plea, Tommy maintained, "Wikipedia says it's Shropshire."

"Wikipedia doesn't always tell the truth," Roger asserted.

"Possibly," Tommy permitted after conferring with Rudolf, "but for the purposes of this quiz, the answer is Shropshire."

Polishing off the residual answers, the adjudicators then gave the marked-up sheets to their team owners.

"Nine out of ten for us," Vera evaluated.

"Should have been ten out of ten," Roger grumbled.

"Okay, Brain of Britain," Charlotte griped, "are you going to give someone else a chance to answer in the next round?"

"Naturally. I know nothing about modern pop music," Roger rejoindered, reading the category sheet title.

After calling for quiet, Tommy initiated round two. "Question one. Who had a top-ten hit with the song, *5 O'clock* in 2011?"

Apart from Charlotte, all of Vera's team rubbernecked Roger. Making a disparaging face, he appeared exhaustively mystified.

Taking the initiative, Darlena stepped in. "T-Pain featuring Wiz Khalifa and Lily Allen."

"*What*?" Roger blurted. "What kind of a nonsensical, stupid name is that?"

"Roger," Charlotte groused, whacking her husband's right calf with her high-heeled left boot.

More modern pop teasers befell, Roger becoming progressively disconcerted by the absurdity of the artist names or their tawdry songs, as comebacks from Darlena.

Then towards the end of the round, to his wonderment, Tommy tabled, "question nine. Which rock band had three of England's greatest lead guitarists pass through its ranks? I'll need both the name of the band, and the names of the three guitarists to get a point."

Registering Darlena's vacant lineaments, Roger glittered.

"The band is the Yardbirds," he unmasked to Vera, "and the guitarists are Eric Clapton, Jeff Beck and Jimmy Page."

Progressing at pace, the remaining rounds embedded film and the arts, Charlotte supplying most of the ripostes, the sciences making Herman come out of his coffin to dominate replies, television mainly monopolised by soap operas and reality shows, Vera, Kitty and Wilf coming to the fore with their knowledge, literature, everybody contributing input dependent on their passions, notably Aubrey, and lastly sport, Vera and Kitty surprising Roger with their knowledge of in-door hang gliding and unarmed combat.

As the team points were being totalled by Tommy and Rudolf, Roger turned to Aubrey. “Sorry to be so verbose about me not being a teacher earlier on,” he indifferently defended, “but as you might have gathered, I have little deference for them, or faith in their abilities to properly teach the young.”

“Quite a controversial opinion, Roger.”

“Incidentally, what is it you do?”

Pouting, he advised, “I’m a teacher.”

Chapter 18: The Pulling of Wool in Sao Paulo

"I've got a real nice assignment for you, Roger," Henry Jacques proclaimed as he nonchalantly strolled into Fraser's temple.

"No such thing, Henry," Fraser refuted, sitting back.

"Believe me, this one is the real deal."

"With no hidden catches?"

"None whatsoever."

"No such thing, Henry," he repudiated again.

"Ha, ha, ha." Jacques became more business-like. "No, I'm serious."

"I like charades, so I'll go along with the illusion. What have you got for me?"

"A trip to Brazil."

"To sell shares to the Guarani?" he mischievously postulated, narrowing his blinkers.

"Not quite. Despite your trouble-shooter commission, I can't see you in the guise of Jeremy Irons playing Father Gabriel in *The Mission*."

"What is it then?"

"The World Bank is holding a toxic debt conference in Sao Paulo, and The Firm has been invited to send a delegate to present a paper on that thorny brainteaser from our angle. All the enterprise-scale investment houses will be there."

"I read about the event in the *Financial Times* a few months ago." Bringing up his diary of world events on his laptop, he blathered, "it's starting Tuesday week. Don't tell me The Firm is only thinking about it now."

"No. A paper was prepared by Carson Calhoun at Pearl Street. He was due to deliver it, but has had to pull out of the forum due to a family issue. His wife is in premature labour."

"Isn't that the guy bearing an uncanny resemblance to Jed Clampett from *The Beverly Hillbillies*?"

"Indeed it is."

"I've often pondered, if he travels to Pearl Street in a donkey-drawn buggy and eats grits, jowls and possums for lunch."

"You're not alone, but beneath his Tennessee redneck temperament lurks a crackerjack business brain. Did you know he graduated from Harvard with an MBA?"

"Yes. Top of his year, wasn't he?"

"Affirmative. As a Harvard freshman, the Ivy League regulars tried to roust him, thinking he was a down-home, Southern boy made good. They soon found as well as intellect, he was pretty handy with his fists, giving many a privileged New England mummy's boy a bloody schnoz for taking the mickey too far."

"Good on him. Anyway—" Fraser simpered. "I take it, the Ayatollah has volunteered my services."

"Mister Bembridge appreciates it's not a trouble-shooter divestiture, but like with the recent Japanese business, he wants to build the London operation's currency with New York by fielding you."

"Huh, I suppose I should be flattered."

~ * ~

Come lunchtime, Fraser walked over to Smollensky's in Reuter's Plaza with Henry and Dennis Passmore for some seafood.

"How's the meditation going, Roger?" Passmore enquired.

"I don't want to pre-empt it, Dennis, but I think you've put me onto a winner. I've disciplined myself to enact the meditation routine twice daily. As a result, I've achieved an inner calm to equal the external calm I exhibit for business. Before, I used to exude the external trait, but often, my mind was in turbulence for all kinds of pretexts, though nobody saw it. Sometimes I'd drop my guard at home, Charlotte sensing something troubled me, but of late, she hasn't given me a puzzled stare and requisitioned if everything is alright."

"I'm glad for you, Roger." Tapping his arm, he encouraged, "keep it up, and soon you'll never have to pretend tranquillity ever again. No matter what hits you from the clear blue sky, your meditation will cleanse your mind of stress and torment and you'll be temperate and serene."

"Well, I'm not so sure about the serene bit, but you're right about the rest."

After voraciously guzzling down flame-grilled sea bass followed by mango sorbet, the three happy analysts were exiting when Fraser saw a recognisable face on the far side of the restaurant.

"I'll see you back at the ranch," he told Jacques and Passmore.

Making his way over to the bar he babbled, "Gene, Gene Millward."

Millward and Fraser were allies at Merrill Lynch, the former on the mutual funds management side of the business complementing the latter's analyst duties. Always a bright and breezy spirit with an abundance of bad will towards delinquent stock traders, Millward had a lot in common with Fraser, the pair often socialising together until Fraser handed in his notice to join The Firm, Millward jumping ship a few years later for Morgan Stanley. Since, the pair had kept in contact with each other, but for one reason or another, rarely met up.

Swivelling about, an echo image of Fraser in terms of his facial presentation, physique and clothing, came toe to toe with his seasoned buddy.

"Roger Fraser, you old dog," he whooped, grasping his hand. "I haven't seen you for ages. How are you?"

"Good. How's life at Morgan Stanley?"

"Oh, it's much the same at Bank Street as its' always been. Pressure, pressure, pressure. How are you doing at The Firm? I hear you are now a trouble-shooter, as well as an analyst."

"Perfectly *bona fide*, and along with the auxiliary command, to quote you, comes pressure, pressure, pressure."

"Typical business, Roger. Nothing ever changes to condense pressure."

"Say, I'm pushed for time right now, but if you fancy a session later on, I'll be available."

"I can't. It's my second wife Tracie's wedding anniversary today. Maybe I'll surprise her with a Fray Bentos Pie."

"You don't want to go spoiling the girl," Fraser jested, "or she'll expect treats every day, let alone on her wedding anniversary."

"Jeepers, you always were witty, Roger."

"By the way, how's Mason Turrell doing? I've not seen him of late either."

"Ahh, the third member of the Merrill Lynch musketeers." Frowning, his buoyant mood decayed. "You know that Delfina Cornell sort, who caused him a lot of grief when he was just getting his feet wet as pension funds mainstay at Merrill Lynch?"

"I do. Glorious girl, but very high maintenance. Must have been in 2004, just after you joined Morgan Stanley."

"Spot on. Well—" Pausing, his demeanour dropped withal down the melancholy scale. "He's got webbed up with her again. I saw him in October, and he reckons he's emotionally equipped to handle her now."

"Mason is too nice for Delfina," Fraser decried, glimpsing to one side and blowing out as he also recalled how Turrell became broken-hearted. "If he wants to keep her, he'll have to tell her what's what in terms of acceptable behaviour, and if she crosses the line, she's out."

"Just what I prescribed, but you know what he's like, as soft as the proverbial, and Merrill Lynch don't run with lame ducks. If she fuck's him up again and his yields deteriorate, he'll be out."

"Yep, for sure. Heart ruling grey matter never has been compatible with the demands of investment banking. Shame. I'll give him a call, arrange for the three of us to meet up, then you and I can make a judgement pertaining to how he's coping with Delfina and if necessary, tell him what's what."

"Good idea. Count me in."

"Oh, before I forget, Gene—" He sniggered. "Guess who I bumped into at the 2011 Geneva investment banking conference?"

"Go on."

"Two Pints Peach."

"Percy Isambard Peach!" Millward bristled, his optics bulging.

"Him known as Two Pints because he has a gigantic two-pint coffee mug, or alternatively pip-squeak because of his squeaky voice and diminutive stature?"

"The very same."

"He's a supine, gutless little prick, Roger."

"Ha, ha, ha. I knew you'd make a reproving valuation, but he's also a legal expert in international governance and compliance burdens. Didn't he get you out of a sticky mess with respect to an imploding Spanish gilts investment?"

"He might be a good corporate lawyer, but he's still a prick of the highest order, a one-man sales prevention team. After the Iberian lash-up, he went around Morgan Stanley slashing and burning any opportunity assessed to be remotely iffy."

Suddenly, Fraser surveyed Millward more scrupulously.

"What? I haven't got a splash of soup on my beak, have I?"

"Have you, er…" Fraser probed his pal again. "Have you been colouring your hair?"

"I cannot tell a lie. *No*."

"Yes, you have," Fraser steadfastly alleged. "I can see where the black tint gives way to a greyer hue."

"Alright, guilty as charged. It's a vanity thing. Your greyish hair makes you look distinguished and rakish, but I don't feel right with grey."

"*Me*, rakish!" He gave the Morgan Stanley man a sideways gleam. "I hardly think so, Gene. So, what's with the colouring?"

"It's an endeavour to preserve my youthful countenance," he resignedly admitted.

"But you're married, twice over. You don't need to be Peter Pan."

"No, Tracie tells me the same." Fanning out his hands, he appropriated, "as I say, it's a vanity thing, but it's nothing compared to what some guys in the industry have done to themselves to stay *jeune* as the French say. Face lifts, tummy tucks and plastic surgery. For a price, you can have most of your body parts altered, refurbished or renewed these days."

"Good god, next you'll be telling me penis extensions."

"Ah, I don't have any malfunctions in the tuna torpedo province.

I can still put a smile on Tracie's face."

"Man alive." Beaming, Fraser came over all juvenile, a condition he readily skated into in the company of put-upon-brethren. "Your acclaim conjures up a chapter from my schooldays."

"What?"

"A kid who wanted to be hung like a big black stud. Someone told him if he tied a heavy weight to his dick with a piece of string, and hung the weight over his bedside as he slept, his desire would be fulfilled."

"Was it?"

"Well, his dick didn't get any longer, but it sure as hell did go very black!"

~ * ~

With the Sao Paulo trip in mind, Fraser worked harder than usual at his analyst undertakings over the balance of the working week, encompassing work he had scheduled for the abutting week, so as to not significantly impact his output delivery.

During the flight to the southern hemisphere, he studied Carson Calhoun's paper and slides on his laptop. Entitled, 'Structural Debt, the Plague of Nations', Calhoun had developed the theme of how national structural debt is fuelled by extravagant public spending, and why spiralling personal debt contributes to the economic downturn effect. Fraser had covered the aspects in different forms, as part of his analyst function for the Firm's London operation since the 2008 meltdown sparked off worldwide recession, Calhoun's analysis of debt stimulants and a prescription to reduce debt very much in-line with his own views. Going through the material repeatedly, he rehearsed the briefing in his own mind, mentally noting cardinal points to emphasise and preparing for the inevitable audience inquisition sequent to the address.

When his laptop battery gave out, he put on some headphones and watched an already inaugurated film on the inflight entertainment system. Not really taking in the dialogue or the action, a new figure permeated the plot instantaneously gaining Fraser's consideration, his disarranged exhibition reminding him of Ronnie Rafferty, an acquaintance he had met during a holiday the Fraser family had in Tuscany.

Hearing their English accents, retired from the Department for Transport via voluntary redundancy, Ronnie and his beleaguered wife Belinda put-down on the Fraser family. Always on transmit and never on receive, unfailingly, Ronnie tabled a query only for the Frasers to be cut off after only getting out two words, droning on at length on whatever paradox he had initiated. An expert on everything from snowboarding in the Alps to Oriental cooking, the complete works of Vladimir Nabokov to laying bricks, Ronnie had seen and done it all, apparently. He even gave Roger some tips on rugby and investment banking.

After a couple of unidirectional chitchat sessions Roger told Charlotte, Ronnie was the living manifestation of a couple of Steve Coogan incarnations, specifically, bipolar constitution Tommy Saxondale with a large dollop of Alan Partridge paranoia.

Like Saxondale, Ronnie claimed to be an erstwhile roadie and an audio technician, as he called it, to the stars, before he became a Department for Transport civil servant. Supposedly, he'd worked with all the greats and not so greats numbering Pentangle, Robin Williamson, Wizz Jones and Man. He played guitar, and had traded licks with Tony Iommi, Richie Blackmore and John Renbourn, was on Christian-name terms with Martin Cathy, John Entwistle and Al Stewart, and taught no end of up-and-coming musicians how to play the DADGAD guitar tuning variation employed by Davy Graham, Bert Jansch and even Jimmy Page.

Whilst at the Department for Transport, such ministerial luminaries as Cecil Parkinson, John Reid and even the formidable John Prescott had consulted Ronnie about transport conundrums.

An altogether powerful piece of manpower, the Frasers theorised how on Earth both the music industry and the Department for Transport survived without him.

Fraser couldn't make up his mind if the character in the movie was played by the multi-talented Ronnie. When the credits rolled, he'd fallen asleep anyway, the Hollywood blockbuster just too predictable, badly written, clumsily acted, and poorly directed to keep him awake.

When Fraser's jet touched down at Guarulhos International Airport in the early evening, he felt a discernment of exhilaration, even expectation. South America had always represented the epitome of excitement to him, especially Brazil.

During his career with Merrill Lynch in the mid-1990s, he had the good fortune to tour Chile, Bolivia, Paraguay, Uruguay and Brazil, as part of a precious metals and natural resources investment campaign, the trip introducing him to the magnificent South American geography; the sheer scale of mountain ranges, deserts, tropical forests and enormous grasslands, dwarfing anything he had formerly seen in Europe and the United States.

Moreover, astounding him, the major cities with their soup of art nouveau and Greco-Roman montages, supplemented by the odd tilt at art deco mingling with modernist and high-tech, sharply contrasted with the near-to shanty towns growing around mines in the outback, their distances so far from city urbanisation that complementary local government amenities had never taken root. These were labour intensive domains, workers and management alike traveling there by coach or sometimes transport aircraft, their domestic and social lives ordinarily subsumed in La Paz or Asuncion.

In the main, he'd found the people to be cheerful, markedly the local agents accompanying him on business, their enthusiasm infectious. Being an English businessman, many of the company officials he met valuated him to be a curio to their experience. Normally solely using Spanish or Portuguese language in the business habitat, accommodating Fraser with the use of English became a pleasurable necessity, many of his counterparts enjoying the banter and gags they made during negotiations, thus forging good working relationships.

Meeting Fraser in the arrival's concourse, Chief Analyst for The Firm's downtown Sao Paulo setup, Antonio Ribeiro, quickly whisked him away to his car. Fraser had met Ribeiro at The Firm's 2007 analyst's symposium held in their Pearl Street New York HQ. Typically Brazilian in his outlook and disposition, Fraser took to him immediately, his diligent attitude to all things reminiscent of his South American experiences on the Merrill Lynch tour.

Ribeiro's ancestors had emigrated from their native Portugal in the early 1880s to work in the rubber boom in the Amazonian part of

Brazil, the country still raging between kingdom and republic factions. When the rubber bonanza ended abruptly in the 1920s, most of the Ribeiro family moved south to the fast-developing city of Sao Paulo, Antonio's grandfather working as a clerk for Banca do Estado de Sao Paulo S.A. By the 1980s, Sao Paulo had become Brazil's main centre for commerce, contributing a noteworthy amount of business to the national GDP.

Joining The Firm in 1997, Antonio Ribeiro had previously worked for Banca Garantia and Banco Real as a stock analyst. When Fraser originally met him, he had risen to the rank of chief analyst. Married with a brood of offspring and an immense extended family, directly he struck Fraser as being a very contented man, his constant smile, positive body language and perky communication, all attributes of fulfilment and satisfaction.

"How are your family, Antonio?" Fraser explored as they hurtled southwest along Highway 116 towards the city, Ribeiro's foot-to-the-floor speed typically Latin-American, just like Fraser's Italian pal, Alfredo Bachelli.

"My wife Isabel and all our children are fine. Our eldest daughter Teresa graduated from the Geosciences Institute at the University of Sao Paulo two summers ago, and now works for the State of Sao Paulo environment directorate. Fernando, our eldest son, married May 2011. He still works for Banca Safra as an asset manager, as I told you in New York. The rest are still at school."

"And your protracted family?"

"Growing with every passing year, Roger. My brother's and sister's sons and daughters are producing children like shelling peas. The senior members of the family incorporating my father, have all retired. They spend their days with my enduring grandparents reminiscing about their youth and talking about the fabulous winning 1970 World Cup Brazilian team, pre-eminently Pele."

"Yes, as a young child, I saw much of the 1970 World Cup on television with my father and my elder brother Colin. The save Gordon Banks made against Pele in the group stage is still regularly televised in England."

"I remember it. Pele shook Bank's hand in admiration." Pausing, he appealed, "now tell me, how is your family fairing?

"Causing a few heartaches for me, my wife Charlotte has gotten herself embroiled in arts & crafts and latterly drama studies at our local technical college."

"Why heartaches?"

"Oh, the people she has met have influenced her thinking. She's assumed a Che Guevara-like philosophy to life, not quite advocating outright revolution, but more erring towards trendy, left-wing politics and PC causes."

"Hhmm, the PC bug has yet to infect Brazil's middle-class women. Fortunately for us men, our women still tend to be family centric and traditional in their mindset. And of course, Catholicism is the unbeatable neutraliser of anti-Status Quo rebellion." He grinned at Fraser. "Heretics still fear the confessional box. How are you remedying Charlotte's rebellion?"

"I'm not sure I am. I gave her unrestrained latitude to pursue her newly acquired doctrine, in the hope it was a fad, burning itself out."

"But it continues to blossom?"

"Regrettably, yes. From New Age food through to load-bearing Keynesian economics, she has become the archetypal PC warrior, not just to my horror, but her parents as well. Even our children bide unconvinced about much of her moralistic standpoints. I love her dearly, but arguing her stance on some controversial policies has no punch on government decision making, inevitably falls on deaf ears."

"What about your children?"

"All still in the educational system. Wendy begins her final A-Level year this September, and has ambitions to go into economics after university. James is still undecided about his future, apart from a pipedream to be in the contiguous generation of *The Inbetweeners*."

"What's that?"

"Ohh—" Fraser wafted a dismissive hand. "A juvenile TV comedy about dopey schoolboys who swear a lot."

"And your youngest daughter. Heather is it?"

"Yes. She's doing fine at junior school, and we fancy her to pass her eleven-plus and go on to Chelsfield Grammar School for Girls." Dwelling, he reminisced. "Heck."

"What?"

"The w-penetrations still pour out of her like a waterfall in response to virtually any conversational topic. It often makes for embarrassing episodes, expressly for me."

"Nonetheless, Roger, you sound very happy," Ribeiro cajoled glancing at his compatriot. "I'm pleased for you."

Fraser had been booked into the Tivoli Sao Paulo for three nights by April Harrington. After escorting the Englishman into its cyclopean reception atrium, Ribeiro said he'd pick him up at eight the forthcoming morning, Fraser wandering up to his sixth-floor room, and after a long bath and an even longer meditation session, quickly falling asleep.

~ * ~

Driven by kudos factors, Sao Paulo City Council had put the Matarazzo Building City Hall conference facilities at the disposal of the World Bank. After registering and going through a fairly extensive security procedure at the venue for the launching session, Fraser and Ribeiro began to comprehend the scale of the event. Additional to speakers and their aides, delegates from around the world, Sao Paulo City Council officials and World Bank officials, the vast foyer forward of the conference hall was filled with security guards, policemen and media hacks.

"Have you been to a World Bank forum before, Roger?"

"No, I've been a speaker or a delegate at a few investment banking seminars in Europe over the past twenty years, but the World Bank is new to me."

"My experience matches yours in both respects. I hadn't anticipated it'd attract so many security and media representatives."

"Toxic debt is affecting most countries nowadays, distinctly in the developed world, so it makes this conference newsworthy." Furrowing his brow, he tendered, "I'd imagine the billions monitoring the event are envisioning a miracle coming out of it, in terms of an instant cure to the debt crisis."

"True, but it's both sad and naive. There's no quick fixes to debt, only a long hard struggle to draw down the obligation, making sure it does not happen again."

"Precisely, but we never learn from history," Fraser ironically proposed. "Despite economic crashes and out-of-control structural debt situations from the past, both governments and investment houses can never keep the purse strings closed."

Out of the corner of his eye, Ribeiro discriminated the crowd starting to move into the conference hall. "We're underway. Just prompt me, when are you indexed to speak?"

"Tomorrow at 11:00 hours."

"Good, it affords you scope to judge the lay of the land from today's session and slant your message accordingly."

Predictably, the opening day of the conference saw speaker after speaker review world debt and its agitators, some prescribing ways of managing how essentially structural debt could be handled without excessive tax rises or wide-ranging reductions in public services. Nothing Fraser had not heard before or even considered, he realised Calhoun's take on the stumper resonated with other notable authorities, but like them, in no way did it set forth anything other than to quote Churchill, 'blood and sweat and tears.'

Dawning on him the event was nothing more than a cosmetic workout, designed to defend the existence of the World Bank in the minds of the world's population, he sighed at the hoodwink. Of course, such an overarching and regal body ought to have seen the economic cataclysm coming, told governments to stop spending and investment houses to stop speculating, primarily with derivatives stock, long before the crash.

Soon, the repetitious text of the talks from World Bank speakers centring on assurances they were cognizant of the calamity, and doing everything they could to make the recovery swift and painless made him drowsy, ostensibly, the conference utilised as a public relations exercise to vindicate the World Bank. In Fraser's appraisal, it amounted to yet another modernist absurdity, the pulling of wool, the enactment of more smoke and mirrors, anything to deflect awareness away from the guilty, anything to disguise the fact, the powers that be had royally fucked up.

"I can't believe how blasé these spokespeople are about the subject matter," Ribeiro slammed.

"I expected nothing less," Fraser quipped. "Remember, amateurs built the Ark, professionals built the Titanic!"

Cogitating at the Tivoli Sao Paulo in the early evening, Fraser determined how in place of platitudes and false apologies, he could pitch Calhoun's presentation in such a way as to make The Firm stand out from the pack in terms of tendering a durable and believable methodology for tackling toxic debt. Calling Calhoun, still at work at Pearl Street, he suggested some modifications and changes in emphasis to his pitch, the streetwise and book-smart Tennessean straightaway tuning into Fraser's imaginative schtick. Mutually agreeing on an update, Fraser refreshed the slides as they spoke, then emailed them to Calhoun for his approval.

Come the appointed slot for his briefing, Fraser left Ribeiro's side in the auditorium, confident his revised data contributed some revolutionary ploys to handling national structural debt and sidestepping toxic debt. Thunderstruck by the content of his treatise, speakers, delegates and the media alike, bombarded Fraser during his Q&A session, Ribeiro near to dazed by the intensity of the exchanges. Some doubters poured scorn on Fraser's prescription. Others hailed it as a giant step forward, needing in-depth rumination.

Coming out of the hall, media people engulfed Fraser, all squealing they wanted a quote from him or an interview. One particularly motivated female TV reporter didn't so much as collar him, but more like abducted him in her drive to get an exclusive.

Stopping him in his footfalls, she hollered above the din, "Mister Fraser, Connie Elsmore with Fox News. I'd really value a few minutes with you."

Staring at the mass of TV cameras and photographic flashes going off behind her, his jaw dropped and he flinched.

Sensing 'hot-news' Fraser wanted to get out of the limelight, Connie imparted, "I've got a small room booked in the media centre."

Acutely fazed by the burgeoning pandemonium he assented, "you've got a deal."

While she got on her mobile phone to have the room set up by her support crew, Fraser peeked into the melee, Ribeiro coming into his line of sight. "*Antonio*," he shouted, waving him on.

"Well, Roger," Ribeiro saluted, "unconditionally, you brought the house down."

"Come on, Miss Fox News is offering us sanctuary."

"Are you going to give her an interview?"

"Not necessarily. I just need somewhere quiet for a few minutes."

Moments later, the Fox News contingent whisked Fraser and Ribeiro into their news room, Connie Elsmore checking the setup for the interview she aspired Fraser would give.

Facing him, she praised, "pretty mind-blowing stuff you were saying at the rostrum. Are you willing to go on the record apropos your balm for debt?"

"I'd need to clear it with The Firm's Corporate VP of PR in New York."

"Elliott Ravenhall?"

"You know him?"

"We've met."

Heedfully, Fraser investigated, "if Elliott did give his approval, what do you plan to ask me?"

Outlining the interview, she satisfied him that whatever he said, Fox News always reported verbatim without editing.

"Okay, I'll call Elliott."

Twenty minutes later, after Ravenhall had perused Connie's interrogations and given his provisional approval on the basis Fox emailed the recorded interview to him for inspection before permitting it to be televised, Fraser and Connie sat opposite each other in chairs, set at an oblique angle to the camera.

Ticks after, the Fox News field director counted them in and Connie introduced Fraser.

"This is Connie Elsmore for Fox News at the World Bank's toxic debt symposium in Sao Paulo. I'm with Mister Roger Fraser, Director of Market Analysis for The Firm's London operation. Earlier today, Mister Fraser dispensed some remarkable cures to easing the burden of toxic debt austerity, currently being experienced by many nations after the 2008 meltdown and subsequent worldwide recession. His *avant garde* solutions attracted both criticism and cheers from conference delegates." Facing her interviewee, she commenced, "Mister Fraser, could you summarise your suggested remedy to the problem of toxic debt management?"

"Put simply, I applied the principles of bond issue nationally as a means of reducing structural debt. The idea is, in place or at least partially in place of government austerity measures, predominantly hoisting taxes and reducing public spending to shroud structural debt repayments, governments issue bonds or gilts to the general public and investment houses with the caveat they cannot be sold on, thus avoiding derivative trading toxic debt. The capital raised in a bond issue would be invested in low-risk stock by governments, and the yield on the investment identically divided between bond investors and government, the latter using its share to draw down structural debt."

"So, the general public get to own part of the national debt, and make money on bond profits?"

"Yes. Rather than amplified taxes on income to service the debt, probably they'd prefer to examine the option because a financial benefit accrues to them."

"This is such an obvious secondary string to the bow of any chancellor charged with bringing down structural debt. Why do you think it's not been schemed before?"

"Let me be clear. This paradigm is not new. Government bonds and gilts have been around since the early sixteenth century in Europe. In part, they've bankrolled wars, infrastructure development and transport requirements. It'd not rock me, if the specific conviction I sketched to the conference has been privately rendered in other quarters."

"I see. So why do you think government bonds aimed at structural debt have not seen the light of day to tackle the here and now crisis?"

"The relationship between governments and financial institutions is often complex and multi-layered. Fiscal policies are discussed between both parties behind shut doors to establish the possibilities. Often the limiting factor is how they might impact other national tactics."

"Do you think your method might fly?"

"Now it's been made public, perhaps governments will give it deliberation and run with it."

"Thank you, Mister Fraser." She pinpointed the camera. "This is Connie Elsmore for Fox News at the World Bank toxic debt conference in Sao Paulo."

~ * ~

Later, after freshening up and changing into casual clothes, Fraser took a taxi to Ribeiro's family home on the western outskirts of the city, the Brazilian inviting him to dine with his family and close friends the foregoing day.

Materialising to a warm greeting from Ribeiro, his host then made at least forty introductions to Fraser, ranging from junior school children through to octogenarians, his paw becoming limp at the frequency with which it was grasped and firmly shook.

Amazed by the scale of the gathering and the intergenerational camaraderie, he revered Ribeiro must never have been short of company throughout his life, from the day of his birth, through childhood and into his adult life, a conveyor belt of family members and friends safeguarding loneliness and despair never overtook him. Albeit somewhat smaller in terms of numbers, the Fraser family gave him the same benefits, whereas he was aware of many people in his wide social and business circles, though successful in their careers, lived a near to a hermit existence and would give their right arms just to have one tenth of the family and friend relationships available to Ribeiro.

Taking place under a towering canopy in the back garden, the *al fresco* style traditional Brazilian dinner comprised of savoury appetisers, main courses of *pão de queijo*, *feijão tropeiro*, *moqueca de camarão* and *feijoada*, followed *by créme de papaya* and *brigadeiro* for dessert, all washed down with *Pizzato Reserva Tannat 2008* and coffee so thick, a spoon could be stood up in it, everyone finding pleasure in the feasting process. Making for topical communion during the early part of the evening, Fraser's watershed newscast monopolised the airwaves before powwows segued into domestic polemics, various diners enthralling the Englishmen with their experiences.

As the evening wore on, Fraser got talking to recently returned to Sao Paulo from roosting with other Ribeiro family members in Brasília, Mama Constantina, Antonio's ninety-one-years-old grandmother. Slight of build, gnarled and with a lifetime's struggles etched into her face, she evoked *Whistler's Mother* in Fraser, her long black dress and white shawl blanketing her noodle, outwardly the universally adopted uniform of elder women.

"Tell me, Mama Constantina," Fraser neutrally voiced, "what did you miss most while you were up in Brasilia?"

Shimmering at him like he'd posed an ask to her liking, she took a drag on her small cigarillo, put her mitt on his knee and rejoindered, "cccccoooccccckkkk," in an eerie, rasping howl.

Flinching and recoiling, Fraser's pallor went deathly white.

During the flight to London, Fraser meditated at length in an effort to get the image of Mama Constantina probing his tender body in her quest to find his 'cccccoooccccckkkk', as she had indelicately put it. Decidedly receptive to most sexual advances, categorically, necrophilia was not within his preferred menu options.

Long ago in the mists of time before Charlotte materialised on the scene, he hankered after sex beyond the usual conventions with Giselle Charpentier, a sexually provocative French girl he met the summer before firstly going up to Cambridge. She had introduced him to the delights of French teasing before allowing him to fulfil 'an Anglo-French exchange of bodily fluids contract', as he later called it to confidant Alan Mallory. Other out-on-the-rim expeditions into the heartlands of overt sex occurred during his late teens-early twenties, but apart from eternally fancying the ever-out-of-reach Joanne Lumley, his appetite for the older woman, and certainly cigarillo-smoking, cock-hungry octogenarians fell outside his sexual appetite palate.

~ * ~

Ensconced once more at Canary Wharf, Fraser had just about

settled into his daily analyst's routine when Toby Chalcroft's PA, Miss Chadderton, summoned him to the equities director's executive suite.

"Good morning, Roger," Top Cat briskly greeted as Fraser made his way towards the customary *Mastermind* seat.

"Good morning, Toby."

"I won't beat about the bush, Roger." Hands behind his back, his carriage authoritative, he gawked at the analyst, making Fraser think he was in for a pasting. "Mister Bembridge and I are very pleased with your performance at the World Bank conference." Fraser's countenance lightened. "That interview you did with Fox News was a stroke of genius. If your collateral rode high with New York before the Brazil trip, it's now off the scale. I believe CEO Benton Pascoe III tuned into Fox News when your interview was broadcast in the States."

"*Really*?" Fraser gingerly retorted, flabbergasted by the tidings.

"Yes. Of late, apart from members of the executive board of directors, our esteemed CEO has become somewhat of a Howard Hughes-like recluse with The Firm's staff. Elliott Ravenhall mentioned to him The Firm formed part of the Fox News evening broadcast. After watching your interview, he called Elliott, soliciting who you were and praising your statesmanship-like measured responses to the queries tabled by Connie Elsmore."

"I must be dreaming," Fraser muttered, thinking he was still in a meditative flux.

"The initiative you displayed when you pitched a bond resolution to handling structural debt at the conference, has resulted in The Firm becoming categorised in many highly-influential quarters as the guiding beacon in debt management strategies."

"If you'd heard the prior presentations regarding toxic debt at the conference, Toby, you'd have done the same thing."

Gratified, TC simpered. "Thank you for the praise, but I'm not so sure I'd have seized upon the opportunity so quickly. The point is, Roger, you did. It's what counts. To use a baseball analogy, as the Pearl Street folks are fond of doing, he who goes to the plate and strikes a home run, enabling his team to win the pennant and go to the World Series, is hallowed with messiah-like reverence." Moving frontwards, he peeped at Fraser with absolute pride. "When you're next in New York, don't be overcome if you are invited to the lofty heights of the CEO's executive suite to press the flesh with Benton Pascoe III."

"*Bloody hell*!"

~ * ~

Arriving home jubilant in the early evening, Roger told Charlotte about his meeting with Top Cat.

"*Good gracious*, they're definitely going to knight you on this occasion," she cryptically prophesied after taking in his dispatch.

"Well, I'd not go as far as that, but not many people in The Firm's entire worldwide network at my grade get to meet the indefatigable Benton Pascoe III."

"You make him sound like a deity."

Puckering his lips, he promoted, "*he is* in investment banking circles."

"Well, when the monumental day comes, and you are ushered into the great man's *sanctum sanctorum*, don't forget to bow and curtsy."

Roger scowled. "Very funny."

Chapter 19: Have it Away Day

As the spring gave way to early summer, The Firm's annual fete came into sharp focus at the London nucleus of pre-eminence. Set to take place the closing Saturday of May, the event donated an opportunity for Firm employees to bring their families and loved ones into a shared environment, the objective from The Firm's perspective, to boost good relations with those affected by their husbands' and wives' professional lives, pouring oil on the inevitable troubled waters invoked by work versus domesticity conflicts.

Selected as the venue for the 2012 event, seventeenth century grade-one listed Petworth House and Park in West Sussex, containing priceless works of art by J.M.W Turner and Van Dyke accompanied by extensive Capability Brown landscaping was deemed to be a suitably agrarian and bucolic setting, providing the counterpoint to London Dockland's daily hustle and bustle.

An event universally acclaimed by Firm employees and their families alike, quondam venues incorporated Waddesdon Manor, Aylesbury, Polesden Lacey House, Great Bookham, and within Fraser's venerated Kent, Scotney Castle and Chartwell. Topping the function, The Firm hired an events company to set up marquees in the venue grounds, allowing their guests to dispatch *cordon bleu* delights and slurp the beverage of their choice, whilst being surrendered by string and wind octets, playing Bach, Mozart and Vivaldi family favourites.

On this occasion, Petworth House had been chosen because the London operation's Chief Executive Officer, Quinton Talbot-Forshaw, known as 'Q' after the MI6 research and development quartermaster in James Bond novels, had his own country pile at Pulborough, less than four miles away. Set to touch down from a business trip at Gatwick Airport early on the Saturday morning, he intended to collect his family at Pulborough before they journeyed to Petworth.

Taking up the placement of chief financial officer, Talbot-Forshaw had joined The Firm's London board from Goldman Sachs in 1987. Old school and with a roster of iron-clad Establishment qualifications, he'd been headhunted by the New York parent company after their undercover agents investigated him and reported his stalwart standing in the London financial district community. Nine years later, when erstwhile incumbent Gerald Rimmington retired, New York elevated Talbot-Forshaw to London SBU CEO. Nominally elusive in his CFO role to other than his executive fraternity, sightings of him became progressively less during his early CEO years, until the chance of spotting him became rarer than a glimpse of Lord Lucan or Shergar getting odds to win the Epsom Derby.

In all the years Fraser had been with The Firm, like most non-executive employees, he had only ever seen Talbot-Forshaw either coming into or leaving The Firm's Canary Wharf skyscraper, his chauffeur carrying his briefcase. Not quite Howard Hughes incarnate like Benton Pascoe III, Talbot-Forshaw occupied the floor above the executive suite inhabited by the likes of Bembridge and Chalcroft. From there he ran the London dealings, sometimes going down to the executive level for meetings, but mainly staying aloft and summoning executive board members as required. Like Talbot-Forshaw, his PA, Miss Templeton, also tarried elusive, her entire working life spent in the office adjoining the CEO's, marshalling his elite forces at the executive layer and arranging his business schedules.

Like ordinary folk innocently mentioning the word 'Jehovah' in Monty Python's *Life of Brian*, only to be instantly stoned by religious zealots, Talbot-Forshaw's name seldom came into business repartee between the executive layer and the troops, non-executive employees sensing saying the CEO's name, even as part of an investment contemplation would be frowned upon by Bembridge, Chalcroft *et al.*

Firm social-gatherings like the one intended for Petworth House seemed to be the only occasion when both Talbot-Forshaw and the ever-present Miss Templeton were seen by non-executive employees. Every so often, like the Queen randomly selecting people in an adoring crowd to speak to, the CEO and his PA bestowed deity-like benediction on a few lucky blighters from the rank and file. Never amongst their number, Fraser had gasped in astonishment on several occasions, when the patron-like figure meshed in social discourse with the likes of Essex boy traders, Lawrence Springs and Brendan Kirkman, thinking whatever can they be talking about, Porsche 911s and tequila slammers?

~ * ~

As part of the checks and balances for the A. B. Garwood plc investment Fraser and Pension Fund Manager Oscar Giddins had brokered, Fraser had to substantiate the credit rating of one of the private equity backers, necessitating a visit to Chief Accountant Warren Whitney. Strolling through the accounts department, Whitney's deputy Craig Sadler caught Fraser's attention.

"Looking forward to this year's company away day?" Fraser beseeched nearing him.

"You mean, have it away day?"

Mystified, Fraser responded, "derp?"

"I thought you knew," Sadler tentatively ventured, retreating at the thrown reply.

"Knew what?"

"*Wow*, clearly you don't." About to recount some shenanigans, Sadler took on a fraught expression. "A couple were caught *in flagrante delicto* in Polesden Lacey House at the 2011 outing."

"A couple of what?" Fraser facetiously quizzed.

"Hah! Sanford Birbeck from private equities was nabbed having it away with Lara Corley from mergers & acquisitions."

"Isn't he meant to be a doyen of the reformation and a lay preacher, spouting the evils of lust and debauchery?"

"Yep."

"The old *dog*."

"I understand the *faux pas* dented both their careers."

Spying around Sadler into Whitney's empty den, Fraser ticketed, "Warren about?"

"He's probably gone for the main event," Sadler volunteered, glancing at his timepiece. "That's code for number twos. He does everything in a regular pattern, *inter alia* his daily swallowing of syrup of figs, ensuring at precisely 10 a.m. every morning he makes an excursion to the gents."

All at once, Sarah Williams, the well-endowed accounts department secretary, who had chased Dave Stratton around the office for impersonating I.T Support Specialist Nigel Brooks obsession for her overdeveloped chest pranced in, giving Fraser a black mug. "I've not forgiven you, Roger, for your part in the joke certain members of this department played on me last summer."

"*Me*!" Fraser remonstrated. "I was an innocent bystander."

"Maybe so," she doubtfully conceded walking away, "but you still guffawed hysterically like the rest of them."

Taking in the admonishment, he murmured to Sadler, "I thought she'd have got over the incident by now."

"Not our Sarah. She doesn't forgive and forget easily."

As fate had it, who should enter the accounts department but the lust-sick Nigel Brooks, Fraser and Sadler rubbernecking as he passed Sarah's desk, exchanged a hello with her, then went on his way with a soppy sneer emblazoned across his face, and walking in a manner suggesting his big dipper had come alive.

"I think Nigel's gone to make a deposit in the sperm bank," Fraser gibed.

"For sure. Ha, ha."

"Say, how's the new gal in accounts working out?"

"Mixed metaphors, Roger. Greta Neilsen is easy on the eye and very good at her job, but she's too talkative, her north and south always on the move. I'm sure she could whittle down wood to a pulp, her jaws move that fast and relentlessly."

"Shucks, faultlessness is always hard to find, but at least she can do her job, unlike the nitwit now running the post room."

"Kaylee O'Keefe."

"Dear me," Fraser ridiculed gaping to the heavens. "She couldn't find her own arse with both hands. I think she was hired when the PC brigade put The Firm under pressure to hire numpties. Fancy sending a parcel intended for Pope-Benedict, Roe Green to Pope Benedict, Rome. There's quite a difference between a management consultancy company and the pontiff. She's as inept as Nicola Murray."

"Oh, the cretin character in *The Thick of It*?"

"The very same."

"Warren and I were talking about *The Thick of It* cast being on *Question Time* the other day. Can you conceive puritanical, PC fanatic David Dimbleby trying to control the likes of Malcolm Tucker and James McDonald, the twin Celtic strikers for Scotland's premier league swearing and blaspheming team?"

"An impossible job, Tucker would eat Dimbleby alive. Coming back to O'Keefe, it begs the scepticism, how do some of these newer recruits ever get through the hiring process? I'm not so sure Jaclyn Hulme is as robust an interviewer as her HR Director predecessor Matt Landman."

"*Oh—*" Wrinkling his lineaments, Sadler distinguished, "Landman was the original double-hard bastard. Interviewing was a bit of a euphemistic term applied to him, no one not meeting muster got past him."

"How do you mean?"

"He had a reputation more for truth extraction rather than any softly, softly, two-way exchange to get to the heart of a candidate's makeup. Some say, it was more like an exorcism to draw out any hidden peculiarities and anachronisms detrimental to The Firm's well-being."

"By George, he must have treated yours truly with kid gloves when he interviewed me all those years ago."

"It's because you were sought, Roger. Someone inside the organisation wanted you."

"Yes, Henry Jacques."

"If you'd have come in via the normal application route, you might have been the recipient of Landman's dark side."

"Quite. Just regressing to the Petworth House gig." He chuckled.

"I wonder who Q will select to engage in conversation with this year? For some inexplicable motive, he always gravitates towards simpletons like O'Keefe, or the socially and etiquette defied Essex boy dealers."

"Yes, I agree. It's almost as if someone in the executive structure, like the Ayatollah, identifies those not endowed with an overabundance of grey cells, or not readers of Debrett's guide to social graces, and points them out to Q."

"Taken to its logical conclusion, it can be deduced if Q comes in your direction, the Ayatollah or another exec views you to be either a dunderhead or a social misfit, or both."

"Food for thought, Roger, which brings me to another juicy thought. Can you picture one of Q's chosen ones misinterpreting his patronage and going on the rampage proclaiming beatification was nigh?"

"Case stories confirm it's always a possibility. Julius Jukes for example. Q graced him with kind words at the Scotney Castle event. Subsequently, he told everyone in investment assessor services he'd be the upcoming departmental monarch, much to the annoyance of current *meister* in residence, Roslyn Joyce."

"Yes, a total lack of perspicacity led to a purely semantic incongruity becoming a show stopper. Roslyn had no choice but to fire his arse after he surreptitiously arranged a leaving shindig for her." Glowering, Sadler declared, "I never felt comfortable in Jukes' presence anyway."

"Oh."

"Well, he was one of those, wasn't he?"

Bemused, Fraser went into heedful mode. "One of what?"

"Don't be obtuse, Roger. You know perfectly well what I'm talking about. He was a whoopsie. Give me a man like no-nonsense, stake all the bastards while they're still in their coffins Lord Flashheart as a business colleague, rather than limp-wristed, effeminate Nancy boys." His condemnation on overload, he yowled, "I can't stand namby pamby, pinko, poofy types."

"There's one standing behind you."

"*What*!"

"Only joking."

~ * ~

Validating the weather forecast ahead of schedule for tornadoes and tsunamis, Roger found the day set for The Firm's jamboree to be a clement and sunny, so he decided to exercise the M3.

During the drive down to Petworth, James pumped his father about sustaining one-upmanship in social situations, not that he intended to use anything he might learn at The Firm's away day. On the contrary, he'd already arrived at a point in his adolescent development whereby he found the profound need to stand out from his contemporaries by fair means or foul.

"So," Roger began, "if I comprehend you correctly, you're seeking to rise head and shoulders above other James gang members, like Neville Matthews and Billy 'The Mountain' Swan, and equip yourself to confront potential adversaries."

"Yes."

"You don't want to use it, as a means to impress girls?"

"No…well, maybe."

"Right. The preeminent asset to master in the gentle art of supremacy, as your mother's drama teacher will attest to…" Sending Charlotte a recapping glare, she tutted at him. "…is to purposely get someone's name wrong, if you want to perpetuate the upper hand during a foremost introduction, indicating the other fellow has not dazzled you. Very disconcerting, it can put even the most determined adversary on the defensive. Notwithstanding, James, that kind of ruthless attack without justification is really an attempt at intimidation, brought about by lack of confidence. Instead of thinking negative aggression, I'd counsel foresight, meaning preparation will equip you better to undertake potential adversaries."

"Got it. What else, Dad."

"Oh, I'm no expert, but I'd also recommend whatever you brag about, make sure up front your capabilities in the given domain are better than your adversaries. For example, before you challenge someone to a game of tennis, go watch them. Fathom their strengths and weaknesses and plan your game proportionately."

"Isn't that just common sense?" Wendy interceded.

"Quite right, elder daughter. Most things in life are common sense. In all situations, not just tennis combat, it quantifies as forward planning." Pausing, he harvested more pearls. "I'll also integrate this in my free-of-charge advice to you, James. Never run with the crowd if you want to stand out from it. Invert whatever your chums are intending."

"He's talking about side and back doors, James," Wendy qualified.

"Right again, Wendy. If you can come up with a lateral or a novel approach, inherently it will empower you with cageyness. Such an aptitude is heralded as positive gamesmanship and will gain you admirers."

"Can you itemise an example?" James supplicated.

"Well, I tend to be drawn towards non-conformist, maverick film directors such as Ken Russell and Lindsay Anderson. I admire them for rejecting the status quo. They were natural born rebels, refusing to fly other people's flags and agendas. Sometimes, you have to think outside of the conventional box in order to differentiate yourself from the rest. Does this resonate with you?"

"Yes. Got it," James emphatically inveterated.

"Now Grandmaster Flash has finished his lesson for the day," Charlotte groused, "can we talk about something else." Twisting about, she browsed the back-seat occupants. "Heather, you're unusually quiet. Have you got anything you'd like to talk about?"

"Mmmmm…"

"Well?"

"I'm thinking, Mummy."

"Sorry."

"Are there deer at Petworth?"

Her dilemma meter pinging on danger level, Charlotte exchanged worried physiognomy with Roger.

"Yeessss," her father providently replied.

"Can we take a deer home with us?"

"*Ohh*, Heather," Charlotte exclaimed, "we've gone through this before. Wild animals and home do not mix."

"But we could put a deer in the back garden. There's lots of room for it to run around."

"Heather, darling," she sold, "it's not practical."

"You say that about every animal I want. A badger is much smaller than a deer, and you didn't let me have one of those either."

"But you see, it—"

"You won't even let me have a cat," she interrupted, "like Uncle Colin's and Aunt Louise's cat Morpheus."

"But," Charlotte began again before Heather cut her off.

"It's my birthday soon, and if you don't get me a pet for my birthday, I'll be leaving home to live at Adelaide Perrett's house," she adamantly foretold. "Her parents bought her a cat, so I don't see why I can't have one."

Exchanging weakened visages, Roger nodded to Charlotte.

Facing Heather, her mother propositioned, "okay, you can have a kitten for your birthday."

"*Yeahhhh*," she jubilantly squealed. "I'm going to name it Bilbo, and I'll build it a little house to live in, and give it bacon rolls and cream to eat. Then I'm going to…" And so it went on, Heather happier than a gullible Gillingham FC partisan, having been told the Gills were in the FA Cup Final.

Pulling up at the entrance to Petworth House, Roger attracted the gatekeeper. "Can you direct me to the BMW car park, please?"

Startled by the solemnity of the request, he earnestly apprised, "I'm afraid we don't have a separate car park for BMWs, sir."

"I suppose I needn't be bowled over," Roger disclosed. "There's a lot of it about these days. I had the same response at the 2008 Harlequins versus Leicester match at Twickenham, and the 2009 British Open held at Turnberry. Gone are the days when event organisers set aside special car parking facilities for BMWs."

"Yes, sir," he cajoled, thinking pedantic twit. "If you follow the drive around to the right, you'll find adequate parking facilities."

As the M3 edged away, Charlotte griped, "*really*, Roger, when are you going to accept BMWs are no different from any other car?"

"Never."

Walking through the proscenium of Petworth House and Park, the Frasers were starstruck by the prospect of the mastodon, baroque country residence in the background with rolling hills and a lake in the median.

"I thought Waddesdon Manor was spectacular," Charlotte reminisced, "but this prospect of Petworth House is remarkable."

"Absolutely, "Roger underwrote. "Maybe the house itself is not as breathtaking as the manor building, but this milieu is paradise on Earth. Phew, it's evocative of Chatsworth House with the River Derwent in the forefront. As young boys, brother Colin and I were taken there by our parents."

"*The childhood shows the man, as morning shows the day*," Wendy recited.

"Aah, *Paradise Regained*," her father recognised.

"Yes, I studied Milton's epic poem for GCSE English Literature."

"What do you think, James?" canvassed his father, noticing whilst the remainder of the family gazed at the recondite beauty of the Petworth House setting, his son's vision had locked onto Lorelei Birkbeck, a junior in the investment archiving subsection with a fondness for flaunting off her splendid legs in next-to-nothing skirts.

"Ugh," he cooed, still totally spellbound by the leggy lassie.

Miffed, Roger gave him a stern sulk. "Have you been eating red meat again?"

"What?" James uttered, realising he was being censured.

"I thought you made a New Year's resolution not to stare at girls."

"Er, er…zounds," he blathered, having entirely forgotten about the commitment.

"*Peu importe*," Roger sanctioned. Turning to Charlotte and his daughters he confabulated, "right…" Smiling gleefully he clapped his hands, "…let's go and enjoy ourselves at The Firm's expense."

Over the hereinafter few hours they chatted to Firm employees comprising Toby Chalcroft, Dennis Passmore, Ricky Henshaw and their invitees, then went around the plush house interior and inspected the park, before retiring to one of the marquees for luncheon with Henry Jacques, his wife Kristen and their two sons, Aubrey and Jerrold.

Having feasted on a melange of Fortnum & Mason's finest food hampers, the junior members of the Fraser and Jacques families went off to explore the grounds further, and more importantly the gift shop, permitting the adults to chill out under the influence of equally chilled *Chateau de Ligny Chablis* and *Domaine Vincent Girardin Meursault*.

Affording them a panorama of the winding road linking the house, Henry spied a white 1955 Rolls Royce Silver Cloud drophead coupe with white wall tyres, accompanied by an entourage of top-of-the-range Mercedes and BMW saloons. "Looks like Q and Bembridge are about to join the entertainment."

Swinging around to see the cavalcade, Roger adduced, "Q's roller must be worth a small fortune."

"I was told he bought it for £250,000 in 2002. It's probably worth twice that by now."

Pulling up in the house forecourt expanse, the spectators gaped as CEO Quinton Talbot-Forshaw and his family, chaperoned by the ever-present Miss Templeton, plus the Luther Bembridge clan, embodying uncontrollable flatulence sufferer Missus Bembridge senior, exited their highly-polished vehicles.

"I say," Kristen observed, "Miss Templeton is very fetching in her Christian LaCroix summer dress and hat."

"Yes," Roger and Henry propped in unison.

"How old is Miss Templeton?" Charlotte pried.

"Perhaps thirty-two to thirty-five," Roger estimated.

"She really keeps herself in peak condition," Kristen eulogised.

Gawking at the tall, elegant brunette, very reminiscent of Madeleine Stow at her most foxy, Charlotte plumbed, "does she furnish all of Q's required services?"

Roger and Henry made prurient faces at each other.

"Why Charlotte," Roger clucked, "whatever do you mean?"

"Well…she's a very attractive woman. Perhaps Miss Templeton tends to all his needs."

Mortified by the hypothesis, Roger gloomed. "Even if she did, it'd be a career threatening action to broach the suspicion anywhere within The Firm's influence. What say you, Henry?"

"For that very rationale, such possibilities never penetrate my consideration."

Slinking down in her chair, Charlotte drew her hat down over her peepers, making Roger think she'd got the delicate message.

As the Q caravan made its way into the refreshment's bailiwick, Talbot-Forshaw occasionally stopped to converse with someone, while his cortege, incorporating Luther Bembridge, stood behind the CEO, waiting to be called into play, if required.

"Oh, look," Henry entreated. "Q is talking to nervous Trevor Evans."

"I'll bet the sweat is pouring off Trevor," Roger remarked. "He's fragile at the best of times. *Crikey*—" He sparkled. "I recall Walter Hoskyns, another nervous wreck, telling me Q had surprised him in Davos—"

"*Davos*!" Kristen interrupted.

"Yes, it's where the Daleks are made." Glistening, he gently pushed her arm. "Only kidding. A lot of economic conferences are held in Davos. Reportedly, Q made an unexpected visit to the 2009 Worldwide Investment Banking summit. Walter nearly jumped out of his skin when the CEO confronted him. Huh, he also stunned the rainmakers."

"Rainmakers?" Kristen queried.

"Heavy duty money makers," Roger deciphered. "Brokers doing anything necessary to make the mark cough up the readies…persuasion, blackmail, electroconvulsive shock therapy. Evidently, even valiant, old school dealer Wallace Ferrier, a man renowned for his *savoir faire*, went as white as a ghost when Talbot-Forshaw and Miss Templeton stepped onto The Firm's stand."

Upholding their fascination, they beheld Q conversing with more Firm staff, mainly women, encircling Marcia Knight and Kellie Chadderton, PAs to Bembridge and Chalcroft respectively, and HR Director Jaclyn Hulme.

"Assuredly, he likes the ladies," Kristen stipulated.

"Yes, it's widely known," Henry outlined, "Q feels more comfortable in the company of women."

"Well, he's not alone," Roger exulted. "What man in his right mind, wouldn't prefer to be surrounded by the opposite sex."

Prodding Kristen, Charlotte conveyed, "my husband has some experience of being ringed by adoring schoolgirls," Roger's expression reciprocally darkening.

"What's this, Roger?" Henry affably postulated. "Been communicating with the gymslip brigade?"

"Oh, it's nothing. Charlotte is exaggerating. Earlier in the year, I did some supplementary evening sessions for Wendy's A-level business studies class at Chelsfield Grammar School for Girls." Wrinkling his nose, he conceded, "some of the girls got a little carried away with their affections."

"*Bread of life*, that's an understatement," Charlotte contended. "When Missus Greenwood and I entered the classroom, you certainly appeared to be the centre of attraction. Mister Bryant told me you got mobbed."

"Also an exaggeration," Roger insisted, playing down the incident.

"By Jove," Henry gabbled. "Q has moved on to Beavis and Butthead."

"Who on Earth are Beavis and Butthead?" Kristen interrogated.

"Jasper Gilham and Todd Charnock," Roger enlightened. "A couple of traders who, let's say, have a very close relationship."

"You mean," Charlotte began, "they're woofters, to use one of your quaint phrases?"

"Nothing has ever been proved, but conjecture is rife. They go everywhere together."

"Including The Firm's away day outings," Kristen noted.

Smirking, Henry speculated, "I wonder what Q will make of them?"

"Difficult to predict," Roger vouched. "Poofery hadn't been invented when Q was a lad. He'll probably think Jasper and Todd are just good friends."

A while later, after Henry and Kristen departed to reconnoitre the house, and Charlotte reacquainted herself with Ricky Henshaw's current love interest Vivian Karlsson, whom she'd met at the Horton's frolic in deepest Surrey, Roger got talking with Ricky about a convoluted situation involving ex-Firm employee Clarence Darrington, an investment house appraiser nowadays at Ogilvy & Jerome.

Knowing Ogilvy & Jerome were in the market for investment opportunities, The Firm had targeted the enterprise scale FMCG conglomerate as a new client for 2012. However, with no love lost between Darrington and those at The Firm categorising him as a blind, fly-by-night, never mind the risk, just feel the width of the profit equities manager, once working for Toby Chalcroft, the need for exceptional care had to be honoured. Never one to hide his speculator light under a bushel, Chalcroft had fired Darrington for one too many seat-of-the-pants concessions in 2006. Word went around the street Darrington was toxic, no reputable investment house willing to employ him. Consequently, he submerged into marine insurance brokerage for a while before gaining his current highly influential post with Ogilvy & Jerome.

"Darrington is not one to forgive and forget," Henshaw warned. "And—" He leaned in towards Roger to secure not being overheard. "He has some leverage."

"How?"

"Put it this way, he knows where the bodies are buried at The Firm. That's why he's fireproof."

"What does Chalcroft say?"

"Top Cat wants Darrington neutralised." Henshaw simpered. "Could encompass an adjunct to your trouble-shooter contract, Roger. One granting you 007 status to rub out unwanted nuisances."

"Jeepers, don't jest, Ricky. Knowing the nature of the beast, it's not beyond the realms of possibility as far as TC is concerned." Alarmed, he screwed up his mien at the notion. "Surely there are other primary decision makers at Ogilvy & Jerome we can get onboard to counteract Darrington's influence."

"The exploit process is torturous, requiring careful nurturing of the client's consignant officers." Stopping, his temperament became subdued. "It's not so simple."

"*Yes, it is*," Fraser boldly averred, "only you choose to dress it up in complexities to vindicate its failings."

"Oh, a little harsh, Roger. I'm only reflecting what Chalcroft has told me."

"Hhhmm, it's unusual for Toby to play soft ball. He must be perturbed about whatever he thinks Darrington is going to possibly expose."

"Well, huh—" Wavering, he dropped into a vigilant timbre. "When I told TC Darrington was a key advisor, if not a decision maker on the Ogilvy & Jerome team, he really steamed, threatening to beat him up with a cactus, if he set foot on The Firm's premises."

Facetiously, Fraser sucked in breath. "Sounds painful."

"More like gruesome. Howbeit, outdoing Darrington, there's another spook Toby despises coming to light as an intermediary evaluator on behalf of the client."

"Who?"

"Malissa Gabler."

"Mercy." Shrinking, Fraser contested, "wasn't she the one who bad-mouthed The Firm on the Botswana precious metals covenant two years ago?"

"The very same."

"She really was a nasty piece of work, vicious an underestimation. Accordingly, I cerebrated I'd rather French kiss a skunk or worse still Jannette Spliff Snorter, than go within gobbing distance of Malissa Gabler." Displaying disconcerted features, he relayed, "I never figured out why she had such a hard on for The Firm. I investigated her antecedents and no preceding history with us came to light."

"You should have searched on the name Aldo Beck."

"If memory serves, Beck used to work out of our Frankfurt branch for Obergruppenführer Heinrich Metzer." Roger winced. "Did Heiny can him?"

"Yep, for not making his quota. Malissa Gabler's surname before she married was Beck. Aldo Beck is her brother."

"So that's why she hates The Firm?"

"On the dot. I unearthed the connection after the Botswana business plummeted south."

"So er, does Top Cat want her neutralised as well?" Anticipating an affirmative riposte, he nervously licked his lips.

“Like I said, Roger, your trouble-shooter mandate could be changing. You might have to get in some practice with your Purdey.”

Gulping, his countenance fracturing into anxiety, he mumbled, “I need my meditation manuals.”

“Anyway, enough business,” Henshaw propounded, neglecting Fraser’s refrain. Leering lustfully at his bewitching girlfriend, he joyfully heralded, “I’ve got to give Vivian my full attention for the residue of the day.”

“Well don’t get caught having it away with her in Petworth House,” Fraser cautioned, bringing to mind Craig Sadler’s ‘have it away day’ anecdote. “It could climax, if you’ll forgive the pun, in your career ambitions at The Firm being severely impacted.”

Chapter 20: Finale

An absolute must in the Hazelwood regional social calendar for the Frasers, Steve and Colette Hunt had invited them to a garden fete to celebrate Steve's forty-fifth birthday, Colette stipulating after the water fight debacle at the Fraser's 2011 summer garden party, their soiree would be a water-free zone.

When Steve pushed out the boat, it was always certain to be a memorable affair for those attending. Invariably assenting to just about every sort of social tomfoolery and misdemeanour, his *carte blanche* palette knew no bounds, pleasing those prone to unintentional gaffes, such as Roger, and infuriating others of a more sensitive makeup, like Colette and Charlotte.

Remarkably, Steve even got a dispensation from Colette agreeing for him to invite members from the Lunt, Hunt and Cunningham solicitor practice. More essentially, virtually everyone from Kappa Corinthians Rugby Club received summonses. Balancing what she perceived to be the madcap element, Colette invited her arts & crafts friends from Orpington Technical College, the intoxicating mix of grunt and intellect guaranteed to make for a fascinating event.

Steve had also invited many members of his extended family, counting his nephew Milbern, son of his elder brother Jordon and his wife Paige. Aged twenty-four, and about as subtle as an air raid, Milbern was in the habit of rushing up to people, and making the most incongruous, if not foul proclamations. Whether for sheer devilment or to parade his knowledge of some notably obscure axiom was not clear to those on the receiving end of his pronouncements. Delivering the edicts in such a convincing, whole-hearted way, his phizog free from pretence in toto, people were stranded with the supposition they had missed some vital information, staring them in the face.

On the occasion of his uncle's birthday, like a man possessed, Milbern surged up to Roger, while he and Charlotte were chatting to Gordon and Rachel Anderson and Alan and Francine Mallory. Grabbing Roger's arm, he yelped, "*Roger, Roger.*"

"What is it, Milbern?"

"Do you know, over a lifetime, the average person produces five tons of crap and 10,000 gallons of slash?"

"Fascinating fact," he drily jeered, "but no."

"Where does it all go?" Nonplussed, Milbern gave him an incredulous mope.

"I think you'll find," he poignantly educated, "drainage systems feed sewage plants where biological waste products are treated."

Bamboozled by the precise retort, Milbern retired without disputing the explanation, leaving Roger bewildered. "Hard to believe he comes from the same gene pool as Steve and Jordon."

"Perhaps he gets his hare-brained, if not impudent tendency from Paige's side of the family," Rachel offered.

"*No,*" Roger resolutely bonded. "When Milburn initiated his asinine hyperbole, Steve checked out Paige's ancestry, discovering nothing untoward." Baffled by the dichotomy, he twisted around to see Steve's nephew affronting another group with his ludicrous outpourings. "Milbern has a quite unique embodiment."

"My," Charlotte blabbed, scoping about aghast, "there must be approximately a hundred guests here already. Our summer garden celebration was positively small in comparison."

"Yes, well," Roger soberly began, "if you'd allowed me to invite more people from the rugby club, we'd have had a ball as big as this."

Riled, she flung her husband a black lour.

"Oh, I don't think your do was so far removed in terms of numbers," Alan credited, diffusing the fast-approaching discord.

"Interesting choice of music blaring out of the PA," Francine remarked. "I didn't think Colette liked the Sex Pistols."

"She doesn't," Roger apprised. "Steve is the Johnny Rotten lover.

We're always joshing him *Anarchy in the UK* is the traditional recalcitrant solicitor's beloved hymn."

"At this rate, *Basket Case* by Green Day will be on next," Alan predicted. Putting his paw to his ear, the culminating strains of *Anarchy in the UK* gave way to *Basket Case*. "There you go."

"I didn't realise Steve was such a punk addict."

"It goes hand in glove with his, 'let's kill all the bastards before they kill us' solicitor's philosophy," Gordon claimed.

"Where's Charlie and Julianne Farley?" Roger raised to Charlotte, scanning the gathering. "I thought they followed us in."

She shrugged her shoulders.

"They got purloined by Colette," Alan advised. "She wanted Julianne to see her new pottery creation, and Charlie got dragged along."

"How do you know?" Roger ticketed circumspectly.

"Because I only narrowly dodged going the same way, by pointing out a very unusual cloud formation to Francine, thus distracting her concentration."

"Yes, you did, *didn't* you," his wife scorned, facing Charlotte. "He only told me about the subterfuge after we'd been milling around for five minutes, and before we joined you."

"Ouch, it's the kind of trick Roger pulls."

"True," he candidly admitted with more than a touch of pride, before surveying the garden again. "I still can't see Charlie and Julianne. You don't think Colette has them entombed scrutinising her whatever it is?"

"Probably," Alan submitted. "She once kept Francine and I immersed in inspecting one of her welded-metal constructs for an entire hour. Damn it, the item was so minimalist that the assessment should have taken seconds." Recognising he might have blundered; he made a help-me face at Roger. "Once bitten, twice shy."

"Yeah," Roger approved, coming to his aid. "I've known Colette to lock the door to ensure onlookers gave a hulking dollop of their precious time to agonise over some macabre wood sculpture or misshapen ceramic cup."

"Is that…Fay Farrow, I can see on the other side of the garden?"

Rachel drawled, jolt spread-eagled across her face.

"Yes," Charlotte accredited, focusing on the given direction. "I know what you're going to say, she's put on a lot of weight."

"Bloody hell," Gordon piped up, "the double, king-size clothing she's wearing is a very tight fit. It's breaking at the seams."

"Palpably, Fay has developed an eating disorder," Charlotte clarified.

"You mean, she can't stop cramming Mars bars and iced cakes down her gullet?" Roger wickedly enquired.

"A little unkind," his wife rebuked. "But there's some truth to what you say."

"So, the eating disorder is a ruse?" Rachel surmised.

"Well, it's the official line," Charlotte confirmed.

"Official line or not," Gordon touted, "unequivocally, she's a candidate for that TV programme, *Embarrassing Bodies*."

"*Gordon*," Rachel snapped. "Shush, she might overhear you."

"What, from the other side of the garden?" Roger quizzed. "She must either have unparalleled hearing or can lip read."

"*Roger*!" Charlotte reprimanded.

"The woman ought to have more self-control," Alan beefed. "Fancy getting into that state through an inability to resist temptation." Unimpressed, he made a disparaging face. "I have no sympathy for her."

"It's said, everybody looks good from at least one angle," Roger stipulated whilst casting an eye over the humongous Fay Farrow. "But I guess there are exceptions to the rule."

~ * ~

Later, after Charlotte went off to talk to Colette and other arts & crafts devotees about what their husbands considered to be trendy, nondescript, trivial, vacuous dribble, Roger got talking with Steve.

"Well, forty-five hey?" Poking out his lower lip, he developed a compassionate kisser.

Tottering at the bombshell, Steve reminded him, "you'll be hitting the same age in a few months, Fraser, so let's have no false sensitivity."

"Don't I know it."

"Besides, age is a frame of mind." Confident of his proposition, he fabricated a poised quality. "I feel just the same as I did when we were in our teens."

"Yeah, count me in on the sentiment, at least in mind, if not always body."

"Blimey, harking back, you, me, Gordon, Charlie and a host of others, all thought we were invincible."

"A bit like Liverpool Football Club in the 70s and 80s."

"Yeah. In those days, we thought we could do anything, and there were no barriers to stop us, particularly with girls."

"For sure, and we all had some crackers."

"Yeah." Steve beamed. "Angelique Freebody amongst them."

"Geez…Angelique 'Goodbody' as I re-christened her, had all of us at her beck and call. She eventually went off with Darius Thornly, didn't she?"

"Indeed she did."

"I could never see what she saw in that ugly git. I mean, if she'd played her cards right, she could have had Fraser's seventeen inches of pulsating pleasure."

"You're exaggerating again, Roger."

"No, I kid you not. She could have."

"*No*, the dimension, nitwit," he bawled. "Not the intent."

"Ha, ha, ha…bollocks, Hunt."

"Some of those guys we used to knock around with in our teens have vanished from the scene altogether."

"For sure, but it's the way of the world," he granted. "Some people change, move on, discard existing relationships, and establish new lives for themselves in toto."

Disregarding the edict, Steve babbled, "do you remember Wally Wescomb?"

"Oops, Wally by name, wally by nature, but difficult to dislike."

"He always called at an inconvenient juncture, either when I was up a ladder, taking a dump, or having a shag."

"Yes." Amused by his friend's candidness, Roger chuckled. "I'm sure it was never intentional, just…" He unfastened his hands. "…bad timing."

"He dropped out after A-levels. Zoinks—" Stimulated by the recollection, Steve glittered. "We're being generous. Veritably, he really was an out-and-out, undiluted, asinine dick."

"Yes, an undivided, inarticulate, unthinking twat." Flummoxed, he queried, "what happened to him?"

"He went to Trinity College Oxford."

"Figures. He'd be in the company of all the other moronic dopes that gravitate to that bastion of ineptitude."

"Yeah."

"Ollie Padbury is another whizz we used to knock around with."

"You mean, the master of the undiplomatic."

"That's an understatement. I recall when he bumped into Rosemary Benfield at a party, and you know God had not been kind to her in the beauty stakes. '*Holy shit*,' he howled, 'have you got a license to be out in public with a face like that? In Wales you'd be done for sheep scaring.' Of course, poor Rosemary fled, and Padbury got pummelled by a flock of her girlfriends."

"Oh yeah, though good company, he was a total bastard with girls. Huh—" Steve twinkled. "He had an ambition to go out with a girl who had a large wart on the end of her honker. Damn well achieved it as well. I was at a Chislehurst shindig when he came up to me with a girl he had picked up and said, 'take a look at this!' There before me stood his heart's desire encapsulating a humongous wart on her snout. He crows, '*great*, isn't it', and waltzes off with her."

"They don't make 'em like Ollie Padbury anymore, do they?"

"Regretfully, no."

"Another crackerjack coming to mind is Two-Dinners Thomas."

"Who?"

"You must remember him from our schooldays. The guy with the large appetite. He used to have two-school dinners, hence the nickname Two-Dinners Thomas."

"Him who was a dead ringer for the Pink Panther?"

"Nooooo…you're thinking of Jerry Jaffer, and anyway, he looked more like Snagglepuss. Two-Dinners was a kind of cross between Felix the Cat and Yogi Bear. Golf fanatic. Used to pitch everything in golf vernacular. When he was on the job, he'd say to the girl, 'tee it up.' Later, he claimed he had ditched double lunches in favour of muesli for breakfast, boiled white fish for lunch and a sliver of beef, turning out to be half a cow for dinner!"

"Oh yes. I know who you mean. What happened to him?"

"Last I heard, he'd become a model aircraft designer. Designed one big enough to house a pilot."

"Isn't that what's called an aircraft?"

"Yeah. How many other ex-Chelsfield Grammar students can claim they achieved flight?"

"None to the best of my knowledge."

"I think we're starting to talk gibberish."

"Collette says I always talk gibberish."

"Speaking of Collette, what did she get you for your birthday? A signed copy of *Anarchy in the UK*?"

"Ha, ha, if only. No, my darling wife gave me a Prada two-piece suit, Charles Tyrwhitt shirt and a pair of Christian Louboutin shoes."

"Very nice," Roger congratulated, nodding appreciatively. "Colette always has had panache and good taste."

"Yowzah, you'd not bestow such praise if you could see her first thing in the mornings. Talk about moody-bitchyitous!"

"*Jesus*, they all suffer from that," he upheld. "Charlotte is capable of throwing a wobbler with the best of them, as my repeat incarcerations in the doghouse testify to. Now, if you want an example of a person of the female persuasion with permanent moody-bitchyitous, look no further than Charissa Coleman. She even puts my arch-enemy Brigit Hammond, aka Cruella de Bitch, in the shade."

"Who?"

"She's a member of the arts & crafts clique."

Apprehensively, he foraged about the garden. "Good god, she's not here, is she?"

"I haven't seen her, but you'd have to examine Colette's guest list to be sure. Anyway, what do you—"

About to seek Steve's opinion on the proposed changes to rugby scrums, a crucial if not game-changing topic requiring thorough deliberation, the pair saw a posse from the arts & crafts set coming their way.

"*Oooh*, incoming," Steve yapped.

"I wonder what they want?" Roger whispered. "They look like psycho-bitches on heat."

"Perhaps they heard us, er you, denigrating Clarissa Coleman and Brigit Hammond."

"Oh, no. I get enough bollockings from Charlotte for having the audacity to speak the truth about some of her friends. I don't want it from other arts & crafts aficionados."

"Hello," nattered the pack chairwoman, a tallish, clearly cerebrally-superior woman with a florid complexion, exuding an air of authority. "You're Steve, the birthday boy, aren't you?"

"Y-y-yes," he stammered out, unsure of his standing.

"We'd like to offer you our congratulations."

"*Oh*, thank you."

"Colette tells us, given the opportunity, you're still quite a mover."

Dizzy, Steve blinked at Roger, as if seeking guidance *vis-à-vis* how to reply to the assertion, his pal tarrying as befuddled as him.

"You see," she continued, "we're having a September bash at the tech, and we need as many skilled operators there as possible, giving encouragement to the rest to join in."

Withal befogged, Steve and Roger glowered at each other, the penny still not dropping, the woman indexing their addled states.

"You can dance, can't you?"

"*Can he dance*," Roger indignantly fended flinging his arms outwardly. "Not only that, but he's also a man of many parts. In his youth he attained fully-qualified chicken-plucker status. Show them your repertoire."

Gurning profusely, Steve embarked on unzipping his fly.

"No, no, no," Roger gushed, halting his friend's action. "I mean, your dance steps."

After the misinterpretation had given way to recognition of the article under investigation, Steve gave his audience some dexterous examples of the soft-shoe shuffle and his Gene Kelly *Singin' in the Rain* caricature, the arts & crafts cadre retiring into the midst of their clan at its conclusion.

"That was a close one," Steve spluttered. "When she said dance, I thought she implied in the context of a horizontal samba."

"I know. As soon as you went for your zip, I deciphered that both of us had misinterpreted the crux of the enquiry."

"Hey," he gabbed, pushing Roger's arm. "You see the woman to the right of the woman who led the ballroom delegation?"

Gyrating his bonce like a fox about to enter the chicken coup, he ascertained, "you mean the fetching, candy-blonde with azure blue blinkers and curves in all the right places?"

Amazed at the exactness of the description, Steve's jaw dropped. "Not much gets past you, when it comes to the female form, does it."

"I think she's quite…"

"Shaggable?"

"I was going to say, well ripened."

"Well, she is married, but—" Heedfully, he perused to his right and left. "I'm reliably told," he murmured, "she goes ape, if she doesn't get it regularly."

"What does she do when hubby is not there, use a dildo?"

"No, apparently," he benignly divulged, "a Coca-Cola bottle is her joystick of choice. It gives her far more satisfaction."

"*Get away*."

"It's genuine, Roger."

"And—" His voice became a faint sigh. "She likes to do it doggy style."

"Oh, well," Roger blurted, "we all like to do it that way."

"Yeah, but she's not a man, she's a woman."

"Your powers of observation astonish me."

"No, no, no…what I mean is, men are usually synonymous with sexual perversions. Women tend to only like the missionary technique."

Hesitating, he calculated if a very direct or a gentle riposte might set his friend straight. "I don't know what you and Colette have been getting up to in the bedroom domain of late, but if Charlotte is anything to go by, women like to experiment just as much as men."

Astounded, Steve nearly passed out.

~ * ~

With the merrymaking in full swing and people getting progressively blitzed on the Hunt's array of alcoholic delights, many couples began to hop, skip and gambol to the infectious gangling of the Buena Vista Social Club.

"Come on," Charlotte instructed Roger, "it's rumba time."

Taking his hand, she led him away from the group they were in to a relatively secluded part of the garden, and began twirling her arms and legs in concordance with the music, her husband doing his best to keep up with her.

Motivated by the flaunt, Gordon and Rachel followed suit, and soon a miscellany of couples were shaking and twisting as the music took hold.

"Can you fetch from memory the first time we danced together?" Roger begged.

"The May Ball at Peterhouse College, Cambridge. You spent an eternity gazing at me, before you plucked up the courage to come over and ask me to dance."

"I was in awe of you…still am."

"*Gee whiz*, next you'll be claiming, I'm just as attractive now as then."

"Stop putting words in my mouth."

She laughed. "You never quit being the wordsmith, do you? On that spectral evening in 1988, you looked quite the sophisticated gent in your penguin suit, but your banter set you apart from other suitors."

"Aahh, it was work in progress I'd been developing since my early teens. I'm not sure I'll ever complete the undertaking."

"When you walked towards me, my girlfriend imparted, 'Here comes the tall, raven-haired one with the sparkling spiers and the devilish smile.'"

Subconsciously, he pushed his fingers through his hair and burbled, "it's not so raven anymore."

"No, but you developed from a cute undergraduate into a very handsome man." She kissed him on the cheek.

"Oh, Charlotte, you'll make me weep."

"All those women from the tech think you are quite a catch, you know."

"*Really*? I thought they classified me as a philistine."

"They do, but they also think you're gorgeous to look at."

"Oh, I never fly in the face of public opinion," he teased tongue-in-cheek.

"Seriously, Roger."

Never one to feel comfortable with acclaim, fleetingly he peeked to one side. "I'm sure they're exaggerating."

"Ha, ha." She gleamed at him. "Adulation never did sit well with you. It's another reason why I love you so much. Modesty does become you."

"What is this? You're not buttering me up for something you know I'm not going to like, are you?" Suddenly his mien went dark. "You haven't booked us on another New Age happening with Kali and Fortuna, the sisters grimm, have you?"

"If you mean Jacquenetta Underdown and Daina Kirkbride, no."

"Thank god. I nearly died of starvation and alcohol denial the weekend we spent at the Spa Hotel Tunbridge Wells being force fed a New Age witches brew diet."

"You always think a compliment from me comes with strings attached."

"No, well…er, yes. Well, it does sometimes."

"On this occasion, it comes gratis with no ulterior prerequisites. You look at your supreme best this evening, and I've always considered the Armani suit you have on to be the best of many complementing your skin tones."

"Well, if we're paying each other commendations, you don't look so bad yourself in your Claudie Pierlot cocktail dress."

"Glad it meets with your approval."

"Everything you wear from your high-heel court shoes and slingbacks to your 1940s film star wide-brimmed hats meets with my approval. Not many women can come across as a million dollars in anything they grab from their wardrobe to keep out the cold. I even like you in tight jeans, t-shirt and high heels, a rig really trotting out your long, shapely legs, and high-rise derriere."

"Oh, Roger, now who's flinging around the felicitations."

"*Hey*," they heard someone call from the edge of the dancing area. Facing the summoning source, Roger saw John 'the Revelator' Hillibrand. "We're going to have a good old-fashioned rugby club sing-song to celebrate Steve's birthday."

Charged up at the prospect, Roger and Gordon exchanged gleeful twinkles.

"Count me in," Roger hailed.

"Me too," Gordon added.

"Ohh, *really*," Charlotte bleated. "I've just got you in a romantic mood and now you're going off to hoot some silly songs."

"What can I do, darling? Duty calls. If I don't join in, I'll be a social pariah at Kappa Corinthians."

"But, but…"

He pecked her on the cheek. "Be back soon."

Breezing into the Hunt's extensive kitchen, Roger and Gordon saw some familiar faces from Kappa Corinthians, embracing Dusty Maltman, Martin Gayle, Damien Chapple and coach Mason Harvey amongst the legions of rugby players, Steve Hunt sat at their centre, pint glass in hand slurping Master Brew and coming across as extremely content.

"*Roger*," Dusty shouted, "you and Gordon come and sit with the try makers and try scorers."

"You got it," he called in response.

After some re-charging of glasses and sorting out the assembly into boiler room forwards, and 'cherry-picking backs' as Steve called them, to form a horseshoe, Coach Harvey and club toastmaster John 'the Revelator' Hillibrand stood stage-centre and called for silence.

"Right, gentlemen," the Revelator began, "once again, we are gathered together to celebrate the birthday of one of our most colourful members. I speak of none other, than that stalwart of the scrum and the lineout, our veteran team's illustrious hooker." Pausing, he leered. "Some say *happy hooker…*" An ear-piercing yawp went up. "…six feet of pure muscle and grunt, weighing in at sixteen stone, the often grouchy and misunderstood master of the upper cut when all else fails, the player who coined the expression, 'never let them pass without first drawing blood'…Mister Steevvvve Hunt."

Boisterously reciprocating, the players cheered so loud, the roof nearly came off the Hunt's house. Spurred on by the repartee, Harvey and the Revelator then led the hearts of oak choir through renditions of *Birthday* by the Beatles accompanied by the ultimate Liverpool combo on the PA, *Happy Birthday* by Altered Images with Celtic muscle man Evan McGinley playing the Claire Grogan part and *It's My Party* with Steve in the Lesley Gore role, non-singing socialites comprising hostess Colette, Charlotte, other player's wives and girlfriends plus members of the arts & crafts group gathering in the kitchen entrance, and along its outside wall to witness the festivity. More facsimiles ensued, with Steve's solicitor contingent joining the ensemble for a rousing execution of The Beastie Boys *You Gotta Fight for Your Right to Party*, most onlookers equating solicitors with beastie boys, and *I Want a Boy for My Birthday* by The Smiths, with Dusty Maltman getting down on one knee to serenade Steve for the chorus lines.

Beforehand, six barrels of Shepherd & Neame's finest had been set up on one of the kitchen work surfaces. During the thereafter song to be delivered by the choristers, The White Stripes anthem *Seven Nation Army*, a perennial favourite with sports crowds worldwide, somehow one full barrel got punctured, sending a fountain-like spray of Master Brew upwards hitting the ceiling and splashing down on everybody within a ten-yard radius.

Clutching Colette's arm, Charlotte remarked, "I thought you said this soiree would be a water-free zone."

"I did," she hollered, flustered and foaming at the mouth. "My beautiful kitchen has been ruined. *Arrrrrggggghhhhhh.*" Grinding her teeth, she peered into the uproarious multitude, all the rugby players and solicitors oblivious to her presence and laughing hysterically. "Steve, Steve, Steve," she shouted, twisting her eyeline to and fro, struggling to see him in a deluge of soaked but very merry men. "Steve, Steve, Steve…"

~ * ~

Come the hereinafter morning, Roger awoke with a steaming headache.

"Oooohhh," he moaned as the morning sun produced flickering shapes dancing across his peepers through the leaves of the tree adjoining his and Charlotte's bedroom. With the door ajar, he heard her talking to someone on the hall phone, then he marked a little blonde cherub sitting at the bottom of their super-king-size bed. "Heather."

"Hello, Daddy. You don't look very well."

"No, I think an incubus crawled inside my ear during the night, and is running around my cranium birthing havoc."

"What's an incubus?"

"Ermmm," Roger began flexing his facial muscles for relief, "it's er, it's a demon, a hobgoblin."

"You mean, like in the *Dungeons and Dragons* video game?"

"Yes, what, no…I've got no idea." Starting to achieve *compos mentis* condition, he frowned. "Have you been playing underage video games?"

"Well, Adelaide Perrett's elder sister Sabina had her Play Station on, so Adelaide and I couldn't resist having a play. It was *Dungeons and Dragons*."

"Ohh…I'm too zonked to tell you off. Whatever you do, don't tell your mother."

"Don't tell mother what?" they heard Charlotte cry as she came through the bedroom doorway.

"Ohh…nothing," Roger replied.

"Well, whatever it was, I'll deal with it later. Aunt Jemina was on the phone. She wanted to know if we're going to this year's Summer

Exhibition at the Royal Academy of Arts."

"We went last summer."

"I can see there's nothing wrong with your long-term memory this morning. Yes, we did. She's asking if we're going to this year's event." Disinclined to acquiesce, Roger produced a less than enthusiastic face. "I told her, yes."

"*What*!" he exclaimed, levering himself up and instantaneously regretting it as the incubus in his napper played hard-ball against his skull.

"You enjoyed the day out," she impelled before producing a dubious muzzle. "Well, you did eventually, when we journeyed to Jemina's for tea."

"That's right, Daddy," Heather interjected, "especially when you thought a dongle was a man's—"

"Enough, Heather," her mother cut in. "Anyway, we're going, and that's an end to it."

"But I'm never going to get to see Lee Westwood sink a thirty-foot putt live on TV at the British Open, if I have to attend some post-modernism exposition for loons and airheads to exhibit their airy-fairy garbage."

"Well, you'll just have to get the British Open organisers to move the tournament to a weekend when Aunt Jemina doesn't want to go to the Royal Academy."

Faced with the mammoth scale of the proposal coupled with his present groggy shape, he didn't debate the mandate.

Wandering over to where Roger's suit lay draped over a chair, Charlotte clocked the beer barrel explosion aftermath from Steve Hunt's birthday sing-a-long had impregnated into its surface. "Your suit is a mess. It'll have to go to the dry cleaners." She pitched her dishevelled husband a critical sulk. "Come to think of it, you need to go to the dry cleaners as well."

"I'm a little unclear apropos what happened Saturday night," he confessed.

"Let me clue you in."

Folding her arms, always a bad sign of worse to come as far as Roger was concerned, Charlotte reviewed after the singing session, the bawdy choir had taken to playing rugby in the back garden using a melon for the ball, the fruit eventually ending up lodged down Freda Fortescue's ample cleavage when Damien Chapple mishandled a pass from Roger. Undeterred by Colette's demands to refrain from more horseplay, the merry men then indulged in a beer drinking contest, birthday boy Steve Hunt eventually coming out as the winner after his nearest competitor, veterans-fifteen captain and openside flanker Gareth Ross threw up over unlucky Virginia Loos-Smyth, also the recipient of a water soaking at the Fraser's garden fete the foregoing summer.

Not satisfied with their drinking bout, the players then moved on to polish off the gallons of rum punch Colette had tenderly prepared, whilst trampling on a mountain of savouries and sweets displaced off a table in the players' rush to gulp more alcohol. Finally, the evening's crowning glory became a game of leap frog culminating in a massive pile-on after Gordon tripped up Steve on purpose, fell on him, and the lingering Kappa Corinthians leapt on the pair to form a human mountain of flailing arms and legs.

"Get the picture?"

"Kind off," he admitted before his over-sensitive ears began to hear an impending rumble.

Ticks later, Wendy and James bound into their parent's bedroom.

"Goodness me, Dad," Wendy exclaimed, "I haven't seen you this bad since the rugby club stag night."

"Holy kamoly!" he yowled. "Thanks for your support, Wendy."

"She's right, Dad," James sustained. "You look like a train wreck, and I bet your mouth feels like an Abo's armpit."

"*James*!" his mother scolded. "No doubt you picked up such a vulgar phrase from those foul-mouthed juveniles in *The Inbetweeners*."

"Actually, I heard Dad say it to Uncle Steve, the forthcoming day after they had been to a session of the Hazelwood & District Gentlemen's Club at Chapter One."

Jabbering, "*et tu*, *Brute*, *et tu*," Roger pulled the bed sheets over his noodle.

"It's no good battling to escape between the sheets," Charlotte ardently forewarned.

Roger re-emerged, a dazed mannerism covering his fragile face.

"Come on," Charlotte berated, "there's things to be done."

"What?"

She bent down towards him. "You might recall, you promised to take us to Cinema de Lux at Bluewater to see *The Avengers*."

"Did I?" he judiciously probed.

"*Yes*," she emphatically inveterated. "But before the excursion, the lawns need mowing."

"Ooooohhhhhh—" Pouting pleadingly, he submitted, "can't James do it?"

"He's on potato peeling detail for lunch."

"How about if I peel the spuds and James mows the lawns?"

Scowling at him, she sanctioned, "I think you're more in need of fresh air than James to sweat out the aftereffects of Saturday night." Bending towards him, Roger cowered away. "Wouldn't you agree?"

"Huh, a woman's work is never delegated," he moaned. "Who said that?"

"Nevermind. Time for you to rise and shine."

An hour later, after Alka-Seltzer, a lot of Alka-Seltzer, coffee, a lot of coffee, and a piece of toast, Roger donned his darkest sunglasses and set to work on the lawns, mumbling to himself, signing up for the Foreign Legion must be less vexing than being tied to the yoke of domestic servitude.

By lunchtime the combination of the fizzy pain reliever and physical work had sweated out excess alcohol trapped in his body, and near-to neutralised the incubus running rampant travailing to escape in his dome.

After a traditional Sunday lunch, Charlotte took the wheel of the MPV, and the Fraser family set out for Bluewater.

Glimpsing at Roger as they sped along the A21, Charlotte said, "you usually sing *I've got the Chicken Shack, Fleetwood Mac, John Mayall can't fail blues* on these family occasions."

"Only when I'm driving, and it's to take my mind off the single-brain-cell endowed malcontents and Chelsea FC patrons using the Queen's highways to test out their modified Subaru Impretzas' and

Mitsubishi Lancer Evos' weaving in and out of traffic and cutting me up."

"Funny, I never have those curses when I'm driving. Nobody cuts me up."

"They wouldn't dare," he muttered under his breath.

"What?"

"I pleaded, be careful when you join the M25 at junction 4 where there are temporary road works."

"No, you didn't, but it's a lovely day, and I can't be bothered to react to your gibes."

"Oh, I forgot to tell you, Dad," Wendy began, "Furtive Freddie arrived unannounced when you were mowing the back lawn. He wanted to know if you're interested in buying some Rolling Stones bootleg CDs."

"*Hah*, he's strictly a Sexton Blake."

"He's what?" Wendy prudently cross-examined.

"A fake. He sells moody goods."

"What?" Charlotte catechized.

"Shady…half inched…stolen property. He's definitely Stoke-on-Trent."

"What?" she uttered again.

"*Bent*. I know he comes across as a genial entrepreneur, like Hazelwood's retort to Arthur Daly, but I've always suspected his so-called import-export business is not kosher, and endures adjacent to the taxman's dark shadow. The Cricketers landlord Norman Sykes reckons he's had one or two pulls from the feds. Nothing proven, but categorically he's on their radar."

"Norman's got a colourful imagination," Charlotte proclaimed.

"No, it's true, Mum," James validated. "He tried to sell Jeremy Payne's father some antique brass horseshoes. Mister Payne refused him on the basis the articles were front page news in the Orpington & District Gazette."

"That's right," Heather supplemented. "He attempted to sell Zoey Harvey's mum the same stuff, and she's a big brass collector."

"*What*?" Charlotte blathered briefly glancing at her youngest daughter. "I hope you're not being exposed to criminal activities, Heather."

"Oh, Mummy, I keep on telling you, I'm eight, nine next week. I'm nearly an adult, so you shouldn't be shocked I'm aware of people like Furtive Freddie."

"Roger," Charlotte initiated prodding his arm.

"What?"

"Tell her."

"Tell her what?"

"Tell her, no, I'll tell her." Swivelling about to address Heather, she inadvertently rotated the steering wheel making the MPV veer towards oncoming traffic.

"Keep your concentration on the road," Roger bellowed.

Resuming an eyes front mode, she counselled, "Heather, you might think you're grown up, but let me assure you, you have a long way to go before officially becoming an adult. As such, your father and I want you to keep away from controversy, and before you ask it means contentious squabbles and situations."

"Oh, Mummy, I know what controversy means…I am eight."

~ * ~

Like an approaching tsunami, the mega-sized Bluewater mall represented just as much of a physical and mental test to Roger's sensibilities as supermarket shopping. Past expeditions with Charlotte had seen him run out of energy during their trek through its seemingly millions of designer goods shops, resulting in him begging passers-by for water or to call for an ambulance.

As the MPV neared the exit sign for Bluewater on the A2, memories of previous visits brought a shudder to Roger. Though the current quest only targeted the Cinema de Lux, the slightest of stimulus might lure his wife to set off on a gargantuan hike in search of the lost designer label, dragging the residual of the family behind her kicking and screaming.

Miraculously, miraculous as far as Roger was concerned, after parking the MPV and roaming through the mall concourses towards the cinema complex, Charlotte abided on message, a barrage of Estee Lauder,

Gucci and Vivienne Westwood advertisements not distracting her.

"Oh, there's Mungo Madsen," James chimed waving to a callow-looking, spotty youth accompanied by two adults.

"Who's he?" Roger queried, "a flunked applicant to the James gang?"

"He's a happy slapper."

"He's a what?"

"A happy slapper. Just for fun, they go around slapping heads."

"Well, he'd better not try it on me. He won't get a reciprocal slap, I'll plant him."

On reaching their destination, Roger bought five gallery seat tickets and the Frasers made their way into the cinema, the lights quickly dimming, Pearl & Dean doing their Joe's café and Matilda's massage parlour advertising before the main feature hit the silver screen.

"It's not what I foresaw," Roger whispered to Charlotte.

"How?"

"Well, we're five minutes into the movie, and Steed and Emma Peel are yet to appear. You know, like in the TV series."

"This is not a remake of the 1960s television spy series," she informed, producing an aporetic gloom. "It just happens to have the same name."

"You mean—" The penny dropped. "There will be no men in bowler hats defeating arch villains with their brollies, or women dressed in leather catsuits karateing psychopaths to death?"

"No. *The Avengers* is an action fantasy film, based on the Marvel comics superhero team of the same name."

"So, it's going to be like 'Iron Man', 'Spider Man', VAT Man and all those other childish films I despise?" he quacked.

"There's no such film as VAT Man. It's a figment of your hyperactive wit, but yes, and by the way, this *is* an 'Iron Man' movie."

"*By all the saints*," he wailed, "then I'm here under false pretences. If I'd known it was a comic strip for lamebrains and the intellectually subnormal, I'd not have come."

"I'd have thought you were adequately qualified in that department."

Ignoring her swipe, he folded his arms in disgust and glared at his wife. "If it ever gets out I attended a kid flick, I'll never be able to hold my noggin high at Kappa Corinthians Rugby Club ever again."

"It's not exclusively a kid's film, it's a family film, justifying why I suggested it."

Disgruntled, Roger stared at the contrivance for a few minutes. "It's not even scary."

"It's not meant to be," she explained. "It's a good versus evil theme."

"Balderdash," he rebutted, his voice merciless. "I've seen better stuff on the Film Channel, and that really is the pits."

"Just give it a chance," she castigated, her voice also ramping up in volume.

"Will you two be quiet," Wendy admonished, "or we'll get thrown out."

With herculean effort, Roger kept his volcano in check until Nick Fury, Captain America and Black Widow traded punches with an extra-terrestrial race known as the Chitauri, the CGI treatment engendering a collage of gory colours and a farrago of shrieks and howls from the rivals. "Dear me," he cried. "Utter dribble."

"It's not dribble, Dad," James insisted. "It's state-of-the-art, astral warfare foretelling what will happen when aliens invade our world."

"Heavens above, I think you'll find it's already happened on Chatham High Street and more critically, the London Underground's District Line," his father maintained, remembering the Lazoonland mishmash of spooky humanoids he and Heather saw in Chatham and the alien-like creatures he often observed on District Line trains.

"Will you lot *shut up*," barked an irate man pirouetting around to sight Roger from the seat row immediately forward of where the Frasers sat. "Some of us are trying to watch and listen to this film."

About to delve out vitriol in equal measure, Roger found his arm grasped by Charlotte. Scintillating gracefully at the man, she petitioned, "I'm very sorry." She scoured at her husband. "One of my children in particular is having tantrums."

Fuming, nevertheless Roger resisted the temptation to test his wife's patience further.

All remained hushed until the juxtaposition of the film, when the Avengers rallied in defence of New York City, housing a wormhole through which the alien hordes had invaded Earth forming the battleground.

"*Nonsense*," Roger denounced, "you don't need superheroes to defeat this scuzzy bunch of ugly space cadets. There are parts of Brooklyn and downtown Manhattan where outsiders are dispatched by raw muscle and Colt 45s every day. These intergalactic *dummies* wouldn't present a problem to native New Yorkers. Who needs gay-boy trolls like Loki and Thor?"

"Right, *that's* it," screeched the irate man to the Frasers front. Standing up, he made his way to the rear of the cinema, returning with an usherette.

"I'm sorry, sir," she articulated to Roger, shining her torch in his kisser making him lurch sideways, "but you and your family will have to leave the theatre."

"*What*!" he remonstrated. "Just because this Herbert can't take some constructive film criticism?"

"It's not just this gentlemen, sir. We've had a lot of complaints about you during the screening."

Gawking around, Roger saw a myriad of cinema goers glaring at him. "But, but, I was only getting into the spirit of the occasion."

"Might be so, sir. Nonetheless, you must follow me and decamp from the theatre."

"Including my family?" he stuttered out, knowing he'd be in for a pasting if the usherette corresponded in the affirmative.

"Yes, I'm afraid it does, sir."

Returning to the foyer, Charlotte whined, "you've embarrassed me on multiple social occasions over the years, Roger, but this latest exhibition of your intolerance has hit new heights." Perusing about, she berated, "it's a good job nobody we know saw what happened."

"Somebody we know did see what happened," Heather advised.

"*What*!" Charlotte and Roger exclaimed in unison.

"Who?" Charlotte enquired.

"Georgina Pender and her elder sister and parents were two rows behind us."

"Oh no," Roger squawked, "Marian Pender is a fully paid-up member of the gossips union, and—" Grimacing he bit his bottom lip. "She knows your nemesis Deborah Stapleton. If Marian tells Deborah, and she tells her husband Ben, he'll use it to blackmail me into giving away The Firm's innermost secrets."

"But Ben used to work with you at The Firm. When we saw them in Chiquito's after the 2011 Summer Exhibition at the Royal Academy of Arts, you two got on fine."

"Yes, but Ben loves dropping people in the nasty stuff, and he works for Oakley & Ainsworth, one of The Firm's most prestigious clients." Fully cognizant of the impact, he winced. "And…he's on the buy side. *Jesus*!" Envisaging the worst, his lineaments darkened. "Ben will see this as an opportunity to hold me to ransom on pain of my minor contretemps being leaked to The Firm."

"Topping that," Charlotte grumbled, "Marian will tell everybody she knows at the tech, and my name will be mud." Inevitably, as the upshot of her husband's indiscretion hit home, her foot began to tap incessantly.

"Don't tell me," he sarcastically posed, noticing the kinesics. "I'm in for a session in the doghouse."

"Far more than that," she stipulated, the rebuke just dying to jump off her lips. "As well as the usual penance, I'll be tearing up your membership of the Hazelwood & District Gentlemen's Club. Apart from work, you will be confined to barracks until this salacious furore burns out in the publics' mind, and I've restored our good name in the neighbourhood."

"Ohh!" Landed and filleted, he lolled in abject resignation. "*Not again,* God preserve us!"

Despite his self-imposed commitment not to become embroiled in freedom-threatening tangles, and hours passing like centuries bent double in the *I Ching* position meditating like fuck, once again the doghouse beckoned for Roger Fraser.

About the Author

Clive Radford began writing at school, then university but mainly through subsequent life experience.

His poetry has been published in numerous poetry magazines such as The Journal, The Cannon's Mouth, Poetry Monthly, Poetry Now, Storming Heaven, Poetry Nottingham, Scripsi and Modern Review, plus in many compilations by United Press.

A series of his short stories and poems have been published by Ether Books. The Arts Council has sponsored publication of his novels 'One Night in Tunisia' and 'The Sounds of Silence'. His contemporary satire 'Doghouse Blues' was number one in Harper Collins Authonomy chart and has been awarded gold medal status. It has been published by Black Rose. His spy thriller 'Zavrazin' has been published by Triplicity Publishing. It's companion sequel 'Nexus Bullet' is published by Ex-L-Ence Publishing. His three-book series 'Disclosures of a Femme Fatale Addict' is published by Wild Dreams Publishing. His science fiction novel 'Maggie's Farm', suspense-thriller 'Incident at Lahore Basin' and his satire 'Doghouse Blues 2' are published by Rogue Phoenix Press.

'One Night in Tunisia', 'Zavrazin' and 'Bullet' have all been converted into three-act screenplays.

The 'Zavrazin' screenplay is under contract with Story Merchant/Atchity Productions for film production.

Wild Dreams Publishing re-published 'Disclosures of a Femme Fatale Addict' as a deluxe edition, May 2020. Miraclaire Publishing has also re-published his 'Disclosures of a Femme Fatale Addict', October 2020.

Rogue Phoenix Press will be publishing his satire 'Doghouse

Blues 3', June 2021. Melange Books will be publishing his mystery thriller, 'Monsoon in the Making', April 2021, and his 'The Spiral Staircase and other Novellas', a mix of psychological, modern satire and rite of passage sagas, November 2021.

Currently, he is crafting a number of works including the satire 'Doghouse Blues 1 Revised and Remastered', 'Alpha Centauri', a contemporary thriller, 'Oklahoma City Looks Oh So Pretty', a rite of passage sojourn along Route 66, 'Three Cheshire Boys' a comedic thriller, and 'Colby Richmond: The University Years', the coming of age sequel to 'Disclosures of a Femme Fatale Addict'.

His work has a distinctive voice setting it apart and appealing to those fascinated by intrigue, and who question status quo accepted views.

By the Atuthor
at
Rogue Phoenix Press

Incident at Lahore Basin

Whilst on business in Pakistan, ex-RAF officer and businessman Dale Latham comes close to death when his helicopter is downed by a ground to air missile. Hospitalised, he meets Chanda Govinda, a persecuted Christian Indian and helps her escape across the Pakistan-India border. Although there is no evidence linking Latham's involvement with Chanda, Muslim zealot police chief Aman aims to imprison him.

With his top-secret knowledge, HMG fear Latham will end up in the hands of Pakistani intelligence. MI6 agent Ross Hunter is dispatched to appraise the situation, and if necessary, liquidate Latham. When Latham is abducted by terrorists, Hunter rescues him, saying that Aman set him up for the ultimate fall. Without evidence, Aman is forced to allow Latham to leave Pakistan, avoiding a bullet from Hunter.

Chapter 1: Tempest

Flameout! Pilot Wing Commander Dale Latham's Tornado zoomed groundward. As the aircraft stalled, rolled and flipped over into a spiral dive, its altimeter decremented at an astonishing rate.

He had to act fast. Initiating the engines start-up procedure, he managed to engage one RB199. Singing into life the turbofan generated thrust, allowing Latham to push the stick forward making the aircraft nose down, then increase throttle setting to full power. Miraculously, the Tornado settled, enabling him to apply back pressure to the stick levelling the wings, the aeroplane regaining steady-state flight, Latham recovering altitude as he tried to ignite the second RB199.

Approaching RAF Lossiemouth, backtracking from a combined RAF-Luftwaffe sortie over the Rhineland, navigator-weapons officer, Flight Lieutenant Harry Beaumont, warned of severe hailstorm conditions ahead. As the Tornado slowed from supersonic speed and descended from 30,000 feet over the Moray Firth channel, she hit the inclement weather. Far worse than expected, a freak set of climatic conditions had conspired to generate the mother of all storm clouds, cumulonimbus building a trail blazer of epic proportions.

As the Tornado passed beneath 15,000 feet, she encountered heavy rain and tennis-ball- sized hailstones, the contaminants ingested into the engine's inlet ducts leading to dual-turbofan flameout.

Whilst Latham struggled to re-start the second RB199, Beaumont contacted Lossiemouth Air Traffic Control, advising their predicament. Asked if the Tornado wanted to register a Mayday call, Beaumont answered in the negative. Confident of Latham's flying skills, he knew the pilot would be reluctant to pull the ejector seat handle, releasing the canopy and sending both aircrew into space, abandoning the Tornado to crash into the Moray Firth.

Latham had never lost an aircraft. He certainly did not intend to let the £14m fighter-bomber end up in the drink. Albeit, the second engine refused to spark into life, further ingestion of the life-threatening hale defeating his attempts. Though capable of flight on a single engine, prudence dictated under the tempest onslaught, having both turbofans operational equated with minimising further danger. Gaining height, the Tornado rose above the cumulonimbus wrecker, permitting the second engine inlet duct to clear of ice debris. Sustaining the re-start protocol, at last the stagnant RB199 burst into life, the gained extra thrust making the aeroplane nose-up. Deciding not to risk landing at Lossiemouth through the storm, Latham called RAF Leuchars, requesting permission for an emergency landing.

South of Lossiemouth by 90 miles, Leuchars allowed the Tornado to land without any further troubles, her aircrew reporting the flameout incident, and staying until clement weather prevailed over the Moray Firth locale, allowing then to return to Lossiemouth.

Beaumont's assessment of Latham had been spot-on. Wholly aware that the UK taxpayer owned the platforms he carried out missions on, spanning his RAF flight career, Latham had made it his business to ensure any aircraft allocated to his charge remained in one piece from take-off to landing. A trait inherited from his father; a sense of responsibility in all matters came to dominate his life from an early age.

Sometimes the quality resulted in gladness and fulfilment, whereas on other occasions, it got him into hot water, his innate sentiment to duty subduing imperilment factors.

Also by Clive Radford
at
Robue Phoenix Press

Maggie's Farm

Cody and Carolyn Redford enjoy a carefree lifestyle in Kent County, with friends Gavin and Melanie Maynard. In Cornwall, the Redfords encounter a soothsayer predicting a bleak future for mankind. The foursome then notes some unexplained changes in the behaviour of wild animals and migrating birds, giving credence to the prediction. When a terrorist outrage in South Africa leads to further major atrocities in Israel and India, détente finally fails. Global nuclear war is sparked off by an unforeseen source, resulting in the superpowers exchanging H-bomb punches like drunken boxers. In the midst of survival, Cody Redford becomes aware of the artificial insemination and incubation (AI2) programme, an initiative hatched in the Cold War years to store the sperm of prominent scientists with the objective of using surrogate hosts to factory farm children in a post-holocaust world. Though appalled, nonetheless, he resigns himself to supporting the programme, unaware of the significant down the road consequences to the nature of human life.

Doghouse Blues 2

Roger Fraser, the ever optimistic but perpetually put upon investment banking stock analyst-trouble shooter and occasional rugby player has more work and domestic issues to challenge his sensibilities. He skilfully manoeuvres from one demanding situation to the next, barely managing to extinguish the callous flames of fate seeming to constantly blight his endeavours and bite at his flesh.

During his excursions into shocking social scandals and battling with egotistical megalomaniacs, he endlessly verges on disaster, but somehow always manages to survive. Roger pokes irreverent fun at the new Establishment, single-handedly takes on female dragons, prevails against rampaging supermarket shoppers and trades wisecracks with a Brummy vicar, but invariably finds himself tethered to the doghouse, singing the blues.

www.ingramcontent.com/pod-product-compliance
Lightning Source LLC
Chambersburg PA
CBHW060153260626
47160CB00001B/241
* 9 7 8 1 6 2 4 2 0 6 3 2 0 *